Praise for the novels of Robyn Carr

"Carr has hit her stride with this captivating series."
—*Library Journal* on the Virgin River series

"This book is an utter delight."
—*RT Book Reviews* on *Moonlight Road*

"Strong conflict, humor and well-written characters are Carr's calling cards, and they're all present here…. You won't want to put this one down."
—*RT Book Reviews* on *Angel's Peak*

"This story has everything: a courageous, outspoken heroine, a to-die-for hero and a plot that will touch readers' hearts on several different levels. Truly excellent."
—*RT Book Reviews* on *Forbidden Falls*

"An intensely satisfying read. By turns humorous and gut-wrenchingly emotional, it won't soon be forgotten."
—*RT Book Reviews* on *Paradise Valley*

"The Virgin River books are so compelling—I connected instantly with the characters and just wanted more and more and more."
—#1 *New York Times* bestselling author Debbie Macomber

ROBYN CARR

TEMPTATION RIDGE

mira

Recycling programs for this product may not exist in your area.

ISBN-13: 978-0-7783-8660-5

Temptation Ridge

First published in 2009. This edition published in 2022.

For questions and comments about the quality of this book, please contact us at CustomerService@Harlequin.com.

Mira
22 Adelaide St. West, 41st Floor
Toronto, Ontario M5H 4E3, Canada
BookClubbish.com

Printed in U.S.A.

This novel is dedicated to Liza Dawson, my right arm,
my clear head, my arch and my spine. Your insight is like a beacon,
your encouragement like a warm blanket. Thank you from my heart
for the incredible affection and energy you give to me.

VIRGIN RIVER

TEMPTATION RIDGE

1

Shelby was within ten miles of her Uncle Walt's ranch when she had to pull over to the side of highway 36, the busiest stretch between Virgin River and Fortuna, behind an old pickup truck that looked vaguely familiar. Although 36 was the highway that ran across the mountains from Red Bluff to Fortuna, it was mostly two lane. She put her cherry-red Jeep SUV in Park and stepped out of the vehicle. The rain had finally stopped, giving way to a bright summer sun, but the road was wet and splattered with muddy puddles. She peered way up the road to see a man wearing a bright orange vest holding a stop sign toward a long string of cars, closing both lanes. The turnoff to her Uncle Walt's would be on the other side of the next hill.

She picked her way around puddles to the truck parked in front of her, intending to ask the driver if he knew what was going on. When she got to the driver's window she smiled. "Well, hey, Doc."

Doc Mullins looked out the open window. "Hey, yourself, little girl. Up here for a weekend of riding?" he asked with his usual grumpy tone.

"Not this time, Doc. I sold my mother's house in Bodega Bay," she said. "Packed up the bare essentials and am moving in with Uncle Walt for a while."

"Permanently?"

"Nah. For a few months, though. I'm still in transition."

Doc's grimace melted slightly, but only slightly. "Once again, condolences on your loss, Shelby," he said. "I hope you're doing all right with that."

"Better all the time, thanks. My mom was ready to go." She tilted her head up the road. "Have any idea what's holding us up here?"

"Soft shoulder gave out," he said. "I passed it on my way to Valley Hospital. Dumped half this lane down the hill. They're repairing."

"Guardrails would be nice," she observed.

"Only around the tight curves," he said. "On a straight-away like this, we're on our own. Damn lucky a car or truck didn't go with that soft shoulder. It's going to be like this the next few days."

"Once I get to Walt's, I'm not planning to be on this road again, for a while anyway," she said with a shrug.

"What *are* you planning, if I might ask?" Doc said, lifting one of his bushy eyebrows.

"Well, while I'm visiting the family, I'll be making applications to schools. Nursing," she said with a smile. "A fairly obvious choice for me after taking care of my mother for years."

"Ach, just what I need," he said with his usual scowl. "Another nurse. Drive me to drink."

She laughed at him. "At least we won't have to drive you far."

"There's just what I mean. Another impertinent one, at that," he clarified.

She laughed again, loving this ornery old guy. Shelby turned, Doc leaned out of his window and both of them watched a man approach from the truck that had stopped behind Shelby's Jeep. He walked toward them. His hair was shaved down in that military fashion she'd been accustomed to all her life; her uncle was a retired army general. A black T-shirt was stretched tight over broad, hard shoulders, his waist narrow, his hips slim and legs long. But what fascinated her was the way he came toward them, with an economy of movement. Deliberate. Confident. *Cocky.* His thumbs were hooked into front pockets and he sauntered. When he got closer, she could see his very slight smile as he looked at her, or looked her over, to be more precise. Sizing her up with glowing eyes. *In your dreams,* she thought, which caused her to smile back.

As he passed her Jeep, he glanced inside at all the packed-up boxes, then continued to where she was standing beside Doc's open window. "That yours?" he asked, jutting his chin toward the Jeep.

"Yup."

"Where are you headed?" he asked.

"Virgin River. You?"

"The same." He grinned. "Any idea what's going on up there?"

"Collapsed shoulder," Doc said with a grunt. "They have us down to one lane for repairs. What's your business in Virgin River?"

"I have some old cabins along the river there." He glanced between them. "You two live in the town?" he asked.

"I have family there," Shelby said. She stuck out her hand. "I'm Shelby."

He took her small hand. "Luke. Luke Riordan." He turned toward Doc, putting out his hand again. "Sir?"

Doc didn't extend a hand, but rather gave a nod. His hands were so twisted with arthritis, he never risked a handshake. "Mullins," he said.

"Doc Mullins has lived in Virgin River all his life. He's the town doctor," Shelby explained to Luke.

"Nice to meet you, sir," Luke said.

"Another jarhead?" Doc asked, lifting one white, spiking eyebrow.

Luke straightened. "I beg your pardon," he said. "Army. Sir." Then he looked at Shelby. "*Another* marine?"

"A few of our friends who work in town are marines. Retired or discharged. Their friends come around sometimes—some of them are still active or in the reserves," she explained. "But my uncle, who I'll be living with for a while, was Army. Retired." She grinned. "You won't stand out that much with your hairdo. I don't know what it is with you guys and the buzz cuts."

He smiled patiently. "We've never been checked out on those dryer things."

"Ah. Blow-dryers. Right."

As they waited in their stalled lane, the second lane was opened up to let a big yellow school bus pass. Judging by the number of vehicles waiting in their lane, they weren't going anywhere anytime soon, so there was no great rush to get back to their cars. They remained standing on the road, which ended up being a big mistake for Luke. As he saw the bus barreling down the other lane, Luke also noted a sizable puddle in front of it. He quickly put himself between Shelby and the bus, pressing her up against Doc's open window. With a hand on each side of her, he covered her with his body, barely in time to feel the splat from the puddle against his back.

Shelby stifled a chuckle. Macho man, she thought with some humor.

Luke heard downshifting, then the squeal of brakes. "Jesus," he muttered as he backed off the girl and glared after the bus.

As Luke turned and scowled at the bus, the driver leaned out the window. A round-faced woman in her fifties, rosy cheeked with a cap of short dark hair, grinned at him. She *grinned!* "Sorry, buddy," she said. "Couldn't hardly help that."

"You could if you went a lot slower," he yelled back at her.

To his astonishment, she laughed. "Aw, I wasn't going too fast. I got a schedule, y'know," she yelled. "My advice? Stay out of the way."

His scalp felt hot under his short hair and he really wanted to swear. When he turned back to Shelby and Doc, he found her smiling behind her hand and Doc's eyes twinkling. "You got a little splatter on your back there, Luke," she said, trying to keep control of her lips.

Doc's face was the same—cranky and impatient, but for the glittering eyes. "Molly's been slinging that big yellow tube around these mountains for thirty years now, and ain't nobody knows these roads better. Guess she didn't see a pothole this once."

"It's not even September yet!" Luke protested.

"She drives year-round," Doc said. "Summer school, special programs, athletics. Always something going on. She's a saint—you couldn't pay me enough to do that job. What's a mud puddle here and there?" Then the old doctor put his truck noisily in gear. "Our turn coming up."

Shelby jogged back toward her Jeep. Luke started to walk back toward his truck, which pulled a camper. Then he heard Doc, shouting at his back, "Welcome to Virgin River, son. Enjoy yourself." And it was followed by a cackle.

Shelby McIntyre had been fixing up her deceased mother's house for months, but she'd been able to drive up to Virgin River from Bodega Bay nearly every weekend through the summer to ride. And her Uncle Walt had paid many a visit to her to oversee renovation work that he'd personally contracted. By the end of summer Shelby had roses on her cheeks. She had rolled up her shorts and her legs were tanned. Her thighs and butt had developed firm riding muscles and her eyes sparkled with health. It had been years since she'd benefited from that type of regular exercise.

But when she pulled up in front of Walt's house now, in mid-August, it was a completely different feeling. The house was sold, her belongings were in the back of her Jeep, and at the age of twenty-five, she was embarking on a brand-new life. She gave the horn a toot, got out of her Jeep and stretched. In just moments, Uncle Walt came out the front door, stood there with his hands on his hips, a big grin on his face. "Welcome back," he said. "Or should I say, welcome home?"

"Hey there," she said, walking into his arms. Walt was six feet with thick, silver hair, dark bushy brows and shoulders and arms like a wrestler's. He was a powerfully built man for just over sixty.

He hugged her tight. "I was just about to go to the stable and saddle up. You too tired? You hungry or anything?"

"I'm dying to get on a horse, but I think I'll pass after riding in a Jeep for over four hours," she said.

He laughed. "Backside pretty well broken in?"

"Ohhh," she said, rubbing her butt.

"I'm just riding down along the river for an hour or so. Vanni's down at the new construction, getting in Paul's business, but she's going to be back in time to cook you a nice welcome-home dinner."

Shelby looked at her watch. It was only three-thirty. "Tell you what—I'm going to run into town while you go for your ride and Vanni inspects her new house. I'll say hi to Mel Sheridan and see if I can talk her into a beer to celebrate my change of residence. I'll be back in time to help with the horses before dinner. Should I get this stuff out of the Jeep first? Take it inside?" she asked.

"Honey, leave it be, no one's gonna bother it. Paul and I will unload you before supper."

She grinned at him. "Let's make a date for tomorrow morning. We'll have that ride together."

"Good deal. No trouble closing on the house?"

"It was a little more emotional than I expected. I thought I was ready."

"Regrets?"

She turned her large hazel eyes up to his face. "I cried for the first fifty miles," she said. "And then I started to get excited. I'm sure about this."

"Good," he said, giving her a squeeze. "I'm so glad you're here."

"Just for a few months. Then I'm going to travel a little and get a head start on school. It's been so long since I've been a student."

"Life here is usually pretty laid-back. Take advantage of it."

"Yeah—" she laughed "—when you're not having shootouts or forest fires."

"Well, hell, girl, we want to keep things interesting!" He walked her to her Jeep.

"Wait for me to get back to muck the stalls and feed the horses."

"Enjoy a little girlfriend time," he said. "It's something you haven't had enough of the past few years. You'll have plenty of horseshit to muck while you're here."

"Thanks, Uncle Walt," she said and laughed. "I won't be too long."

He kissed her forehead. "I said, take your time. You took good care of my sister. You've earned piles of it."

"See you in a couple of hours," Shelby said, heading for town.

★ ★ ★

Luke Riordan pulled into Virgin River, his Harley strapped into the back of his extended-cab truck, pulling his small camper. It had been seven years since he'd seen this town and there had been a few changes. The church was now boarded up, but what he remembered as an old, abandoned cabin in the center of town was renovated, had cars and trucks parked around the front porch, and an Open sign in the window. It looked like some construction was under way behind the cabin; it was framed for an add-on. Since he was considering a renovation project of his own, he wouldn't mind having a look at what had been done to this place. He parked off to the side, out of the way, and got out of the truck. He went into the camper and changed out of his muddy shirt before going inside.

The August afternoon was warm, with a cool, refreshing breeze; the night would be chilly in the mountains. He hadn't been out to the house he planned to live in, which had been vacant for a year. If it was uninhabitable, he had his camper. He took a deep breath. The air was so damn clean, it stung the lungs. Such a huge change from the deserts of Iraq and El Paso. Just what he'd been needing.

He walked into the renovated cabin and found himself in a good-looking little country bar. He stood just inside the door and looked around appreciatively. The hardwood floors gleamed, hot embers glowed in the hearth, hunting and fishing trophies hung mounted on the walls. There were about a dozen tables and a long, shiny bar behind which there were shelves full of liquor and glasses surrounding a stuffed king salmon that must have weighed about forty pounds at the catch. A television, mounted high in a corner, was tuned to national news, the volume turned down. A couple of fishermen, identifiable by their khaki vests and hats, sat at one end of the bar playing cribbage. A few men in work shirts and jeans were having drinks at a nearby table. Luke looked at his watch: 4:00 p.m. He walked up to the bar.

"What can I get you?" the bartender asked.

"A cold draft, thanks. This place wasn't here the last time I was through town."

"You've been away a while then. I've been open more than four years now. I bought it and turned it into this."

"Well, you did a helluva job," he said, accepting the beer. "I'm going to be doing some remodeling myself." He stuck out his hand. "Luke Riordan," he said.

"Jack Sheridan. Pleasure."

"I bought some old cabins along the Virgin that have been sitting empty and going downhill for years now."

"Those old Chapman cabins?" Jack asked. "The old man died just last year."

"Yeah, I know," Luke said. "I was back here hunting with one of my brothers and a couple of friends when we first saw them. My brother and I thought the location, right on the river, might be worth some money. We noticed the cabins weren't in use and wanted to buy 'em and fix 'em up for a quick resale, turn 'em fast and make a couple of bucks. But old Chapman wouldn't even listen to an offer...."

"It would have left him homeless," Jack said, giving the bar a wipe with a cloth. "He wouldn't have had too many options, and he was all alone."

Luke took a drink of his icy beer. "Exactly. So we bought the whole property, including his house, and told him he could stay there, rent free, for life. It turned out to be seven years."

Jack grinned. "Sweet deal for him. Smart deal for you. Property doesn't come available around here that often."

"We could see right off the land under those cabins was worth more than the buildings, right on the river like that. I haven't been able to get back here since, and my brother has only been up here once, just to have a look—he said nothing had changed."

"What held you up?"

"Well," he said, scratching the stubble on his chin. "Afghanistan. Iraq. Fort Bliss and a few other places."

"Army?"

"Yeah. Twenty."

"I did twenty in the Marine Corps," Jack said. "I thought I'd come up here and serve up a few drinks, fish and hunt for the next twenty."

"Yeah? Sounds like a good plan."

"My plan got derailed by a cute little nurse midwife by the name of Melinda." He grinned. "I would've been fine, but that woman does something to a pair of jeans that ought to be against the law."

"That so?" Luke asked.

"Anyone can go fishing," Jack said with a satisfied smile.

Luke didn't mind seeing a man happy with his life. He smiled back. Then he asked, "Did you do most of this work yourself?"

"Most. I got some help, but I like taking credit where I can. This bar is a custom job, delivered to me finished. I installed the shelves and laid the hardwood floors. I didn't trust myself with the plumbing and I screwed up the wiring enough to have to hire someone, but I'm good with wood—I managed to add a large one-room apartment onto the back to live in. My cook, Preacher, has it now and is adding on again—his family's growing, but he likes living at the bar. You going to work on those cabins?"

"I'm going to look at the house first. Chapman was already pretty old when we bought the whole business—that house probably needs work. And I have no idea what shape the cabins are in, but I don't have anything better to do right now. Worst case, I can fix up the house and live in it for a while. Best case, I can renovate the house and the cabins and put 'em on the market."

"Where's your brother?" Jack asked.

"Still active. Sean is stationed at Beale Air Force Base in the U-2. It's just me for now."

"What did you do for the army?" Jack asked him.

"Black Hawks."

"Shew," Jack said, shaking his head. "They go in some real hot spots."

"Tell me about it. I came out the hard way."

"You drive one in?" Jack asked.

"Hell, no," he said indignantly. "I had to be shot down."

Jack laughed. "Man. At least you got your twenty."

"It wasn't even the first time," Luke said. "But in a moment of sheer genius, I decided it should be the last."

"Something tells me we've been in some of the same places," Jack said. "Maybe even at around the same time."

"Saw some combat, did you?"

"Afghanistan, Somalia, Bosnia, Iraq. Twice."

"Mogadishu," Luke confirmed, shaking his head.

"Yeah, we left you boys in a mess. I hated that," Jack said. "You lost a lot of brothers. I'm sorry, man."

"It was bad," Luke agreed. What started out as a relief mission sanctioned by the UN ended in a horrible uprising after the Marine Corps was pulled out and the army was left behind. Somalian warlord Aidid launched an attack that left eighteen U.S. Army soldiers dead and over ninety wounded in a bloody conflict. "One of these days, Jack, we'll get drunk and talk about the battles."

Jack reached out, grabbed Luke's upper arm and said, "You bet. Welcome to the neighborhood, brother."

"Now, tell me where to go for a night out that might include women, who to call if I need help with the house or cabins and what hours I can get a beer here," Luke said.

"Been a long time since I've been looking for women, buddy. The coastal towns have some nice spots—try Fortuna or Eureka. There's the Brookstone Inn in Ferndale—nice restaurant and bar. Old-town Eureka is always good. Then for something a little closer, there's a little bar in Garberville with a jukebox." He shrugged. "I remember seeing one or two pretty girls there. And I have just the guy for you if you need help with the remodel. A buddy of mine just moved a part of his family's construction company down here from Oregon and he's doing Preacher's add-on. He helped me finish my house. He's a helluva builder. Let me go get one of his cards."

Jack went into the back and hadn't been gone a minute when two women came into the bar and almost gave Luke a heart attack. A couple of pretty blondes, one in her thirties with curly golden hair and the other, much younger, with an unforgettable thick, honey-colored braid that hung down her back to her waist. The girl from the roadside; the one he saved from a muddy bath—Shelby. Both of them were wearing tight jeans and boots. The golden girl had on a loose-knit sweater, while Shelby wore the same crisp white shirt from earlier, sleeves rolled, collar open and tied at the waist. He tried not to stare, but he couldn't help looking at them, though they hadn't noticed him at all. His immediate thought was that he wouldn't have to go as far as Garberville. They jumped up on bar stools just as Jack came from the back.

"Hey, baby," he said, leaning across the bar to the older of the two women, kissing her. Ah, Luke thought, those would be the illegal jeans that keep him from fishing. What man wouldn't give up fishing to spend more of his time with a woman like that? "Meet a new neighbor. Luke Riordan, this is Mel, my wife, and Shelby McIntyre—she has family here."

"Pleasure," he said to the women.

"Luke here owns those old Chapman cabins on the river and he's thinking of renovating. He's ex-army, so we're gonna let him stay."

"Welcome," Mel said.

Shelby said nothing. She smiled at him, letting her eyelids drop a bit. He judged her to be about eighteen, just a girl. In fact, if she'd been any older, he might've gotten a phone number out there on the muddy road. Eureka or the Brookstone couldn't beat this, though both these women were obviously completely off-limits—Mel was Jack's woman and Shelby appeared to be a teenager. A very sexy teenager, he thought with a slight flush of warmth. But their appearance held promise. If two such beautiful women could be found in a little bar in Virgin River, there had to be a few more scattered around these mountains.

"Here you go," Jack said, sliding a business card across the bar. "My buddy Paul. Right now he's also building a house for my younger sister, Brie, and her husband next door to us. Plus one for himself and his wife."

"My cousin," Shelby said.

Luke lifted his eyebrows in question.

"Well, Paul's married to my cousin Vanessa. They're staying at my Uncle Walt's and I'm staying with them."

"You want a beer, Mel?" Jack asked his wife. "Shelby?"

"I'll have a quick soda with Shelby, then I'm going home to relieve Brie of the kids so she can have dinner with Mike," Mel said. "I just wanted to swing through and tell you where I'll be. I'll feed the kids and put them to bed. Will you bring us some of Preacher's dinner when you come home later?"

"Be happy to."

"And I'm going home to help with the horses," Shelby said. "But I'll have a beer first."

Well, at least she was twenty-one, Luke found himself thinking. Unless Jack had some very relaxed age standards in this little neighborhood bar, which was entirely possible.

"I'd probably better get going—" Luke said.

"Hang around," Jack said. "If you don't have to go, five o'clock usually brings out the regulars. Perfect opportunity to meet your neighbors."

Luke looked at his watch. "I guess I can hang out a while."

Jack laughed. "Buddy, the first thing that's gonna go is that watch." Jack put a beer in front of Shelby, a cola in front of his wife.

Luke talked with Jack a while about the renovation of the bar while the women were occupied with their own conversation. Not ten minutes had passed when Jack said, "Excuse me, I'm going to walk my wife out," and Luke was left at the bar with Shelby.

"I see you changed clothes," Shelby said to him.

"Um, that was pretty necessary. The schoolmarm got me good."

She laughed softly. "I never thanked you. For saving my blouse."

"No thanks necessary," he said, sipping his beer.

"I've seen those cabins," Shelby said. "I like to ride along the river. They look pretty awful."

He chuckled. "I'm not surprised to hear that. With any luck, they're not beyond hope."

"They were built a long time ago when people used quality materials," she said. "I learn these things from my cousin— some of these old houses are built like brick shit— Um. Well. So, do you expect your family to join you here?" she asked him.

He grinned into his beer. And the question, so quick and

to the point, surprised him. He lifted his eyes from his beer and looked at her. "No," he said. "I have a mother and brothers scattered around."

"No wife?" she asked, one corner of her mouth tilting upward along with the slight lift of one pretty brow.

"No wife," he said.

"Aw. Too bad," she said.

"You don't have to feel sorry for me, Shelby. I happen to like it this way."

"Solitary kind of guy, are you?"

"No. Just an unmarried kind of guy." He knew this was his cue to ask her if she was attached to someone special, but it was irrelevant. He wasn't going there. And while he knew getting to know her better probably wasn't wise, he put an elbow on the bar, leaned his head on his hand, met her eyes and said, "Just visiting, huh?"

She took a drink of her beer, nodding.

"How long are you in town for?"

"That's still kind of up in the air," she said. Jack was back behind the bar and Shelby put down her glass, still half-full, and a couple of dollars on the bar. "I'd better go take care of those horses. Thanks, Jack."

Jack turned toward her. "Shelby, why don't you just ask for half a beer?" he said.

She shrugged, smiling. She put out her hand to Luke. "Nice seeing you again, Luke. Later."

"Sure," he said, taking her hand. As she left, he watched her walk out. He didn't want to do that, but the view was impossible to resist. When he looked back at Jack, Jack grinned, then got busy behind the bar.

Before seven o'clock Luke had met Preacher—or John to his wife and young stepson. He met Paige, Preacher's wife, and Jack's younger sister Brie and her husband, Mike. He saw

old Doc Mullins again and passed the time with some of his
new neighbors. He feasted on some of the best salmon he'd
ever eaten, heard some local lore and was already feeling like
one of the gang. While he was there others passed through for
dinner and drinks, greeting Jack and Preacher like old pals.

Another couple entered and Luke was introduced to Paul
Haggerty, the builder, and his wife, Vanessa. "Jack gave me a
call," Paul said. "He tells me we have you as a new neighbor."

"That's optimistic," Luke said. "I haven't been out to the
property yet."

"Is that your camper out there?" Paul asked.

"As a precaution," Luke said with a laugh. "If the house
isn't habitable, I won't have to sleep in the truck."

"Be sure and let me know if you need me to look at any
of it."

"I appreciate that. More than you realize."

Luke found himself staying at the bar far later than he had
intended. In fact, when Jack's friends were saying good-night,
he was still there, having a cup of coffee with Jack. These
seemed like nice people, though he was a little shell-shocked
by the women. He could accept the idea that Jack had found
himself a young beauty right in Virgin River, but it seemed
they were everywhere. Shelby, Paige, Brie and Vanessa were
all damn sweet-looking. He held out great hope of landing
himself at least a little diversion in the next town over.

"You're going to want to meet Paul's father-in-law, Walt,"
Jack said. "He's retired army."

"Yeah?" Luke asked. "I think Shelby mentioned that."

"Three-star. Nice guy."

Luke groaned in spite of himself. He actually dropped his
head. And apparently Jack was reading him.

"Yep. Shelby's Uncle Walt," Jack said.

"Shelby. The eighteen-year-old?"

Jack chuckled. "She's a little older than that. But I admit, young. Looker, though, isn't she?"

That was impossible to miss, Luke thought. "I took one look at her and felt like I was going to get arrested," he said, making Jack laugh. "How much more dangerous could she be, huh? Young, sweet and living with a three-star."

"Yeah," Jack laughed. "But hell, she's all grown up now. Grew up fine, I'd say."

"Hey, I'm not getting near that," Luke said.

"Whatever you say," Jack said.

Luke stood up, put money on the bar, put out his hand and said, "Thanks, Jack. I really didn't expect this kind of welcome. I'm glad I shot through town before going out to the house."

"Let us know if we can do anything to help. Nice having you with us, soldier. You're going to like it here."

2

It was typical of the Sheridans to have their dinner together at the bar, often with friends and family, and then Jack would load up his little family and send them home so Mel could put the children to bed while he stayed on, serving until closing. On this particular night, Mel had hurried home to relieve Brie of babysitting. Jack snuck out of the bar a little early and brought their dinner home.

It could still amaze him, the satisfaction he felt when he went home to his family. Three years ago he was a single man, living in a room built onto his bar, completely disinterested in a domestic tether like this. Now he couldn't imagine any other kind of life. He kept thinking that the strength of his feelings for his wife should settle into a kind of complacency by now, and yet his passion for her, the depth of his love, only grew by the day. She had wound her sweet love around his heart and owned him, body and soul. He didn't know how he'd lived so long without it; didn't know why other men evaded it, and he finally understood his friends who'd lived this life for years.

It was nothing fancy: a meal at the kitchen table, some conversation about the building at the bar, the new guy in town, Shelby's return for a nice long visit while she applied to colleges. But for Jack it was the most important part of his day, that time he had Mel all to himself, the kids tucked in for the night.

When the dishes were cleaned up, Mel headed for the shower first. Jack brought in logs and laid a fresh fire in the master-bedroom hearth—the nights were already getting brisk. Fall came early in the mountains. When that was done, he went around the house collecting trash to take to the town Dumpster in the morning. He pulled off his boots by the back door and as he passed the laundry room, he tugged off his shirt and socks and left them on the washer. By the time he got back to his bedroom, the shower had stopped running. He hung his belt in the closet and went to the master bath.

As he stood in the doorway, he caught Mel in front of the mirror, quickly pulling her towel closed over herself. She had a guilty look on her face as she met his eyes in the mirror. "Melinda, what are you doing?" he asked, unzipping his jeans to take them off and take a shower of his own.

"Nothing," she said, averting her eyes.

He frowned and stepped toward her. He lifted her chin and looked into her eyes. "Were you covering up? In front of me?" he asked, astonished.

"Jack, I'm going to pot," she said, cinching the towel tighter.

"What?" he asked, laughter in his voice. "What are you talking about?"

She took a deep breath. "My boobs are drooping, my butt fell into my thighs, I have a potbelly, and if that's not bad enough, I'm so covered with stretch marks, I look like a de-flated balloon." She put a hand against his rock-hard chest. "You're eight years older than I am and you're in perfect shape."

He started to laugh. "I thought you were trying to cover a tattoo or something. Mel, I didn't have two children, a year apart. Emma's only a few months old. Give yourself a little time, huh?"

"I can't help it. I miss my old body."

"Oh-oh," he said, putting his arms around her. "If you're thinking like that, I'm not doing my job."

"But it's true," she said, laying her head against the soft mat of hair on his chest.

"Mel, you are more beautiful every day. I love your body."

"It's not what it was…"

"Hmm. But it's better," he said. He tugged at the towel and she hung on. "Come on," he said. She let go and he pulled it away. "Ah," he said, smiling down at her. "This body is amaz-ing to me—incredible. More lush and irresistible every day."

"You can't mean that," she said.

"But I do." He leaned down and touched her lips with his, one hand on her breast, the other moving smoothly down her back and over her bottom. "This body has given me so much—I worship this body." He lifted her breast slightly. "Look," he said.

"I can't bear it," she complained.

"Look, Mel. Look in the mirror. Sometimes when I see you like this, uncovered, I can't breathe. Every small change just makes you better, more delicious to me. You can't think I'd have anything but complete admiration for the body that gave me my children. You give me so much pleasure, some-times I think I might be losing my mind. Baby, you're perfect."

"I'm twenty pounds heavier than when you met me," she said.

He laughed at her. "What are you now? A size four?"

"You don't know anything. It's much more than a four. We're headed for double digits…"

"God above," he said. "Twenty more pounds for me to gobble up."

"What if I just keep getting fatter and fatter?"

"Will you still be in there? Because it's you I love. I love your body, Mel, because it's you. You understand that, right?"

"But…"

"If I had an accident that blew my legs off, would you stop loving me, wanting me?"

"Of course not! That's not the same thing!"

"We're not our bodies. We've been lucky with our bodies, but we're more than that."

"It was my butt in a pair of jeans that got your attention…."

"My love for you is a lot deeper than that, and you know it. However—" he grinned "—you still knock me out in those jeans. If you've gained twenty pounds, it went to all the right places."

"I'm thinking—tummy tuck," she said.

"What nonsense," he said, leaning down to cover her mouth in a bold and serious kiss. His hands were moving up and down her bare back and before seconds had passed, she was losing herself in his touch. "The first time we made love, I thought it was the best love I'd ever had. Ever. The best experience of my life. I really didn't think it could get better—but it does. Every time, richer and deeper than the time before."

"I'm going to stop eating Preacher's fattening food," she said, but she said it a little breathlessly. "I'm going to insist he start making salads."

He took her hand in his and put her palm against his belly, sliding it down. "I'm not going to have time for that shower," he said, his voice husky. His lips went to her neck. "Unless you want to get back in, with me."

"Jack…"

"You know how much I wanted you that first night?" he whispered against her cheek. "I've wanted you more every night since. Come on," he said, bending and lifting her into his arms. "I'm going to show you how beautiful you are." He carried her to the bed, laid her softly on the sheets and knelt over her, an arm braced on each side. "Want me to light the fire?" he asked with a chuckle.

She ran her hands down over his narrow hips, sliding his jeans lower. "Jack, if you start to find me unattractive, will you tell me? Please? While there's still time for me to do something about it?"

He covered her mouth, kissing her deeply. "If that ever happens, Melinda, I'll be sure to tell you." He kissed her again. "God, you taste good."

"You don't taste bad," she whispered, letting her eyes fall closed.

"Any special requests?" he asked her.

"Everything you do is special," she whispered.

"Fair enough," he said. "We'll just do everything.…"

When Luke pulled up to the house and cabins in the dark of night, he used a big flashlight to illuminate them. The electricity had been shut off last year when old Mr. Chapman passed. All he could really make out was a house black as pitch and a few cabins with peeling shingles and some boarded-up windows. A closer inspection had to wait until morning.

But the sound of the rushing river was awesome. What a great locale this was for the time being. He remembered how much he'd liked this place the first time he'd seen it— the sound of the river, the owls, the wind through the pines making that whistling sound, the occasional bark of a goose or quack of a duck. Although it was cold, he pulled out extra blankets and planned to sleep with one of the camper's windows open so he could hear the river and the wildlife.

At the first light of morning, he pulled on his jeans and boots and went outside to a morning that was just turning pink, the air crisp and damp. Just down the bank he could see the river rushing over natural waterfalls where, in fall, the salmon would be jumping upstream to spawn. On the opposite side of the river were four deer having a drink. And—unsurprisingly—the house and cabins looked like hell. What a pimple on the face of this beautiful landscape.

Exactly what he expected. A lot of work ahead, but great potential. They could sell it right now for the value of the land, or he could improve the structures and get a much better price. And he needed something constructive to do while he plotted his next move. He could scout around for a helicopter flying job. There were news choppers, medical transport, private industry. He took a deep breath. But for right now, this little piece of river land was perfect.

He went first to inspect the house. The porch out front was nice and big, but would have to be reinforced, sanded and stained or painted. The door was stuck and he had to force it, splintering some of the rotting wood around the jamb. Of course the place was filthy—not only had it not seen a good cleaning in a long while before Mr. Chapman's death, in the year since, a couple of animals had burrowed in and taken roost. He heard the sound of scurrying, saw footprints on the dusty floor, and the countertops suggested a menagerie. The place would be full of mice, raccoons, maybe opossums. Hopefully the bear didn't have a den in here. He'd be sleeping in the camper for a while.

It didn't have a good smell, either. Everything was left as it was the day Mr. Chapman passed—the bed was even mussed as though he'd just gotten out of it. Dirty clothes littered the floor, there was rotten and petrified food in the kitchen, all the furniture was still in place. Nasty, musty, stained furniture that was on its very last legs. The appliances also seemed to be about a million years old and the refrigerator had never been cleaned out before the electricity was shut off. It was completely destroyed by odors that would have to be blasted out.

Right inside the front door was a decent-size living room with a good-looking stone hearth. To the immediate left was a large, empty dining room separated from the kitchen by a breakfast bar that was sagging. The kitchen was big enough for a table and four chairs or, better still, a butcher-block island.

Straight ahead was a short hall—on one side a big bathroom with a clawfoot tub, on the other, a utility room. Straight ahead was a bedroom. No walk-in closet here—this was an old-fashioned house. The old man had left large, man-size bureaus and wardrobes. The bed was a big, wooden four-poster. Luke didn't much like the furniture, but he thought since it was solid, heavy, durable ash, it was probably valuable.

He made a U-turn and went back to the living room. There he found a staircase to the second floor. He went up cautiously, not sure of the reliability of the steps. Plus, it was dark up there. If he remembered, there were two good-size bedrooms and no bath. More scurrying. He ran back down the steps. He could look up there after the exterminator had paid a visit.

Standing in the living room, he did a mental inventory. The good news was, it didn't appear the place had to be gutted and completely remodeled to make it livable. The bad news was, what had to be done was going to be expensive and time consuming. Everything but the ash bedroom furniture needed to go away. Far away. It wasn't even up to secondhand standards. The floors would have to be sanded, the cupboards torn out and replaced, new countertops would have to be installed, the old wallpaper stripped, windowsills, doors, frames, baseboards sanded and stained, or maybe just replaced.

But first, the amount of trash hauling and pest removal was going to be a giant pain in the butt. At least this was work he could do, with the help of an exterminator. He'd inspect the roof later.

He walked out of the house and pried open the door to the first cabin. More of the same. The furniture was rotting, the floor was covered with debris. The cabins were all one-room efficiencies that hadn't been used in years, so the small stoves and bar-size refrigerators were outdated and probably didn't work. He was good with wood and paint, but he didn't trust himself with gas and electricity. He was looking at six empty cabins, all in need of new hot-water heaters, stoves, refrigerators and furniture. He'd have to get up on the roofs and see how they had held up through the years, but from where he stood, it looked as though the shingles were mostly missing or rotting. And the wood on the outside of the cabins, all in need of scraping, sanding and painting. Every window would have to be replaced.

He did a mental calculation. It was nearly September. From January to June, before the summer people came for camping and hiking, things were slow and wet around this part of the world. If he could get the house and cabins in shape by spring, he could put them on the market or open them up for rent to vacationers. If it turned out he was bored with the mountains by then, he'd lock the whole business up and make tracks to either San Diego, where his brother Aiden was stationed and there was plenty of beach and swimsuits, or to Phoenix, where his widowed mother lived and would be forever grateful for his presence. He could always chase a flying job if he wanted to.

He unhooked the camper from the truck, unloaded his Harley from the truck bed and parked it up on its stand in front of the house. He grabbed a pair of work gloves, broom and shovel from the bed of the truck, got his toolbox out of the trailer and began scooping out the house. He could at least fill the back of the trunk with trash and, on his way to Eureka to have the utilities turned on, hire an exterminator and rent a big Dumpster; he could also dispose of a big load at the dump.

By noon he had a huge pile of trash in front of the porch. He got to work on loading the trash into the back of the pickup. The bright afternoon sun had warmed up the air and he was sweating like a farmhand, so he took off his shirt. He was just hefting a big three-legged overstuffed chair into the back of the truck when he spotted her. Holding it over his head, he froze.

She was sitting in the clearing astride a big American paint. She smiled at him. Pure, innocent honey. Luke couldn't move. The horse was beautiful, at least fifteen hands. She was wearing khaki shorts, rolled up high on her tanned thighs, a pair of what appeared to be laced hiking boots with white socks rolled over the tops, a white short-sleeved T-shirt and a khaki fishing vest. With that long, pale blond braid down her back and a Stetson on her head, she could be fifteen, tiny and built solid. The thought that she looked like a statutory offense came instantly to mind and he felt every day of his thirty-eight years.

The horse danced and pawed at the ground, snorted and reared his head, but this little girl in the saddle didn't even notice. She handled him with ease and finesse.

"I just had to see this for myself," she said. "You're doing it. You're at work on this mess. Wow," she laughed. "Looks like you're going to be busy."

He tossed the chair in the back of the truck and took a rag out of his pocket to mop his sweating face. "Maybe you can't see the potential here," he said. "I'm going to impress you, in that case."

"I'm already impressed," she said. "It looks like a monumental job. Where I grew up, there were a bunch of old cabins just like this, out on the beach. I was a teenager. They were almost never in use and the local kids used to sneak in. To smoke pot and...other stuff. Then one day they were gone. Razed."

"When you were a teenager," he said, shoving the rag back into his pocket. "Last week?"

"Hey," she laughed. "I'm talking ten years ago."

"In which case, you don't age."

"Why don't you just ask?" she challenged him.

"Okay. How old are you? Exactly?"

"Twenty-five. And you?"

"One hundred and ten."

She laughed again. When she did, she threw her head back and that braid rippled down her back. "Yeah, I thought you were probably really old. How old?"

"Thirty-eight. Pretty well out of your range."

"That depends," she said with a shrug.

"On?"

"On whether I have a range."

Oh God, he thought weakly. She liked him. Not a little teasing, but private flirting, just between the two of them. Luke was a man with few scruples and even less control. It wasn't a good idea for her to do this. She was too alluring for her own good. "You're pretty good with that horse. He's a beautiful paint."

"Chico," she told him. "All little boy. Uncle Walt adopted him as colt—you'd think he'd be better behaved. You know your horses."

"I've flown over a lot of horses running wild in the desert. Incredible creatures."

"You ride?" she asked.

"Haven't been on a horse in years."

"You fish?" she asked.

"When I get a chance. You hunt?"

"No," she said, shaking her head. "I'd never shoot anything. But I shoot skeet, and I'm good, too. Lately I garden and babysit. And I read a lot."

"What are you doing here?" he asked, stepping toward her.

"In Virgin River? I came to spend some time with my family for a while before going back to school. Uncle Walt, Vanessa and Paul, my cousin Tom—he's at basic training, soon to have leave—they're my family."

"No," he said, smiling. "Here. Checking me out."

"Get over yourself, I'm checking out the cabins," she said, returning the smile. "I rode here a few times last summer. I really thought these cabins would disappear someday. Wouldn't it be easier to build new ones?"

"It might be easier, but it wouldn't be cheaper. And I was looking for something to do."

"Why? You get fired from your job or something?"

"I retired from the army."

Her eyebrows shot up. "Like my uncle!"

"No, not like your uncle. Like a warrant officer, helicopter pilot. Jack said your uncle is a retired three-star. A whole different thing, kid."

She grinned at him, but her cheeks took on a little flush. "Just remember, he's retired. He really isn't in charge anymore."

He took note of the pinkened cheeks. She wanted to do this, obviously, this flirting. But it wasn't natural for her, he could see that. He could make it easier for her. He knew how to calm a woman down, put her at ease. In fact, he enjoyed it.

He was having an attack of pure lust and he told himself to nip it in the bud. She said twenty-five, but he thought there was a good chance in any bar other than Jack's, she'd be carded. He grabbed his shirt off the porch railing to shrug into it.

"You don't have to do that," she said. "Not for me—I'm

not staying. Just dropping by to see your project, that's all. I was in the neighborhood."

He chuckled and pulled on the shirt, but he left it unbuttoned. "Yeah. We're neighbors," he said, smiling up at her. "I should be getting back to work, unless there's something you need."

"Nah," she said. "I'm sure I'll be seeing you at Jack's."

"Only place in town to get a beer, so I'm sure you will."

"Well then. Good luck here," she said, lifting the reins. Chico reared, ready to be set free. "Later," she yelled, leading her gelding away and out of the clearing to the river's edge. Luke watched the sight of her departure. Once she was through the trees, she kicked her horse into a run. She got low in the saddle and made that braid ride out behind her, she went so hard and fast. I'm in for it now, Luke thought.

He watched her tiny, young butt move with the horse, confident in the saddle. Sweet heaven, what am I thinking? he asked himself. What am I feeling? She couldn't possibly know what a trim little beauty on a big horse did to him! This was almost the hugest mistake he'd ever considered. But he couldn't escape the fact that he'd like to get his hands all over her. He began to pray that he'd have both intelligence and restraint where this one was concerned. But it would be a first.

Shelby rode back to her Uncle Walt's and all the way she was thinking how Luke might think she'd been flirting, but he was absolutely *not* her type.

Shelby was totally focused on her plans. While waiting for acceptance to a school, she'd travel some. Alone. She remembered the exhilaration of flying off to the East Coast or Europe to spend a couple of months with her cousins during summer. But she'd never seen the Caribbean islands, Mexico, Italy, France or Japan. She'd like to take a cruise, then a vacation—maybe in Italy, the south of France or Cabo San Lucas. After she'd had a nice little break to recharge, she would get herself set up at school, find a part-time job and take a few classes before her degree program officially began in the fall. Just to get herself back in the study groove.

But maybe she'd have herself a little adventure in there somewhere. Maybe on her cruise, on one of her trips.

Not with this kind of man, of course. He was too mature, for one thing. One look convinced her—he knew everything about men and women, while she knew very little. He looked a little dangerous and very, very physical. Scary. He had that warrior appearance, complete with tattoos.

The sight of him bare-chested had rattled her, but the big horse beneath her had given her plenty of confidence. His shoulders were so large, strong and muscular, and he had a barbed-wire armband tattooed on his rippling left biceps. His belly was flat and hard with a trail of chest hair that disappeared into his jeans. The stubble along his jaw made his grin a little taunting and definitely naughty; it had made her shiver. And he had an aura of carelessness. He would take a bite of her, then pitch her out, forgetting her before morning.

But while Shelby had looked him over, everything inside her had grown warm. Something about him, a forbidden quality, was absolutely delicious. Even the damn dirt looked good on him. Despite her common sense, she wondered, wouldn't that be interesting? And her very next thought was, no, no, no, not him! My adventure will come in a polo shirt, cheeks as smooth as a baby's butt, styled hair, no tattoos and hopefully an advanced degree. Not some scary Black Hawk pilot who has a Ph.D. in one-night stands!

Mel stormed right into the bar's kitchen. Preacher had his hands in the sink, his back to her. "Hey, Preach," she said.

But he didn't turn around. "Preach?" she asked again. Nothing. "John!" she yelled.

He jumped in surprise, turned toward her and pulled earplugs out of his ears. "Whoa, Mel," he said. "You snuck up on me."

"Well, not exactly," she said. "I yelled."

"Yeah, well, after a while all that noise makes my head pound. I'd just go fishin', but I have things to do here."

"Listen," she said, sitting on the stool at his work island. "We have to talk, you and me."

"Sure."

She took a breath. "I've gained twenty pounds since I came here. Almost ten pounds a year. By the time I'm forty, I'll weigh two hundred pounds."

He frowned. He wasn't sure what he was supposed to say. Finally he smiled a small smile and said, "Well, good for you."

"This is not good!"

He almost jumped at the angry tone in her voice. Then he frowned.

"Listen," she said, "you have to start doing some cooking that isn't so fattening. Understand?"

"No one's ever complained about the cooking before, Mel. It tastes good…"

"I know, I know—but you're cooking for men with real physical lives. Except you—you stand in the kitchen all day and I know you sample everything. I don't know how you keep from getting fat."

"I clean a lot," he said. "I lift weights—but not as much with two kids."

"Yeah, well, you have a lot of muscle, and that eats up calories. Women don't have that kind of muscle, John. You have to stop using so much cream and butter, that sort of thing. It's unhealthy anyway—not good for weight, cholesterol and blood pressure, not good for the heart. Make some salads, more vegetables not swimming in butter. I can't be the only person in this town who's getting fat on your food."

"Salads?" he said. "I don't usually make a lot of salads."

"I know this," she said wearily. "But we need to make a couple of changes. Just minor changes. Buy some low-fat, whole-wheat bread for sandwiches. Don't do pastas, breads and potatoes at every meal. Make salads, stock fresh fruit."

"There's plenty of fruit around here," he said.

"Yeah, and it's all in the pies."

"You have pie almost every day," he pointed out. "You love my pies. You more than anyone, I think."

She scowled, then grimaced. "I'm going to stop doing that. Listen, can you make some lighter meals available, please? Or else I'm not going to be able to eat here all the time. I'll have to pack a lunch, make my own dinner at home. This madness has to stop. I can't keep gaining weight like this. I am not going to be fat!"

Preacher tilted his head. "Jack complaining about the way you look?" he asked cautiously.

"Of course not," she said in frustration. "He thinks I'm perfect."

"Well, there you go."

"John, I don't think you're paying attention here. I have to go on a diet. You want me to write down what I need?"

"No," he said unhappily. "I think I've got it."

"Thanks. That's all I wanted. I need a little help here, that's all."

"We want you happy," he said, caution in every word.

"It would make me happy." She slipped off the stool. "Thanks, that's all I wanted to talk to you about."

After she left, Preacher stood in his kitchen for a long time, thinking. Then he went out back where the men were at work.

He spotted Jack standing in what used to be his bedroom, talking with Paul. They both wore hard hats while Preacher's head was bare. He waited. Finally Paul and Jack turned to look at him and Paul sighed and shook his head dismally; he took two giant steps away, grabbing a hard hat and handing it to Preacher.

"I'm not going to tell you again," Paul said. "You don't come out here without protection for your head."

"Yeah, right," Preacher said, putting it on. Too small, it sat high on his head.

"You have the biggest head out here," Paul said. "We're framing the second story. You're an accident waiting to happen."

"Yeah, I get it. Listen," Preacher said, turning his attention on Jack, "Mel was just here. She's complaining about the food."

"Huh?" Jack answered. "Mel?"

"Yeah. She says my food is making her fat."

Jack chuckled. "Oh, that. Yeah, she's making noises about that. Don't worry about it."

"She didn't make it sound like I shouldn't worry about it. She was pretty much loaded for bear."

"She had two babies in fourteen months, plus a hysterectomy. And—she doesn't like to be reminded about this—she's getting older in spite of herself. Women get a little thicker. You know."

"How do you know that?"

"Four sisters," Jack said. "It's all women ever worry about—the size of their butts and boobs. And thighs—thighs come up a lot."

"She yelled at me," he said, still kind of startled. Paul laughed and Jack just shook his head. "Did you tell her that?" Preacher asked. "About women getting thicker with age?"

"Do I look like I have a death wish? Besides, I don't think

she's getting fat—but my opinion about that doesn't count for much."

"She wants salads. And fresh fruit."

"How hard is that?" Jack asked.

"Not hard," Preacher said with a shrug. "But I don't stuff that pie down her neck every day."

A sputter of laughter escaped Paul, and Jack said, "You're gonna want to watch that, Preach."

"She wants me to use less butter and cream, take a few calories out of my food. Jack, it isn't going to taste as good that way. You can't make sauces and gravies without cream, butter, fat, flour. People love that stuff, salmon in dill sauce, fettuccine Alfredo, stuffed trout, brisket and garlic mash. Stews with thick gravy. People come a long way for my food."

"Yeah, I know, Preach. You don't have to change everything—but make Mel a little something, huh? A salad, a broiled chicken breast, fish without the cream sauce, that kind of thing. You know what to do. Right?"

"Of course. You don't think she wants everyone in this town on a diet? Because she says it's not healthy, the way I cook."

"Nah. This is a phase, I think. But if you don't want to hear any more about it, just give her lettuce." He grinned. "And an apple instead of the pie."

Preacher shook his head. "See, I think no matter what she says, that's going to make her pissy."

"She said it's what she wants, right?"

"Right."

"May the force be with you," Jack said with a grin.

3

The first couple of weeks in Virgin River, Shelby had to make some adjustments she hadn't expected. At the Booth household she was part of a family—an active, busy, very present family in which she was the fifth member. It was a new experience.

When Tom came home from boot camp shortly after her arrival, for ten days of leave before going to West Point, the family grew again. Vanni and Paul brought the baby into their room and Shelby took the combination guest room/nursery so Tom could have his room back. And, if Tom wasn't missing from the household, his girlfriend, Brenda, was present with him—they were inseparable. The Booth house was spacious, but Shelby felt they were packed in like sardines. She was used to having a lot of space in her tiny Bodega Bay house with just her mother. Periods of solitude. Quiet. There was no solitude now unless she went for a ride. And invariably, someone wanted to go with her.

There was a new development that took Shelby by complete surprise; she never even smelled it in the wind. Vanni whispered it to Shelby one night when Tommy was with Brenda and Walt was heading out the door. He said he was going for a beer, but Vanni said, "Beer, my eye. I'll bet he's going over to see Muriel and that beer takes a long time to drink. We won't see him for dinner." Then she winked. "Daddy's got a woman."

"No way!" Shelby said.

"Believe me," Vanni grinned. "I suspected they were getting to be more than just neighbors, but then you arrived and Tom came home on leave, and he's been sticking around a lot."

"Do you know her?"

Vanni smiled. "Ever see that movie *Never Too Late?*"

"Yeah," Shelby said, perplexed. "I *loved* that movie."

"Muriel St. Claire. She played the new divorcée."

Shelby gasped. "She's *here?*"

"She bought the ranch downriver a little over a mile. She retired to Virgin River, is done making movies and is restoring the house herself. I've only seen Muriel and Dad in the same room three times—they're playing it real cool. But let me tell you—their eyes twinkle when they're together. I've asked Dad if we can have her to dinner soon and he says he doesn't mind an evening away from the house now and then. He also says there's plenty of time for that. I think he's trying to keep her to himself. I'd bet my life something hot's going on there, but neither of them will fess up. The second I ask questions, he clams right up."

"Uncle Walt has a *woman?*" Shelby asked in shock. "A famous *actress?*"

"Well, it took him long enough. I don't think it even

crossed his mind after my mother died, five years ago. It's high time. Everyone needs someone. Age certainly has nothing to do with it. But I wish they'd loosen up. I'd like to hear about all the famous people she knows."

Now they all had a special someone, her young cousin, even her Uncle Walt.

As a teenager, Shelby had been in most ways a typical girl, if a little on the shy side. She got good grades, had girlfriends, was active in school activities. She'd had a nice little part-time job at the library after school and had even gone through a few boyfriends. She went to games, slumber parties, dances. Her friends tended to run in a pack more often than as dating couples; some had high-school boyfriends who were serious, but most of them, including Shelby, were damn happy if they had dates to the homecoming dance or the prom.

She might've been a little more cautious than the average teenage girl—her mom had been very honest about her accidental pregnancy at the age of eighteen, her short marriage that had become a nonevent as she was divorced when Shelby was just a baby. No way Shelby was letting something like that happen to her. She knew she'd be a late bloomer.

She hadn't thought it would be quite this late....

Shelby was only nineteen when the life typical of a girl her age halted and a whole new set of responsibilities took over. Uncle Walt had been more than willing to cover the cost of nursing-home care for his sister, but Shelby had said, "This isn't going to be an issue for long. In fact, much sooner than I like to think about, she'll be gone. She gave me her whole adult life, always putting me first. If I don't give her a few years of mine, the rest of my life won't matter a damn."

Then it was over and time to think about what was ahead for her. Before Vanni had even uttered those words about Uncle Walt, Shelby had been thinking, I want to join the ranks of women my age, women who are my friends, both old and new, and have what they have—the relationship building, romantic and physical love, idealism and passion and even the struggles. She wanted all of it. She was due. She wanted to be *whole*.

She wanted a *man*.

Walt gave a couple of taps on Muriel's guesthouse door, then pushed it open. Muriel had fixed up the old bunkhouse to live in while she worked on the larger house. Unlike most of the times he called on her, finding her in her work clothes and waiting for him to arrive before cleaning up, she was not only showered and changed, but had set a small table with plates and utensils and a candle in the middle. He smiled and handed her a sack of takeout from Jack's bar, then bent to scratch behind the ears of two excited Labs, Luce and Buff. "Looks like a celebration," he said, indicating the table.

"It is. I finished the floors upstairs. One coat of paint in the bedroom and hall and I could live there if I wanted to. And yesterday I bought a pie safe for the dining room. I found it up near Arcata at this little antique shop. It's big—I can't get it out of the truck bed, so I parked it in the barn. Maybe you'll help me tomorrow?"

"Sure."

She looked in the sack. "What is it?"

"Brisket, steamed red potatoes, green and wax beans."

She inhaled. "Pie?"

"Of course pie."

"Where did you tell your daughter and your niece you were going?" she asked, tilting her head and smiling at him.

"I told them I was going out for a beer," he answered. And grinned.

"Walt," she admonished. "Don't you think you're having a

little too much fun with this? I bet you're not fooling anyone. Besides, I'm not sure how I feel about being hidden like this."

He got a startled expression on his face. "Muriel, I'm not hiding you. Not at all! And I did have a beer, while I waited for the food."

"Then why haven't you invited me to dinner with the family?"

"You want to come over for dinner?"

"Walt, I'm not going to let you get away with this. Remember, I know what I'm doing, I know about men. You're not moving forward, you're not backing off. I'm more than happy to be your good friend, as long as nothing's wrong."

He looked down briefly. "All right," he said uneasily. "You caught me. I'm enjoying the hell out of this, Muriel. The riding, the dinners here with you, even when I'm helping you paint or sand or move furniture. But... I'm waiting for you to say something very Hollywood to me, like, I find romantic relationships pedestrian and beneath me. And I'm dreading it."

She laughed at him. "What's this? Isn't this a relationship? And I'm enjoying it, too. Besides, that's not what they say in Hollywood."

"What do they say?"

"Well, it's almost always in newsprint, right near the grocery checkout stand, and it usually sounds something like, St. Claire Caught In Sordid Affair. Or, St. Claire's Husband Seen With Swimsuit Model. Or hooker." She shrugged. "Or something equally gauche." But he had such a soft expression on his hard, handsome face, it startled her eyes open wide. She put the take-out sack on the table and her hands on her hips. "Oh Jesus, you think I'm letting you come over and pester me all the time because you're the only available man in my age group!"

He lifted one black bushy brow. "But am I?"

"That's so irrelevant! Chasing a good-looking thirty-year-old was *never* beneath me!"

She made him laugh. That was the linchpin—she always made him laugh. "That doesn't surprise me. Not that there are many of those, either."

"Walt, for God's sake, I have my own transportation if Virgin River isn't amusing enough for me." She stalked over to him, put her arms on his shoulders, got up on her toes and laid a lip-lock on him that shocked his eyebrows up high and his eyes round. But she kept at him until he finally put his big arms around her slim body, pulled her hard against him, let his lips open, opened hers and experienced, for the first time since they met almost three months ago, a wholly passionate, wet, deep kiss. It was *fantastic*. Delicious. And long. When he finally relaxed his arms a bit, she pulled back and gave him a whack in the chest. "Now stop being a fool or you're going to mess this up. I'll come to dinner Friday night. You cook. I'll bring wine."

"Okay, fine," he said a little breathlessly. "Dinner. With the family."

"*Not* because I'm getting ready to propose, but because I'd like to know your family. And more to the point, they'd like to know me, to be sure you're in no danger." She went to the sack and began removing cartons, placing them on the table.

"Do you suppose we'll be doing that again?" he asked. "That kind of kissing?"

"Beats the hell out of those little pecks and pats, don't you think?" she asked.

"I have to agree with that, yes," he answered. Leave it to some aging starlet to bring a tough old general to his knees. In fact, he thought he felt his knees wobbling and a slight vibration under his skin. Given a little more time, he was going to feel something else; something he didn't feel all that often, but often enough to know it still worked.

"Maybe after brisket. I'm a little annoyed with you at the moment."

"Shame," he said. "I'm completely happy with you."

"I shouldn't have to make the first move," she complained. "Jesus. Men. They're either too ambitious or not ambitious enough." Her phone rang and she said, "Excuse me one second."

He listened to her side of the conversation. "Hmm... Well, much as I appreciate you keeping me in mind, it would take something monumental to pull me back into films.... A year from now? We'll see what you have a year from now, Mason. But really, I'm not going back to Los Angeles for some shitty little supporting role in a B movie—I'm having too much fun. And I have horses and dogs—they don't transport all that easily. No, it's not about the horses and dogs, it's about being *retired* from acting, and not convinced you have a worthwhile project where I'm concerned. Fine, fine—send the script and I'll look at it, but I highly doubt it's going to change my mind, so be prepared for that. Yes, Mason—you, too." She hung up.

Walt had an unpleasant look on his face. "You mind if I ask..."

"Mason. My agent."

"And ex-husband? Fifteen years older than you? Isn't he getting close to retirement himself...at seventy-one?"

"You'd never know it. The man's going to be dancing on my grave."

"Trying to get you to come back?" Walt asked.

"Trying to get me to *work*. And I'm not inclined to do that...." She looked at Walt and for just a second frowned at his frown. Then she laughed. "Oh, Walt, are you worried? Relax. He calls almost every day. He sends scripts sometimes—

nothing but junk. But Mason has always been one to throw everything he has at the wall to see what sticks." She walked up against him and rubbed her hands over his chest. "Really, he'd have to come at me with something as good as *Cat on a Hot Tin Roof* or *Gone with the Wind* to even get my attention." She smiled at him. "Now, can we please have some of Preacher's brisket? You've been a little high maintenance tonight. Not like you. And I'm starving!"

He ran his big rough hands through her soft blond hair. "You're starving? When we met, you didn't eat anything but celery and hummus."

"Yeah, I know. And hanging out with you is starting to show on my rump."

"Looks damn fine to me, Muriel. Light the candle and load up your plate." And he smiled.

A few days later, Vanessa and Shelby were in a fever of excitement as they tidied the house for their famous dinner guest. They would have her captive, to ask all the movie-star questions they were kicking around, trying them out on each other. They wanted the scoop, but didn't want to be a tabloidlike invasive. Of course, they wanted to know things like, who was the sexiest man you ever slept with?

"You can't ask that!" Shelby said with a gasp.

"Of course not," Vanessa agreed. "Try to think if there's a way to ask her which big Hollywood hunk turned out to be the biggest dud?"

Giggles erupted from both of them.

Walt listened to a lot of this from the kitchen. He had insisted he was cooking—it was what he had promised Muriel. And he found himself wondering about the answer to those questions, himself. Vanessa and Shelby shouldn't ask, but given time, he might.

Tom, who had only a couple more days of leave before West Point, brought Brenda. They arrived just minutes before Muriel, and once Brenda got with Vanni and Shelby, the level of excitement rose again.

When Muriel stepped into his house, she handed over two bottles of wine. Then she turned to find herself being stared down by three very expectant, excited, flushed female faces. She laughed. "Well, now, before you get started, I don't kiss and tell."

Three pair of cheeks flamed, but they also melted into laughter.

Things went easy after that. They sat together at the big dining-room table and had wine and hors d'oeuvres and Hollywood questions. Vanni, Brenda and Shelby could give as good as they got—they shared all the Virgin River gossip from as far back as they could remember or had heard. The thing was, if these young women had been true stargazers, they would know that Muriel only told stories that had already been reported and were common knowledge. She was crafty—she'd been down this road before. Her lifestyle was fantasy for the civilians. But she was being completely honest, she didn't kiss and tell. She knew things the *Enquirer* would pay good money for. It was in the vault of her memory.

As far as she could tell, all the Virgin River stories, from hot romances to fights, deaths, despair and victories, were real. "And one of the most talked-about romances in town at the moment is between a certain very popular, accomplished high-school senior and a West Point cadet," Vanni said, lifting an eyebrow.

"No!" Brenda said in shock. "People talk about us?"

Everyone laughed that she could be so naive.

"Do they say anything bad?" she wanted to know, and they laughed harder.

Finally it was Muriel who said, "Of course not, Brenda. You're the darling couple. Everyone roots for you to make it through West Point and college, staying together. You seem perfect for each other."

"Really?" she asked, lifting her head, straightening her neck proudly. It was quite something at seventeen to be complimented by someone like Muriel St. Claire.

Although they were at it till quite late, through coffee and cheesecake, eventually the evening had to come to a close. Walt and Muriel insisted on doing the dishes together. "It's what Muriel promised, since she'd donate a kidney before she'd actually consider cooking," Walt said.

And once they were alone in the kitchen, he came up behind her at the sink and kissed her neck. "You handled that whole interrogation beautifully. Classic recon—evasion, resistance, escape. We could have used you in the army."

She turned in his arms. "What I did for a living was much more dangerous. But I agree with you, I *am* good."

"Then let's get this kitchen cleaned up so I can follow you home, spend a little time away from the kids."

"I can get into that idea," she said, grinning.

At the other end of the house, Tom led Brenda out the front door, pulled her into his arms, making her giggle. He covered her lips in a passionate kiss and against them asked, "How does it feel to be the pretty half of the darling couple?"

"I can't think about it," she said. "It reminds me, we only have two more days together before you go."

"Then we better get alone. How about that?"

"Hmm, please. The sooner the better."

And in the family room, in front of the fireplace, Paul sat in a large leather chair with Vanessa on his lap. She ran her fingers around his ear and put little kisses on his temple. They could hear the general and Muriel laughing in the kitchen, the sound of Tom's little truck firing up in the driveway as he took his girlfriend away. "How's the countdown on the house?" she whispered.

"I'm working as fast as I can. I can't wait until we have our own place." He kissed her lightly on the lips. "As soon as I get a little caught up on the building, let's sneak up to Grants Pass and not tell anyone we're there."

She giggled. "Paul, all we have to do is park the baby with your mother. No one will bother us if she has her hands full of little Matt. We can do whatever we want."

He growled and nuzzled her neck. "Is there any question in your mind about what I want?"

She sighed, snuggling closer.

Outside the great room on the deck, hearing the laughter in the kitchen, the engine of the little truck, the smooching in front of the fire, Shelby looked up at the cool, early-fall sky. She tried to imagine her mother's face amidst the stars, the way she looked before she got sick—so energetic, so pretty and full of good humor and sass. As she so often did, she transported her thoughts to her mom.

I wish you could have been at the table with us tonight; it was so fun. Everyone was laughing, poking fun, telling jokes, gossiping. They were all so loud. And seeing Walt with a woman—it's so different than the way he was with Aunt Peg. More playful. He's happy, Mom, having fun like I never thought he could. And Muriel, for a famous person, she's so silly, so funny. And you should see Vanni and Paul together. There were times I worried so much about Vanni, after losing first her mom and then her young husband—I was afraid she'd never be truly happy again. Paul is such a blessing to her, to the whole family. And I know that Tom and Brenda think only about how difficult it's going to be for them to be apart, but just the way they look at each other... Ahhhh, it reminds me a little of all those chick flicks we watched together. Man oh man, there's so much love in the air around here. Really, I didn't think this little town could hold so much life, so much romance. I'm so lucky to have this place, to be here with my family....

Sometimes, even with all these people around, I still miss you so much....

Sometimes I'm still so lonely....

Do you think my turn will ever come? I wonder that all the time.

Mel Sheridan had worked with Doc Mullins for over two years and in that time had married Jack and produced two children. The job hadn't been easy, Doc being a cantankerous sort, but they had developed a close working relationship and a very special friendship. They didn't agree on all that much, but they understood each other quite well. She was all about following the legal statutes to the letter while he was more concerned with being sure his people, his town, got by as well as they could, regardless of little things like laws. Getting down to it—Doc Mullins would risk anything to see his job was done, and done well.

Mel came to realize he'd probably delivered most of the town; at least everyone under forty. He'd been so much more than just a doctor here. He was the backbone of this town; their confessor, friend and healer. He didn't have any other family. Virgin River was his family.

And Mel and Doc, while neither of them was the least sentimental, had come to love each other. There was a grudging mutual respect—he maintained he didn't need some uppity nurse to get the job done, while she chided that he was so stubborn and difficult he could make those asshole surgical residents she'd worked with in Los Angeles look like a bunch of candy asses. It was true love.

He didn't see her as a daughter nor did she see him as a father figure, but he did regard her children as one might grand-

children. He never said as much, but the twinkle in his eyes
when he picked one of them up was enough. And it filled her
heart with pride and affection.

Mel was at the clinic first thing in the morning, leaning
up against the kitchen sink sipping a cup of coffee, when he
limped into the room. "Morning," he growled.

"Morning, sunshine," she said with a grin. "How's the arthritis today?"

"Worst day of my goddamn life." He reached into the cupboard over the sink and grabbed a bottle of anti-inflammatory
capsules, shaking a couple out.

"Worse than yesterday, which was the worst day of your
goddamn life?" she asked.

He turned to look at her and lifted one white, bushy brow.
"Yes," he said, swallowing the pills without water.

"Hmm, sorry then," she said. "Must be awful. Say, listen—
I've worked out a couple of things with Shelby. She's going
to do some babysitting. She's a godsend, really. Brie's getting
pretty pregnant and though she loves keeping the kids for
me on Wednesdays, I think it's a good idea to spell her, let
her contemplate her uterus and her own bundle of joy. Plus,
Shelby loves hanging around here. So we'll let her help out
here, watching kids, assisting in exams, learning the work-
ings of a country clinic. She'd get to see a side of medicine
that's not limited to caring for someone who's terminal. She's
so anxious to pitch in. How's that sound to you?"

"The babysitting will help you," he said. "I don't know
if we'll ever have enough work here to ask her to pitch in."

"I know. But she has time on her hands. And nursing is different than caregiving. I realize it's not the experience she'll
get when she's finally in school, but it's something. You can
always loosen up and tell her stories of country doctoring—
she'd love that. And when I have patients, I'll have her with

me. Plus, I enjoy her company. She's sweet and sharp. I think
of her as kind of a protégée. I've never had one of those before. I've always been one." She grinned at him.

"Melinda, we're going to bore her to death," he said.

"You can always teach her to play gin. Maybe you can find
a girl you can actually beat."

"When I think about one more woman around here, it
gives me heartburn," he said.

"You shouldn't be having so much heartburn, especially
with your gallbladder gone. Maybe it's acid reflux. Are you
having pain?"

"Ach," he said. "I'm seventy-two with arthritis. What do
you think?"

She shrugged. "I think we should check it out."

"Bah," he scoffed. "I'm fine. I'm old, that's all. I've been
ridden hard and put up wet."

She laughed at him. He hadn't changed much in her two
years there. He was using his cane a great deal more these
days—the arthritis was wearing him down. He was an old
seventy-two—his life had not been an easy one. He'd worked
his way through college and medical school with no help from
family and spent the next forty-five years caring for the needs
of a town single-handedly, with only the most rudimentary
equipment, and with no liability insurance. When she had
lifted her eyebrows at that, shocked, he merely shrugged and
said, "We don't sue each other here. At least not over medical aid."

Doc had never married, had no children, and had told Mel
there was no extended family. Mel had a great deal of affection for him, even if he did ruffle her feathers from time to
time. He had, indeed, been ridden hard.

"If it's acid reflux, they have some really good stuff for that
now," she said.

"I know this, Melinda. I'm a doctor."

"And not just any doctor," she said with a smile. "The biggest pain-in-the-ass doctor in three counties. Suit yourself." And then she thought of something. "You know, you could ask Preacher to come up with some meals that don't stir up that heartburn so much...."

"Why would I do that? He's a dream in the kitchen."

"Well, I've asked him for some low-fat meals. He was very agreeable, for Preacher. I've put on some weight since I got here."

He lifted his glasses to his forehead and peered at her lower half. "Hmm," he said.

"You did *not* just do that!"

"Did I say a word?" he asked, letting his glasses drop into place. She hmmphed and crossed her arms over her chest, glaring at him. "Quit complaining about your weight," he said, rubbing a hand over his big belly. "At least you have the advantage of giving birth to most of yours."

She lifted a mean little eyebrow. "You could give up that whiskey you have at the end of every day. That might help with the heartburn."

"Melinda," he said gravely, "I'd rather have needles in my eyes."

4

It didn't take Luke long to make enough adjustments so he could sleep in a real bed, in a real house, make use of a real shower. First, the exterminator plugged holes and placed traps. Luke did some serious clearing of trash and cleaning. Then there was a new mattress-and-box-spring set and a working refrigerator, both of which he could transport in his truck and move with a dolly. A couple of weeks made all the difference. But every day was long and dirty. His muscles ached. There was an endless amount of work to be done.

It wasn't yet five when he was showered and headed for a beer and some of that excellent food at Jack's. He'd only been there a minute, waiting for someone to come from the back to serve him, when Mel struggled into the bar, baby against her chest, toddler in hand, diaper bag slung over her shoulder. Right inside the door, the toddler took a tumble down onto his knees and sent up a wail. "Oh, punkin," she said. She spied Luke and said, "Oh, Luke, here." She thrust the baby into his hands so she could stoop to lift up the boy. "Oh, you're okay," she said, brushing off his knees. "Don't cry now, you didn't even break the floor. It's okay." She was just about to stand, when she heard her husband's voice.

"Mel," he said.

She looked up from the floor. Jack was behind the bar. He inclined his head toward Luke with a smile on his face. Luke was holding the baby out in front of him at arm's length, a startled expression on his face while Emma kicked her little legs and squirmed.

Mel burst out laughing, then covered her mouth. She rose and went to him, taking the baby. "I'm sorry, Luke," she said. "It's been such a long time since I've been around a man who didn't know exactly what to do with a baby."

"Sorry," he said. "I don't have much experience with this."

"It's okay—my mistake." She couldn't help but laugh again. "The first day I met Jack, there was a newborn at the clinic and he scooped her up like an old pro."

"Because I *was* an old pro, Mel," Jack said, coming around to the front of the bar. "Four sisters, eight nieces and one on the way," he told Luke.

"Prolific family," Luke observed. "I don't know much about babies."

"If you're looking to learn babies, this is the place," Mel said. "I don't think there are any virgins left in Virgin River. The birth rate around here is on the rise."

"Me and babies—incompatible. And I like it that way."

Jack crouched in front of the bar. "Come on, cowboy," he said, holding out his big hands to David. "Come to Dad."

"Da!" David cried, waving his chubby arms and toddling at high speed toward Jack.

Jack hoisted the boy up onto his hip and went back around the bar. "What's your pleasure?" he asked Luke.

"Cold draft?"

"Gotcha," he said, expertly drawing a beer one-handed. He put it on the bar. "How's the house look?"

Luke picked up the beer, much happier holding that than a baby. "Like a train wreck. A complete disaster. I should probably have just put a match to it." He took a long pull. "But, I have the trash out of the house and I've cleaned it up enough to sleep and shower in there. I've started clearing out the cabins. I'm going to have to ask Paul for some advice."

"You may have already gathered Paul is a great guy to work with if you want to do a lot of it yourself. He can step in and get the things done that are outside your expertise. Wish I'd had him around when I was working on the bar."

With precision timing, Paul came in for a beer, still dusty in his work clothes. Right behind him, old Doc Mullins limped in and joined the men at the bar, raising one finger to Jack to set him up a whiskey, and Jack immediately knew exactly what he wanted. A few neighbors arrived, taking tables. The bar had settled into a nice little family watering hole with everyone knowing their places, relaxing into an end-of-day libation before dinner.

Paul inquired about the house and cabins and Luke said, "I'm going to ask you to take a look, but first I have to finish clearing the trash out of the cabins. I got a Dumpster from Eureka and hired an exterminator. If you saw them now, you'd run for your life."

"I don't scare easy," Paul said. "But you go for it. I'm ready when you are."

Luke tried not to watch the door. He had told himself for two weeks he wasn't coming here to see *her*. He came to Jack's because the people and the atmosphere were just what he was looking for in a small, friendly country bar. The men were good-natured and helpful, the women impossibly beautiful. The fact that he kept imagining her in his mind atop that big horse, the braid standing out as she rode, well...that was just that guy thing. He couldn't help it.

Jack leaned on the bar and said in a low voice, "Some of my boys are coming in a few weeks to catch a piece of hunting season."

"Jack," Mel said from across the room. "Not again!"

He ignored her while Paul chuckled. "She thinks we torture the deer," Jack explained, his voice normal again. "She loves to see the boys, but hates that we hunt. Why don't you buy yourself a deer tag and license. Join us."

"Sounds like a plan," Luke said.

"Luke, I had high hopes for you," Mel shot across the room.

"Run by the bank and make a withdrawal," Paul advised. "There will be poker."

Luke grinned. "Deal me in."

An old woman with muddy rubber boots, wiry white hair and big black-framed glasses came into the bar and jumped onto a stool beside Doc. Jack said, "Luke, meet Hope Mc-Crea, town busybody."

"Mrs. McCrea," he said politely.

"Another jarhead?" she asked Jack.

"No, Hope. We're letting some army in here, as long as there aren't too many of them."

"You do anything special?" she asked him point-blank.

"Special?" Luke returned, tilting his head.

"I'm looking for a teacher and a preacher for the town," she answered. "Bad hours, low pay." She lifted her finger to Jack, who set up her drink. "Dream jobs."

He laughed at her. "I sure can't fill either of those slots."

Then she came in. The girl. Luke gulped. He felt a shimmer all the way to his knees. She wore her hair unbound and he saw that it was full and springy, something a man could get his hands all tangled up in. He had a mental image of his large hands on her slim hips. She had a fresh face. Except for something shiny on her lips, she appeared to wear no makeup, but she didn't need any. When she saw him, she lowered her lashes briefly, but smiled. Demure. Vulnerable and in need of a strong man. Oh, crap.

Then stepping into the bar right behind Shelby was a tall, broad-shouldered, silver-haired man of about sixty. Not exactly Daddy, but close enough. It hit Luke in the pit of his stomach. He came instantly to his feet—force of habit. He knew a general when he saw one—in or out of uniform.

With one hand on Shelby's shoulder, Walt extended the other toward Luke. "This must be the new guy. Walt Booth. How you doing, son?"

"Sir," Luke said, taking the hand. "Luke Riordan. Pleasure to meet you."

"At ease," he said with a quick smile. "Welcome. Jack, how about a beer?"

"Yes, sir," he said, fixing one right up.

Shelby gently tugged Paul out of the way so she could have the stool next to Luke, causing Paul to lift his eyebrows curiously. But Luke wasn't sitting. At least not until the general did. He hadn't been out of the army quite long enough to relax about things like rank. He did glance at her, however, and she smiled at him, her eyes glittering slightly, maybe enjoying his obvious tension around her uncle. What he noticed was how rich and sultry her hazel eyes were. And he thought, oh God, I have to get beyond this. There were fifty things about the stirring he felt every time he saw her that were all wrong. He didn't get into things like protective, high-ranking

uncles and innocent young women who were clearly looking for true love.

Luke didn't fall in love. He'd been in love once, when he
was much, much younger, and it had left a hole in his heart
big enough to drive a tank through. The experience left him
a man who couldn't form attachments; he was a dabbler, a
player, not the kind of man who settled down. He never stayed
in one place, nor with one woman for long.

This young Shelby was so transparent, she left little doubt
as to what she wanted. Needed. She'd like to wrap her emotions around a man and tether him right up against her heart,
breaking him in half. Then, in making his getaway, he'd
hurt her bad. Annihilate her. Leave her young, tender heart
in shreds and spoil everything for the guy who might come
along later to do right by her.

The general finally sat and made army small talk. They
went over their various commands and combat tours, and all
the while he spoke with the general, he could smell Shelby's
sweet fragrance. It was swirling around his head, confusing
him, addling his mind.

When Walt finally turned his attention to Doc and Hope,
Luke felt Shelby's breath soft on his cheek as she leaned toward him and asked, "Have you made much progress on the
house and cabins?"

He wanted to be hardened toward her, oblivious to her,
even cruel and indifferent would work, but when he turned
to look at her, his eyes warmed because she melted him into
soup. "As much as possible. I have a place to live that's not
on wheels. It's going to be a bigger job than I thought. What
have you been doing?"

"I've been helping Mel with the kids while she works,
sometimes helping her with patients. I ride, babysit Vanni and

Paul's little one, keep an eye on Uncle Walt… Hardly anything, really. I should come over and help you haul trash."

"You shouldn't," he said. "It's miserable work. Way too dirty for you."

"I could just watch," she said, and smiled so prettily that his heart almost fell out of his chest.

"If you do that, Shelby, I won't get anything done. You're a distraction."

She looked completely surprised. "How nice of you to say that," she said. She briefly covered his hand atop the bar with hers, and a sizzle shot through him at her merest touch. Damn, he thought, I'm in serious trouble. He wasn't sure what he feared most: never having more of her or repercussions from the general if he ever did. "Isn't this the greatest place?" she asked him.

"Virgin River?"

"Sure, that. But Jack's. This little piece of town. I love dropping in here and always seeing a friendly face."

"I've been here a few times over the past couple of weeks and haven't seen your friendly face," he said, then silently cursed himself. Don't push this, he warned himself.

"Oh," she said, laughing. "My cousin Tom was home on leave. We came in a couple of times, but mostly it was all about family. Quite a crowd at my uncle's, with all of us and then Tom and his girlfriend. He's gone to West Point now, so I imagine I'll be around more often."

"And you like Jack's," he observed.

"I grew up in a small town on the coast—way bigger than this, but still cozy. There was this old dive called the Sea Shack—nets and shells on the walls, lots of locals, but also bikers and tourists. You could always count on some of the same people being there. You never had to worry that you'd be alone."

"Where?" he asked her.

"Bodega Bay, south of here. While this is all redwoods, deer and bear, Bodega Bay is ocean, fishing boats, some rocky cliffs above the sea, whales and dolphins."

He leaned his head on his hand, being hypnotized slowly. Thoroughly. He imagined her on the beach; the bathing suit would be very, very small. "It sounds great," he said. "Is that home for you?"

"Not anymore," she said. "My mother passed away last spring, left me the house and I sold it."

He was momentarily surprised. "I'm sorry," he said.

"Thank you. So, I won't be staying in Virgin River—I'm going to college, finally. This is just a vacation. While I'm hanging out here, I'm also applying to schools."

"How long is this vacation?" he asked in spite of himself.

"A few months, probably. After the first of the year, I plan to take a couple trips—I'm surfing the Net, looking at package deals. Then decide on the college and go find an apartment, get a part-time job, take some classes to get back into the rhythm. But I'm hanging around to see Tom again. He'll have leave over the holidays."

Walt interrupted them by getting Luke's attention. "What's this Jack says? You have a brother in Black Hawks, too? Is the whole family crazy?"

Luke turned toward the general and hoped it didn't show in his eyes that he was over the edge in lust. "Lighten up, sir," he said. "At least it's not tanks."

"Boy, I happen to like tanks."

When Luke left the bar, he drove straight to Garberville, when what he really wanted was sleep. His body was bone tired, but his brain was working overtime. And there was one part of his anatomy that was a little too alert for its own good. He hadn't had a reaction like this in a long, long time and coincidentally, the last time had also been from a general's daughter. It was years ago, and he'd been unusually smart—he walked away and never looked back. She had been a prison sentence waiting to happen.

He was trying to drive the thoughts of that sweet young thing from his mind; he'd like to stop the hot little darts from shooting through his body.

He had no trouble finding the local bar—a little hole in the wall that actually made him feel overdressed and totally military with his close-cropped hair and pressed shirt. There were a lot of men in plaid or chambray shirts, long hair, ponytails, mustaches and beards. It looked packed; plenty of cars and big trucks parked around outside.

The place was full at nine o'clock. He made his way inside, finding a stool at a very crowded bar in a noisy room. He ordered a shot of whiskey and a beer. Time to settle everything down and stop thinking about the girl. By the time he'd left Jack's he had started having visions of putting his hands on her and being shot by her uncle.

He threw back the shot and nursed the beer. Good move, Riordan, he lectured himself. Move to a new little town where the same dozen or so people meet at the same little watering hole a couple of nights a week and within twenty-four hours get the instant hots for the one woman to be avoided at all costs. But lust was a beast in him and he was impossibly attracted to her.

He understood very well that touching her wasn't the problem. They were all grown-ups, not teenagers. He could seduce Shelby, get her in his bed, enjoy her and be enjoyed by her, and there wouldn't be too much trouble. He got the impression the general and Paul actually liked him. What would come after would create trouble—he would fail to get serious, move on, make her cry. He'd get into her without falling in love when she was a young woman clearly designed for true love, for permanence. And that would have a bad ending—with him it wasn't just a premonition, it was destiny. He hadn't been able to feel anything like what Walt Booth would want for his niece in over a dozen years.

After about twenty minutes passed, another beer was put in front of him and he looked up at the bartender. "The ladies across the bar," he said.

Luke hadn't even noticed anyone else. His mind had been on exactly one sweet thing. He glanced up and felt his lips lift in a slight smile. "Thank them," he said.

"They'd like to know if you want to join them for a drink."

"Ah, I'm going to have to leave pretty soon," he said. But he was thinking, that's more my speed. Some good old-fashioned, all-American, slutty girls, hanging out in the bar and buying drinks for strange men.

"I'd think that over," the bartender said, lifting an eyebrow.

"Yeah?" He grinned. "Why not," he said. He put some money on the bar to pay for his drinks and, lifting the beer, walked to the other side.

There were three of them. One in each flavor—a redhead, blonde and brunette. They seemed to be in their late twenties and headed for sloshed. "Ladies," he said. "Thanks for the beer. Having girls' night out?"

Giggles all around. "Well, not anymore," one of them said. They parted seats so he could have the middle stool.

"You ladies from town?" he asked.

"Yeah, we're from Garberville," one of them said. "How about you?"

"I'm just passing through," he lied. "I have some property on the river. I thought about some hunting. Fishing."

They were named Luanne, Tiffany and Susie. They were

secretaries and had been in the bar since happy hour, and there didn't seem to be a designated driver among them. Two were divorced and one, Luanne, claimed to have never married. They were wearing their out-to-be-seen bar clothes: short denim skirts to show off their long legs, heels, fitted tops that accentuated cleavages. They had high, perky boobs and fluffy hair. In spite of himself, he briefly considered how much sexier Shelby was in her jeans and boots, her white shirts with rolled-up sleeves and fresh face, leaving everything to the imagination.

He learned they'd all grown up in the area, so he asked about their favorite nightspots. He admitted to being recently discharged from the army after flying helicopters for a long time, but avoided the topic of any kind of combat. These girls weren't that interested in international events and after he said he'd been last stationed in Texas, they didn't push him for details. They wanted to know more expedient things: Was he married? Would he be here long?

Within ten minutes Luanne had her hand on his knee under the bar. He almost jumped in surprise. Then she slid it along the inside of his thigh and he grabbed her wrist. "I'd like to be able to stand up from the bar, Luanne," he said. And she thought that was very funny.

That's when he knew—if he wanted to unload some tension, it wouldn't be hard to negotiate. Embarrassingly, it wasn't exactly a rare move for him. He briefly considered this alternative, but very briefly. He just couldn't get into the idea.

As if a pact had been arranged, the girlfriends, Tiffany and Susie, wandered off, ostensibly headed for the ladies' room, except Luke noticed they were sidetracked at other tables in the bar and didn't return. They were leaving Luke and Luanne alone to proceed. He tried carrying on a conversation with Luanne, who seemed only able to talk about her secretarial job, clothes and girlfriends. She had a very annoying hair-tossing habit. Every few seconds she flapped that fluffy mane over her shoulder.

He had to remove her hand from his thigh another time. He leaned toward her and whispered, "Listen, you don't want to get me stirred up. All right?"

And, leaning far too close and brushing her cheek against his, she said, "What if I do?"

"It would be a mistake. I'm not exactly available." Then he wondered why the hell he said that. He was worse than available, he was verging on desperate.

"I don't exactly care," she whispered.

He was not in the best shape for this kind of horseplay. He excused himself and said he'd be right back, leaving her at the bar. Whew, he thought, headed for the men's room. There was no safe place, he realized. He wasn't safe with Shelby, wasn't safe away from her. This Luanne was more his type— she looked like lots of mindless sex with no attachments. One small problem—she just didn't do it for him. And the more she came on to him, the less she appealed to him. The guileless-ness of the general's niece had already spoiled him for a nice, uncomplicated one-night stand. He decided that rather than go back to the bar, he'd slip out the back way.

He came out of the bathroom and found himself in an in-stant body slam against the wall in the narrow, dim hallway. Luanne had him pinned. "Whoa," he said, hands up as though he was being arrested to keep from touching her.

She lifted her sultry, half-drunk eyes up to his face, smiled a lopsided smile and cleverly tucked something into the front pocket of his jeans. From his vantage point he was looking down at an impressive cleavage and two very healthy breasts pressed against him. It distracted him for a minute—he loved breasts. He often thought that if God had given him breasts, he wouldn't be able to keep his hands off himself. He'd be seen walking around town with his palms pressed over his own chest.

She had her arms around him in the dark hallway that led to the restrooms, pressing him against the wall. A man walked past them, glanced at them, smiled slightly and moved on. Luanne stood on her toes and pressed her lips against his. Holy shit, he thought, his groin beginning to tighten. With her arms around him, she pulled him around and into the ladies' room. He found himself pushed up against the sink while she flipped the lock on the door. She accomplished this with such deft skill, it was clear she'd done it before.

Again, embarrassingly, it wasn't his first time for this, either. He couldn't remember ever being appalled, though. Last he could remember, this was about the time he'd pull a condom out of his pocket and just go for it. It had been quite a while since he'd been with a woman; it wouldn't take long. She was willing. She was past willing—she was obnoxious. He slipped his hand down to his pocket to see what she'd put in there. He pulled out something soft and lacy. A very tiny pair of panties. Red and black. And *off*. "You're fucking kidding me," he muttered, stuffing it back in his pocket.

"Does it look like I'm kidding?" she said sloppily.

He put a hand against her black hair. "Luanne, this isn't going to happen. I'm not doing this here."

"You want to go somewhere?"

"No, baby. We're not going anywhere. I'm not tapping this tonight," he said, giving her hip a little pat.

"I bet I can change your mind."

He shook his head. "Nah. Not gonna happen. Want to let me out of the ladies' room, please?"

"Why not? I don't usually get turned down."

Fantastic résumé, he thought. He felt a slight chuckle escape. "Twenty reasons, kid. You're drunk, you're out of control, you don't know me and I don't know where you've been. But I suspect—lots of places." He put his hands on her upper arms and firmly but gently pushed her back. "You shouldn't do this. You could get hurt."

He moved past her and unlocked the door. When he opened it there was a matronly woman waiting to get inside. He nodded. "Ma'am," he said. He brushed past.

Luke moved, not slowly, to his truck, hoping to clear the parking lot before he found himself assaulted by a pantyless Luanne in the dark of night. Despite his better judgment, if she followed him, he was afraid he'd have a momentary lapse and get under that short skirt. Hmm. He'd never been afraid of something like that before. When he was on the road, he opened his window and let a little piece of red-and-black lace fly.

Then he stopped at a store on his way home to buy a six-pack of beer. He was going to have to avoid Jack's for a while. Until his brain disengaged from his nether parts.

Dinner with the Booths had gone so well while Walt's son, Tom, was on leave, Muriel was invited back the next week. She had secret hopes it would be a regular event. It was lovely. Muriel pulled her truck up to her little bunkhouse after the next such dinner. She'd left a light on for the dogs and could hear them barking before she even had her truck door closed. This is the family I come home to, she thought. Buff, only a few months old, had to be kept in the kennel when she was away from the house; he was still full of all that destructive puppy stuff and for Labs it was almost an art form. Luce was safe on her own now at almost two, but she spent most of that time right up against the kennel, watching over Buff.

She released the puppy from his kennel in the corner and got down on the floor to scratch and cuddle and play.

She had the most wonderful time with Walt and the kids. They were energizing. So full of life and laughter, despite the fact that each one of them had been through some incredibly tough times. Obviously Walt treasured his family, that was without question. They were fantastic fun. But did he know how remarkable they were? she wondered.

They wanted to know how she got into movies. "It was a ridiculous accident," she had told them. "I was about fourteen when I was chosen from my freshman class to appear in a public-service commercial. This agent appeared and talked my parents into letting me try out for a part in a movie. For a fourteen-year-old with virtually no experience or training, I lucked out and did well. Then there was a slightly larger part, then slightly larger, and I grew. By seventeen I was rushing through my senior year to finish all my classes ahead of time so I could be in another movie."

"Didn't your parents freak out?" Vanessa asked.

"I didn't have those kind of parents. They were amazed it was happening for me. I was making money and making film-industry waves—Hollywood focus has always been on the new entrant, the incredibly young wannabe. But—at twenty-one I married my agent, who was thirty-six. That almost sent my father to the moon. But he was a tough country rancher; he came around. Life was different back in these hills in my younger years. With common country folk, when a fifteen-year-old girl was keeping company with a guy over thirty, the girl's father got them married. Today—he'd have the guy arrested."

"Were you married to him long?"

"Five years," Muriel said. "He's still my agent of record. And friend."

"But why didn't you stay married?" Shelby asked.

Muriel shrugged. "He didn't really love me like I wanted to be loved. I wanted a home, a family, a life. Roots. He wanted an Oscar."

"Forgive me for being completely uninformed," Vanessa said, "but did you get the Oscar?"

"I was nominated three times," she said. "I was robbed."

And never got the family. Or the marriage that would have the kind of commitment and devotion that, even in the absence of children and Oscars, could have sustained her. After getting to know Walt's family, she thought that even if she'd had the chance for a family, there was no way she could have produced such strong, independent, well-adjusted adults. Not in her line of work.

So she ruffled the ears and necks of her two Labs, cooing to them, kissing them, telling them she loved them.

And then she heard an engine. A truck engine. The vehicle stopped, the door slammed and booted feet landed on the porch. All these sounds were familiar. There was a knock. Wasn't this unexpected.... "Come on in, Walt."

He stood in the door frame in his suede jacket, jeans, hat. He looked at her on the floor with her pups and smiled. The dogs abandoned her to rush to him, weaving in and out of his long legs, Buff jumping on him. She'd have to break him of that before it got out of control, she thought.

"Any chance you brought more of that delicious dessert with you?" she asked, getting up.

"I'm sorry, I didn't," he said.

"Are you looking for coffee?" she asked.

"It would keep me up," he said, tossing his hat in the chair and reaching out a hand to pull her to her feet. "Come here." He pulled her against him. He ran a hand down her cheek and along her jaw. "Where do the dogs sleep?"

"On the bed with me." She laughed, tilting her head up to him. She wondered if he knew how good-looking he was. And how solid; a man you could hold on to confidently. He didn't waver, not literally, not figuratively. She liked that in a man.

"Think they'd be okay on the floor one night?"

"You making that move, Walt?" He kissed her in a way that should have sufficiently answered the question.

"Muriel, I'm sixty-two years old. I didn't see this coming."

"Aren't you afraid of us becoming an item?"

"Girl, I've been dressed down by a president. You can't scare me with a little gossip. What worries me is that you'll find me old."

She laughed at him. "You're just a few years older than I am. And you're almost irresistibly handsome."

One black brow shot up. "You find me handsome?"

She nodded. "And sexy."

"Well, now. That so? Muriel, I want to touch every part of you. And then I want us to watch the sunrise together." The dogs were whirling around their legs, wagging, butting, trying to get someone to play. "You might have to do something about these animals."

"They'll settle down in a minute," she promised. "But don't you."

5

On what had lately become a fairly typical afternoon, Shelby, Mel and Doc were having a game of gin at the kitchen table in the clinic while the babies napped. Doc wasn't doing much better against Shelby than he had over the last couple years playing Mel. These women were wiping him out. "I think I've gone through my retirement. You're ruthless females."

"I think I remember you winning a couple of hands last week," Mel said.

"Bah," he said, struggling to his feet. He grabbed his cane and hobbled out of the kitchen.

"Is there anything I can do around here that would help you two more than being a third hand in a card game?" Shelby asked. "Need someone to organize charts? Clean up a drug cabinet or treatment room? Inventory? Lab or supply run?"

"Tomorrow is appointment day and I have three prenatals

and four Pap smears. Since you're working here, you can assist. How does that sound?" Mel asked.

"Like a very slow day."

"The thing about country medicine is that it runs hot and cold," Mel said. "This town is so small that days, sometimes weeks, go by without anything exciting. Then everyone will pass around a virus and they're all hacking up a lung, and while they're doing that, everyone else is having an accident or going into labor. You have to be ready for everything, and nothing."

Shelby never tired of Mel's stories drawn from her nursing career, from the wild days of big-city emergency medicine, to the transition to small-town doctoring. For Shelby, working in a hectic urban E.R. sounded exciting, though she wondered if she'd really enjoy living in a big city. But being a nurse in a town as little as this didn't seem to have enough jazz for her. More and more she thought she might end up in an emergency or operating room in a place like Santa Rosa—something between big and small. Or perhaps Eureka or Redding.

"Having come from a big-city hospital, there was one thing about small-town medicine that took me by surprise," Mel said. "In no time at all, your patients are your friends. If there's some intervention you can't get to them in time, you feel not only that you've failed a patient, but let down a friend. For example, hardly any of the women in this town had been having regular mammograms, and when I finally got a nonprofit foundation to bring a portable X-ray unit to Virgin River to examine the women over forty, one of my best friends was diagnosed with aggressive, advanced breast cancer. She died—and I keep kicking myself for not getting the thing done sooner."

"You must feel you can never do it all."

"To the contrary," Mel said. "I feel I have to think of everything, and I *must* do it all. To many of these uninsured rural women, Doc and I are all they have. These Pap smears—I've cajoled almost every one of them. I call them, I push them, I get them in here and charge only lab costs."

"It's an easy thing to let slide, I guess," Shelby said.

"But you wouldn't let it slide," Mel said.

"Well, that hasn't exactly been a priority the last few years," Shelby said with a laugh. "But I've been meaning to talk to you about that...."

Mel's back stiffened instantly. "How long might you have let that go?"

"I haven't had one," Shelby said.

"What?"

"I'm an extremely low risk," she said. Then she lowered her eyes. "I haven't had sex."

Mel sat forward. "That's kind of unusual. At your age."

"I haven't had a boyfriend. Oh, I dated a little in high school, but not seriously. I'm the product of an accidental pregnancy and my mom raised me alone. If we hadn't been lucky enough to have Uncle Walt, life would have been a terrible struggle for us. My mom always felt so guilty about that, about taking all his help. I was scared to death of something like that happening to me. Mostly, I was afraid of disappointing my mom and my Uncle Walt."

"You were very cautious...."

"Well, yes. And I was shy. And then I became nearly a recluse, taking care of my mom. The only men I came into contact with were married doctors, male nurses or hospice volunteers. And here I am, probably your first twenty-five-year-old virgin." She made a face. "Please, I really don't want the whole town to know I'm a helpless, recovering introvert who lived with her mother for twenty-five years."

"Shelby, you know everything in this clinic is confidential—you took the oath when you decided to help out here.

Besides, what you did for your mom gets nothing but admiration around here," Mel said. "It was very selfless. And if you don't mind me saying so, you seem quite sure of yourself."

"Oh, I got over a lot of that shyness while I was taking care of her. I had to be assertive to be sure she was getting what she needed medically. Once you learn to stand up to a high-falutin neurologist, you can handle the bag boy at the grocery store just fine. I'm not crippled by shyness anymore, just a newcomer into the big, free world," she said. "And I don't want to be unprepared...."

"Honestly, I don't want the first thing inside you to be a speculum, but you should be examined. There are other concerns—not just cervical cancer. There's uterine cancer, ovarian cancer. And then you should be protected. Ready. When that time comes, you shouldn't have too much to be worried about—I can't imagine you still have a hymen with all that riding...."

Shelby sighed. "I wonder if it will ever happen."

"It'll happen." Mel smiled. "Let me ask you something—how important is it to you that the first time be noticeably the first time?"

"That's not a big issue with me."

"I think I can get you through an exam without changing the whole landscape too much." Mel took a breath. "Let's do it."

"Now?" she asked squeamishly.

Mel nodded. "Get naked. I'll meet you in the exam room. You know where the gowns are."

A few minutes later Mel let herself into the exam room to find Shelby seated on the table. "Take a deep breath," Mel said, smiling. "It's going to be fine." She helped to ease Shelby into the position, keeping a hand on each thigh so she wouldn't slide too far. "The good news is, I have really small hands."

"Thank God for that, huh?"

Mel chuckled and took her stool, snapping on the gloves. She selected a speculum, then selected a smaller one. "Easy does it," she said, slipping it in. "Well, here's a surprise. Hymen is still partially intact. After all that riding, I'm amazed." She collected the Pap smear and removed the speculum. "I was able to slip past it with the swab, but what's left of the hymen might be sacrificed when I palpate the uterus and check your ovaries."

"It has to go sometime," Shelby said. "I was sort of hoping to lose it the way the other girls do."

Mel chuckled. "This is going to work out better for you. We'll get everything checked out and find you a dependable pill. No shocking surprises for you, Shelby."

"A twenty-five-year-old virgin. How often do you see that outside a convent?"

"You're not the first," Mel said, standing. She gently palpated the uterus. "Since you don't have any symptoms or problems, I'm not going to stretch my hand in there any farther today. Your periods are regular?"

"Extremely."

"No pain between periods?"

"None."

"It's all good, Shelby." She pulled off her gloves. "I usually do the breast exam first, but under the circumstances I wanted to get the pelvic out of the way. Let's have a look," she said, pulling the gown to one side, then the other to gently examine her breasts for lumps.

"I'll take you up on the birth control pills, even though I don't have any use for them at the moment," Shelby said.

It would be unethical for Mel to ask Shelby if she had someone in mind for that position. Another handicap of being a small-town practitioner—seeing the hot little glances exchanged in a neighborhood bar. "Well, I think it's healthy to have a sex life with a responsible partner," she finally said. "I think it's unhealthy to have an unplanned pregnancy. Choose very carefully. Be prepared. Play it smart," she said. "There's one more thing. I probably don't have to lecture on this, but—"

"Condoms," Shelby said. She smiled and a flush reached her cheeks. "I should probably have some of my own, in case..."

Mel patted her hand. "I love having beautiful, intelligent women for patients. Get dressed and I'll round you up some supplies."

Shelby was leaving the clinic for the day when something caught her eye. She made a U-turn and went right back inside. "Mel?"

"Hmm?" Mel said, looking up from the computer. "What's up?"

"Is there some old guy living in the boarded-up church?"

"What?"

"Come and look," Shelby said.

Mel walked out on the porch and looked across the street. Slumped in the doorway wearing a ragged coat, baggy men's pants and boots, Cheryl Chreighton. "My God..."

"What?" Shelby asked.

"She's back."

"Who?"

"When I first got to town, I met Cheryl. She's an alcoholic and young, only about thirty years old. I was determined to find a way to get her into some kind of treatment, but she disappeared. We haven't seen her in about a year. I could have asked around more, but... Well, I didn't pursue her because she wasn't my patient. And I was pregnant, then pregnant, then..." She sighed. Then had two babies and a hysterectomy, she thought. It was hard enough to keep up with the patients in her actual care. Cheryl might not be a patient, but still, a resident of the town. And Mel couldn't stand the idea of a thirty-year-old woman being the town drunk. It ate at her. She should get a second chance.

And she was back.

Luke stayed away from Jack's for a while; stayed away from Shelby. He hoped he'd forget about her, but lust has a life of its own. He thought about her, then damned himself for being an idiot. But, nonetheless, she preoccupied his thoughts. And while she rested in a sweet place in his mind, he made progress on his house and cabins and drank his own beer.

The army delivered his household goods, things that had spent almost as much time in storage while he was in barracks or out of the country as in a home.

Luke had owned a duplex in El Paso, renting the other half to another G.I., which he sold upon discharge from the army. He didn't have a lot of furniture, which turned out to be a good thing, but what he had was quality stuff. He had decided to put his big, old-ash bedroom furniture in one of the upstairs rooms. He had a plush velour L-shaped sectional, an extra-large chair and an upholstered piece that doubled as a coffee table or bench—a little something to put your feet up on. He kept a tray on the ottoman to rest a glass or cup on. He put everything in the living room and covered the furniture with sheets until the sanding, painting and staining could be completed.

There was a nice Pottery Barn dining set that was perfect in the dining area; a dark, square table and eight chairs—a real good poker table. He could get matching bar stools, but he planned to rebuild the breakfast bar first. The kitchen looked a lot better with new appliances, but it would really shape up when the countertops and cupboards were replaced. He made a trip to Home Depot in Redding to place his order—he could install everything himself. While he was there, he bought the stain, varnish and large area rugs for the hardwood floors.

Among his household goods were kitchenware, linens, stereo, large-screen TV for which he had a satellite dish on order, tons of tapes, DVDs, books, CDs. Not many clothes; he'd been in uniform a long time. His closet had always been pretty lean and functional, which suited him fine.

He was ready to venture back to Jack's. There was a part of him that hoped she wouldn't be there so he could be at peace with his decision to stay away from her. Another part wanted her there, within reach, because the decision just didn't seem final.

She did something to him. At first he figured the attraction stemmed from being in this little town with so few options, but then he remembered Luanne and that bar in another town and realized it wasn't quite that. Even if Luanne hadn't appealed, it was very likely a more alluring woman would come along. Usually if he got the hots for a woman he shouldn't be around, it didn't exactly take an act of Congress for him to move on to someone who didn't jam him up so bad. Whatever it was about Shelby, he was having a damn hard time letting go of it.

But he just wasn't done with her. Not hardly.

Luke was just coming out of the shower at the end of a long workday when he happened to see a figure pass too closely to the house. The river was far enough away so that people walking, fishing or jogging there should not come so close. With a towel wrapped around his waist, he looked out the bedroom window. Nothing. He went through the living room to the kitchen and looked out the dining-room window. There was a large boy or man digging through his Dumpster. He was heavy and slightly humped. He'd heard there were transients living in the forest. He could have yelled at him to get out of there, but what did it hurt, him digging through the trash? He wasn't making a mess or anything. Besides, with the threat of bears, he didn't leave food scraps out there.

The man turned and Luke nearly jumped back in surprise. He couldn't be sure of his age, but two things were glaringly obvious. He had Down syndrome. And a big, nasty black eye.

Luke stayed out of sight. He didn't want to frighten him.

An hour later he was leaving the house for an early-evening beer at Jack's and as he went down the driveway to the road, he saw the door to cabin six slowly swing closed. The farthest cabin from the house.

So. He had a tenant.

Luke had been putting in some real long, solitary days. Nothing was going to fix him up better than a cold beer and a little company. When he walked in, Jack welcomed him like an old friend. "Hey, man. Haven't seen much of you lately. How's it going?"

"Dirty and ugly." Luke grinned. "But I'm making incredible progress."

"Beer?"

"Oh yeah. What's Preacher got cooking tonight?" Luke asked.

"He's got some venison stew going back there," Jack said. "It's about the best I've ever tasted. You staying for dinner?"

"I'm going to have to now," Luke said.

By the time Luke was halfway through his beer, Paul walked in, still dirty in his work clothes. He looked down at one upturned boot and walked back outside. The banging that could be heard in the bar was Paul kicking the porch steps, knocking the dried mud off his boots. Then he was back, up on a stool beside Luke.

"How you doing, Luke?" Paul asked.

"Pretty good. I was planning to give you a call. Can I get you to send someone out to look at a couple of things? I need to have a professional examine the roofing on the house and cabins and check wiring for me."

"Be glad to. In fact, I'll do it myself. Jack," he said, lifting a finger. A cold beer instantly appeared in front of him. "How's tomorrow afternoon? Say, around five, when I'm wrapping it up out at the houses and we still have light?"

"Perfect." Luke glanced over his shoulder a couple of times. He hadn't seen her in too long. He hoped she'd stay away, prayed she'd be there soon. "You staying for dinner?" he asked Paul.

"Nah," he said, taking a deep drink. "A beautiful redhead's cooking for me tonight. And if there's a God, the general has other plans."

The bar filled up, some neighbors, a few fishermen and a small gang of young hunters wandered in. Luke had a second beer, opting to wait on the stew a while, and then it happened. She finally came in. He had just about convinced himself he was going to escape temptation tonight. But no, it was going to be worse than usual. Tight jeans, silky blouse under a denim vest, all that hair unbound and flowing free, begging to be crumpled up in his hands.

She came right up to the bar. Paul dropped an arm around her shoulders immediately. "What's up, kiddo?"

"Not so much," she said. "Hey, Luke."

"Hey, yourself," Luke said.

"Getting any better out at your cabins?" Shelby asked.

"Yeah," he said. "A lot better."

"I'm heading home," Paul said, draining his beer. "Coming home for dinner?" he asked Shelby.

"Uncle Walt's out for the evening," she said. "Why don't

I have dinner right here. Luke looks lonely," she said with an impish smile. "I'll be home later."

Paul kissed her forehead and said, "God bless you. And God bless Muriel." And he was gone so fast it made Shelby laugh.

"Do you think he could be any more obvious?" she asked Luke.

"Muriel?" Luke asked.

"A beautiful neighbor lady moved in, right across the pasture. Uncle Walt's been tied up a lot of evenings ever since."

"Really?" Luke asked, eyes widening slightly. The general was into a woman?

She leaned her elbow on the bar, her head against her hand. "You don't mind a little company, do you?"

"Actually, I think I'm going to have to shove off…"

Then Jack was standing in front of them, obviously hearing that last comment. "I thought you were staying for dinner? Beer, Shelby?"

"Thanks," she said. When the beer was delivered and Jack gone again, she said, "You were going to stay till I got here? That's not very flattering."

A little embarrassed, he said, "I guess I could manage dinner."

"Don't put yourself out," she said. "I can find someone to have dinner with."

"No, this'll work."

"I don't come here every night, so I thought maybe we just missed each other. But I asked Jack—you haven't been around for a beer at all. A couple of weeks, I think…."

Eleven days, he thought miserably.

"And you were going to make a break for it once I showed up. I hadn't even considered you were avoiding *me*. Do I make you nervous or something?" she asked.

"Whew," he answered, shaking his head. "I haven't been

out of the army long enough to get over that rank thing. Your uncle—"

"Isn't anywhere in sight," she said, cutting him off. "Is it just my uncle?"

"You're a pretty girl, Shelby," he said. "And you're just a girl. Puts me on edge, yeah."

"Well then, we're even," she said. He gave her a perplexed look and she said, "You're a good-looking guy, obviously been around a lot more than I have, and you're older. Scary."

He laughed at her candidness. "There you go—like water on a grease fire. Let's play it safe, huh? Now tell me about your day."

"Nothing to tell. Besides, this is interesting. I'd like to know what's going on here. So, it's pretty much that I'm a lot younger than you are. Or you just don't like me." And then she blushed, which made him squirm. It obviously took guts for her to push on this issue. But she wanted to know. So he decided to tell her.

"You know what it is, Shelby," he said. "You're young and tender. A sweet young thing. I'm hell on sweet young things."

She laughed at him. "I bet anything you usually find a way to get past all that."

Well, she didn't scare easy, Luke realized with some admiration. And here was what had him screwed up—it wasn't just that he had taken one look at her and felt that familiar tug of lust. Sounded like maybe the same thing had happened to her. Except that she had feelings deep enough to fall into and drown, and his feelings were all superficial, physical. Once his lust had been satisfied, he wouldn't have much left for her. She'd end up sorry. He had always been able to avoid things like this, but this one, she was real tough on the nerves. It was going to be torture, just holding back. And it could be suicide, giving up the fight.

"I just wish your Uncle Walt was a retired master sergeant," he said.

Luke usually confined his prowling to a town or two over so when the affair had run its course, he didn't keep bumping into the woman again and again. Or her uncle. Before crawling between the sheets, he'd always give them "the talk": he didn't fall in love; wasn't interested in long-term deals or commitment. He had his reasons, serious and personal reasons, for believing that a serious relationship wasn't possible for him.

He wondered how Shelby would take to "the talk." Given her age, she would probably cry.

He had been attempting to give not touching her a try, but just sitting next to her, having a beer, smelling her sweet scent and looking into those large hazel eyes, it was increasingly apparent he was destined to fail. It was just a matter of time; maybe a matter of hours.

"Well, I admit, you're not exactly what I have in mind, either. I was thinking around twenty-six, more hair, polo shirt, or maybe a sharp, crisp, white button-down," she said, and then she grinned at him.

He was totally shocked. He'd spent all this time fighting the attraction and she had something else in mind anyway? "I'm too old for you, plain and simple," he pointed out.

"Probably, but there don't seem to be many single men around. You kind of stand out."

"You should throw your net wider," he suggested.

"Until I do, let's not get ridiculous. It's a beer and some dinner. It doesn't really matter how old we are or who my uncle is."

He smiled. Sometimes she seemed a little older than twenty-five. She was awfully bright. Quick. Usually the problem with girls her age was they were dimwits. Not this one. She was honest and direct. Luke respected that. "You've been riding," he said. "Your cheeks are sunburned."

"Every day. Sometimes twice a day."

"How long have you been riding?"

"Since I was real young. I'm Uncle Walt's only sister's only child, and my parents were divorced when I was just a baby, so my uncle kind of took me under his wing. He taught me— he thought it would build my confidence to learn to handle big animals. It turned out I only got more confident around big animals." She shrugged and looked down. "I used to be real timid."

The memory of seeing her on that big American paint came to mind. "You're sure not timid on that horse," he said. "And you're not so timid with me."

"I know. I've worked through a lot of that. I don't know very much about you besides that you flew helicopters in the army. What about your family? All I know is you have a brother in Black Hawks in the Middle East."

Luke's dad had been a hardworking teamster, an electrician, and while he was a good provider, there hadn't been a great deal left over for things like college educations. There were five boys to raise and educate. "I was the oldest and first one in. It wasn't a hard decision for me—I always liked the idea of the army. It was a place for me to show my stuff—and I did fine. Loved the challenge. Colin followed me—into the army out of high school, into Warrant Officer School and the Black Hawks. Aiden upped it a notch—went into college ROTC and got a navy scholarship for med school. Don't ask me how—but Sean scored an Air Force Academy slot and got into the U-2. Sean is the brother who went in on the cabins with me. Paddy—Patrick—got into the Naval Academy and F-18." He smiled because her mouth had dropped open.

"Holy crap, there are five of you!"

"Yeah," he said. He thought he was going to have to sit on his hand to keep from touching her hair. "Prolific Irish family. Sean and Patrick and their jets—they think faster is cooler. But they think that because they've never been in the Black Hawks."

"Faster, higher and maybe safer," she said.

"Possibly." He laughed.

"How many times have you crashed?"

"I've never crashed," he said, straightening proudly. "But I've been a damn good target three times. Mogadishu, Afghanistan and Iraq. I'm all done getting shot out of the sky. Right now, I want my most dangerous experience to be hammer versus thumb."

They talked about building for a while, about the plans he had for the cabins. He would concentrate on the exteriors while the weather was still nice and when it cooled off and the Pacific winds brought the wet and cold, he could work inside. "Chapman left the house a wreck, but the structure seems sound. It's going to take some doing to get it right. It's small, but big enough for me. And if a brother or two shows up, there's room. But this is temporary for me. By the time the work is done, I'll be looking for a flying job—rescue or news chopper, or maybe even private industry. But chopper jobs are pretty tight, so it's good I have something to keep me busy while I check out the job market."

"Where will you go?" she asked.

"I'm flexible," he said with a shrug.

She learned the brothers were close—when they were in the same part of the world, they got together. His father was deceased, but his mother was in Phoenix and they met there regularly. And each of them was willing to travel if there was a chance to meet. When she asked if he had a lot of nieces and nephews, he said, "All single. No kids anywhere."

She didn't tell him a whole lot about herself, just that she was finally ready to get on with her education, that she would be applying for degree programs. "I have my tuition money set aside from the house sale. I'd like to take a couple of trips first, maybe a cruise, since I can't get back to full-time school till next fall anyway. I'm pretty nervous about that, it's been a long time since I've been a student."

"You'll kick ass," he said, taking curious pride in her ambition.

"For now, I'm just hanging out."

"For how long?" he asked.

She answered with a shrug. "Till the first of the year, anyway, that's the plan. There's not too much for me to do except help everyone out, and I'm already getting a little bored."

He made her laugh, put her at ease. She had a second beer and he had another. "You about ready for some dinner?" he finally asked her.

"I'm starving," she said.

By the time Jack put stew in front of them, many of the locals were leaving, but there were still a few fishermen, so there was no hurry for Luke and Shelby to clear out.

They asked Jack for coffee and talked for another hour before Shelby looked at her watch and said, "Do you think I've given the lovebirds enough time alone?"

"By the look on Paul's face, there isn't enough time."

"Tell me about it." She stood up and slipped a hand into her jeans' pocket.

"Nah, Shelby. Let me," Luke said. He pulled out his wallet and put some bills on the bar.

"Careful, Luke," she teased. "If you buy my dinner, I'll think you like me."

He put a hand on the small of her back. "That's the problem," he said. "I do." He was past the jitters about her age, her uncle. He was moving on this. And when it was over, he was going to be shot, he was pretty sure. But he was into her; she had him. He hoped his death would be quick and painless.

An excited shiver ran through her as she preceded him out the door. When she got outside, she stopped on the porch and looked up at the clear, cool sky, peppered with a million stars. The wind through the pines made a whirring sound; an owl occasionally hooted.

Luke moved behind her and, with his arms around her waist, drew her back against him. She let her eyes softly close, enjoying the feeling of his sturdy body so close to hers. He nuzzled her hair and despite the noise of the wind through the pines, she heard his breath as he inhaled. Then she felt him move her hair aside; his lips and tongue were on her neck. "Hmm," he said. "That's nice. Real nice." Then she felt him sucking and she tilted her head to one side to give him more of her neck.

That tilt of the head, that was more invitation than Luke usually required. He pulled her away from the bar's front door to the edge of the porch, to a dark corner. He'd begun feeling light-headed just from the sensation of her neck against his lips. Her soft, sweet fragrance swirled around him and he wanted to take her somewhere, undress her, taste the rest of her body.

He faced her and looked down into her eyes. "I'm sure this is a huge mistake," he said in a throaty whisper.

She rubbed her hands up and down his upper arms and just smiled that soft, sweet, beguiling smile.

"You're pretty irresistible, Shelby. And I never did have much willpower."

"I'm kind of new at this flirting with dangerous older men," she said. "Is this where I apologize?"

"New at it?" he asked. "I think you might be a natural. It's working."

"Well, maybe I have more social skills than I thought," she said with a laugh. There was no maybe about it—she had made a sudden and crazy decision. She wasn't going to wait for the younger, more stylish man. The very thing he was warning her to be careful about, she decided, would work to her advantage. He was experienced. He knew what he was doing. She needed that. His arms around her and his lips on her neck felt wonderful. He would do nicely.

"Do you know what it means to get mixed up with someone like me?" he asked, his voice husky.

"Danger? Heartbreak?" She took a breath. "Adventure? You don't scare me as much as I scare you, Luke."

He slowly lowered his lips to hover over hers. "You sure about this?" he asked. "Because I think you know where all this flirting is headed. I'm no kid. This is headed someplace real naked."

"Don't get ahead of yourself," she said with a weak whisper. "I'm not taking my clothes off."

"Not yet?" he asked, his lips so close to hers she could feel his breath in her mouth, warm and sexy.

"Maybe never," she whispered.

"Maybe," he whispered back. "I like that word, *maybe*." Then he lowered his lips to hers and pressed against them softly. He ran his hands up her sides, catching her under the arms and stretching them out, bringing them around his neck, showing her how to hold him. His arms went around her waist and he pulled her against him, kissing her more deeply. He could feel her firm breasts against his chest and he'd like nothing so much as to lower his lips to one, but this was not a woman to ravage. This was a woman to lead. Besides, Jack's front porch was not the place. For the things he wanted to do, they needed to be assured of more privacy. He opened his lips, sucking at hers. And she opened hers, letting her tongue make a gentle, silken swipe of his mouth, bringing a deep and passionate groan from him. He ran a hand down over her bum and pulled her hard against him. He was already aroused; she just knocked him out.

Something like a whimper came from her as she pressed herself against him, opening her lips more to admit his tongue. His kiss was hot, wet, deep and long. He had been right about one thing—she could mold her small body against him in a way that made him think he might go completely crazy. The one thing that helped him keep his sanity was the belief that when this was finally consummated, it was going to be sweet. And good. For both of them.

"I have a feeling I'm not what you were expecting," she whispered against his lips. "I'm not very experienced."

"I already know that," he said. "I am." He kissed her again, holding her tight, and he felt a slight trembling in his arms. He pulled away from her lips, still holding her small bottom and pushing her hips against him, and whispered, "You're right, Shelby. You're pretty much all surprises."

She expelled a small huff of air, smiled and said, "You have no idea."

He ran a hand along the hair at her temple. "Shelby, how does a young woman as beautiful and sweet as you not have a man in her life?"

She glanced down briefly. "There was no time for that. My mom… She was completely dependent on me." She looked up into his eyes. "I took care of her. That was my full-time job. Until she died."

He was stunned speechless for a moment. "For how long?" he asked softly.

"Five years or so."

"Aw, Shelby…"

"It was my choice. It's what I wanted."

He leaned toward her and pressed his lips tenderly against her head. "Not many people would do that."

"Oh, probably more than you think."

He was surprised at how much that moved him, touched him. He lifted her chin with a finger and brushed his lips across hers again. He threaded his hand under her thick mane of hair at the back of her neck and put soft kisses on her mouth and temples and eyes. Then her lips again. And he said, "No. Only a certain kind of person takes on something like that. Your kind of person." This young woman was every beautiful thing he'd ever imagined, from her body to her spirit. He gave her lips another light kiss. "I'm going to put you in your car now."

"Seems like maybe you changed your mind about this... this flirting...."

He shook his head. He wished he could. He knew he should. But he hadn't. When the time was right for her and the tension gave way to need, when there was no more maybe about it, she was going to come to him, soft and willing, and he was going to make long, slow, fabulous love to her—damn the consequences. And he would be sure she'd have no regrets about the experience. It wouldn't be too fast and it wouldn't be too soon—and it would be exquisite. It wasn't a good idea, but it was the only idea he had.

"Nah," he said. "I have a one-track mind."

She laughed at him. "Big surprise."

"Before this goes any further, we're going to talk about some things," he said.

"What things?"

"Expectations. Needs. You have to know what you could be getting yourself into. While there's still time for you to come to your senses."

She put her hand against his cheek. "I look forward to that."

He gave her a brief kiss and said, "Come on. Time for you to go home."

6

Shelby wasn't quite ready to leave Luke; she was in the mood for more of that kissing and touching. But, sensing he was right to put a little space between them if she wasn't ready to go further, she let him put her in her Jeep and went home. She let herself into Walt's house and found it dimmed and quiet. A light was left on for her in the great room and Uncle Walt's big Tahoe was missing from the driveway. It was only ten, but there was no doubt in her mind that Vanni and Paul had turned in the minute the baby was asleep.

She was too stirred up for sleep. She pulled off her boots, built a fire, pulled the throw from the couch around her shoulders and curled up in the big leather chair near the hearth. She hugged herself dreamily.

Only about fifteen minutes had passed when Vanni came out of her bedroom wearing her robe and furry slippers. She smiled at Shelby, then went to the other chair facing the hearth, kicked off her slippers and pulled up her bare feet, tucking the robe around her legs.

"Did I wake you?" Shelby asked quietly.

"I wasn't asleep."

Shelby laughed conspiratorially. "Did I disturb you?"

"Not at all. In fact, I was thinking about you, wondering when you'd get home."

"Are you staying awake for me? To be sure I get in safely?"

"No," Vanni said. Then she laughed and said, "Yes. Paul said you stayed at the bar to have dinner with Luke."

"Yes. And not only did Paul come home and report on me, every person there glanced at us as they left Jack's. Good thing I'm not trying to get away with anything, huh? Good thing I'm not fifteen, right?"

"I think maybe Luke's a little too old for you."

"He is. And he's made it real clear that I'm too young for him." Then she laughed softly. "Oh brother, he doesn't know the half of it."

"You know, I grew up around soldiers. Honey, they have some real rough edges. It's the nature of the beast. The life they lead, the things they're required to do, it puts them on the tough side of life. They harden up, you know? They can become insensitive, brash and... Well, they learn how to live in the moment, without looking back, if you know what I mean."

"Would you say that about Uncle Walt? Jack or Paul?"

She shook her head. "They're pretty special men." She was quiet for a moment and then said, "You've been locked in with your mom for so long, you practically missed the real beginning of young womanhood. And now when you could really use a mom to talk to, she's gone. Maybe you and I should go over a few things. About men. About relationships."

"Aw, Vanni—you're worried about me."

"I can't help it. I know how old you are. But I also know how inexperienced you are."

But *he's* experienced enough for both of us, she almost said. "You know, you can't have the kind of talk with me as you would with a thirteenor sixteen-year-old girl. True, I haven't been around, but I'm not ignorant. While I was housebound, postponing my life, I still had books and television. I might not have experienced much firsthand, but I've been watching from the sidelines. I've witnessed women's romantic problems from Scarlett O'Hara to Anna Karenina. And that's not even taking into account prime-time TV. But you go ahead, Vanni," she said with a smile. "Anything you think I should know—lay it on me."

"You like him," Vanni said.

"I do. I didn't expect to, but I just can't help it."

"And you know *exactly* what you're doing."

She laughed. "No. I know what I'd like to do, but I'm such a clumsy novice, it's amazing he's not bored to death by me. I'm a twenty-five-year-old going through puberty. When I was supposed to be learning these things in high school, I was too shy. I was afraid to flirt, afraid the boys would laugh at me. I could have learned a little later, when I was older and braver, but I was busy." She shrugged. "So here I am. Trying this out for the first time. With a guy whose first time probably came before I was born."

"I don't want you to be hurt," Vanni whispered. "You're the sweetest, kindest person I know."

"Vanni, I barely know Luke Riordan, but it's real clear he's not my knight in shining armor. He's done everything he can think of to discourage me, but let's be honest—this was no frontal attack from him. He admitted he's avoided me because of my age. The coward."

Vanni laughed at her.

"When you get down to it, my first choice was a completely different kind of man. Closer to my age, less seasoned, someone who doesn't come right out and promise to ravage you—"

Vanni sat up straight, eyes very large. "He *said* that?"

"Not in so many words, but I got the message." A wonderful shiver passed through her. "Besides, even if I found myself attracted to a younger man, he'd still be more experienced than me, he might even be divorced with kids. There are a couple of things I know about Luke, though. He might be a little on the rugged side, but he's actually very tender. Gentle. Patient." Her eyes glistened when she looked at her cousin. "He kissed me," she whispered secretively. "I've *never* been kissed like that. It was unbe*liev*able."

"Whew. Really?"

Shelby nodded. "You just can't imagine how good he is at it. Shew. But don't worry—I told him I wasn't taking my clothes off. I wanted to, though. Boy, did I."

"Shelby!" Vanni said, stunned.

"Well, I did, but the porch at Jack's bar didn't seem the place. Plus, it's pretty cold. I mean, I wasn't cold—Luke was wrapped around me like a straitjacket."

Vanni giggled in spite of herself.

"And he likes me. He hates that he likes me—Uncle Walt has him scared to death. And you know what? I love that in spite of that he can't resist. Do you have any idea what that means to someone like me?"

Vanni was quiet for a long moment. Finally, she said, "What can I do?"

"Let's have that talk. It would be nice to have someone to talk to about this. About where it's going, which I think I'm pretty clear about. Can you do that without telling Paul all my personal business?"

"Sure," Vanni said with a smile. "Men don't care about these things anyway. Where should we start?"

"Why don't we start with you telling me about your first experiences with this," Shelby suggested.

"Well," Vanni said, looking into her lap for a second. "First of all—I wasn't shy in high school. Or in college. Or while I worked with the airline...."

Shelby giggled. "Oh God, this is going to be delicious! I can't wait!"

Luke was up early the next morning, as was usual for him. But this morning he had a mission in cabin six. He got out the bread, mayonnaise and mustard, bologna and cheese and made a half-dozen sandwiches. He wrapped them, put them in a sack and grabbed a big bag of chips and two canned sodas. The sun was just coming up when he pushed open the cabin door.

The man was curled up on a broken-down sofa in the corner in a big, chubby ball, sleeping, his jacket spread over his body. He rested his head on an arm. Luke crouched down beside him, but the guy didn't move a muscle. He was pretty filthy; Luke wondered how long he'd been homeless. He gave his shoulder a little shake and the man's small eyes opened slowly.

He rolled slightly, rubbed his eyes and scrambled into a sitting position.

"How long have you been sleeping in here?" Luke asked.

He shrugged. He yawned. "A couple nights," he said. "I'll go."

"I brought you something to eat," Luke said, handing him the bag.

"I don't have any more money," he said.

"It's free. It's from my kitchen and I'm sharing with you. What's your name?"

"Art," he said, opening the bag and digging out a sandwich. He nearly stuffed the whole thing into his mouth.

"Slow down," Luke said and laughed. "Who hit you, buddy?"

"He din't mean it," he said, chewing and gulping. "He said he din't mean it."

The guy was starving. "Who didn't mean it?" Luke asked.

"Stan," he said. He made a final gulp and reached into the bag for another. "My boss at the grocery."

"Hmm. Where are you from?"

"Eureka," he said, unwrapping another sandwich. "I came through the big trees. I like 'em. The big trees."

"The redwoods. You walked all that way?"

He shrugged and swallowed. "I hitched some. You're not supposed to hitch, you know. Then I walked through the big trees."

"Through the grove, huh?" Luke said. "Yeah, they're nice. How old are you?"

"Thirty. My birthday is in November. Then I'm thirty." He dived into another sandwich.

"Your parents live in Eureka?"

He shook his head. "My mom's gone now. I have a group home, but if I stay there I have to work at the grocery. For Stan."

Luke was still crouched, sitting on the heel of his boot. He'd only known one kid with Down's while growing up—a neighbor kid. He'd been younger—his brother Sean's age— and Luke and his brothers all looked out for him. No one dared give him any trouble—they'd have to answer to the scrappy Irish Riordan boys. He was the sweetest kid on earth; Luke had learned they had a reputation for being the gentlest-natured people alive. But this guy's boss had slugged him in the face. Now, why would a person do something like that?

So Art is on the run from an abuser. Wouldn't his caretaker be onto that? Make that right? Unless the caretaker was also abusive...

Luke thought about calling someone, get this guy some help. But he only thought about it for five seconds. He couldn't have some agency toss this guy back into a group home where he was mistreated. "You need a job where nobody hits, buddy?"

He shrugged and chewed.

"I could use some help. Maybe if I let you have a place to sleep while I'm working around here, you could do some chores for food and clothes and stuff. Any interest in that?" Art nodded without making eye contact. "Can you count?"

Art looked up, swallowed and said, "'Course I can count. I'm not stupid."

That made Luke smile. "'Course you're not. Okay. I can let you sleep in the trailer a few nights till we get a cabin straight for you. There's some plumbing that works in the trailer. I'll find you a sleeping bag and something clean to wear. How's that?"

He gulped down the last of his sandwich. "What's your name?"

"Luke," he said, standing up.

"Okay. Luke."

"When you're done eating there, go down to the camper and wash up. The water's not real hot, but I'll get you a bar of soap and a couple of towels. I'll meet you down there in a little while, how's that?"

"Okay. Luke."

"It's a roof and a bed. We'll get a cabin in shape for you so you have a little more room, but the trailer's not so bad. It's better than this."

"Thanks. Luke."

"You're welcome, Art."

Luke went back to the house and dug around in his things. Luke was a big guy, but his waist was trim, so nothing of his would fit Art. He finally settled on a bathrobe he never wore, and with towels, soap, pillows and a sleeping bag, he went back down to number six. It was empty. He hoped Art hadn't panicked and run, because the guy needed a little assist.

But Art had gone, as he was told, to the trailer. The shower, barely warm and tiny as hell, was running. Luke knocked on the door. "Art? Hey, Art?"

"Yeah?"

"Can I hand you over some soap? Leave you a bathrobe and some towels?"

"Yeah," he said. "Don't look at me."

"I won't. You put on this bathrobe and I think I'll wash these clothes for you. They're nasty, Art."

"They're dirty," Art corrected.

They were way past dirty. Luke handed a bar of soap into the shower and left the towels and robe hanging on the hooks right outside. Then he gingerly plucked the clothes off the floor and, leaving the shoes, carried them to his house. But before he entered, he changed his mind. They were so awful and probably infested, he didn't even want them in his washing machine. They were also threadbare, the underwear gray...yet the bruise was new. Suddenly Luke realized this was how Art had been dressed in the group home. So, Luke dug around in his toolbox for a tape measure and went back to the trailer. He walked in to find Art in his blue terry robe. Art jumped in surprise.

"Don't worry," Luke said. "I looked at your clothes and they seem to be in bad shape. I don't have anything that will fit you, but since you're going to work for me, I'm going to buy something in your size. Any chance you know your size?"

"Forty."

"What's forty, Art?"

He shrugged his shoulders.

"Okay, no problem. Let me measure your waist. I bet it's your waist. But I'll need—" He stopped. He couldn't measure the man's inseam. Art had asked not to be looked at and Luke had a momentary concern that maybe something uncomfortable, if not horrible, had happened to him. He'd measure the inseam of the discarded pants. That would do.

Art stood still for him while he put the tape measure around his waist. Forty—the guy was fairly competent. Time would tell how competent, but Luke had made his decision. He was going to give him a chance to not be homeless or beaten. He'd work out the details later.

"What size are your shoes?"

"Ten," Art said. "Wide. Very wide."

"Good. Here's what I'm going to do. I'm going to get you some clothes because yours are ruined. Then I'm going to make sure you have dinner. And tomorrow we can talk about your chores. Can you stay here, inside, until I get back? It'll be more than an hour."

He looked at the rolled-up sleeping bag on the bed in the trailer. "Can I open that? It's okay?"

"Sure. Have a nap if you want to." Luke smiled at him. "You look good all cleaned up. How long you been on the road, buddy?"

He shrugged. But it couldn't have been too long—the bruise was still fresh. He must have had some rough experiences in a short time to get so filthy.

"I'll be back. Stay inside. I don't want you scaring anybody in your bathrobe."

"It's your bathrobe," Art said. He was clearly very literal.

"I'm giving it to you, pal. I never once put it on. I think my mother gave it to me. I think she gives me one every Christmas. Maybe she's trying to keep me from walking around naked."

"My mother's gone now."

Luke reached out and squeezed his upper arm. "Yeah, you told me that. I'm sorry, man."

"I have a group home. But I don't want to have that job anymore."

"I understand, Art. You don't have to do that job. No one on this job will hit you. You clear on that?"

He smiled a small smile. A small, tired, hungry, beaten-down smile. "Clear. Luke."

Two hours later, Art had new clothes. Functional clothes. Loose blue jeans and soft denim shirts, new tighty-whities and clean socks, new tennis shoes—black, because his chores would get him dirty. He also had a toothbrush, paste, comb, disposable razor and shaving cream. Luke made him a hamburger for dinner, made sure he knew where everything was in the trailer. Then he observed the shaving to be sure Art handled the razor safely. "You'll be okay here by yourself tonight?" he asked.

"I like it," Art said. "I wished it was mine when I first saw it."

"That right? You won't run off, will you?"

"I'm helping you now, Luke."

"I got you some bottled water and a few protein bars in case you get hungry before morning. If you have a problem, you know where I am. I'm in the house. Okay?"

"Okay," he said, sitting on the small bed and circling his chubby knees with his arms, rocking.

"You need anything else, Art?"

"No."

"See you first thing in the morning, then. We'll have some breakfast together."

"Okay. Thanks. Luke."

Luke went back to his house. He was staying in tonight, in case Art needed anything, even though it meant not running into Shelby. He felt briefly disappointed; another fifteen or twenty minutes of feeling her pressed up against him, kissing him, that wouldn't hurt. But now he had another project, one he hadn't prepared himself for. If Art proved at all competent, it could turn out to be a good decision for both of them. If Art needed more assistance than Luke could provide, he could find him some help. But for now, at least he'd found a home for one of his mother's many bathrobes.

A couple of days later, Shelby rode Chico into the clearing that fronted Luke's cabins and stopped before getting too close. She had saddled and pulled Plenty along. The September afternoon was pleasant and sunny and she could see that Luke was crouched atop one of the cabins tearing off rotting shingles. Although it was cool enough for her to need a jacket, his broad sunburned bare back was facing her—it was a very enjoyable sight and she drank it in, silent. Then Plenty whinnied and Luke glanced over his shoulder. He stood and carefully turned toward her, balanced on the sloping roof. A smile found its way to her lips. What a sight he was, bare-chested, whiskers on his cheeks and chin, wearing jeans and a tool belt. She briefly wondered what it was about a tool belt... What was it she had said about the guy she had in mind? Clean-shaven, starched and pressed, polo shirt...? Nah....

"Looks like you lost a rider," he called down to her.

"I'm looking for a rider," she said. "Want to take a break? See if you can sit a horse?"

"Is this a test of some kind?" he asked.

"No." She laughed. "I'll still like you if you fall off."

He came down the ladder, grabbing his shirt off the lower

rung and shrugging into it. It hung open and her eyes stayed riveted on that tool belt. His hands were on the buckle to remove it, but they didn't move. When she lifted her eyes to his, she found him grinning. Caught. What the hell? she thought, smiling back.

"What are you doing here?" he asked her.

"I haven't seen you in a couple of days. Are you avoiding me again?"

"I should, but I haven't been. I've had stuff going on. Does the general know you're doing this?" he asked.

"Of course. They're his horses."

"Aw, Shelby," he said, sounding a little miserable. He took off the tool belt and buttoned up his shirt. "What did he say?"

"He said, 'You be careful of that Black Hawk pilot. They have a reputation for abusing women.'"

He shoved his shirt into his pants. "God," he moaned. "Why don't you go away and leave me alone before you get me shot."

She laughed. "He didn't say that. He said, 'Be sure to tell Luke that Plenty nips and bolts.' So—Plenty, short for Plenty of Trouble, nips and bolts. You'll have to pay attention."

"Bolts?" he asked a little nervously.

"Not usually with a rider. But if you get off, keep the reins. She can be a handful when she acts up, but she's a pretty good ride."

"Aw, man. I have a feeling this is going to be humiliating. Where are we going?"

"How about upriver a ways to check out the turning leaves?" she asked. "Think you can handle that?"

"I'll give it a go," he said. "Be with you in a minute." He walked down to the first cabin and stuck his head inside. Art was doing exactly as he'd been asked, sweeping debris into a nice neat pile in the middle of the cabin that had been emptied of furniture. "Hey, Art," Luke said. "I'm going to be gone a little while. You'll be okay, right?"

"Right," Art said, not looking up from his job.

"I'll let you know when I'm back."

"Okay. Luke," he said.

Luke went back to Shelby and the horses, cautiously giving Plenty's neck a slow stroke. She pulled her lips back as if she'd like to bite him, but she managed to control herself. "You have anything with you? Like a gun?" he asked Shelby.

"What for?"

"Bear. They're still out. Fishing."

"Oh, I have some repellent. Plus, I'm really fast."

"Yeah." He grinned. "I saw that the last time you were here. I'm not. I'm just hoping I can stay in the saddle." He went to his truck and pulled his Remington .338 rifle out of the rack. "I'll feel a little better if I don't have to rely on you to protect me."

"Ninny," she said, smiling. "That's pretty, but way more gun than you need."

"It makes me feel manly," he said.

By the time he was tying his rifle onto the saddle straps, Art was standing in the doorway of the cabin, watching them, broom in hand. "Who's that?" Shelby asked.

"I'll tell you in a minute," he answered, swinging into the saddle. "Lead the way."

He followed her to the river and as they rode away from the cabins, Luke said, "That guy, his name's Art. I found him camped out in one of the cabins—filthy, hurt and on the run. So he's working for me in exchange for food and a decent place to sleep."

"He's staying with you?" she asked.

"No. I put him in the camper while we get one of the cabins fixed up enough for him, which is why I haven't been at the bar in a couple of days—I wanted to make sure he was all right on his own. All he needs is hot water, cereal in the morning, bologna-and-cheese sandwiches for lunch, dinner and something soft to lie on. The guy's pretty incredible. He's not fast, but he's careful and he tries real hard. Turns out to be a good helper, but let's keep it quiet that he's here until I figure out what he's up against. Okay? I don't know exactly who he's running from, but he doesn't want to go back. Someone gave him a black eye. He doesn't have family anymore."

She looked at him in surprise. "You're protecting him."

"He was digging through my trash, like he needed something," Luke said with a shrug. "I didn't go out of my way."

"You could've told him to take off."

"Nah, no reason for that. He has Down syndrome—just a plain old good-hearted soul. But if some asshole who hits him is looking for him, I don't want word to leak that he's hiding out here. Not till I figure out what to do about his situation."

"You know, you try to hide the fact that you're nice," she said. "I think it's natural for you to be kind."

"Nowwww," he warned. "You'll ruin my reputation."

"You haven't even established one yet," she said. "No one knows quite what to make of you." She lifted her chin, looking up at the tall pines, the enormous sequoia, the clear, bright sky. Interspersed were oak and madrone with leaves turning yellow and orange. "Is this awesome or what?"

"Awesome," he agreed. "How does it compare to living down the coast?"

"So far, a wonderful change." She looked over at him and her eyes glittered. "I see great potential for this place."

"Playing with me again," he teased. "Don't you worry that you're biting off more than you can chew, little girl?"

"Aren't you?" she asked.

He groaned. "I *know* I am." And she laughed at him.

As they rode up the river into the hills, Luke couldn't help but find the horse a good diversion, a real pleasant experience. As long as Plenty was beside Chico and not behind him, there were no bad manners, like nipping. They talked only a little while they rode, and after about twenty minutes along the river, Shelby stopped Chico at the base of a trail that rose steeply into the hills. It was marked with well-worn trail that led to a plateau. "Think you can do that?" she asked. "The view from up there is pretty awesome."

"I can give it a try," he said. "Let me go first so this horse doesn't bite Chico's behind."

"Go," she said.

The trail was wide enough for an easy ride, made up of switchbacks that went right, then left, then right again in a zigzag that took the strain out of the climb. It took about twenty minutes to get to the top and once there, the valley opened up in front of them, the river behind them, and what looked like a vineyard was spread out below. He took a deep breath and admired the scenery. He could see a number of hiking trails and a couple of old, abandoned logging roads that had probably been used in years past for the harvesting of lumber.

Shelby came up alongside and inhaled in much the same way, experiencing the view. They could see for miles over the tops of the ponderosa and fir. She pulled off her hat and shook out that single braid, letting the fall breeze cool her.

They sat for a long time, saying nothing. Minutes passed and then Luke heard a sound. There was a rustling and not exactly a growl but something like a deep whine. A mewling. He looked to his right and saw that at the base of a tree a large bear cub rolled around playfully. Even though the cub was probably four months old and good-sized, he was still just a kid. "Shit," he said. "Oh shit." Where there was a cub, there was always a mother. And sure enough, coming at them from the left was Mama. They had somehow inadvertently gotten between the cub and the mother. And damn, Mama was *big*.

"Down, down, down," he said to Shelby. "You go first," he said, backing out of her way.

Shelby took off for the trail that led down the hill, Luke close on her heels, but moving at such a quick pace that Plenty didn't have the opportunity to nip at Chico. Bears have front legs shorter than their back legs and it was a bad idea to run up a hill or on level ground or, God forbid, up a tree, but if you traveled downhill, they were at a disadvantage. Ten or twenty feet and they'd trip and roll. But bears could get up a hill with those short front legs faster than any man. Or any horse carrying a man.

Shelby whacked Chico with the end of her rein and Luke dug his heels into Plenty. He hoped he could stay astride—he wasn't nearly the horseman Shelby was. And it wasn't a straight shot down—there were all those switchbacks to traverse. Behind them, Mama let go with a huge and frightening growl. If she got close, he hoped he could level the rifle in time. While Shelby and Luke had to make use of the switchback trail, Mama Bear was making a straight line down, through the trees and shrubs.

Ahead of him, he saw Shelby managing Chico with one deft hand, her other reaching behind her for the repellent spray. It occurred to him to get back a little, in case she decided to use it and he caught the drift downwind. But getting away was the first priority—he didn't want to have to shoot the mother of a cub.

About twenty feet into their descent, it happened. The bear stumbled over her short front legs, curled into a huge furry ball and began to roll out of control. Both Shelby and Luke pulled back on the reins and watched her roll right by them and down about twenty more feet. "Stay," Luke said softly. He pulled the rifle off the saddle ties and had it at the ready.

"Don't shoot her," Shelby pleaded.

"Only if I have to," he said. "Easy does it."

Mama recovered, shook herself off, stood at full towering height, treated them to her meanest snarl and scrambled up the hill in the other direction, back to her cub at great speed, avoiding them.

"What'd'ya say we get the hell out of here?" he suggested.

Shelby whacked Chico on the butt and urged him forward, and to Luke's amazement, he heard her laughter ring out as she descended. He was right on her heels, keeping up with her pretty well for someone who was reluctant to put down a rifle that was longer than his arm.

When they got to the bottom, she didn't slow down. She put her heels to her mount and flew down the riverside, laughter echoing through the tall trees as she drove the horse. Even Plenty's Arabian heritage wasn't helping Luke keep up with that paint. There weren't any people along the river, but he couldn't help but wonder what an onlooker might think, him chasing her with a rifle in his hand. But she was laughing wildly. Shelby had hunkered down in the saddle and showed her stuff; she was amazing. Lightweight, skilled, unafraid and fleet. She raced all the way back to the cabins and once there, her cheeks flushed, eyes aglitter, she grinned victoriously as he came into the clearing.

Luke learned something that moment that he hadn't expected. This was a young woman who liked an adventure. She liked speed. A little bear scare lit her up brighter than the sun, that was for sure. Now, he didn't kid himself that he knew everything about women, but he knew when to pay attention. Shelby was suddenly more alive than she'd been all afternoon. It turned him on almost unbearably.

"That was fun," she said.

"Yeah, once the bear was gone. You're a show-off."

"There are very few places where I'm able to show off," she said. "I'm good on a horse."

"Yeah, you are," he agreed. He brought Plenty up next to her so that he was facing Shelby. "Come here," he said.

He moved forward and she met him willingly, leaning toward him. He tilted his head and pressed her lips for a brief, sensuous kiss. Luke moved over her mouth slowly, deeply. Each kiss put him closer to the very thing he thought was the worst idea he'd ever had, and the most fated. He slipped an arm around her waist and held her; she put her arms on his shoulders. When he left her lips, he said, "You're killing me. Come inside with me for a few hours."

"No. Not yet," she said. Then she shrugged. "Sorry if I'm teasing you."

He pulled away and dismounted. "Shelby, I don't think you're sorry. I think you're in control here, trying to make me sorry," he said, but he couldn't help smiling.

"See you tonight. For a beer."

"Maybe."

"Come on," she laughed. "It's not possible I'm more brave than you. You've been in combat how many times?"

"This is so different. This is a small town. You're a general's only niece."

"Yeah," she said, taking Plenty's reins with a naughty grin. "Man up."

Luke manned up enough to get himself to that little bar five nights running. When the general was with his niece, Luke shoved off before dinner to bring Art and himself some of Preacher's fixings, including pie, which Art lived for. When Shelby was alone, he stayed. It had been about a hundred years since he'd played kissy-face with a girl without groping her, but he was able to do that with Shelby and even look forward to it. It wouldn't be much longer before he pressed the suggestion of more, the talk, and finally the event, the thought of which sent sparks shooting through his body.

During the days, he worked hard. He always made sure Art was set up for eating reasonably good food—his cereal and fruit for breakfast, his sandwiches for lunch and at least a microwavable TV dinner that included vegetables for supper when Luke was absent for the evening.

Almost a week had passed since the bear scare. Luke had since pushed all the furniture into the dining room of his house and was now sanding hardwood floors in the living room. He'd just started thinking about a shower and a refreshing beer at Jack's with Shelby, hopefully accompanied by a few meaningful kisses, when he heard the blast of a horn. He turned off the sander and went to the porch. His brother Sean pulled right up to the porch and jumped out of his Jeep SUV, all grins and a bright eyes. Luke frowned. This wasn't at all what he had in mind.

"Hey, buddy," Sean called. "Wassup?"

"What are you doing here?"

"I snagged a few days out of the squadron and thought I'd pleasure you with my company. Have a look at what you've got going on here."

All Luke could think about was how much longer it would be until he could be alone with Shelby. "Good," he said without enthusiasm. "That's good. Why didn't you call?"

"Since when do I call? You leaving town or something?"

"Nah. Just put in a long day…"

"Get cleaned up. Let's go over to the coast. Have a couple, see if we can find a couple."

Code for couple of beers, couple of girls. "Go ahead, buddy. I'm not into that tonight."

"Since when? Come on."

"I'm just going into town for a beer. There's a little bar there. Nice little family place. You can come with me or go to the coast on your own. Or there's a closer place you can try—a bar in Garberville. I've seen girls there."

"Sounds really exciting. What are you, getting old?" Sean asked.

Luke frowned. This was not great timing. He was getting close to closing the deal with a twenty-five-year-old beauty and who shows up but the younger brother who is all of thirty-two. The hotshot spy-plane pilot. Younger, better-looking, plenty of money, exciting life. An *officer*. The general would no doubt prefer that. He looked Sean up and down—he was tan, had dark blond hair, a dimpled bad-boy smile and no shortage of lines for picking up women. Good lines; Luke had actually borrowed some of them.

"You are *not* happy to see me," Sean said. "What's going on?"

"You going to work while you're here?" Luke asked testily.

"In daylight. When the sun goes down, I'd like to enjoy myself a little. I sense that's going to be a problem around here."

"Tonight, I'm going to Jack's. We'll talk about tomorrow night tomorrow," he said, heading for the house.

"Shew," Sean said, annoyed. "This is going to be wonderful." Just then Art stepped into the doorway of cabin number three with his broom. "Um, who is that?" Sean asked Luke.

"Art, come here, buddy," Luke called. Art walked down toward the porch. "Art, this is my brother Sean. Sean, this is Art. He's helping out around here. He's sleeping in one of the cabins."

"Hey," Sean said, putting out a hand.

"Hey. Sean," Art said, shaking his hand. Then Art turned and went back to the cabin he was sweeping up.

"Luke, what's going on around here?"

"Just getting the job done, pal. Art turned up looking for a place to stay and he works hard all day long for room and board. But we're not telling anyone he's here. He's going low profile for now. On the run from a bad group home."

"Jesus, Mary and Joseph," Sean said.

Forty minutes later Luke and Sean were in Luke's truck, on the way down the river to the town. When Luke pulled up in front of Jack's, he saw General Booth's Tahoe parked there, and hoped Shelby was inside with him. He put the truck in Park, but before turning off the ignition, he said to his brother, "If you get a whiff of anything in there that has my scent on it, back away. If you touch it, you're a dead man."

Sean grinned. "Okay, now I'm catching on. Oh man, this is going to be fun." He jumped out of the truck and bounded up the stairs, clearly dying of curiosity.

Luke was right behind him, but almost plowed into him. Sean stopped short right inside the door. Walt and Shelby were sitting up at the bar and both turned at the sound of someone entering. Luke put a firm hand, a reminder, on Sean's shoulder. "Holy shit," Sean whispered. Luke gave his shoulder a little shake and pushed him forward.

"General Booth," Luke said. "Shelby McIntyre. Meet my brother Sean."

"Sir," Sean said. "Miss."

Standing behind him as he was, Luke couldn't see Sean's dimpled grin, but knew it was huge. It made Luke's frown a little deeper. God, he thought, why couldn't I have had sisters?

Jack put up a couple of beers and Sean began to entertain himself at Luke's expense. "So, I invited my brother to go over to the coast to have a beer, check out the women, and what does he tell me? Not interested in doing that—he wants to go to this little bar in Virgin River. But he doesn't tell me why. What an incredible coincidence that you happen to be here, Miss McIntyre."

She laughed at him, finding him darling and playful, two things Luke definitely was not. "Please, it's just Shelby. He knew I'd be here. It's almost a standing date."

"Is it, now? Is there another one of you at home?"

"I'm afraid not," she said. "But I understand there are more brothers."

"Aiden, Colin and Paddy. But I'm the richest and most handsome."

"And the biggest pain in the ass," Luke inserted.

"Where do you fall in the pack?" Shelby asked.

"Number four. Luke's the oldest." He looked over his shoulder at Luke. "He's very old, you know. And I think my family and your family were at war for thousands of years," he teased. He sipped his beer. "Yeah, the McIntyre-Riordan wars. Sure am glad that's over."

"And none of you married?"

"At last count, two of them tried it and blew it. They insist it wasn't their fault," he said, grinning.

Luke was going to take him home and beat the shit out of him.

But Shelby was loving it. The sly grin on the general's face was unmistakable and the amused crinkle at the corners of Jack's eyes suggested he was getting too big a kick out of this as well.

And right on cue, the others began to file into the bar. Luke dutifully introduced everyone to Sean. After a few minutes Sean leaned across the bar and said to Jack, "Look at these women, man. What is this place? Stepford?"

"All taken, buddy. Unless you can get this fresh young thing away from your older brother."

The general and Sean carried on a lengthy conversation about the Riordan boys. "How'd you get an entire military family?" Walt asked.

"I don't know, sir," Sean answered. "No imagination, I guess. Luke went first, right out of high school, but he scored a warrant officer promotion, flight school, and made it look fun. Big Irish-Catholic family like ours with a Da who's an electrician, he wasn't sending the lot of us to college, so we had to come up with alternate plans. ROTC, military scholarship, active duty—whatever. But it turns out I like the life."

Then Shelby told Sean about merely being here for a visit, and for the first time Luke had a catastrophic thought—what if he wasn't quite ready for her to leave when she decided to go? He'd spent so much mental energy on the disaster that would befall him when he was through with her, it hadn't occurred to him it might just go the opposite way.

If Luke was quieter than usual, it could be explained by the fact that Sean never shut up. That, and the fear he was losing a major chance with Shelby to this upstart who would be gone in a few days. A few *long* days.

Tables were pushed together as those present collected for dinner, and Sean grabbed the chair next to Shelby's, entertaining her, making her laugh. Luke didn't make her laugh so much. He wasn't the comedian Sean was to start with, plus he was sulking. Sean stole the show. So after the plates were picked up, Luke stepped outside into the cool fall night.

He wasn't out there long before she joined him. She gave him a little smile and shook her head. "You're so unhappy," she said, humor in her voice.

"I hate him," Luke said miserably.

"Come on," she said. "You don't have to be so cranky. I

like your brother." She got a little closer to him. "You're the jealous type, I guess."

"I guess," he grumbled. Truthfully, he was feeling old. Feeling thirty-eight, soon to be thirty-nine. Feeling less educated than Sean, boring and retired.

"Seems a little ridiculous for you to be jealous when you keep telling me I'm making a big mistake flirting with you."

"I was going to stop saying that pretty soon," he told her.

"I wasn't exactly fooled," she said. "You tell me that and then rattle my bones with a kiss that goes all the way to my belly button. You're kind of obvious, Luke." Shelby did something that a year ago, even a month ago, she couldn't envision. But she'd had a couple of glasses of wine and Sean had made her laugh the night away even if Luke had not. She walked right up to him and put her arms around his waist. His arms went instantly around her. "It's been a while since you kissed me like that. Couple of days," she reminded him.

Finally, after all this time, he smiled. "Believe me, I know."

"And now you're in a bad mood."

"It has nothing to do with kissing you. Kissing you is good."

"Why not try that again? See if it's still good?"

His arms tightened around her. "What about the general?"

She laughed. "It would probably thrill him. He's been awful worried about my arrested development. I'm sure he thinks I'm pathetic and manless."

"You're not."

"Pathetic?"

"Or manless," he said, covering her mouth in a powerful and deep kiss, a possessing kiss. He moved over her mouth and her lips opened for him. It briefly ran through his mind that he had to have her this minute, but first he should remind her, she couldn't count on him for the long haul. At best, it would be a fling. A fabulous, satisfying fling. Instead of talking to her about that, he received her small tongue into his mouth and moaned his pleasure. He didn't want it ever to end and he concentrated on making it the longest kiss in history, hoping to get caught, hoping everyone would go on notice— this was his girl. His woman. He could feel her firm breasts pressing against his chest and knew nothing would feel quite so good as to have one in his hand. At length, he released her lips. But didn't let them get too far.

"Your brother is very cute," she said against his lips.

"I'm going to take him home and beat the shit out of him."

It made her giggle to hear that. "Would you two like to go for a ride tomorrow?" she asked. "We have another good riding horse. A beautiful Appaloosa named Shasta. All spotty and gentle."

"I don't want him to go anywhere with us."

"Luke," she scolded.

"Seriously. I want him out of here. I have things to do with you." He shrugged his shoulders. "Riding and beers and dinner and...stuff."

"You better be patient," she said.

"How patient?" he asked.

She gave him a peck on the lips. "How long will Sean be here?"

"Seriously, I'm going to kill him and hide the body."

"How long?" she demanded, though she smiled.

"He says a few days. But he doesn't know about his impending murder."

"How about tomorrow morning? After it warms up a little bit. Come to my house and we'll ride along the river."

"Is that what you really want?"

"I think it would be very neighborly of me."

He sighed. "All right. But don't laugh at his jokes. It makes me crazy."

7

Walt gave Shelby and Luke a little time alone on the bar's porch. Not too much time, though. He walked outside noisily. He briefly glared at Luke, just to see if he could make him tremble in guilt and fear. To Luke's credit, he didn't. But he did pull his arm from around Shelby's shoulders slowly, reluctantly. So, there it was. Walt had suspected.

"I'm headed out," Walt said. "Coming now or later, Shelby?"

"I'll go with you, Uncle Walt."

On the way home Walt said to Shelby, "I bet those Riordan boys were a handful to raise." Shelby only sighed. Dreamily, Walt thought.

Once Shelby was dropped off at home, Walt said he'd be going over to Muriel's place for a nightcap. He had a couple of things in the Tahoe already—a surprise for Muriel.

He loved that Muriel knew the sound of his Tahoe engine, his boots on the wooden planks of her porch, his knock. "Come on in, Walt." It gave him a crazy lift, that there couldn't possibly be any other caller. He walked in, shifted his stuff to under one arm so he could greet the pups, who would not leave him alone until they had a piece of him. She was wearing a comfy sweat suit, sitting on her bed, what looked suspiciously like a script in her lap and her reading glasses balanced on her nose. "What have you got there?" she asked.

"A little entertainment I didn't want to get into alone." He put a portable DVD player beside her on the bed along with four DVDs he'd gone to a great deal of trouble to find. Not so many of her films were available on DVD.

She fanned through them. "Oh, Walt!" she exclaimed. "What did you do?" Then she flipped one aside. "Not this one. I'm naked in this one."

"Muriel, I've seen you naked. It's a brilliant sight."

"I know, but you've only seen me naked in the dark while we're trying to keep the dogs off the bed. In this I'm naked with an actor, a director, an entire film crew and I think everyone from janitorial to the roach coach that brings lunch."

He sat on the edge of the bed. "Is that hard to do? Get naked like that?"

She made a face. "You won't get this, but it's easier for me to do that than it was to get naked in front of you. I couldn't care less what those people think of me—it was just work. It was right for the script or I would have declined." She shrugged and added, "Plus, my parents were dead."

He put a little kiss on her lips. "It was hard to take your clothes off for me?"

"It was," she admitted. "I wanted to live up to your expectations. I'm getting better at it since you decided to be insatiable. Are you sure you're sixty-two? You certainly haven't slowed down much."

"I feel twenty years younger with you. And you not only

lived up to my expectations, you pretty much blew my mind."
He picked up the rejected DVD. "Let's watch this one first."

It made her laugh.

"Is that a script?" he asked, glancing at the sheaf of pages
she held.

"Yeah. Don't worry, it's crap."

"Good. Muriel, you have to start coming to Jack's for dinner with us. It's getting more interesting by the day. You
wouldn't want to miss it."

"Really?" she asked, sitting up and crossing her legs in
front of her.

"My innocent little Shelby has picked out a man. I'm sure
she's made a rash choice, he's too much for her—a thirty-eight-
year-old roughneck who flew Black Hawks for almost twenty
years. He looks like he could take apart a big gang of Huns
with his bare hands. But when he looks at her, sins of many
varieties glitter in his eyes. And I scare the hell out of him—a
thing of beauty. Well, tonight he showed up with his younger
brother, who was a surprise visitor—better-looking, funnier, a
lot more socially acute, more sure of himself around Shelby..."
He laughed. "Almost caused the roughneck to take his own
life. You don't want to miss too much more of this stuff."

"Shelby picked out this guy?" she asked. "This older guy?"

"Oh, there was no question about it. I suspect it was almost
the second she saw him."

"But he's a roughneck. How do you feel about that?"

Walt leaned over and took off his boots. He straightened
and looked at her with those scary general's eyes. "If he does
anything to hurt her, I'm going to kill him."

Muriel shook her head and pulled the DVD out of the
sleeve and loaded it in the portable player. "Shelby must be
very grateful," she said facetiously.

He climbed up next to her, leaning back against the wall,
stretching out his long legs, shooing first Buff and then Luce

off the bed. "I think she's secretly enjoying his fear. I can't wait for this movie."

"It's a chick flick," she said.

"Clint Eastwood's in it," he said, settling back. "I like Clint Eastwood."

"You won't like him in this. He's romantic. He doesn't blow anyone's brains out or say 'Make my day' even once."

"But you took your clothes off in front of him. I want to see the look on his face."

"Well," Muriel said, "if you look very closely you might see an expression that approaches oblivion. He's seen a huge number of actresses in the nude, and remains very much in control of his emotions. He wasn't tempted in the least."

"Poor fool." Walt pushed Play.

"Are you determined to watch this?" she asked.

"I can't wait."

"This is going to bore me to death," she said tiredly, leaning back against her pillows and yawning.

"Want me to wake you up for the naked part?" Walt asked her.

"Wake me up when *you're* naked," she said, yawning again.

Mel received a very important phone call at the clinic. She hung up, took a deep breath, looked at her watch: 10:00 a.m. She picked up the phone and called Shelby, but there was no answer at the ranch—they could be out riding. She called Brie. "Hi. I need a sitter. I can try to find Jack if you're—"

"I just saw him leave the bar in his truck," Brie said. "I'll come and get the kids, how's that?"

"Thanks. I have an errand and could be a few hours."

After hanging up, she went into Doc Mullins's office. "I did it," she said. "I got a county rehab placement for Cheryl Chreighton."

"How'd you manage that?" he asked, impressed in spite of himself.

"It wasn't easy. I had to make a hundred phone calls. It would have been infinitely easier if she had committed a crime and could blame it on booze. She could have gotten treatment in sentencing. This was way harder."

"She have any idea you did this?"

"Nope," she said, shaking her head. "I didn't want to give her time to think about it. She'd just get drunk and change her mind. But if I blindside her, get her over there and they dry her out and get her in the program, she has a chance."

"Exactly one," he stressed.

"Yeah, I'll never be able to pull that off again if she relapses. So—I'm going over there. I'll take your truck and leave you the Hummer for patients."

"Jack's truck would be a better ride," he said.

"Can't do that," she insisted. Jack and Cheryl had history. There was a time, long before Mel, that Cheryl had a fierce and embarrassing crush on Jack, and Jack had to put her down rather harshly. "I can't get Jack or even his truck involved. It might send the wrong message. Besides, I keep reliving that nightmare of riding to the hospital in the back of your pickup with a patient, holding a bag of Ringer's over my head. I'll take your truck and leave you the Hummer," she said, holding out her hand for the keys.

"Good luck," he said, handing them over.

After Brie had taken the kids back to her RV, Mel drove a few short blocks to the house she now knew to be the Chreightons'. It was in disrepair, which several of the houses on this block seemed to be. People tended to get used to things like peeling paint, sagging roofs. Plus, this was not a family with money. No one worked but Dad, and he only worked when there was work, piecemeal, probably with no benefits.

She knocked on the door and it was a long time before a morbidly obese woman answered. She had never seen Cheryl Chreighton's mother before, which in a town this size was incredibly strange, but it was apparent why—the woman had probably not been out of the house for many months, perhaps years. She had a cigarette in her yellowed fingers and a frown on her face. She answered the door with a barking hack. Mel gave her time to catch her wheezing breath.

"Is Cheryl at home?" she asked.

"Who are you?"

"My name is Mel Sheridan," she said. "I'm the nurse-practitioner and midwife. I work with Doc Mullins."

"You're the one," she said, looking Mel up and down. "Jack's woman."

"Yeah, that's me. So. She here?"

"Sleeping it off," the woman said, turning to waddle back into the house, leaving Mel to follow.

"Can you get her up for me?" Mel asked, letting herself in despite the lack of invitation.

"I can try," she said. Mel followed the woman into the little kitchen, which was obviously where she had set up camp. There was a collection of newspapers and magazines, stained coffee cups and empty Coke cans, an overflowing ashtray, an opened box of doughnuts, a small TV sitting on the counter. Mrs. Chreighton went into a room off the kitchen, a crude add-on in the back of the house. The door didn't close, didn't seem to have a mechanism for closing—there was a hole where the doorknob should be.

Mel heard her in there, yelling, "Cheryl! Cheryl! Cheryl! There's some woman here to see you! Cheryl!" After a bit of that, there was some muffled protest. Mrs. Chreighton came back into the kitchen, went back to her chair, which sagged under her weight.

It was a household of addiction, Mel thought. Mom is hooked on food and cigarettes, Cheryl's hooked on alcohol, and Dad's drug of choice was anyone's guess. He was probably hooked on these two women and their problems.

Cheryl appeared in the doorway of her bedroom, wearing yesterday's clothes, straggly hair hanging in her face, her eyes swollen and barely open. Mel took a breath. "Got a minute?" she asked.

"What for?" Cheryl asked.

"Let's step outside and talk," Mel said. She walked out the front door, leaving Cheryl to follow. Mel stood on the sidewalk in front of the house until Cheryl came out and stood on the front step. "How drunk are you right now?" Mel asked her.

"I'm okay," she answered, rubbing her fingers across her scalp, threading fingers through her limp and greasy hair.

"You have any interest in getting sober? Staying sober?"

"I do sometimes. I don't drink a lot of the time…"

"I can get you in treatment, Cheryl. Get you detoxed and cleaned up and in a program. You'd get twenty-eight days of sobriety therapy and a real good chance of going straight, off the booze. But you have to decide right now."

"I don't know…"

"This is your one shot, Cheryl. I'll take you, check you in. The county will pick up the tab, but you only get this one chance. If you say no right now, that's it. That's all I can do."

"Who told you to do this?" she asked.

"No one told me. I thought you could use a little help, so I found it for you. All by myself. And no, I haven't even mentioned it to Jack. You could try this. You know you can't do it on your own."

"You ask my mom?"

"I haven't asked anyone. You're over twenty-one, aren't you? You want help? Go shower and pack a bag—you don't need much. They have washers and dryers. Clean sheets and towels. Healthy food. And a lot of people just like you who are trying to sober up. It's hard for everyone, but they're the experts and if anyone can help you, they can."

She looked at her feet, her dirty, unlaced boots. "I get the shakes real bad sometimes," she said.

"Just about everyone does. They have medicine to get you through the first days." Mel looked at her watch. "I'm not hanging around while you think about it."

"Where is this place?" she asked.

"Eureka."

Cheryl shuffled her feet a little bit. Finally she lifted her head. "Okay," she said.

"Fine. Go shower and pack. I'll be back for you in thirty minutes."

She came back and picked up Cheryl, who carried her belongings in a brown grocery bag. She had cleaned up; her hair was washed but only towel dried. She probably didn't own a blow-dryer. She smelled of soap and a touch of liquor—a little nip to help her get into the truck, Mel suspected.

"Did you tell your parents where you're going?" Mel asked.

Cheryl shrugged. "My mom. I told my mom."

"And is she glad you're going?"

Cheryl shrugged. She looked away from Mel as she answered. "She said it's probably a waste of time and money."

Mel waited for Cheryl to look back at her. Then she said, "No. It's not." She took a breath. "Come on, let's get going."

They didn't talk much on the long drive to Eureka, but Mel did learn that Cheryl had been at a cousin's house in some other mountain town for the past year until her father brought her home. And Cheryl had had some delusional and grandiose aspirations—she'd wanted to join the Peace Corps, travel to foreign lands, be a nurse, a teacher, a veterinarian. Instead, she drank her dreams away. She didn't have any friends in Virgin River anymore, just her mother and father.

"You don't have to tell me anything you don't feel like talking about," Mel began, "but I'm curious. I know you don't go to Jack's. How did you manage to get liquor?"

"Hmm," Cheryl started. "There's a liquor store in Garberville, but usually my dad would get me something to keep me from driving his truck."

"Ah. I understand," Mel said.

"I try to stop all the time," Cheryl said. "But if I get shaky and crazy, my dad takes care of it. Just enough to get me straight."

So Dad was the enabler, Mel thought.

The aftercare was going to be a huge problem, Mel realized. Because Cheryl had nowhere to go but back home to her parents, who seemed unable to support her in getting healthy. That would have to be her sponsor's challenge—maybe they would find a place for her in Eureka where she could work, live, go to meetings, get a grip on sobriety before landing back in Virgin River, doomed.

It was late afternoon by the time Mel got back to town. She went into the clinic to give Doc his keys.

"Mission accomplished?" he asked.

"All taken care of."

"Your husband's been looking for you."

"Swell. What did you tell him?"

"That you were on a mission. A medical mission."

"I bet that thrilled him. I guess I'll go tap-dance around Jack and grab the kids from Brie. I'm going to call it a day, Doc."

"I'll phone you if anything exciting pops up." She turned to leave and he called her back. She turned to him. "That was a good thing you did. I don't like her chances, but that was a real good thing."

"Thanks, Doc."

"All my years here, all my years watching her go downhill, I never gave her that much hope. Glad someone did. Glad you did."

She felt a small smile come to her lips.

★ ★ ★

Over the course of the previous three days, Luke had taken Sean over to the Booth house for a couple of morning rides. He hadn't done it for Sean, certainly. But for Shelby, because it made her happy to have someone with whom to share the rides. And although it irked Luke, she found Sean amusing.

The rest of the time Luke and his brother worked together. They finished the floors in the house, then concentrated on cabin number one for Luke's new tenant.

"We should have this ready for you in a couple of days, Art," Luke told him. That put Art in a fever of excitement, that he was going to have his own little house. "Ever had your own house before?" Luke asked him.

"By myself?" Art asked. "Not by myself."

"Think you're ready for your own little house?"

"I am," he said with a nod.

"So let me ask you, Art—at the group home, who did the laundry?"

He shrugged and said, "We had to sign up for it."

Luke was perplexed. "Sign up? I don't get it."

"On the clipboard," Art said impatiently. "You have to sign up on the clipboard when you want to use the washer and dryer."

"No kidding? So you did your own?"

"We did our own."

"And did you have other chores at the group home?" Sean asked him.

"Make the bed, put away the clothes, keep a neat room. Dishes. Vacuum. Bathroom cleaning."

Luke lifted a brow. "I think you are ready for your own house. With some OJT on the washer…"

Art frowned. "OJT?"

Sean slapped him on the back. "On-the-job training, buddy.

Come with me. I'm going to show you how to scrape the dead paint off the outside of this cabin so we can prime it."

"OJT?" he asked.

"Exactly."

When Art was settled into his chore outside, Sean went inside and asked Luke, "What are you going to do with him?"

"He just got here, Sean. He just needs to feel safe right now."

"He's going to get attached to you."

"Maybe." Luke shrugged. "Look, the guy had a job. And from what he says, he took care of himself. Sounds like all he needs is a little supervision. Since I'm not going anyplace, what's it hurt if he just hangs out here?"

Art stuck his head in the door. "Sean? Can I have some more OJT?"

Luke looked at his brother. "He's going to get attached to *you*."

"I won't be here long enough."

Between the three of them, they managed to get a lot done. At the end of the day, Luke fixed Art a grilled cheese and some soup and then, at Luke's insistence, he took Sean to Jack's for dinner again. Shelby and her uncle, as well as Muriel, the Booths' new neighbor, were there. Before leaving, he was briefly and wonderfully in possession of her lips. But Sean, unfortunately, had nothing to do with his lips but talk.

The next day Sean said, "Tonight we're going over to the coast or at least Fortuna. I'm only here another day and I'm tired of entertaining your girlfriend for you."

"She's not my girlfriend, but I'm tired of you doing that, too."

"I bet you've already got a girl someplace else—a girl with girlfriends. Do a brother a favor and make a call."

"I'm not doing that, man. You go. Knock yourself out."

"What is your deal, Luke?"

He took a deep breath. They had managed not to talk about this, though it was as obvious as a punch to the gut.

"You know what my deal is, Sean. And I don't need you to jam me up right now."

"Come on, Luke. You can pick up your threads when I'm gone."

"Not interested. I have things on my mind."

"Yeah—Shelby things. Since we can't share the girl, let's go find some action. Besides, her uncle is watching her like a hawk."

"I'm working that angle," Luke said. "Brother, you have to get out of my way here. I have things to do with the girl."

"You are heading for something not so good," Sean said. "She's young and innocent, anyone can see that. She's sweet. And she's got that look—like she'd bruise easily. You'd better think about this."

"It's under control," he said. But it wasn't. He felt about as far from control as he ever had. There was just no way in hell he could stop this now. He was like a runaway train where Shelby was concerned.

"She's vulnerable. Maybe needy," Sean stressed.

Luke knew this. Ordinarily twenty-five wasn't too young, but Shelby, despite everything, seemed much more tender than the average twenty-five-year-old woman. Maybe it was the fact that she'd spent the years from nineteen to twenty-four held hostage, taking care of her mother, and had limited worldly experience. And he was more than a little aware of her vulnerability, that soft underside that a man like Luke, with his careless ways, could damage. And yet, even knowing all that, he wasn't having any success at cooling himself down.

"I'm going to have to go pick up some supplies," Luke said. "I'm going to get a hot-water heater and new sink for Art's cabin. You do whatever you want and tonight I'll take you out to a nice dinner, not at Jack's," Luke said, because he wasn't in the mood for any more of Sean's interaction with Shelby. "But I'm not interested in women. We'll take two cars."

"Sounds like a plan," Sean said. "A pathetic plan, but a plan…"

It was executed in exactly that way. They had a steak dinner at the Brookstone in Ferndale and while Sean retired to the bar, Luke headed home. Sean returned to Luke's in the early morning. He was smiling privately and there was no question he was more relaxed than when Luke left the bar the night before. The Riordan men carried the tension of abstinence in their necks and shoulders.

Luke was surprised he could still turn his head.

"If you don't mind me saying so, I've never seen you like this," Sean said.

"Like what?"

Sean rolled his eyes. "Oh, brother. You're going after the baby and you are so tight you're going to grind your molars flat. Not only isn't she good for you, you're poison for her."

It occurred to Luke to try to explain that he hadn't been able to think of anything else for weeks, and he couldn't remember when that had happened to him last. That when he got his arms around her, he was out of his head. But he'd been running with his brothers a long time and they were all the same with women—fast and loose. They didn't get like this.

Sean put a hand on Luke's shoulder and gave it a squeeze. He shook his head almost sadly. "Good luck with this, man."

"It's not what you think."

"Oh—it is what I think. You're so into this woman, you're done for. I can't wait to see how this turns out."

"Yeah. Me, too."

8

The last weekend in September, Jack's bar had to be closed because Jack, Preacher, Paul, Mike and their wives were all going to Grants Pass, Oregon, for the wedding of one of their boys. Joe Benson, marine and architect who designed all their houses and had worked with Paul for years in Oregon, was getting married. It was no coincidence that Joe was marrying one of Vanni's best friends from flying days—they had met in Virgin River when Nikki was visiting Vanessa. Their wedding brought together a few of the available marines, but was a small flight-attendant reunion as well.

For a wedding that was thrown together in just over a month, it was beautiful and classy. Unlike those casual, low-key Virgin River weddings, this one was held in a charming downtown chapel with a fancy reception dinner and dance in the city's prestigious Davenport Hotel's ballroom. It was loaded with tuxedos and limousines, not to mention some amazing floral arrangements and a dinner menu that impressed even Preacher. Nikki had been Vanessa's maid of honor twice, and Vanni was happily returning the favor. Also with them were their other two best friends, Abby and Addison.

When the four women started flying together, Abby and Addison had shared an apartment in L.A., while Nikki and Vanni had been roommates in San Francisco. The four of them bid all their trips together so that for three or four days every week, they had layovers in the same cities, at the same hotels. They had shopped together, partied together, gotten each other through a bunch of rotten boyfriends, kept each other afloat through the rough times, laughed through the good times. Now, with Nikki's marriage, all four would be wed.

But Vanessa asked Addison, "Is Abby a little too quiet?"

"She won't talk about it, but her husband has been on the road with his band since right after they were married…which has to be about a year ago."

"I could tell it was a bad situation," Vanni said. "Does he go home at all? Does she go to him?"

Addison shook her head. "I don't think so. It's like pulling teeth to get her to say anything at all about him. And of course, she's here alone."

Abby and her husband wed after a very short courtship and almost immediately Ross disappeared, along with Abby's flush of romance and happiness. She grew evermore silent and distant.

"Abby, are you all right? Is everything okay with Ross?" Addison asked her in a whisper.

"Shh," Abby said. "This is Nikki's day. I don't want to talk about that stuff now."

Abby held it together pretty well, smiling for the pictures, raising her glass at the toast, but she disappeared from the reception at about the time the dancing started. Addison and Vanessa noticed at once. They talked about going after her, talking her through a bad patch. But in the end they decided to leave her be. She hadn't wanted to talk about whatever was going on with her marriage, especially not at one of her best friend's wedding. Maybe she just needed a good, strong, cleansing cry without a bunch of girlfriends in her business.

The Steak House in the Davenport Hotel was one of the nicest restaurants in Grants Pass and a favorite of Dr. Cameron Michaels'. Once a month he had dinner with his partners and their spouses and quite often, they chose this restaurant. He shared a practice with one female and two male pediatricians, all excellent doctors, all married. As had become typical lately, Cam didn't have a date. He could've found a woman to accompany him. Women liked going out with him, and his partners were always offering fix-ups. There were plenty of pretty nurses signed up to take on that duty.

But he was thirty-six and heartsore. He'd been looking for the right woman for a long time, though it appeared he wasn't going to find her. He had even felt himself beginning to fall in love with the beautiful Vanessa a few months ago and it had stung pretty bad when she let him know she'd given her heart to another man. She not only loved someone else, she married him immediately. Last spring; not all that long ago.

He wasn't carrying a torch, he even admired the man she married—Paul Haggerty. He was a good man, strong and decent. The problem Cam was having wasn't a broken heart so much as a tired one. He was a good-looking guy—dark hair and heavy brows over blue eyes, dimples, a bright smile. He was successful, masculine but tenderhearted—women were drawn to him. By now he should have found a woman he was just as drawn to. He wanted to fall in love; he wanted to love someone deeply enough to make her his wife. He was a family physician and pediatrician—having a wife and kids would mean a lot to him.

The women who fell for him were always the wrong ones. Plenty of the young mothers who brought him their children fixed big, vulnerable, doe eyes on him; young, pretty, married women. He was in the market for a wife, not an angry husband coming after him.

He'd had a couple of serious relationships that hadn't lasted long. There had been a lot of women to fill the time—brief, superficial affairs. Frankly, he could have a woman whenever he wanted one, but he was so tired of that long string of meaningless relationships, weary of the nurses' jokes about the playboy pediatrician and exhausted from looking.

So he remained the solitary seventh wheel, lately refusing his friends' offers of blind dates and introductions. He had grown bored with it all and realized his failure to hook up had put him in a real mood. And sex without any feelings of involvement left him empty inside. He was better off alone.

When dinner with his partners was over, he watched them go off together, home to their marriage beds and children while he would go to his too-large, too-quiet house.

The prospect had him feeling gloomy enough to go to the hotel bar for a nightcap. It was late and the bar was nearly deserted; it seemed most of the hotel guests were caught up in a loud and annoyingly happy wedding reception in the ballroom. At the bar, he asked for a Chevis, neat. He didn't feel like a drink so much as he didn't want to go home yet, so he spent more time staring into it than sipping. Thirty minutes passed and he still had most of the drink in his glass when he started thinking about facing the loneliness of his house. He stood and pulled out his wallet to put a bill on the bar when he noticed her. A woman sitting at a small table in a dark corner. Also staring into a drink, also alone.

Cam thought about talking to her, but reminded himself how these encounters usually played out. He didn't feel like another empty connection or worse, finding someone he liked and being let down. But she was pretty and looked a little sad...

The bartender wandered over. "Anything else, Doc?" he asked Cam.

"No, thanks. She been here long?" he asked, tipping his head toward the table in the corner.

"Longer than you."

"Alone?"

The bartender shrugged. "Couldn't tell you. I guess."

Oh, what the hell... Cameron put down the bill and picked up his drink. He wandered over to her table. As he looked down at her, she lifted soft brown eyes to him. She had that classic, sophisticated look, her shiny ash-blond hair curled under on her shoulders. High cheekbones, oval face, arched brows the identical shade as her hair, and a sweet pink mouth. But she didn't smile. "Can I buy you a drink?" he asked her.

"I'm just having seltzer," she said. "I don't think I'd be very good company."

"I'm no prize tonight either, which is why I was killing time in the bar. I bet we'll be able to tell in five minutes if we're just two miserable people."

Her shoulders gave a little lift with a silent huff of laughter. "May I sit down?" he asked.

"Really, I think I'd rather be alone..." she said.

He sat down across from her anyway and said, "You sure I can't get you something a little stronger? Something tells me you could use it."

"No. You should really go."

He chuckled lightly. "Man, I thought *I* was in a bad mood," he said. "You're working up a good funk. What's wrong, kiddo? What happened?"

She sighed. "Could we please not do this? I'm not in the mood to be picked up or talk about my troubles, all right?"

"Okay," he said. "I won't pick you up or ask you about your troubles." He finished the last swallow of his drink and got up. Cameron went to the bar and ordered another Chevis and a champagne cocktail, returning to her table. He put the cocktail in front of her and took his seat again.

"What's this?" she asked.

"Champagne cocktail. I figured you for something sweet and sexy."

Her smile was mocking. "Great line," she said facetiously.

"Thank you." He smiled. "You obviously need a few lessons in how to feel sorry for yourself. You don't do it with seltzer, for one thing."

She lifted the glass and took a sip.

"There you go," he said, smiling again. He reached across the small table and placed his hand over hers. "Sure you don't want to talk about it?"

"I'm sure," she said, removing her hand. "You want to talk? Let's talk about you. You said you're in a bad mood."

"Fair enough. I was out to dinner with friends and when they left the restaurant, I decided I wasn't ready to go home. See, I screwed up—I bought this house. Nice house, but way too big. Way too quiet and empty."

"Buy furniture," she said.

He grinned at her. "It's full of furniture, ah...what's your name?"

Abby thought for a second, trying to decide if it was a good idea to get that familiar. She glanced away from him, toward the bar, then back. Finally she said, "Brandy."

"Nice to meet you, Brandy. I'm Cameron. Friends call me Cam. I have plenty of furniture. That's not what's missing."

"I get it. You're looking for a woman. There must be something in the Yellow Pages..."

That made him laugh. He picked up his drink and had a sip. "No, Brandy. In fact, that's about the last thing I'm after tonight." He leaned back in his chair. "Well, I take that back, maybe that's what I am looking for. But it's not what you think. I'm not looking for a date. I've had more than enough dates. I'm kind of amazed to find myself thirty-six and still single."

"Never married?"

"Not even close," he said.

She tilted her head to one side, looking at his face. "What's wrong with you?"

"Couldn't tell you. I have a good job, good friends, nice big house, I brush and floss..."

"You're not that bad-looking," she said. "You shouldn't have any trouble finding a woman who'd want to marry you, spend your money." The corners of her mouth lifted slightly.

"Amazing. You don't look like my mother, but you sure just sounded like her."

"You're an escaped convict? Serial killer or something?"

"In Grants Pass?" he asked, laughing. "You can hardly get away with unpaid parking tickets in this town. Nah, I'm boringly law abiding. I don't even speed."

Abby lifted her drink to her lips. "I think you were right about the seltzer," she said. "Not a great pity drink." She took another sip. "How long has it been since you were, you know, involved?"

He slipped over into the chair next to her instead of across. "Hmm. Long," he said. "I was working up a pretty good crush a few months ago, but before I could close the deal, she married someone else. Real fast. He'd been on her mind the whole time I was staging my seduction."

"Oh," she said. "Broken heart."

"No, not at all. We weren't involved. I was hoping to get involved, but once it was over I could see that it never really got started. She wasn't into it at all. How about you? How long?"

"God," she said, lowering her eyes and shaking her head. "That's pretty hard to say. I think maybe we have that in common—I was involved. He wasn't."

He touched her hand again and this time she allowed it. "Just break up?" he asked.

"No. It was over quite a while ago. He's been with someone else for at least six months."

"Yet you're hurting?" Cameron asked her.

She took a deep breath. "I was just at a wedding. Weddings are awful places for women alone. It works great in the plot of chick flicks because it's tragically funny."

"You look like you might've just escaped from a wedding," he observed.

"Just the thought of the bride throwing that bouquet and knowing I was qualified to line up with the single women to catch it sent me running for the bar."

"To lick your wounds with a seltzer? Thank God I came along." He turned around, caught the bartender's eye and lifted a couple of fingers. "Tell me about the wedding," he said.

"Oh God," she said, lowering her head to rest it wearily in her hand. "Don't ask."

"Why?"

"Because there was enough true love in that room to make a person throw up."

He laughed. "That right? You represent the bride's side or the nauseating groom's side?"

"Bride's," she said, laughing in spite of herself.

The bartender brought them two more drinks.

"Trying to get me drunk?" she asked him.

"No, I'm trying to get you over the hump. You're sad. And a woman as beautiful as you has no business being sad. Drink it. It's going to make you feel better." He grinned. "Or at least stupider."

She laughed at him. "Yeah. Like that's possible…"

"These bad nights, I've had a ton of them," he said. "When it just feels like things work out for everyone else. But if I was trying to get you drunk, you'd be drinking the Chevis and I'd be drinking the champagne. That's Kool-Aid. You'll be fine. I, however, am slowly becoming pain free. Tell me about it. The wedding. Come on, make me laugh."

She took another sip, getting to the bottom of her first drink and sliding the glass away from her. "Well, let's see. They met five months ago when they had this passionate first date or something, then didn't see each other for two months, then got back together. They've been a couple for two or three whole months. Both of them claim it was love at first sight. They can hardly keep their hands off each other. There was enough steam in that room to make my hair go straight."

If that wasn't disgusting enough, she told him, the whole reception was loaded with longtime girlfriends of hers who were madly in love with wonderful, loving, sexy men whom they'd found in the most unexpected places. She, however, had had lousy luck with the opposite sex. Since about the fourth grade.

That got them started, talking and laughing about the worst dates and relationships imaginable. They went over the disastrous dates, hookups that looked like they might turn into stalkers, their most embarrassing setups. For a while it was like horror-dating one-upsmanship, but it began to put them both in a better mood. Someone to find the humor in all of it helped. It seemed they were two people who just never scored good partners at all. He was thirty-six and she was thirty-one and neither had found the right one. While they talked, he occasionally held her hand, the hand that rested on the table. With either of them hardly aware, more than an hour had passed, and it had passed with some laughter and pleasure, surprising her more than him. He lifted two fingers; two more drinks were delivered.

"What kind of odds do you give them?" he asked. "The bride and groom?"

"I'm the last person you should ask about that," she said. "Turns out I'm not much of a judge."

"Join the club," he said. "Well, I wish them the best." He grinned at her. "And I wish you the best, Brandy. This thing you're going through—it's going to pass. Just looking at you, talking with you through a couple of drinks, you're going to land on your feet, find the right guy. Tell me something. What's a woman like you looking for in a guy?"

"Are we talking about a date? Or something more than that?"

"How about both?" he said. "Start with the date."

"Okay, in a date—good manners. That's my only requirement for an evening out, as long as the guy is likable and I have an attraction. For the rest, I have this list. There are ten things, ranked."

He burst out laughing. "Are you kidding me?"

"I am not," she said indignantly. "My Aunt Kate told me a long time ago, make a list. She's always right about everything, so I made a list. It's a great list. There's one problem. Sometimes I lie to myself about whether he's got list qualities. When I do that, I pay. Big."

"I gotta know, Brandy. Give me the list."

"I can't. It's very private."

"Listen," Cam said. "I might need a list. Maybe that's my problem—no list. Tell me about it. I promise, I won't tell a soul."

"Well," she said reluctantly, "I might get some of the order mixed up. Four through seven are kind of interchangeable. And I can't talk about number one, you'll just have to let that go."

"Okay," he said. "Go."

"Number two is humor. Then honesty. He has to be committed. Trusting. Tidy. Not anal and fussy, just not an unbearable slob. Good-looking—I mean to me. Not necessarily a hottie hard-body, but a man I find attractive, you know? And bear in mind, I think Liam Neeson is hot," she added, making Cam laugh. "He has to like children. I know it's the kiss of death to say that to a new boyfriend, so I try to keep it to myself, but I want children. At thirty-one, I don't have all that much time left. He should make a decent living. And find me irresistible."

He sat back in some surprise. "That's a very good list. A well-thought-out list."

"Thank you. I put a lot of time into it."

He shook his head. If he were to make a list, that one would suffice. In fact, he couldn't think of a thing on that list he couldn't fulfill, if the woman found him attractive, that is. And yet, he was still alone. "A perfect list."

"I consider those things the basics."

"Okay, so where were the men in your life falling short?"

She took a thoughtful sip of her drink. "Hmm," she hummed. "Frankly, in the children and finding me irresistible departments. A little bit in the tidy area. And so far the men I thought were trusting simply didn't give a crap. And that commitment thing? I've run through a long line of cheaters. Which I guess implies they were also dishonest."

She smiled at him. "This isn't Kool-Aid. I'm a little light-headed."

"Good. That'll get your mind off the wedding. So, Brandy, have you compared your counter-list to your list of requirements? You're falling for handsome, funny men who make plenty of money and are good at number one." He smiled at her shocked expression—his deduction was completely accurate. "I'm way smarter than I look."

"You're not at all drunk. That was sharp."

His smile vanished and he looked into her eyes. "I'm really glad you didn't wait for the bouquet."

"I think I am, too," she said.

"You're beautiful when you laugh."

"You're coming on to me," she said. "It was subtle before."

"I've had at least three drinks," he said. "My subtlety is out the window."

"At least?"

"There was wine with dinner."

He lifted her hand, turned it over and pressed a small kiss onto her wrist. The look on her face was one of surprise, maybe apprehension. She started to pull her hand away, but he held it. He slipped his other hand up her arm to cup her elbow and put his lips softly against the inside of her elbow. When he lifted his head and connected with her gaze, he found those warm brown eyes had grown darker. He put a hand on her waist and pressed his lips softly to her bare shoulder; he heard her inhale slowly. He leaned closer, his lips hovering just above hers. He could feel her breath on his mouth. "Brandy," he whispered. She made a small sound as her eyelids slowly fell and he pressed his lips gently against hers. Her lips trembled beneath his so he pressed a bit more firmly, but he didn't hold them long. When he pulled back he said, "I have excellent manners."

"You seem to," she agreed. "I must be drunk. I'm kissing a stranger in a *bar*."

"I think we've gotten to be pretty good friends," he said. "We know each other's darkest, most embarrassing secrets."

"We don't know each other well enough to be kissing in a *bar*."

"Listen," he said. "Did I mention I'm staying here tonight? I probably shouldn't be driving. I'm going to check in and then come back here. We could have a drink or seltzer together, or I could take you upstairs, if you want to. We could watch a movie or something. Talk. Have drinks and not worry about anything. Whatever you like. Be less alone."

"That would be completely nuts," she said. "You do this sort of thing a lot?"

He shook his head. "Not in years. When I was younger, I was game for a lot of stupid things, but then eventually you grow up a little. Something like this didn't occur to me when I came over here, bought you a drink. What do you think?"

"I think you're lying," she said. "And, it's not a good idea."

"I'm telling the truth. I'm not drunk, but I shouldn't be driving. I'm getting a room."

"And when you come back and I'm not here?"

"You'd be playing it smart, I guess. But don't go. Wait for me and if you'd rather not go upstairs, let's stay here a while longer, close the place down, then I'll get you a cab, just to be safe. I like you. We'll just sit here, talk. Laugh. Maybe kiss."

"In a bar?" she asked, but she smiled.

He laughed. "Look around. There's no one here," he said. He gave her hand a squeeze and stood from the table. He leaned toward her and let his lips graze her cheek. "I'll be right back. Wait for me—I'm not going to force you to go upstairs, you're completely safe." He jerked his head over his shoulder toward the bartender. "He's watching, and he knows me—

I'm certainly not going to drag you out of here." He smiled. "Like I said, I have very good manners."

He left the bar and did exactly as he said he would, checking in to the hotel. It was late, there was no one else around the registration desk and it took just minutes. They gave him a king-size bed in a no-smoking room with a Jacuzzi tub and a wet bar. He asked for a shaving kit and when he popped the lid on the little cardboard box, he found the essentials—disposable razor, shaving cream, toothpaste, brush, comb, condoms. Then he walked back to the bar and looked in. Of course, she was gone, as any woman with an ounce of sense would be. He was thoroughly disappointed; he shouldn't have left the bar so soon, alone. But he should have expected this—he knew in five minutes she was intelligent and classy; such a woman wouldn't go to a stranger's hotel room.

But he had hoped she'd stay in the bar a while longer.

Cam could have canceled the room and gone home once he saw that his lame attempt at getting a funny, sexy, beautiful stranger into his hotel room had been rebuffed, but he wasn't on call and didn't have to work in the morning. He decided to take the room anyway, maybe turn on a movie and fall asleep here, rather than listen to the deafening silence in his too-big house. He walked toward the elevators and there, standing right in front of them, beautiful in a soft, gold silk cocktail dress, was the perfect stranger. Brandy. His eyes glowed with warmth. He could feel his smile reaching all the way into his chest.

Cameron walked toward her and took her hand in his. He leaned down and put a soft kiss on her forehead. The elevator doors opened and he pulled her inside, taking her gently into his arms. "You're trembling," he whispered. "Are you scared?"

"To death," she said. "I never intended to do this."

"You don't have to be scared. I'd love it if you came with me, but you certainly don't have to," he said.

"This could be the biggest, stupidest mistake of my life." Then she laughed. "Or at least the second biggest," she added softly.

"You'll see, it's all right. I don't want a woman who doesn't want me. We already know we have plenty to talk about...." He lifted her chin and gently touched her lips with his in a very soft, brief kiss. He kissed her once more, lightly, playing against her lips. "You can change your mind and leave anytime. You won't get any trouble from me."

"What if it's the biggest mistake of *your* life?" she asked him.

"I'm not worried. You're beautiful and sweet and I like you. I don't care." He kissed her again, a little more deeply. Then the doors opened and he led her to the room. Once inside, he tossed aside the shaving kit and put his hands on her face, threading his fingers into her hair, pulling her gently to his mouth. He moved over her lips sensuously, tugging at them with his, running his tongue around them. When her tongue joined his in play, he groaned his pleasure and pushed his tongue in to taste the inside of her mouth; she tasted like champagne and strawberries. Then he felt her tongue enter his mouth, slipping around. Heaven. He couldn't breathe.

"Scotch," she said.

"I can change that taste to Crest, if you'd like me to," he offered.

"I like scotch," she said, leaning in to his kiss again. "You taste good."

He wrapped his arms around her. "God," he whispered against her lips. "I feel better already. How do you feel?"

"Crazy. Completely crazy," she said.

"Yeah," he agreed, laughing. "This is pretty crazy. But I like it so far."

She molded herself against him, her arms going around his neck to hold him. She felt his hand glide down her back, over her butt to rest there and pull her closer still. His arms were strong, firm, but not confining. She could have wriggled out of his grasp without the slightest struggle. Instead of feeling frightened, she began to feel secure. Loved. Of course she knew it wasn't love—it was nothing more than human contact. But while her life was spiraling out of control, this handsome stranger felt like an anchor.

The one thought that came to mind should have brought her to her senses, catapulting her out of these arms, this room. But the opposite happened. She remembered she had a husband. And a prenuptial agreement in which she promised fidelity. In the event of divorce, she would not receive alimony if she had been unfaithful during the marriage. Of course, he had made no such promises and had been living with another woman for six months. He'd asked for the divorce nine months ago, but she hadn't signed the papers or told any of her friends.

She didn't care about alimony; her heart was in shreds. No amount of money would put it back together again.

She pushed against Cam. "This is wrong," she said.

"It's a lot of things, honey, but it's not wrong," he said. "We're single, consenting adults and we're—"

"I'm not," she said.

He was frozen for a second. "Okay, this sure feels consensual, so I'm guessing you mean you're not single."

She nodded and her eyes glistened.

"Oh, boy," he said, backing up a little bit, though he couldn't seem to let go of her completely. "I hope he's not standing outside that door with a big gun…"

"He's been living with another woman for six months. He served me nine months ago. I've been putting off the inevitable. Not because I want him back, but because…" She looked down. "I should have known better than to marry him in the first place. And I never saw myself as divorced after just months of marriage. Abandoned, after a few weeks of marriage…"

He looked down at her, sympathetic. "Aw, Jesus… No wonder you're feeling all broken up inside. I'm sorry, honey. That's a little worse than some lousy fix-ups, that shouldn't happen to anyone. I noticed you're not wearing a wedding ring."

"I had it on at the wedding, in front of my friends. By the time I got to the bar, I had decided—enough is enough. I can't stand this anymore, this pretending. It's in my purse. I'm sorry I misled you. It's not your problem. I should be going now—"

"Relax. Ordinarily I'd run like hell from a married woman, but I'm not exactly cuckolding the son of a bitch. Stay. Put the whole thing out of your mind for a while." And then he pulled her to him and kissed her again, deeply.

She swayed in his embrace, letting her hands run over his back while losing herself in his mouth, in his deep kiss. His hands on her were large, tender and confident, his chest hard against her breasts. She felt a tingling pull between her legs and knew she was going to cross the line, let it happen. She needed to feel something; she'd been in pain or numb for too long. And before morning, she'd be gone. She'd go home and sign the papers and get to work on putting her life back together. It was time to move on.

She met his kiss with hunger that was so real, so hot and bold, she almost forgot everything that had landed her in that bar, feeling sorry for herself. They consumed each other for a minute, then two, then four, completely lost in kisses so strong and penetrating her knees grew weak. She was beginning to feel again, feel something good.

Then she kicked off her shoes. She was staying.

Taking her hand, he led her to the bed where he sat on the edge, looking up at her. He gave her hand a gentle tug, bringing her down on his lap. His arms around her waist, hers around his neck, they were lost in deep, wet kisses that lasted forever. She felt his hand brush against her breast and it sent shivers rippling through her. He held her there, his hands on her waist while her hands moved behind her neck to the zipper of her dress, slowly inching it down. He lifted his hands to meet hers, pulling the zipper the rest of the way. She pulled the soft, gold silk forward, off her shoulders and down until it fell to her waist, leaving her only in her small, lacy bra. "God, you're beautiful," he whispered, burying his face in satin and lace, kissing her through the undergarment.

She held his face against her, resting her cheek against his soft hair. "I've lost my mind," she said against his ear. She slipped her hands down and began to work the buttons on his shirt, opening it, sliding her hands across his hard, hairless chest. "I've completely lost my mind."

"I can stop," he said. "If this isn't what you want, all you have to do is say so. As a courtesy, you might want to say so pretty soon."

"Don't stop," she said. Beneath her, through the sheer fabric of a silk dress and small, thin panties, she could feel him growing hard against her, and pleasure shot through her as she moved against him.

With his hands on her bottom, he pulled her against him, his erection still tucked into his pants. She pressed herself harder into his lap, causing him to growl deep in his throat. He claimed her mouth once more as he made the bra disappear, crushing her breasts against his bare chest. Her breasts felt heavy and needy and she was already starting to ache in the place that had gone empty and unsatisfied for so long. All she could think about was feeling good, feeling loved, feeling full.

Cameron reclined on the bed, lowering her carefully beside him. He kissed her as he filled his hands with her breasts. He lowered his lips to her nipples to kiss then run a tongue over each one, then gently suck, drawing a low, wonderful moan of pleasure from her. Back on her lips, feeling her tongue come into his mouth, it was his turn to moan. She was so delicious. Her mouth was slick velvet and he made a long, slow sweep of the inside.

He ran a hand over her hip and down, slipping it under her dress. Then he pulled the dress down and she lifted her hips to help. It went down over her knees and she kicked it off into a pile of golden silk on the floor. There was just the tiniest pair of panties underneath and he placed a gentle hand over her soft mound. "I want to get past these panties. Tell me it's okay," he said, his voice raspy.

"Yes," she whispered.

He slipped his hand inside the fabric. "You've been hurting for a while, haven't you, baby?" he asked.

"Don't spoil this."

"Let's talk about what I can do to help," he said, tugging off her panties and parting her legs with his hand. His long, gentle fingers reached until he found the place that was dark and wet and it made him groan softly, deeply. He slipped lower. He found the hard, sensitive knot with his fingers and she gasped; he covered her opened mouth with his and went to work on that vulnerable little spot. Instant response—he loved it. He pulled her tongue into his mouth as he slid a finger inside her, letting his thumb make slow circles around her clitoris. "God," she said, pushing against his hand.

"You're perfect," he whispered against her lips. "Go ahead, sweetheart. Take it—it's free. Feel better."

Her hips began to rock against his hand and he sank his finger deeper while his thumb pressed harder against her. He moved over that tender little knot and in no time at all her hips rose, her breath caught and her entire bottom clenched, bathing his hand in the most wonderful spasms. Instant orgasm. And a powerful one that held her in its possession for a long, shuddering moment until she fell back into his embrace. He stilled his hand, but didn't remove it. He just kissed her little gasping lips, soft and sweet and slow, sensuously sucking on them while she caught her breath. And finally, as her breathing normalized, he slowly pulled his hand away.

"I think you needed that," he said.

"Ohhhh," she answered.

He chuckled. "Better?"

"You have no idea."

"Oh, I have a pretty good idea," he said with a soft laugh.

"Why'd you do that?" she asked him.

"That was what you needed. Anything more has to be what you want. I'm not going to take advantage of you."

"You haven't," she said.

"You about ready to let me out of my pants?"

She ran her hands down his chest to his belly. Her hands went to his belt, unbuckled it, undid the button on his pants and slid down the zipper.

"God bless you," he said in a grateful breath. She took him in her hand and he trembled involuntarily, it felt so good. "Brandy, I have to get protection for us. Give me a second." He went quickly for the shaving kit, kicking off his shoes as he returned. He grabbed a condom out of the box, let his shirt fall from his shoulders and dropped his pants, getting rid of them. Sheathed and ready, he knelt on the bed. He leaned over to press his lips against hers and said, "Anything you want. Any way you say. It's still your turn."

She answered by opening up to him. He knelt between her legs and gently filled her with his aching erection, pushing inside slowly. She moved with him, arching against him, and he groaned with the effort it took to hold back. It had been a very long time for him, which had the disadvantage of making him a less than astonishing lover. He struggled, and welcomed the struggle. Making this a night of no regrets for her was all that mattered. He was in some kind of trance, amazed by how pure and right she felt, how familiar, like he'd been in this place before. The way she met him, thrust for thrust, was natural and felt as though they'd practiced this coupling for years.

He couldn't remember feeling like this before and he wondered if he'd just lost his mind. Then he thought, is it possible there really is one true mate for every man? For every woman? Do you search for years and then stumble onto the right one? The one who smells, tastes and feels perfect?

He pushed deeply, moving in long slow strokes, listening to the little purrs and sighs that told him he was on the right spot. Her hips began to move in rhythm with his and then as her pace picked up, he pushed harder, faster, deeper. He was hanging on for dear life, giving her a chance to grab on to another orgasm before he'd let himself cash in. It didn't take her long; she was sexually charged. She lifted her hips against him, her breath caught and he felt her close around him, pulsing. "Oh, yeah," he whispered. With a shudder, he let go, joining her in a thundering climax.

As she collapsed beneath him, he held her, running his hands over her soft body in a tender caress while she recovered. He was reluctant to let go of her, reluctant to leave her body. He stayed there for a long time, holding his weight off her slender frame, and finally he slipped out, but he kept his arms around her for a while longer.

"You okay, honey?" he asked.

"Hmm. Okay."

"How'd I score on number one?" he asked her.

She chuckled softly in spite of herself. "If there's one thing I've learned, it's a mistake to praise a man's performance in bed."

"You were wonderful," he said. "Phenomenal. Like a furnace, a blast furnace. Hot and strong. God. I thought I was going to faint," he said.

She laughed. "You weren't too bad."

"Thanks. Just out of curiosity, why is it number one?"

She shrugged. "I guess I couldn't think of a compromise. This is an awful important part of being a couple."

"It is," he agreed. He kissed her cheek and said, "Excuse me for just a minute." He withdrew to the bathroom. When he came back, he was wearing a frown and a towel around his hips. He sat on the bed beside her. "Brandy, I have to tell you something. The condom—it broke."

"Jesus," she said in a weak breath.

"It's okay—I'll tell you exactly what to do. I'm a doctor. There's emergency birth control for exactly this kind of problem. If you'll see your doctor on Monday, he or she can prescribe something to prevent a pregnancy. If you can't get an appointment, you can come to my office Monday and I'll write you a scrip."

"I'm on the pill," she said.

"Well, that's a relief," he said. "Damn, I'm sorry, honey. We should sue the hotel."

"It'll be all right, won't it?"

"You should be fine. I take real cautious care of myself— you haven't been exposed to anything." He brushed the hair back from her brow. "I'm so sorry. The last thing I wanted was for you to be worried about anything. Especially now that I know everything you've been through."

She smiled at him. "Aren't you worried that you've been exposed to something? You don't know me."

"I can take care of my concerns." He smiled. "I get a real good deal on lab tests, if I feel they're in order."

"No reason you should believe me, but it was necessary for me to be completely checked over after my... After he moved out. Quite a while ago."

"Thanks for telling me that, Brandy." He lowered himself to the bed and gathered her up in his arms. "As long as you're all right, that's all that concerns me right now. As far as I'm concerned, you have everything on the list covered. Very nicely."

"This should never end," she said.

"It doesn't have to," he said, kissing her neck. "God knows, I don't want it to."

"But it will," she said, a hint of sadness in her tone.

"That's up to you. I'd like to know more of you."

"I'll have to think about that," she said.

"You think," he said. "I'll try to offer incentives." His hands began to move and she moaned, instantly responsive to his touch. He was on the rise again, and it was obvious against her thigh.

She said, "Do you think the next condom will hold?"

"I don't think it much matters. Now."

It was a very long time before they slept. He made love to her again and again, each time sweeter, more satisfying than the time before. It shouldn't have been so effortless, so right, but it was. For someone who had been tense and frightened, she had shed her inhibitions quickly and unfolded at his touch, responding to him with a heat and passion that surprised and thrilled him. The level of physical intimacy was greater than he expected, more profound than he'd imagined. He'd had his share of one-night stands, but he couldn't remember one that felt like this. He wanted more of this woman, and not just more of her in bed.

In the morning, early, when the sun was barely up, she was awake and touching him. "I have to go now," she whispered.

"Not yet," he said, reaching for her. "Not yet."

She ran a hand along the hair at his temple. "It was a beautiful night, but I have to go."

"I want to see you again," he said. "Tell me how to get in touch with you."

"My life is so messed up right now," she said. "You have to understand that much, or last night couldn't have happened..."

"I'm not afraid of a little mess..."

"Let me go and do the things I have to do, straighten things out a little, then get in touch with you. Can you do that?"

He kissed her deeply. "I think if we spent more time together, we could fall in love. I want to know if that could happen. I have a real good feeling about us."

She couldn't help but laugh at him. "Cameron, you picked me up in a bar..."

"I know. What a piece of luck. When does something that great happen? I don't want to let you go."

"You're not going to try to keep me from leaving, are you?"

"Of course not, but I'd like to call for breakfast. If you won't stay, I at least want to see you again. Take you out, talk to you..."

"Write down your number. Or give me a business card," she said.

"Tell me your last name. Give me a number if not an address. You know you don't have to be afraid of me."

She sighed and put a soft hand against his cheek. "It's really important that I feel in control right now. Please understand?"

He thought briefly, then smiled at her. He gave her a little kiss and got out of bed. He found her bra and panties on the floor and picked them up to hand to her. His trousers were flung across a chair and he slipped into them, sans underwear, while she put on her dainties. Then he held her soft, gold dress for her and helped her into it, turning her around to zip up the back. Next he pulled his wallet from his back pocket, flipped it open and produced a business card. "I want you to feel safe and in control, just like you were last night. All night. Go ahead, have me checked out." He pressed it into her hand.

"Maybe you'll want to have *me* checked out," she said with a soft smile.

"No," he said, shaking his head. "I'm going to let you tell me everything you want me to know. That's a better place to start."

"Thank you," she whispered.

"Don't make me wait too long, Brandy," he said. "Even if I can't see you until you get your affairs in order, I'd like to talk to you. Just touch base, that's all. Let me know you're okay. I promise, I'll be patient for the rest."

She smiled and said, "Sure. How could I not?"

9

October flew into the mountains and in the first couple of weeks provided a rainbow of color around Virgin River. Mel, Jack and their friends had been back from Joe's wedding in Grants Pass for two weeks and fall was crisp in the air, the nights cold and the hillsides in full autumn bloom, fiery-colored leaves scattered amid towering green pines.

Doc was at the computer behind the reception desk when Mel came in from the kitchen. "Kids are settled into naps," she said. "What are you doing?"

"Playing around," he said. "I've been meaning to ask you—any word on Cheryl Chreighton?"

Mel shook her head. "It's confidential treatment. If Cheryl didn't put us on the list to call her, we can't get through, can't get information. I called to ask how she was doing and was told I wasn't on her list—which tells me she's probably still there. I could go speak to her mother, but I don't know about that. Her mother is—"

"She's not well, and she's not the least neighborly," Doc said. "Mean as a snake, if you ask me. If I were Cheryl, the mother wouldn't be on my list."

"I was going to say exactly that, but much more nicely," Mel said, smiling. Doc seldom minced words. "Are you going to be around for an hour or two?"

He looked at her over the top of his specs. "Looking to get out of here for a while?"

"I don't want to put you out, but they're asleep in the kitchen…"

Doc looked back at the computer. "I've never been put off by the children. That's some of your best work."

She laughed at him. "If I didn't agree, I'd get a little pissy that you don't give me half that much credit for my actual practitioner work."

"Your head is big enough," he barked. "Go. Take a break. I'll holler when they wake up."

"Are you sure? Because if your arthritis or acid reflux is bothering you at all…"

"Not much bothers me besides you," he said. "Tell Jack it's getting time to get on that river."

"He's on the porch at the bar, tying off flies. I think he's way ahead of you."

When it wasn't appointment day at the clinic, Mel took the kids with her to work. Because David was getting around much faster and fussier, he spent a lot more time with his father than her. Jack would take his son with him on errands to buy supplies for the bar or even keep him in the backpack while he served, but he would have his early-afternoon bottle with his mom at the clinic, then a nap in the playpen kept in Doc's kitchen. Emma, after nursing, would have her nap at the same time as her brother in the little Port-a-Crib, also in the kitchen.

Of course, Doc was more than happy to comfort, change and jiggle Mel's kids. He adored them. He grumbled a little about babysitting, but he never once refused. In fact, if she tried to get someone else to stand in, he seemed disappointed. Maybe offended, as if he'd been considered too old.

This was just such a typical day, a beautiful mid-October afternoon. Mel left the sleeping kids in Doc's charge at about one-thirty and found Jack on the porch of his bar, tying off beautiful, feathery flies. Fishing season was starting to get good—the fall was excellent for salmon, sturgeon and trout. Jack was an amazing angler.

"Things have been really interesting in your little bar," Mel said.

"A little tense and steamy." He laughed. "Think someone should take Luke aside and warn him about this place?"

"I thought you'd finally learned your lesson," she teased him. "You've been in the business of almost every romantic relationship in this town...."

"Yeah, but this one's different. The second Shelby saw him, it was a target lock on. She wants him. Can you see the struggle on his face? He's getting lines."

"Yeah, what's that about?" Mel asked. "She's adorable. You'd think he'd be thrilled."

"Well, the first night he met her he said he took one look at her and thought he was going to be arrested. He might be having a little trouble with her age."

"Phooey," Mel said. "There's quite a nice difference in our ages." She grabbed his thigh. "I'm catching up with you, however."

"Then there's the general," Jack said. "Kind of intimidating…"

"Oh, Walt's a pussycat," she said. "And I think he likes Luke. They have the army in common."

"Luke's either going to give in or explode," Jack said.

"How do you know he hasn't? Given in."

"Have you taken a good look at him? At his posture, his eyes? Believe me, he'd be a lot looser. He hasn't unloaded in a long time."

"Jack!" she said.

"And the funny thing is, Shelby's downright serene," Jack said, completely ignoring his wife's scold. "She's a very unusual woman."

"What do you mean?"

"Have you looked at yourself in the mirror when it's been a long time for us?" he asked. "It's all over your face when you need to be taken care of." He grinned at her.

"It is *not!*" she said, giving him a whack on the arm. But she laughed at him, and secretly knew he was right. She also knew why Shelby didn't look that way. Shelby, virginal, hadn't been satisfied by a man yet; she didn't ache with longing for her lover. "It's hardly ever been a long time for us," she pointed out.

"Which is how I like it," he said. "Then take the general," he said. "Talk about a satisfied man…"

"You can't possibly know that. Walt neither looks nor acts any differently than he ever did," she insisted.

"The general looks like a beautiful woman moved in next door and he's doing his best to be a good neighbor. He's got a twinkle in his eye and a very sly grin."

Mel turned toward him and narrowed her eyes. "Do you really think you know what facial expressions correspond exactly to a man's getting laid?"

"I do," he said with a smile. "In fact, I consider myself something of an expert."

She sat with him for an hour, talking mostly about the new budding romances. In fact, a lot of people were preoccupied with that. No one knew what was going on outside the bar, but Shelby and Luke were there frequently for a beer, sometimes dinner as well, and they were inseparable. They tended to look at each other as though they'd been waiting days to be together just for that little while.

By contrast, the general was seen around town a little less, leaving people to wonder if he wasn't spending that time with the movie star down the road.

It was three o'clock when the empty school bus barreled through town, Molly headed for her pickups. Like all little towns in the area, she had kids at elementary, middle and high schools to gather up at the end of the school day and bring back to town. It was a long day for the farm and ranch kids whose parents drove them into town to meet the bus in the morning, picking them up in the afternoon. As she passed the bar, she gave the bus horn a blast and waved at Mel and Jack on the porch.

"That woman is going to heaven," Mel said. "My idea of hell is being trapped in a school bus full of noisy, bratty kids twice a day. I don't know how she does it."

Mel glanced at her watch; you could set it by Molly's bus run. Her kids were due to wake from their naps and she ambled across the street to the clinic. Her pace was leisurely; it was a perfect autumn day. When she neared the porch, she heard her children crying. In itself, that wasn't a bad sign—they could be just waking up. But Doc would usually alert them if he knew they were nearby. Absent that, he would comfort the little ones.

Something was wrong. She knew it at once, felt it in her

gut, and ten steps before Doc's porch she broke into a dead run. Up the steps, through the door, and what she saw threw her into a panic. Doc was sprawled, facedown, on the floor. Little Emma, only five months old, was right beside him, lying on her back, her face red with pain or fear or both. David, still in his playpen in the kitchen, was screaming loudly.

She honestly didn't know who to reach for first, Doc or Emma. Emma was crying, so she was at least conscious, while Doc was motionless. She did what her instincts seemed to always urge her to do—she turned at the opened front door and screamed, "Jaaaacccckkkk!"

He had seen her break into a run up to the porch and inside. He was already on his way. By the time she screamed for him, he was there, totally in tune with her, sensing her. When she saw him coming, she lifted Emma right into his arms. Then she went to Doc, tucking his left arm to his side so she could roll him onto his back and into a supine position. "See if Emma's all right," she shouted to Jack. "He might've dropped her as he fell."

When she got Doc on his back, his eyes were open and sightless. She checked him quickly—no pulse, no breath. "Oh, goddamn," she said right before starting cardiopulmonary resuscitation. She began by tilting his head back, made sure his airway was clear and blew into his lungs twice—two long breaths. Next she pressed the crossed palms of her hands on his sternum to try to get his heart started and asked Jack, "Is she okay?"

"I think so," Jack said helplessly. "She's pissed off but not bruised or bleeding."

Mel covered Doc's mouth with hers and blew into his lungs again. Then, during thirty more cardiac compressions, she asked. "Any lumps on the head?"

Jack ran a hand over Emma's smooth, bald head. "Don't see anything."

Mel finished pumping and went for the respiratory inflations again. Then, breathless, she said, "Check David, and if he's okay, call someone. Mercy Air," she said. "I need the defibrillator. I need my bag."

Jack bolted for the kitchen. David was standing in his playpen, screaming. The second he saw Jack his cries turned to little gasps and he reached a hand toward him. "Da!" he yelled. "Da!"

"Hang in there, buddy," Jack said, laying Emma in her crib. He ran back to the front of the clinic, found Mel's bag behind the reception desk and placed it beside her, open. Then he ran to the treatment room, grabbed the case that held the defibrillator and took it to her. By the time he got back, she had ripped Doc's shirt open.

"Aw, Jesus, Doc," she groaned, breathing into him again.

Jack was picking up the phone when he heard the sound of heavy, running footfalls and Preacher stopped short in the opened doorway. He took a quick look, assessed and ran into the clinic, kneeling opposite Mel. She was counting. "I can help," he said, brushing her hands away to take over the chest compressions.

Mel immediately flipped open the defibrillator case and turned on the switch. The portable defibrillator was the same as the type carried on commercial air carriers with patches as opposed to paddles. She put the patches on Doc's chest and said, "Pay attention for the shock, Preach." The machine purred and a mechanical voice came from it. *Assessing patient. Stand by. Clear for shock.* "Clear!" Mel said. Preacher pulled back his hands and Mel pressed the button, delivering the jolt. She felt for a pulse. No response. "Dammit, Doc," she muttered.

Mel dug around in her bag while Preacher pushed air into the old man's lungs, then resumed compressions. She started an IV quickly and attached a bag of Ringer's, holding it high. It was taken out of her hands by Jack, automatically assisting. She then examined the labels of two vials and drew two syringes. She added epinephrine to the IV. Next, the atropine.

Jack was beside her, crouched, holding the Ringer's over his head. "Airlift's on the way. I called Shelby to help. And June Hudson in Grace Valley."

"That's all you can do," Mel said, taking the bag of Ringer's. "Bring me an IV stand from the treatment room so you can take care of the kids." When he returned and hung up the bag, she switched on the machine again. "Shocking, Preach." The mechanical voice alerted them. *Assessing patient. Stand by. Clear for shock.* "Clear!" Preacher pulled back his hands and Mel pressed the button again. Doc's body arched with the jolt.

Mel put the stethoscope in her ears, listening to his chest. "Jesus, Doc, don't do this," she said. "God, I *need* you!" She brushed Preacher's hands away and began her own chest compressions. "Breathe for him on thirty—two big breaths," she told Preacher. "Ten, eleven, twelve…"

Mel wasn't even aware that the kids had stopped crying. Jack stood behind her, holding them both against him. Mel tried another eppie, shocked him twice more, listened to his chest. He was completely unresponsive. By the time she could hear the sound of rotor blades, tears were running down her cheeks, falling onto Doc's chest, and she wouldn't stop compressing. Preacher sat back on his heels. "Don't stop!" she barked at him. Slowly, the big man leaned forward and put two more useless breaths into the old man.

"How can you *do* this?" Mel cried to the lifeless form beneath her hands.

Paramedics ran into the clinic and took their places on either side of Doc, scooting Preacher and Mel out of the way. They rushed through a quick assessment while Mel rattled off what drugs had been administered, how many times she'd used the defibrillator. The electrodes for a portable electrocardiogram were attached to his chest as compressions were continued.

Mel backed away and came up against Jack and the kids. He held one on each hip. She turned against his chest. He can't just die like that, she thought in despair. David had been crying so hard that his breath came in jagged little hiccups of emotion and he buried his wet face in his father's shoulder. Mel took Emma into her arms, looked her over briefly to be sure she was all right, then her attention was again focused on the paramedics' resuscitation.

Minutes passed as they worked on him. Shelby arrived, running up the porch steps and into the clinic. "Take the baby," Jack said. "We found her on the floor beside Doc. I think he might've dropped her as he fell. Neither one of us has had a chance to undress her and look her over closely, but she seems okay."

Shelby took the baby out of the reception area and a few minutes later she was back, holding a now-quiet baby against her shoulder. "I took all her clothes off and she seems to be fine. No bumps or marks or anything."

"He might've felt it coming and laid her on the floor," Mel said. "He wasn't on top of her." She turned her watery eyes up to Jack. "Which could've killed her."

Jack squeezed her shoulder.

After twenty minutes, one of the paramedics sat back on his heels and looked at Mel over his shoulder. "Any idea if he has a DNR?" which stood for *do not resuscitate*.

"We never talked about it," she said.

"He's flat, Mel. We're gonna have to pronounce," he said.

"No!" Mel shouted, taking a step forward.

Jack hung on to her shoulder, preventing her from going any farther. "Mel, he's gone. He's been gone."

"No," she said more quietly, shaking her head.

"You didn't have any response. We haven't had any," the man said. "Who's your coroner?"

"You're working on him," she sniffed. "If it's not a homicide, Doc handles it, signs a death certificate."

"He's pumped full of drugs and electricity, ma'am," the other paramedic said. "Would you like us to transport?"

She sucked in a breath. "Take him to Redding for an autopsy. I have to know what happened to him."

"Yes, ma'am. But I bet we know."

She was shaking her head. "He didn't have heart problems."

The paramedic stood up. "Yeah, that's the thing. You can treat heart problems. You just can't make it through a massive coronary, fatal stroke or aneurysm if you don't know the problem exists. I have some paperwork. Stay right here."

The first paramedic went back to the chopper while the second began packing up their things. Mel went to Doc, knelt beside him and gently closed his eyes. She pulled the electrodes from the defibrillator off his chest and then, absently, affectionately, flattened out his sparse, white chest hair. She ran her fingertips across his wild white eyebrows, smoothing them. She leaned down to him and put her lips against his forehead, her tears dropping there. "You are such a pain in the ass," she whispered. "How dare you leave me like this?" She rested her cheek briefly against his head. He was already growing cold.

When the paramedics took his body out, she followed. A small crowd had gathered outside, waiting. Some of her friends—Paige and Brie, Connie and Ron, Lydie Sudder, and others. She looked at them and a large tear ran down her cheek. "I'm sorry," she said. "I'm so sorry. I tried. I really tried."

And then Jack was beside her, pulling her in close.

The night of Doc's death, after Jack had helped settle the kids into bed, he went to the kitchen and poured himself and his wife each a short snifter of brandy. He went back to the great room where Mel was curled into the corner of the couch in front of the fire. He put the drinks on the side table and sat in the big leather chair, opposite her. "Come here, baby," he said, holding up an arm.

She unfolded from the sofa and went to him, settling onto his lap. He handed her a brandy, then with one arm around her back, he picked up the second for himself.

"He was ready," Jack said. "We're going to let him go gracefully, so he can watch over the town from a higher place."

"I'm having a real hard time," she said.

"I know. That's why we have each other." He sipped from his glass. "We have to remember who Doc was and what he'd expect of us. He'd want to be toasted, thanked kindly for his good work and sent off with a minimum of sentiment. He was a tough old codger. He never liked mush."

"I wish I'd told him I loved him," she said, misting up.

Jack chuckled. "He knew you loved him, but if you'd tried that sop on him, he would have barked your head off."

"It's going to be hard for the town to say goodbye," she said.

"Even so, he's moved on, and so will we." He pressed his lips to her temple. "Call the hospital tomorrow, Mel. Tell them an autopsy isn't necessary. Let's not carve him up. There isn't anything more we need to know."

"I need to know if I could have saved him," she said softly.

"What would he say about that?" Jack asked her quietly.

"He'd say, 'Don't waste your breath.'" She turned her head,

looking at Jack, and a large tear spilled down her cheek. Jack pressed his lips against it.

"Okay," she said. "There's a lot to do. To go through his things." Then very softly she asked, "What are we going to do without a doctor?"

"You'll have Shelby to help out for a while. And we'll get looking. Tomorrow morning, I'll go to the clinic with you and we'll have a look at his personal effects, see if he left any kind of journal or last wishes. We'll make arrangements and let this town say goodbye to an old friend as soon as possible, so we can all heal."

"You're right," she said. "He wouldn't want us to carry on."

"He wouldn't," Jack said.

"I don't know what I'd do without you," she told him.

He smiled sweetly. "You'd be miserable." He touched his glass to hers. "To Doc," he said.

"To Doc. The biggest pain-in-the-ass country doctor in three counties." She hiccupped. "God, I'm going to miss him."

Although Mel and Doc had never discussed what would become of the clinic should something happen to him, he had no intention of leaving the town or his nurse midwife in dire straights. In documents dated shortly after Mel had married Jack two years before, Doc had willed the clinic, free and clear, to her in a living trust that would bypass probate. It was funny to think of him doing something so savvy, so modern; impossible to think of him hiring a lawyer. Also, in the top desk drawer, in plain sight if she'd ever bothered to look, was an old, worn bankbook. Doc had been squirreling away little bits of money over forty-five years—and about a year before his death, he had put Mel's name on the account. While she thought she had signed documents so that he could payroll her, she'd unknowingly provided her signature to the account.

He should have taken a big Alaskan fishing trip instead, because Mel had plenty of money. But Doc wouldn't indulge himself any more than he'd leave town for more than a day or two. Still, she was incredibly touched. Without ever saying a word and in fact being somewhat stingy with his praise, he had seen her as a partner within six months of her arrival in Virgin River.

He left a request—not even a letter, but a few sentences in his cramped old hand, tucked into the bankbook—that he be cremated and his ashes sprinkled in the Virgin River. Mel called Harry Shipton, the preacher from Grace Valley, and arranged to have him say a few words when they scattered the ashes at the widest curve in the Virgin. Notices were posted in the bar and at Valley Hospital.

Four days after his death, Mel and Jack closed the bar and the clinic and drove to the river where, it should not have surprised them, they could hardly get down the road. Hundreds of people from Virgin River, neighboring towns and medical staff who worked at Valley Hospital, had gathered on both sides of the river. As they walked toward the river there was a pickup parked in their path, the bed of the truck filled with flowers—gladiolas, carnations, baby roses, daisies and mums. A man handed Mel and Jack long stalks of flowers to hold.

June Hudson from the Grace Valley clinic, her husband, Jim Post, and her father, the Grace Valley doctor before June took over, Elmer Hudson, stood at the river's edge beside John Stone, June's business partner, and Susan, his wife. Mel went to stand by them, accepting and giving hugs and condolences. "If you need any help in the clinic, Mel, John and I can probably lend a hand," June said.

"Thanks. I might have to send patients your way for a while. I don't know what we're going to do for a doctor."

"Lots of little towns around here make do without one—patients just drive a little farther. Meanwhile, they still have you."

"Look at these people," she said, tearing up a little. "You'd think a man as crotchety as Doc wouldn't be able to draw a crowd like this."

"He's always been cranky, too," Elmer Hudson said. "In my case it came with age, but Mullins was in a piss-poor mood since I met him forty years ago."

Mel felt a huff of laughter escape through tears. "My first night in Virgin River, he pulled my car out of a ditch. My brand-new BMW convertible. His first tender words to me were, 'That piece of crap isn't going to do you much good around here.'" She shook her head. "Damn, I'm going to miss that old man. He was like a grandfather to the kids."

"When I go, I want at least this many people at my funeral, plus twenty, just to show him up," Elmer Hudson said. He looked at his daughter. "Hire 'em if you have to, June."

"Sure, Dad," she said.

Harry Shipton walked to the edge of the river. The crowd parted so that he could pass. Dressed in a simple light blue chambray shirt and khaki pants, holding his bible, he said, "We're gathered here today to say goodbye to a good friend. Doc Mullins served the medical needs of Virgin River and beyond for more than forty years, and from what I'm told by people who knew him longest, he never worried about whether he'd get thanked or paid. All that mattered to him was that his town, his family, have whatever medical attention he could provide. He saved lives, nurtured the sick, brought new life into the world and gently closed the eyes of the ones who passed. Let us pray." Heads bowed as he recited the prayer of Saint Francis of Assisi, then the Twenty-third Psalm, and finally the Lord's Prayer.

"There's quite a bit more that could be said about our friend

Doc, but I'm a little afraid a lightning bolt might strike us down if we get too fussy. Doc appreciated a few things in life—he liked some honest, direct words, hard work, good friends and a shot of decent whiskey at the end of the day." He accepted the urn that contained Doc's ashes and sprinkled them over the water. The ashes were followed by a shot glass of amber liquid—a little Jack Daniel's. "Go with God, old friend. Peace and love."

When the ashes began to float downstream, flowers were tossed from the banks to escort his final passage. Slowly, perhaps reluctantly, people began to turn away from the river.

And then Jack opened up the bar for anyone who wanted to raise a glass to their departed friend.

With the people in town saddened by the passing of their old doctor, it was a welcome diversion for everyone to look forward to Jack's marine friends' arrival a couple of weeks later. They always caught the end of deer-hunting season. It wasn't a complete squad, especially since the full throng had just been to Virgin River in late July, lending a hand when a forest fire threatened the town. Josh and Tom from Reno arrived. Joe Benson and his new wife, Nikki, came down from Grants Pass and stayed at the general's house with Vanni and Paul. With Mike Valenzuela, Preacher and Jack, that left only Corny and Zeke missing.

One person who was anticipating their visit but still a bit too preoccupied to take her usual full pleasure was Mel. With Shelby's help, she had been simultaneously running the clinic, making house calls and sorting through Doc's papers and personal effects. More than forty years of accumulation was taxing and emotional. She was clearing out his room, giving away his clothes, books and furniture, and preparing his bedroom as either a guest room or quarters for a new doctor, if one could ever be found.

She missed him so much. Once she and Doc had their little kinks ironed out, she had begun to cherish his grumpy frowns and had found humor in his cantankerous behavior.

Finally she heard the honking of a horn and lifted her head from her chore of reading through Doc's old calendars. "They're here," she said to Shelby.

"Who?" the younger woman asked.

"The boys. Jack's squad. We're done for today. We need their laughter. Trust me." And with that command, Mel snatched up the baby and Shelby grabbed David. They made their way across the street to the bar.

They were barely in the door when Mel found herself instantly whirled around by Tom Stephens, while Josh immediately grabbed David out of Shelby's arms and hefted him into the air to check his weight.

"Shelby, meet Josh Phillips," Mel said a little breathlessly. "He's a paramedic from Reno. And this wild man is Tom Stephens, a news chopper pilot from the same place."

With an arm around her shoulders, Tom said to Mel, "I know you've had a bad couple of weeks, sweetheart. Anything I can do to make it better?"

She patted his chest and said, "Just miss him with me, Tom. That's all we're left with right now."

"Aw, baby—you know no one wanted to see the old boy go. I bet wherever he is, the fishing's good."

"Given his surly behavior, the fish might be fried where he is," she joked. "I'm glad you're here. We need some of what you boys have. This bar has been really quiet. Well, except for the pounding."

"Well, we don't exactly specialize in quiet." He laughed and took Emma out of her arms. "Let's have a look at our girl. Whoa, she's putting on some weight. Thank God, she looks like you, Mel. I'd hate for her to have a face like the ugly mug you married."

"I think he's very handsome," she said.

The alarm of their arrival had somehow been sounded, probably by Jack from the phone in the kitchen. It brought out Mike, Preacher, and from the general's house, Walt, Joe and Paul. By five o'clock the men had all gathered and the neighbors were starting to show their faces—the Carpenters, Connie and Ron of the corner store, Joy and Bruce, Harv, the county lineman, Hope McCrea and finally, Muriel St. Claire.

Mel's delight wasn't as pure as it might have been ordinarily, but her mood was lifted by their presence. At a little after five, Luke Riordan made his appearance and Mel noticed that Shelby's eyes took on a very familiar glow. The early-evening gatherings at the bar had been extremely subdued since Doc's passing; even Shelby grieved. But with the presence of the marines, everything seemed just a little bit better.

Luke was welcomed by the brothers and drawn in with friendly approval. The conversation quickly turned to missions and commands as they compared notes, trying to figure out if they had mutual friends or had served in common battle arenas at the same time. Then more women began to arrive and Luke watched curiously as the men greeted each one as if she could be a sister or girlfriend. When Paige came out of her quarters with the new baby, the tot was passed around from man to man, each of whom took her close and affectionately, praised her beauty and snuggled her like any fond uncle might. Her son, Christopher, was soon riding on various shoulders while Paige was being embraced.

Brie came in from the RV behind the bar, her home until her house was finished, and damned if each one of those men didn't have his hands all over her belly like he'd been the one to put that baby in there. After a quick feel, they'd compliment Mike on his excellent potency. "You got her cooking a good one here, brother," Josh said. "Baby, you are more gorgeous than ever!" said Tom.

Then came Vanessa and Nikki and the whole process was repeated again, with bone-rattling hugs and sloppy kisses. It was a whole new experience for Luke. Even in his own family of biological brothers, he hadn't seen anything like it. But it interested him, the way these men behaved toward each other's women, as though it was expected. As if they idolized each other's wives as much as their own, treating them with a fondness that was hardly superficial; an intimacy that was at once deep and completely respectful. The trust was implicit; the affection appeared genuine. The security they felt in their relationships was obvious.

Luke had never lived in this kind of world.

Preacher was poaching fish, steaming rice and vegetables, putting out snacks. The man's typically serious expression had turned happy and his grin was bigger than Luke had ever seen. Drinks and food were served, the noise grew louder as the evening grew later. Then slowly, the women began to disappear to take care of their children.

Luke had gratefully allowed himself to be pulled into the brotherhood. It scratched an itch he'd had for a while; he'd been missing his own military brothers. But when he noticed that the women had begun to depart, he stole a glance at Shelby. Mel had put on her jacket and with Jack's help with the children, she made her way out of the bar, leaving Shelby momentarily alone.

Their relationship had just started heating up when Doc died. In the couple of weeks since he'd had his arms around her now and then, but she only laid her head on his chest and sighed heavily, tired and sad. The load of Doc's passing had been heavy, both emotionally and workwise. It derailed what would have been a serious seduction from him.

Luke went to her before she could leave or get caught up in conversation with someone else. When he approached her it gave him a lift to see her smile.

"I haven't seen as much of you as I'd like," he said.

"It's been a difficult time. Are you doing okay?" she asked.

"Busy. I've gotten a lot done without you to distract me. Tell me about you."

She shrugged. "We've been going through Doc's things. It hasn't been easy for Mel. I think her heart is breaking, but she's so strong."

"How about *your* heart?" he heard himself ask.

"I wasn't as close to him as Mel was. I gather their relationship was intense, humorous, conflicted but trusting. They gave each other so much crap, it wouldn't be obvious at first sight—but they loved each other. She's been telling me stories about him for days on end—about him going into the backwoods to camps full of transients who could be dangerous, trying to help them without worrying about his own neck. About the way he used to bend the rules to be sure everything would work out for his town, his people. Really, he was an icon. I'm learning a lot."

"You're tired," he said, running a finger along her soft cheek.

"It's hard work. I don't know what Mel would do without me right now, lucky I happen to be here. How's the house coming?"

"The roof leaks, Paul's going to be coming back out to help," he said, smiling. "But I've sanded and varnished the floors, textured and painted the walls, put in new doors, windows and baseboards in the house, installed new cupboards and countertops. The porch is solid and the cabins all have new roofs, thanks to crews Paul could give me." His grin became wider. "I can have a fire at night and the bathroom is functional, though I have to do a lot in there to make it nice. Art has a good little home next door. He's real proud of that. It's the first time he's ever had his own house."

"When we get through Doc's things, I'll come check it out."

"We need some time, you and me."

"That would feel good. But there's hunting…"

"There's hunting," he confirmed. "Then hunting will be done and we'll think of something."

"I've committed to Mel and the clinic every weekday," she said.

"I'm sorry for your loss."

"Thanks," she said. "But I'm going to be fine."

"Then follow me out on the porch," he said. "Let me get my arms around you for a minute before you go."

"That's the best part of my day," she said, walking out the door with him, arm in arm.

When all the women had gone, the cards and cigars came out. The tables were pushed together and hands were dealt. Luke pulled up a chair and eagerly accepted a fat cigar. Everyone sat down except Jack. "I'm going home, guys," he said. "Mel told me to stay, but she's going through a hard time since Doc…"

"Yeah," someone said.

"The girl's hurting," said someone else.

"Tell her we love her," a third chimed in. "This crap's hard on the heart."

"I'll tell her," Jack said. "She's real tough, but there are times that me being around helps. Four a.m.?" he asked.

"Four a.m. Loaded," Preacher said.

"Listen, if I'm not here..." Jack said.

"No need to explain, buddy," Paul said. "Mel comes first."

"She hates it when I shoot at animals. And ordinarily, I'd shoot at them anyway..."

"No explanation necessary, Sarge," Joe said. "This is one of those times..."

"Don't burn the place down," Jack said, going for his jacket.

A few tense and disappointing weeks passed for Cameron with no word from Brandy after their night together. Story of my life, he thought. It seemed that every time he found a woman who came to life in his arms, a woman he could fall in love with, she disappeared before he could grab hold of her.

He went back to the Davenport when the same bartender was on duty. Cameron didn't know the bartender's name, but the latter addressed him personally. "How you doing, Doc? Get you something?"

"Yeah, I sure hope so. You remember the woman I met here a few weeks ago? I haven't been in here since then."

"Vaguely," he said with a shrug that was very telling. Cameron was sure he remembered exactly, as the bar had been nearly empty, but it was his job not to see things.

"I'm trying to find her. I didn't get her name."

"Sorry, Doc. Neither did I."

"Well, how'd she pay for her drink before I got here?"

"Signed for it. She was a guest."

"Thank God! Can you go through your receipts? Anything?"

"That," he said gravely, "would get me fired."

"She said she was at a wedding. What are the chances I can find out what wedding?"

"The manager might give you the names on the billing. There was a marquee up in the lobby. Last names won't tell you anything much, but I bet if you called the newspaper, you could find out if they published an announcement."

That was Cameron's next quest, and it proved easy enough. Of course it didn't turn up any information about the woman to end his search, but he managed to learn it was the Jorgensen-Benson wedding, Joe Benson being an architect in Grants Pass.

He went to Joe's firm, handed him a business card and said, "I met one of your wedding guests in the bar at the Davenport the night of your wedding. Her name was Brandy and I didn't get a last name. I'd like to ask her out. Can you help me?"

"Brandy? I don't know anyone by that name."

"You sure? Beautiful woman, about five-three, dark blond or real light brown hair and large, dark eyes. Thirty-one, wearing a gold dress…"

"Buddy," he laughed. "You just described half the women at the wedding. The bridesmaids wore gold. My wife was a flight attendant and the place was crawling with gorgeous women about that age. How'd you lose track of her?"

"You don't want to know," Cameron said, looking down briefly. "Turns out I'm not real slick with women anymore."

"Doc, I'm sorry. I'll keep your card and ask my wife. Will that help?"

"Not enough, but I'll take it. Did most of the people at your wedding come from Grants Pass?"

"No, as a matter of fact—most came from out of town. My family is here but Nikki's family is from San Francisco. And her girlfriends are from everywhere. Literally."

Cameron was quiet for a minute. "She and I really hit it off."

"Yet you didn't get her name and number?" Joe asked.

Cameron laughed without humor. "She asked that I let her

get in touch with me. And she hasn't. I have no idea why. Really, it was..." He gulped. "I have no idea why," he repeated.

Joe put his hands in his pockets, looked down and shook his head. "Believe me, pal. I feel your pain. I'm just not sure I can help."

"But you'll ask your wife?"

"Sure."

"I'll be in touch," Cameron said.

A few days later he called Joe only to be told that Mrs. Benson had no friends at the party named Brandy. The description of the woman he was looking for could match three of her girlfriends, all married.

The possibilities were endless. She made up her name, maybe she'd had a fight with the husband, it could be a real complicated divorce. Or maybe she was rethinking the divorce. Or he was. If he had a brain, that SOB wouldn't let her go.

Whatever the truth was, she didn't intend to get in touch, or she would have.

That's it, Cameron said to himself. *I'm through. I'm done. No more talking to pretty, lonely girls in bars.*

He realized this did nothing to put him in a carefree mood. One of his partners remarked that he'd seemed depressed lately. He brushed him off, saying it was nothing, but he knew what it was. She had disappeared into thin air. He kept asking himself why. Everything he remembered about that night told him they had a chance together. He had concentrated on treating her as though she was the most special human being alive, and in fact, it hadn't taken any effort. She had been.

One evening when he was the last to leave the medical practice he took it upon himself to tidy up the waiting room. Toys and magazines were scattered everywhere and their current receptionist didn't do a very good job of straightening up at the end of the day. With just another fifteen minutes, he could have it cleared out so the housekeeping staff could do a thorough cleaning. After stowing away the toys, he began to stack the children's books and magazines for the parents.

And there she was—her face stared back at him from a little corner photo on the cover of *People* magazine. He sat heavily in a child-size chair in the waiting room, staring. If it wasn't her, it sure looked like her. Kid Crawford Divorces Third Wife.

He read the story. Oh, it was her. Kid Crawford, a notorious rock star, had chosen for his third wife a flight attendant he'd met while traveling. They'd been married less than a year. He did some math—she had said she'd been served divorce papers nine months before, which made their actual marriage somewhere less than three months. Ouch. Given the source of his current sulk, he could well imagine how tough that would be on the ego. No wonder she was depressed.

There were more pictures in the body of the story, plus pictures of his first and second wives and the new girlfriend, who he had reportedly lived with for six months prior to his divorce. Perhaps the hardest thing to accept was that this classy young woman, so squeaky clean and sweet, had been married to this awful, bearded, greasy guy in torn jeans, dark glasses, gaudy tattoos and chains.

This would explain her pain and loneliness. He took the magazine with him to Joe Benson's architectural firm. Joe stood, stretching out a hand. "Hey, Doc. Sorry, I don't know anything more to tell you about the mysterious wedding guest."

Cameron flashed the magazine. "Do you know her?" he asked.

The look on Joe's face said it all. He couldn't reel in the expression to cover it.

"Abby," he finally said. "I'm sorry, Doc. I had a feeling it might be her."

"But you wouldn't have told me."

Joe shrugged. "I couldn't do that, Doc. To tell the truth, I sympathize with you, I really do. But you have to be careful about making women vulnerable to men you don't know. And even though I'm sure you're sterling, I don't know you."

"I understand," he said.

"According to my wife, Abby's had a real bad year. I'd hate to complicate it further." Joe tapped the magazine. "It's been just awful."

Cameron frowned and shook his head. "How'd she end up with a loser like this?"

"Oh, he's a loser, but this is all theatrics. He doesn't look like this. I'm sure half his fans wouldn't even recognize him. His name is Ross and I've never met him, but my wife was at their little secret wedding and she says he's a good-looking, clean-cut, charming kind of guy. Except not for long, I guess."

Cameron hung his head for a second, taking it in. "Gotcha. You still have my card?" he asked, digging in his back pocket for his wallet.

Joe held up a hand. "I've got it," he said.

"If you could just get word to her that I'd like to hear from her sometime…."

"I could try that."

"If I don't hear from you, I'll consider the matter closed."

"Sure. I'll ask my wife to get in touch with her."

A couple of days went by with no phone call and he knew—there wouldn't be one. If she had any interest, this was a good time for her to reach out to someone who cared about her, wanted to begin a relationship that wasn't like this loony rockstar thing. He forced himself to accept the facts—it was a one-night stand. It was over.

10

Abby MacCall Crawford, aka Brandy one time only, had had a very simple plan when she returned to L.A. from the wedding in Grants Pass. She was going to sign the divorce papers, be free in two shakes and work on rebuilding her life. After all, her marriage to Ross Crawford had been over almost as soon as it began and while technically she'd been Mrs. Crawford for nine months, he'd lived with another woman for over six and she hadn't seen him or talked to him in ten. This should be a mere formality. Long overdue.

It wasn't going to be that easy for Abby.

First of all, she had to hire a lawyer because there were "terms" in Ross's settlement offer. Her husband had run up some impressive bills on credit cards, most of them during their separation, and she was stuck for her half, even though her income wasn't a tenth of his. Just negotiating the amount down to a third of what Ross demanded cost her huge attorney fees and still left her with a bill she could never pay. And she was asking herself for the millionth time how she'd gotten herself in this mess.

Ross Crawford had swept her off her feet with his practiced flirtations and she had fallen hard and fast. He was a musician, the bass guitarist in a band that had several popular albums out. She had met him on the airplane. His appearance in first class was so different from the one he presented while onstage. He was clean-cut in his khakis and crisp white shirt, his hair neatly cropped, face clean shaven, smile dazzling. He had such *charisma,* such *humor!* Onstage he wore ripped jeans, chains, and affected a scruffy three-day growth of beard that he only let grow out before he performed, and long shaggy hair that wasn't his. She knew the band; it made her laugh to think it was the same man. Abby fell in love with a semifamous rock star and even saw her own face on the cover of a tabloid more than once.

When she met him, Ross had been returning to Los Angeles after being in drug treatment, a secret carefully guarded from the public. But the secret wasn't that Ross *had* used drugs, but rather that he'd stopped; there was a certain druggie mystique about rock stars that made them seem more edgy and dangerous, more popular. The fact he was in recovery didn't deter her from seeing him; she was proud of him. He went to meetings every day and couldn't talk about anything but his program. His sincerity was riveting. The other guys in the band didn't use, he said. In fact, they were the ones that did the intervention, demanded the life change if he was going to stay with them. He spoke the gospel; he was clean as a whistle, proven by regular urine tests. He wanted a stable life, a wife, a family, something genuine to come home to.

Abby had married him too quickly because she was with him every day and night anyway. After only a few weeks of marital bliss, Ross was back on tour with the band. The daily phone calls lasted only a couple of weeks and though she could arrange her flying schedule around his tour pretty easily, he told her he was just too busy with the band, rehearsals, travel and grueling performances. But she knew—he started using again right away. She could hear it in his voice—first the slur of alcohol, then the sharp euphoria of cocaine as well. Then he stopped picking up her calls; she went straight to voice mail.

Her own naivete had so embarrassed her that for weeks that turned into months she tried pretending everything was all right, that it was simply difficult being separated while he was on tour with the band. Then his picture started appearing in the media with other women. Then his lawyer called her; she was served papers. Ross had never bothered calling, himself. By the time she gathered with some of her girlfriends at Nikki's wedding in Grants Pass, everyone knew it had fallen apart long ago and she was faced with their pity. So she had slipped away from the reception before it was over, then out of town first thing in the morning.

A turning point for her had been a night of wonderful love in the arms of a stranger. It had been a complete accident. When he left her in the bar to book a room, she had no intention of spending the night with him. She got up from her table and went to the elevators to go to her own room. But when he saw her there, thinking she was waiting for him, the look on his face was so sweet and sexy, she melted. When he took her hand and pulled her carefully into his arms, the need to be held and treated with love surpassed any common sense she might've possessed.

At the time she was glad to have had that night. Something about it showed her that life wasn't over, that after the divorce was final she might actually find happiness someday. It had been her intention to just go back to work, careful not to allow herself to get close to any flirtatious passengers, and go about the business of recovering from the shattered expectations she had had of love. Then she would start anew. When the divorce and her recovery were complete, she thought she might get in touch with that beautiful stranger and maybe get to know him better.

But in the chilly days of late October, her divorce still not final, she was sitting in her doctor's office, tears pouring down her cheeks. "I just don't see how this could have happened. I've been on the pill forever and never before…"

Dr. Pollock took her hand in both of his. "I can tell you exactly how," he said. "You were taking antibiotics for an ear infection and it rendered your oral contraceptive ineffective. Didn't they warn you about that at the clinic? When they prescribed the antibiotic?"

"They might have," she said with a sniff. In fact, who knows what they said? There were many colliding facts—one, she had to have something to heal her ears—she was flying after all. When she realized she couldn't clear her ears without pain and would be on duty in three days, she went to the airline's outpatient clinic right away. If they'd said anything about her birth control being useless to her, she wouldn't have given it a thought—she wasn't making use of her birth control. Her husband was gone; his lawyers had called her every week about that divorce. And then, a handsome young doctor had found her sad and lonely in a hotel bar, bought her a couple of champagne cocktails, led her upstairs and made incredible, unforgettable love to her.

A complete stranger. She had become pregnant by a complete stranger.

"Dear God," she whispered. "What am I going to do?" she wept.

"You have a few options," her doctor said. "But you should

make a decision about whether to continue the pregnancy as soon as possible. The longer you put it off, the more complicated it gets."

It briefly crossed her mind to get in touch with Cameron Michaels. Nikki had called her to ask her if she'd met the man; he'd gone to Joe's office, looking for a way to get in touch with a woman who fit her description. Abby played dumb; she wasn't about to tell even her closest friends what had happened before she had a plan. "Gee," she'd said to her friend, "I ran into a couple of real nice guys in the hotel bar, but that name doesn't ring a bell."

Now it was too late. Now if she saw him again, he'd know he had fathered her child and she'd be stuck with him for life, if only as the baby's father. And what if she learned she didn't want a permanent relationship with him? She couldn't take the risk. That he had been perfect that one night didn't mean anything! Even Ross had been perfect longer than that!

Then everything had become a horrible mess; as if the divorce wasn't enough, being followed constantly by people with cameras, hungry for the ugly details, made it so much worse. Ross had made himself excellent tabloid fodder.

And then there was that other sticky thing—the prenup. Ross's attorney would begin sending her a settlement every month—ten thousand dollars—predicated on her fidelity during their marriage. When she signed the agreement, it seemed almost silly—if she promised to be completely faithful during her marriage, he would pay her that amount in the event of divorce, up to the date of her remarriage. Rich guys had to make deals like that—so short-term wives didn't walk away with millions. She hadn't expected to be a short-term wife.

If her pregnancy became obvious, it was possible Ross or his legal beagles would be able to prove she'd had sex with another man more than a month before the divorce was final. To give up the alimony was nothing to her; she didn't care about that. But the bills Ross had left her with were huge. Cheating him out of alimony wasn't on her mind, but those bills that claimed more than forty grand owing were his, not hers.

She could have this baby if she could find a way to conceal her pregnancy, or at least the time of conception. She had left Grants Pass, returned to Los Angeles, called a lawyer and signed the papers within a couple of weeks—but it was another month before she was a single woman—and a good OB could determine the due date extremely closely with the use of an ultrasound. Any doubt would send her to court, which would cost even more. Abby wasn't a millionaire rock star, she was a flight attendant whose income was completely eaten up by her living expenses, her savings and equity in her small town house zapped by legal fees. She'd have to go into deep cover; she couldn't even return to her family in Seattle to wait out the delivery.

She decided quickly. She was going to give birth, but no one would know about it until it was over and the baby, hopefully, a few months old at least.

When Paul Haggerty decided to relocate part of his construction company to Virgin River from Grants Pass, his mother's only requirement was that he bring the grandchildren back to visit once a month. The only child since his union with Vanessa so far was little Matt, her son from her previous marriage, but to Marianne Haggerty, little Matt was as much her grandson as if he was Paul's very own. And for Vanessa, these little trips to Paul's family were a delightful respite. In fact, she used the trip to make sure Mattie had at least an afternoon with his biological grandparents, Carol and Lance Rutledge, as well.

On this particular early-November weekend, Matt wasn't

finding the visit quite as enjoyable as usual. He'd been teething and had developed diarrhea and a bad cold. When, on Saturday morning, a scary-sounding cough settled into his chest, Vanni and Paul were strongly considering a trip to the emergency room.

But Paul wanted the baby treated by a doctor he knew he could trust. On impulse, he picked up the phone and called Cam. "It's Paul Haggerty, Cameron. Hey, man, I'm real sorry to bother you at home, but we're visiting my folks here in town and the baby's sick. He's got a fever, diarrhea and an awful thick cough. Any chance you're on call? Or maybe you could recommend someone for us to take him to?"

"I'm not busy, Paul. Bring the baby over to the office and let's have a look," Cameron said. "I'll be there in half an hour to unlock the door."

"Hey, man, you don't know how much I appreciate this. I think Vanni's getting herself worked up. Hell, what am I saying—I'm getting worked up."

Cameron beat them to the peds office and when Vanni and Paul arrived with the baby, Vanni was tearing up from worry. "Hey now," Cameron said, dropping an arm around her shoulders. "Let's not get all upset until we know what to get upset about, huh? Hey, big fella," he said, taking the baby out of her arms. "Wow, you've just about doubled in size!"

"Cameron, I don't know how to thank you," she said. "I was doing fine until he started coughing." Right on cue, Mattie let go with a large, deep, gravelly cough that turned him red in the face.

Cameron put the baby on the exam table and listened to his chest first. He took his temperature, looked in his ears and throat, and palpated his chubby little body. "Is he still on the breast?" Cameron asked.

"A couple of times a day. Maybe three—morning, after-noon nap, bedtime."

"Okay, here's what we're going to do—he's not going to love this. This could be croup. At least bronchitis. His color is still good and he isn't having trouble breathing, but that crowlike barking cough is a dead giveaway. I'll need an X-ray, but I'll call ahead for you—I don't want him sitting around a roomful of sick people, or infecting a roomful of people with sprained ankles. I'm going to give him antibiotics and a little oxygen before you leave here, and a nice big dose of baby Ty-lenol for the fever. You're going to have to keep him on clear liquids—Pediolyte works. No breast milk, no formula, no juice, no food. Antibiotics tend to cause diarrhea and you've already got some of that going on—we don't want to aggra-vate it. When you get home, I want you to spend a lot of time in a steamy shower to loosen up his chest. Do that as often as you can stand it."

"Okay," she said.

"Watch him closely. If he has trouble breathing at all or if his color takes on a bluish tint, call me to meet you in the E.R.—I'll give you my cell number. But I think we caught it in time. Lots of clear liquids, Vanni. Tylenol every four hours. Do you know what to do if he spikes a high fever?"

"Cool bath?" she asked.

"Not cold, not warm. Tepid," he said. "Don't leave him in there long, just give him a nice dunk, run a cloth over his little body and dry him off. He's only 101.4 now, before the Tylenol—not scary high for his age. If he gets close to 103, call me immediately. You should be able to keep it under control with regular Tylenol."

Cameron dosed the baby from his drug cabinet. Then he hooked up the oxygen and, holding the baby on his lap, managed to get the cannulas in the baby's nostrils despite his squirming. He held him while the oxygen drifted in and the baby calmed in his experienced hands. "When are you planning to head back to Virgin River?"

"We were going to go tomorrow afternoon," Paul said.

"I'd like you to stick close until it's clear he's recovering. You don't want to be out on the road and have this thing rear its ugly head. I can't think of anything more likely to bring that on than hours on his back in a car seat. Attacks of croup tend to come in the night—you might not get much rest tonight or tomorrow night. Can you shoot for Tuesday for going back?"

"We'll do whatever you say," Paul said, slipping an arm around Vanni's waist.

"Okay, if you don't have to bring him back to me before, let me take a look at him, listen to his chest, on Tuesday morning. If it sounds good, you can hit the road. You should probably have Doc Mullins take a look when you get back to Virgin River. He's probably treated a bucketful of croup in his years there."

Paul and Vanni exchanged shocked looks, then turned those very expressions back to Cameron. "Jesus, Cameron, I'm sorry," Paul said. "I guess you'd have no way of knowing—Doc Mullins died a little over a month ago."

"What?" Cameron asked, surprised. "What happened?"

Paul shrugged. "Not entirely sure. Mel found him facedown on the clinic floor and tried to revive him with CPR, but he never came around. The new baby, little Emma, was lying on the floor right next to him, like maybe he'd been holding her when he had a heart attack or something."

"Aw, Jesus," Cameron said. "That's awful. Emma?"

"Fine. Thank God."

"How's the town holding up?"

"Kinda shaky," Paul said. "Mel's doing her best at the clinic.

Vanni's cousin Shelby has been visiting for a while now and she's going in to the clinic every day to help out with the kids, patients and paperwork. Docs Stone and Hudson from Grace Valley are taking the patients Mel can't cover. But just going through Doc's stuff—over forty years' worth—has really taken its toll on Mel. She's grieving and overworked—and little Emma is barely six months."

"At least she's got Shelby. For now," Vanessa said. "But Shelby is just visiting. She was planning to leave after the holidays. God, Cameron, I'm sorry we didn't think to call you."

"Why would you, Vanni?" Cameron said. "I met the man once, talked with him for less than an hour. I got a big kick out of him in that short time and it was obvious he was a crackerjack small-town doc who cared about his people. Besides you two, we didn't have any mutual friends. But damn, that's a great loss for Virgin River." Matt had drifted off in his arms and was breathing well, coughing less with the oxygen. "I'm so sorry to hear about it."

"Mel has advertised for a new doctor for the town, but who'd want to come to a town that size? I have no idea what the pay is—I guess it's whatever you get. I know Mel and Jack put a lot of produce, wine and meat in the bar from patients paying with what they get off the land."

Cameron chuckled. "Sounds kind of nice, actually. It's gotta beat wrangling with the insurance companies."

Paul laughed. "That's not a problem in Virgin River. Not many folks have medical coverage."

Cameron put the stethoscope in his ears and listened briefly to Matt's chest. "That's a little better," he said. He held the baby a while longer. "Please give my condolences to Mel," he said. His eyes focused on the baby, he said, "Doc was a little snarly, but I bet he had a heart of gold." Then he looked up at Vanessa and Paul and gave a little smile. "How are you two getting along?"

"Good," Paul said. "I'm building in Virgin River. I've got a house under construction for Vanni in addition to a couple of other properties." He kissed her temple. "I think Vanni can convince you she didn't make a big mistake on me."

She smiled at Paul, confirming that she was happy. "We're still living with Dad," she said. "But the house will be ready before Christmas—and it's on Dad's land so we'll be close, but not too close."

"Sounds perfect."

"We're starting to think about the next baby," she said.

"You should. Get 'em while you can," Cameron said.

"Paige delivered last summer, a little girl. Brie's due around Christmas."

"They just keep coming," Cameron said, shaking his head with a chuckle.

"I've heard Virgin River is a fertile place," Vanni said, laughing.

"You fish, Cameron?" Paul asked.

"I haven't done much but doctor in a long time," he said.

"Come on down and fish," Paul invited. "Take a couple of days. I'll take you out to the Virgin. The salmon are starting to run. The sturgeons fat."

"Sounds nice. You fishing a lot?" Cameron asked.

"Nah. I've got houses going. But if you come down, I'll knock off for a couple mornings— I have good supervisors now. Or I'll send Jack out there with you. Jack loves any excuse to get out on the river."

"I'll think about that," he said. He pulled the cannulas out of the baby's nose. "Okay, now hear me on this, Vanessa. No matter how much he fusses, only clear liquids. If we don't treat the diarrhea along with the upper-respiratory problems, he'll dehydrate. And get in the steam, okay?"

"Okay," she said, taking the baby from him. "What do we owe you?"

"Come on." Cameron laughed. "How about a day out on the river?"

"Deal," Paul said, smiling. He stuck out his hand. "You came in real handy, buddy. I can't tell you how much we appreciate this."

"I'm glad you called me. This little guy needs to feel better."

Cameron Michaels didn't call anyone in Virgin River. He had three days off and just drove down. He went first to the clinic, walked in and found Mel at the computer. "Hey," he said.

"Hey," she returned, standing up from the desk. "What brings you down here?"

"I don't know if Paul or Vanni mentioned, I just heard about Doc. I had a few days off and wanted to deliver my condolences in person."

"Thanks. He's a hard one to lose."

"How's your search for a new doctor coming?" he asked.

"No response," she said with a shrug. "But that's not a surprise—we barely started looking. Plus, Hope's been looking for a doctor to help Doc for years and no one ever responded. I was the closest thing and honestly, if I hadn't had special circumstances, I might not have considered Virgin River, either."

"Can I ask—about the special circumstances?"

"Sure," she said. "How about a cup of coffee?"

"That'd be great," he said with a smile.

"Sit tight, I'll be right back."

Shelby was in the kitchen, sitting at the table sorting some paperwork while the kids slept—one in a playpen, one in a portable crib. Mel poured coffee and invited Shelby to join them in Doc's office so as not to wake the children. Once there, she introduced them, and Cameron expressed his condolences again.

"I've been boring Shelby with stories from my years in L.A.," Mel said. "I was widowed when I met Jack. My husband was an E.R. doctor. We worked together for years before he was killed. I was looking for a new start, out of L.A. I found Virgin River at the nurses' registry where I'd placed my résumé. I came here, sight unseen."

"And found it perfect for you?" Cameron asked.

"Far from it," she said. "The town was misrepresented, the pay miserable, the cabin that was to be my rent-free home was a falling-down hovel—but just as I was running for my life, a baby was abandoned on Doc's porch and I stayed a while." She shrugged. "I became attached in no time. Then I fell in love with Jack. Now I'm committed. Medicine here is a whole new scene from what I was used to in the city. It's like taking care of family. These people are my friends. And of course, if Jack is here, I'm here."

"But what's it like doctoring here?" Cameron asked.

"We have to be inventive and flexible. Boy," she said, laughing, "we could sure use a pediatrician, couldn't we, Shelby?"

"Boy howdie, as Mel would say. The babies are flowing into this town."

"I don't like our chances of getting a new doctor, and I'll be honest—I lose a lot of sleep over that. I don't want to be their only resource if something big happens, like a bad MVA," Mel said. "Sorry, Shelby," she said. "That's a motor vehicle accident." Looking back at Cameron, she said, "Or some hunting accident. But this is no place for a doctor to prosper financially. A lot of our patient fees come from services and produce from ranches, farms and vineyards. More food than I could ever eat, less cash than it takes to get by. I've written a grant proposal to cover malpractice insurance. The county is covering mine—they see the merits of having a certified midwife around here. And if you can believe it, Doc was never covered. Never sued, never covered. He always figured if someone got pissed off and put him out of business, so be it." She shrugged. "I'm hopeful that if a physician can be found, the county will step up. I've been contacting medical schools—offering a place for a brand-new family-practice resident to practice rural medicine—he or she could intern here under John Stone or June Hudson. If you know anyone…"

"I might," he said. "I'll talk it around."

"I don't know what I'm going to do when I lose Shelby."

Cameron looked at the younger woman.

"I'm here temporarily," Shelby said. "I cared for my mother who suffered from ALS for a long time and now, before I move on to my own nursing college, I'm staying with my Uncle Walt."

"Walt Booth?" he asked.

"Uh-huh. I'm Vanni's cousin."

"From Bodega Bay," he said. "Yeah, your name was mentioned."

"No kidding? You know them?"

"I was introduced," he said simply. "Nice people."

"I can help Mel for a while longer, but I've been sending out my applications. Nursing is kind of a natural progression for me, given my years as a caregiver. It's going to be hard," she said. "I've been out of school and work for years."

"But what you have done is extraordinary," Mel said, grabbing her hand.

"Good luck with that," Cam said. "So Mel—how are you getting by now? With the patients?"

"Right now, I send a lot of them to Grace Valley and sometimes either June Hudson or John Stone will spend a half day up here, taking patients," Mel said.

"This is a helluva nice place to live," he said.

"Yeah, it's gorgeous. But a person has to make a living. What are you doing here, besides offering condolences?"

"Aw, Paul and Vanni had a sick baby while they were in Grants Pass and Paul offered me a day on the river as payment for my services. Problem is, I didn't tell them I was coming, so I'm not going to hold him to it. I thought I'd see how you're doing and make a house call."

"I heard about Mattie's croup," she said.

"Fortunately, he did well on antibiotics, snapped right out of it. Any chance I could get a tour of your clinic?" he asked.

"You bet. It's a pretty functional little place," Mel said with a touch of pride. She stood up. "Right this way, Doctor." The first thing she did was open the refrigerator and show him that they kept as much blood and plasma on hand as food, something he seemed to get a kick out of. Shelby returned to her paperwork in the kitchen while Mel showed Cameron the exam room and the treatment room. In Doc's old office there were some boxes stacked in the corner. "Personal items of Doc's," she said. "I'm sending that stuff back to his college library. Come on upstairs."

She showed him the only hospital room in town, the roomy bathroom and Doc's old bedroom, completely vacant and freshly painted. "Doc's furniture was almost as old as he was," she said. "I gave it away and will buy new. If we don't get a doctor, it'll make a decent place for me to sleep when we have a delivery here."

"Nice little operation," Cameron said. "But how do you make ends meet?"

"Oh, it's not too hard for me. Jack has income—he's re-tired military and the bar won't make us rich, but it brings in money. I have savings and no longer draw a salary. The clinic is mine now, thanks to Doc's generosity in his trust. It's free and clear. The uninsured patients are almost always able to cover the cost of lab work, X-rays and drugs, and then we get a twenty-dollar bill here and there. Patients on subsistence—welfare or Medicaid—their fees are paid. People around here are very grateful and they do their best—there's often cash in the Christmas card. The most important thing is we never lose money. And all the equipment is paid for. In fact, once Jack had the bar open, he gave Doc almost all his meals. Jack does that—the forest-fire fighters, the police, the game warden or rangers, Jack serves them for free when they've been working here. The sheriff's deputy and his boys drop by for a gratis meal now and then. We have a highway patrolman who visits. Anyone who serves the needs of the town gets served by Jack and Preacher."

Cameron laughed and shook his head. "How can they afford to do that?"

Mel grinned. "When the patients bring in produce as patient fees, it goes straight to Preacher's kitchen where we eat it later. The people in town don't just bring stuff when they're sick—they bring what they can spare continually, sort of like keeping us on retainer. A bushel of apples, several quarts of berries, huge sack of tomatoes, bushel of green beans… Preacher bakes and cans and freezes and loves every second of it. A big patient fee could be as much as a half calf. Or a few months of cream. And besides, Jack has everything he needs, Cameron." Then she got a little more serious. "The first night I landed in this town, I saw Jack as the owner of a bar and restaurant. It didn't take me long to learn he's so much more than that. He does a little of everything, from car and truck repair to building. He never goes for supplies without checking with a half-dozen little old ladies or postpartum mothers to see what they need. And if I'm delivering a baby—Jack is up all night, in case I need something. I hate that he hunts, but when he hunts, we enjoy some of the best venison dishes you can imagine. And most of the fish served in the bar, he and Preacher and maybe even Mike catch in the river. It all evens out." She shrugged. "This is a very simple place, Cameron. Sometimes if feels more like a commune than a town. But Jack... Ask anyone—Jack is at the center of this town, taking care of the people here."

He smiled. "I bet if I ask, they'll say you are, too."

"I do my best. The women—they're my specialty."

"Didn't take you long to fall in love with the place."

"It's rewarding," she said. "I took home a pretty nice paycheck from the hospital in L.A., and I had some very challenging work there, but L.A. is a damn expensive place to live. I'm not sure I was further ahead with that big salary. As long as the clinic can feed me and cover the cost of my gas, it doesn't need to provide me with much else. And I feel a lot better about what I'm doing here. These people really need me."

He just looked at her for a moment, silent. "You've found your niche," he said.

"I have. I have everything." Then she laughed. "Except a doctor. I could sure use a doctor. It's a small town, but we need medical service."

"I think maybe I envy you."

"I'm not surprised." She smiled. "It's a different kind of life."

"Yeah, I can only imagine." He squeezed her arm. "Well. I should check in at the Booth house. Let them know I'm here. You having dinner at the bar tonight?"

"I'm there at five. Just for an hour or so. It's waterfowl hunting now, so Jack stays late and I go home to put the kids to bed."

"I'll see you at five," Cameron said. "And again, I'm sorry for your loss."

"Thanks," she said, sticking out her hand. "He was a pain in the butt, but God, I miss him."

Cameron went out to the Booth household, but found no one was home. He looked first in the stable, then drove out to the house under construction. There was a lot of activity around it, so he walked up the plank that led through the front door and found Paul in the center of the great room, hands on his hips, looking around the nearly finished room. "Hey," Cameron said.

Paul turned. "Cam! What are you doing here?"

"I had a couple of days and really felt the need to express my condolences to Mel. I realize I didn't give you any notice, so I don't intend to hold you to that offer of fishing."

Paul stuck out his hand. "Don't be ridiculous. I can snag a morning."

"Nah, don't worry about it, plenty of time for us to go fishing. I have to talk to you about something."

"Sure, pal. What's on your mind?"

"I'm about to do something pretty crazy. And I can't do that unless you're real clear—this has nothing to do with Vanessa."

The children were napping in the clinic, Shelby was at the bar getting a soda and Mel was sitting on the front-porch steps when Bruce brought the mail. "Any specimens for Valley Hospital today?" he asked her.

"Nope," she said, leafing through the mail.

"Great. I get to knock off early. Have a nice day."

Mel stood, pulled her sweater tighter around her and walked inside. The sun was out today, but it was getting darn cold. She found an envelope from Cameron Michaels and tore it open. Her first thought was that he was such a class act—it was probably a letter of condolence or a thank-you note. She pulled out a couple of pages, stapled together. At the top, in italics, it read: *Résumé for Cameron Michaels, M.D., ABFM, ABP*. Her mouth hung open.

She read through his credentials. He was board certified in family medicine and pediatrics with years of experience—a dream doctor. Her mouth hadn't quite closed when she picked up the phone and dialed his office in Grants Pass. When he said hello, she said, "Have you lost your mind?"

He laughed. "Probably. But just so you know I'm not completely insane, I thought I'd give you a year. I'll know in a few months if it's working for me, so I won't leave you high and dry. I've taken a leave from my practice."

"But, Cameron, don't you have a home there? Attachments?"

"I hate that house—it's already on the market. If I come back here, I'll be looking for something much different."

"But what about friends? Family? Special… You know… Cameron, isn't there a woman in your life?"

"Nothing to hold me here, Mel. And I can bring my own bedroom furniture."

"We've talked about the pay…"

"That really isn't my first concern. I'll live at the clinic, take my meals at the bar, and I know you'll be fair with the salary."

"Holy crap," she said. "Is this really happening?"

"Listen, Mel, I need a change. A temporary if not permanent one. If you find me qualified, I'll see you right after Christmas."

She was speechless for a minute. Then she said, "Ho-ho-ho." And he laughed.

11

The cold and windy days of November made way for an unseasonably warm, clear Saturday with a bright sun—a perfect day for Luke to work on the outside of his house or cabins. Or a perfect day for something else.

He put on his leather chaps, donned a well-worn leather bombardier's jacket over his sweater and checked on Art to be sure he had enough to do to keep him busy most of the day. Shelby should be getting a day off from the clinic. It was still early when he took his Harley down the road to the general's house. He went to the door with the rider's helmet in his hand. Shelby answered in her jeans and sweater, stocking feet, hair loose. "Wanna try my ride for a change?" he asked her. "It's not too cold today."

She looked around him. "On that?"

"Just you and me, Shelby. Want to take a chance?"

She gave him a soft smile. "Am I safe with you on that thing?" she asked.

He presented the rider's helmet. "Well, I'll drive carefully. You should get a jacket and something to wrap around your neck. Boots and gloves. And you might want to tie up your hair."

"Why not," she said. "Come in while I get ready."

He stepped into the house and looked around, impressed. The general had done a good job remodeling this place for his retirement. He heard a baby fussing down the hall in the direction Shelby had gone. Luke walked across the great room to the large picture window and looked across the general's land. The horses were in the corral and not too far in the distance was the home under construction that Paul was building for himself and his wife. There was still a lot of construction mess around the building, but it looked close to finished from the outside. He also saw what looked like a gravestone atop a small rise not far from the stable. He had no idea what that was about.

"Morning, Luke."

He turned to see Vanessa behind him, baby on her hip. "Hey," he said. "Looks like the house is coming along great."

"We'll be in before Christmas, hopefully. You should come out and take a look at it sometime. Paul's a genius."

"I'll do that."

"How's your place coming?"

"Better than I expected," he answered. "I'm taking Shelby out for a ride on the Harley. The general will be okay with that, won't he?"

"Shelby's a big girl," Vanessa said with a smile.

"Ready," Shelby said, popping into the room. She had put on a tan suede jacket with fringe on the underside of the arms, fringe that would slap in the wind. "This will be warm enough, won't it?"

He smiled at her; she was so damn pretty. "You should be fine."

"I have no idea when I'll be back," she told Vanessa. "I hope no one needs me for anything."

"You've been working so hard, just go. Enjoy yourself," Vanni said. "And be careful on that thing."

She has no idea how right she is to warn Shelby, Luke thought. The danger is not on the motorcycle.

Shelby tucked her braid into the helmet and climbed on behind him. She wrapped her arms around his waist and off they went, down the road toward the highway and up through the redwoods. It was cold back in the tallest trees, but when they broke through, he drove into the sunny foothills, up on some of the craggy knolls where sheep grazed. The bike always made Luke feel exhilarated; the cold wind on his face refreshed and energized him.

Luke liked the feeling of her small arms holding him; a cross-country ride with those arms around him was definitely better than one alone. Sometimes she laid her head against his back while he drove them into the country, past the vineyards that lay fallow in winter, past orchards naked of their fruit. The hills were brown now, but in spring this place would come alive in stunning green. When the weather warmed, he'd like to take her to the coast and across the craggy headlands above the ocean. Would she be here in the spring? he found himself wondering. Would he?

They had been riding for a little over an hour when he took the bike up a dirt road that wound around a small hill where livestock grazed. He parked the Harley there, swung his leg over and raised it on the stand. He pulled off his helmet and reached for hers. She took it off and her braid tumbled down her back. Putting one helmet on each of the two handlebars, he mounted the stationary bike backward to face her. Her cheeks were flushed from the cold wind and her eyes glowed. He reached his hands behind her knees and pulled her toward him, draping her legs over his thighs. Then, with his arms around her waist, he leaned toward her, pressing his lips softly to hers. She leaned into his kiss, opening her lips for him at once, so trusting. Besides a few stolen kisses outside Jack's, they had had little contact lately. The demands on Shelby's time had been heavy since Doc's death.

"How do you like the bike, Shelby?"

"I love it," she said.

"You like to go fast?" he asked.

She laughed. "I've always been so cautious," she said. "It feels good."

"I've been trying not to take you too fast," he said, and his voice had gone husky, like brushed velvet. He ran a hand down her back, down her long braid. He pulled her mouth against his and, with a big hand against the back of her head, he kissed her more thoroughly. She melted to him, her arms going inside his jacket and round to his back, holding him closer, her small tongue slipping into his mouth. His world tilted. He probed inside her mouth in a strong kiss, pulling her more tightly against him, until she was straddling his lap. He filled his hands with her butt and held her tight, feasting on her sighs and moans. He rocked her pelvis against him and he became aroused instantly. If they didn't have the barrier of jeans between them, this thing he'd been trying to talk himself out of would be done. "Aw, Shelby," he whispered against her lips. He released her mouth. "Listen, we have to talk."

She smiled at him. "Sure. I've been expecting this. The talk."

"Shelby, you should run for your life, I'm not kidding. I've never been reliable where women are concerned. And I'm not real well fixed with brakes, either. God, I really don't want to hurt you."

"Are you trying to scare me again, Luke?"

"Yeah, I'm trying to scare you. Warn you. Use your head, Shelby. You're young, you're sweet, and I'm just an irresponsible, horny bastard. You'd be making a mistake, getting mixed up with me."

She traced his ear with a finger. "Well, Luke, I'm already a little mixed up with you. And you got yourself mixed up with me."

"Shelby, I'm temporary at best. I'm not staying here."

"Me, neither. Is that it?"

He sighed and shook his head. "I've been known to run through women like sharks run through scuba divers. I wouldn't be good for you."

"Are you sleeping with a lot of women right now?" she asked him.

He hadn't been with a woman in so long, he had a hard time remembering the last one. That fact alone made him even more vulnerable to Shelby's incredibly seductive charm. "There has been only one woman on my mind. My brain is like a frickin' missile and if you don't move out of the target, I'm afraid I'm going to end up doing some things you might hate me for later. And then your Uncle Walt is going to shoot me."

It only made her chuckle. "Do you always warn your women not to get involved with you before you swoop down and devour them?"

"Never. That could keep me from getting laid. But I worry about you. You need to fall in love, I can smell it on you. And I don't fall in love. I don't put down roots and I don't make commitments."

"You know something, Luke?" she asked, smiling. "I think maybe you're more worried you might fall in love with me than the other way around."

"See, you shouldn't think like that—"

"I just said maybe. It's not like I expect it."

"You don't?"

"I'm going to travel and go to school. You're going to fix up your cabins and sell them. You've been very clear. You've warned me a hundred times. And now, I'm just warning you."

"You want a fling? With a guy like me? Who's too old for you?"

She just laughed and he wanted to shake her. "You are pretty old," she said. "Pretty soon, all these long warnings won't even be necessary." She tilted her head back and laughed.

His hands on her fanny, he pulled her against him and rocked her gently. He looked into her eyes and his were as hot as pokers.

"Oh. Apparently, you're not too old yet," she said, leaning toward his mouth for another kiss, drawing a deep, miserable groan from him.

"You should take this a lot more seriously. My track record isn't good. I've been with a lot of women, and never for long."

"I'm sorry, Luke. I'm sure you're very dangerous," she said, but her voice was filled with humor. "I just can't find it in me to discourage you. I love the way you kiss me." She moved her pelvis against his. "And this…? Hmm. I don't know what to make of this."

He swooped over her mouth again, with heat and power. Again, her arms went around him. The taste of her mouth was so delicious it almost sent him reeling out of this world. For all his talk about his many women and his failure to make anything stick, he couldn't remember feeling a rush like this with anyone. He'd been turned on before, stirred up almost to the breaking point, but this thing that was happening to him with Shelby was so intense, it was just about driving him out of his mind. He hung on for dear life, devouring her mouth for two minutes, then four, the sensation of her firm young breasts boring into his chest even through his sweater was getting him high.

She met him all the way, holding him, purring softly against his mouth, joining in his tongue play, sending thrill after thrill vibrating through him. All trepidation and shyness on her part was gone. He was getting damn uncomfortable. Still, he kissed her a while longer.

"Dammit, Shelby," he said. "Don't say I didn't warn you."

"And warned me and warned me and warned me..."

"You should be with a serious young man who will protect you and take care of you, not someone like me."

"Maybe someday. Right now, I just have one requirement. One woman at a time, that's all I ask. I'm not looking to join a harem. Can you do that?"

He sighed. "I'm doing it. I don't even have to try. You're the only woman I want. And I'm starting to want you real damn bad."

"I don't mind that, you know," she said, gently trailing the backs of her fingers along his rough cheek.

"You'd better think about this."

"I haven't thought about anything else. And you know it."

"Okay," he said, running his hand over her shoulder and down to her hand, lacing his fingers in hers. "Here are your choices. Try to be smart. I can take you home now, or take you home with me. Because we either have to stop this here and now, or get it done."

She smiled at him. She leaned toward him and pressed her lips softly against his. "Let's get it done," she whispered.

Luke pulled the bike up in front of his house, dismounted and put it up on its stand. He took her helmet from her and hung it on the handlebar. Then he put his lips against hers as he lifted her off the bike and into his arms. He carried her inside, threw the latch and moved quickly and impatiently toward the bedroom.

His brain was numb; all he could think was that soon he would be cured. Once he had her, he'd be over the insanity. But in spite of his desperation, he was determined that it wasn't going to be too fast. It was going to be slow and sweet and he was going to make her feel so good, she'd faint. *Then* he'd be cured.

He sat her gently on the bed. He let his jacket drop from his shoulders and took hers, tossing them into the chair in his room. He unfastened his chaps and drew off his boots. Kneeling on the floor in front of her, he slowly pulled off her boots and carefully drew her sweater over her head, placing small kisses on her chest, shoulders, breast, neck. She trembled and he pulled her into his arms for a moment, reminding himself to take his time, take it slow, reassure her that he wasn't going to be the shark right now.

Her bra disappeared and his tongue brought her nipples to life, hardening them into peaks. He gently pushed her back onto the bed and unsnapped her jeans, giving them a tug. She lifted her fanny to give assist and they slid down and off. He was left to view an incredible body, naked but for a tiny, transparent wisp of sheer fabric that barely covered her below the waist. He ran a finger slowly under the elastic.

He made fast work of his own clothes, getting down to his boxers. Leaning over her, he began to place kisses all over her body, from her neck to her knees. Then he slid over her, his thighs on her thighs, chest to breasts, devouring her mouth. He heard her moan, felt her arch toward him, and his erection was throbbing against her belly. He nibbled at her lips and said, "You have about ten seconds to change your mind." He looked into her soft, hazel eyes and saw her give a small smile and shake her head. "You're sure?" he asked, wondering what the hell he would do if she tried to stop him now. He was like a runaway train, the blood roaring in his brain.

"Do you have a condom, Luke?"

"I'm on that," he said.

"Then I'm sure."

He ditched the boxers and grabbed a condom from the nightstand. He thought abstractly that it was strange he kept them there when he never brought women home. He had never liked having women in his nest. But Shelby was here, and it seemed perfectly natural. He had the condom on in record time, but his hands on her were slow. He tugged off that tiny wisp of lace; he thought he heard a tear as he was getting it off. He might owe her a pair of panties. Running a hand down her belly, over her pubis and lower, he nudged her legs apart and massaged her, paying special attention to the small, erogenous knot in the middle, a contact that caused her to moan and push against his hand. He let his fingers move lower and dip in, finding her wet and ready to go. And he was ready to give her the ride of her life.

Easy, he told himself. It has to be good for her. He held himself over her and gently probed, pressing himself toward her. He found the path and moved farther as she lifted her hips up, but he met with resistance. He pushed a little, gently, but she was tight. Maybe he hadn't taken enough time getting her ready for this. He looked into her eyes and brushed back her hair. "Honey, you're awful small."

"It's okay," she whispered.

But it wasn't okay; he spent a little more time stimulating her while he kissed her, making sure she was slick and aroused. He wasn't sliding in even though she was ready. He didn't want to force it. There shouldn't be any discomfort with this. It should all be good.

She put her palm against his cheek. "It's okay, Luke. Just do it."

"Something's not right," he said, shaking his head.

"It's the first time," she whispered.

Instinctively, he drew back. It almost deflated him, he was so stunned. "That's not possible," he said in a breath. "You're twenty-*five!*" But she only nodded her head, letting her eyes gently close. When she did that, she squeezed out a couple of tears that ran into the hair at her temples and it tore at his heart. How does a woman this beautiful, this sexy, remain a virgin? was all he could think.

He found himself gently kissing those tears. "Aw, Shelby. This isn't good."

"It's okay," she whispered again. "It's time. I want it to be you."

"But I already made you cry and I haven't even done anything yet."

"Luke, I swear, I'm ready," she said. She reached a small hand down between their bodies and took hold of him, causing him to inhale sharply. "I've been waiting a long time for this to happen. Please don't make me wait any longer."

On the upside, news that she was intact held the advantage of helping him slow down. Way down. In fact, it nearly rendered him incapable of proceeding. But he was mad for her and decided to explore the explanations later and for now, take good care of her. "Okay, baby," he said, placing soft kisses on her lips. "I'm going to make this all right. I'll try to make it nice for you. Trust me and let me do the work, okay?"

"Okay," she answered.

He wasn't exactly an expert on the female body, but he knew one or two things. He wasn't going to get inside her without pain unless she was real soft and loose, and there was only one way to ensure that. He kissed his way down her body until he got to the center and once there, he worked that erogenous spot with his tongue. He groaned in pleasure; she was sweet, intoxicating. Her hands gripped his shoulders as she squirmed beneath him, making small noises that convinced him he was on the right track. He slid his hands up her ribs to her breasts and gently kneaded them, softly running his thumbs over her nipples. Her sighs became pants, which became little cries, and he buried himself in her until he felt the quivering turn to clenching spasms. She dug her fingers into his shoulders and clamped her knees against him, locking him there while she reached a powerful orgasm that seemed to hold on to her forever. He didn't move until it finally set her free and she collapsed beneath him.

Then he rose slowly, a bit reluctantly, kissing his way up her body until he reached her lips. "Better," he whispered.

"I want the rest," she begged breathlessly.

"We're getting there, sweetheart. We need to take a little time with this."

He gave her a few moments of gentle kisses before letting his fingers wander south. What he hadn't expected was for his whole objective to change, from dying to get inside her to free himself of the insatiable craving, to wanting to make this memorable for her, do right by her, especially if this was, insanely, her first time. He found what he knew he would between her legs—her tissues were plump, soft, damp and loose.

When he sensed she had mostly recovered, he let his fingers work that precious little knot, getting her stirred up all over again. When she started to make eager noises and move against his hand, losing herself in the sensations, he gently positioned himself to slowly enter her. He rose above her and watched her face, prepared to stop the second she winced or gasped or showed signs of discomfort. No way he could hurt her. There was still some resistance, but not nearly what he had felt before. A woman's body was miraculous; nothing like a thundering climax to open her up. He moved carefully, just a little bit at a time, until he made his way inside, filling her. He was still, letting her get used to the sensation of having him inside her, and soon he saw her slow, satisfied smile shape her lips.

"You should have told me," he said between soft kisses.

"You would have run for your life."

"I might have been better prepared."

"It turns out you were prepared enough. And I want to know about this. I want you to show me."

He began to move, deep, slow, even strokes, watching her face, taking pleasure in her sweet smile. He reached down and pulled her legs up, bending them at the knees, then his hands went to her hips. "Move your hips a little, honey. Help me find the right spot. We have to find it together...."

He kissed that gasping mouth, again and again. She moved around a little, then suddenly she threw her head back and muttered, "Oh God, oh God, oh God, oh God."

He smiled down into her eyes. "There you go," he whispered. "That's what I'm talking about. The love spot," he said against her lips. He matched his movements to hers, apace with her. He chuckled, a deep lusty sound. "That's my girl. You know what you want, don't you, baby?" he asked her in a hoarse whisper.

"Yes," she said. "Oh, yes."

"Doesn't hurt?"

"No," she whispered. "Oh God..."

Soon the little murmurs once again became more passionate and his strokes faster and deeper. The tempo increased and her hips lunged toward him until finally she lifted her pelvis against him, instinctively digging her heels into the bed for traction to push against him and the storm took her on another frenzied ride. She froze, gasped and closed around him with a heat so intense and power so strong, his brain froze. Again, it held her in its grip for a long, wondrous moment, a pleasure so blinding and spasms so fierce that they pulled his climax out of him. He thought he might lose his mind, it was so good. He'd never felt anything quite like it.

"Oh! Luke!" she cried in a passionate whisper. The sound of his name on her lips made his experience even more incredible.

And then she drifted slowly back to reality in his arms, and he found this to be the most tender part. He held her, ran his hand over her soft, perfect body in long, slow caresses while she caught her breath and calmed.

Something happened to him. The tension was gone, the physical relief was welcome, but he wasn't completely satisfied. He didn't want to leave her body. He found himself thinking, *I'm in a place no one has ever been, and it's the sweetest place imaginable.* The thing he usually did to prove he knew how to treat a woman right, holding her for a long, precious moment after the lovemaking, he was doing now because he simply couldn't let her go. When he thought about her leaving his bed, it made him feel empty inside. Holding her, kissing her, touching her, felt right. Perfect and normal.

At long last she let out a deep, satisfied sigh.

Reluctantly, he let himself slip out of her body. He braced his head on a raised hand and looked down at her, idly toying with the hair at her temple. "Was that everything you thought it would be?" he asked.

"Oh, man," she said, her voice quivering with a small laugh. "Now I know what the girls have been talking about. It's even better than I imagined."

"Okay, even if I can believe you haven't had sex before, it's going to be damn hard to convince me you've never had any kind of orgasm. I started having mine at twelve, all by myself."

"Yeah, I've been there. But there's a definite difference between that and *this*. Whew."

His lips found her neck, shoulder, ear. "You're going to have to help me understand this."

"It's not interesting, Luke. You already know, if you think about it. My mom. She got sick when I was eighteen. I never left her for long." She shrugged. "I got out a little with friends, but I never got involved with any guys. I even had some dates, some very dull dates. The last couple of years were all about helping my mom to the end." She touched the short hair over his ear. "I'm a late bloomer, huh?"

He looked down at her, shaking his head. "I don't know how it's possible. Is everyone in Bodega Bay blind? You just about sent me into a coma the first night I saw you. They should've been beating down the door..."

She stroked his face. "This is a whole new world for me, Luke. To have this kind of freedom. To think about myself. To flirt with a man." She smiled. "A dangerous man." Then her smile faded. "Something like this couldn't have happened while I worried whether my mom was okay at home."

"This is new territory for me, Shelby. I never would have planned this."

She grinned. "Is that so? I suspected that, which is why I decided not to mention it. Until it was too late for you to turn back."

"I don't get into things like this. There are a hundred reasons why I shouldn't be in bed, naked, with you right now." He pressed a soft kiss to her temple. "A hundred and one, now that I know you're a virgin."

"Was," she corrected. "No one had ever been inside me, and you're... Shew." She shook her head.

"I'm what?" he asked, running a hand along the hair over her ear.

She laughed softly. "I admit I don't know much about men, but I suspect you're a little more blessed than the average guy. Plus, you're amazing. I've always heard the first time is uncomfortable." She smiled. "That was great."

"I think if I'd known, I would have moved away. Left town for good."

"I'm really glad you didn't. It was perfect."

"It was pretty perfect. But damn, girl. I've never done that before."

"What?"

"I'm thirty-eight. You're the first virgin I've ever been with. Why did you cry?"

She dropped her lids. "It's a little embarrassing, being this old and…"

"Aw, baby," he said, kissing her closed eyes. "It was sweet. Sweeter than anything I've ever experienced."

He rolled onto his back, looking at the ceiling. Crazy thoughts began filling his head, chief among them was that he couldn't imagine there ever being another man in her life, in her body. He'd never had such possessive, proprietary feelings. He wasn't sure if this was because it was Shelby, or because she'd never been touched inside until he claimed her. "I'll be honest with you," he said. "It shakes me up."

"I noticed," she said with a laugh.

"I'm serious, Shelby. I'm wanting you again. I don't want you to leave this bed."

She rolled over onto her stomach and raised herself up on her elbows. "I'm going to have to go home eventually. Before there's a search party."

"I will shoot anyone who touches that door," he said. "Don't move. I'll be right back." He slipped off the bed and headed for the bathroom to get rid of the condom.

As she walked back into the room, she got her first sight

of a naked man in full form. She smiled. He was so beautiful. It was so awesome to have a gorgeous, lusty man walk
toward her. He stretched out beside her, pulling her against
him again, placing a gentle palm over her soft mound. "How
does it feel? Down here?"

"Lush," she said, snuggling closer.

"There's a little blood."

"Yeah. No surprise. Nothing to worry about," she said.

"Are you sore?"

She shook her head. She felt him against her thigh. Growing. "Am I going to be able to walk out of here?" she asked,
humor in her voice.

He covered her lips with his. "Not soon," he whispered.
"But don't worry. I'm going to be good to you."

Luke took her home in the truck. The motorcycle would
have been too hard on her tender parts. When he pulled up in
front of the general's house, she leaned toward him. He cra-
dled her jaw in his big hand and pulled her lips to his. They
were all going to know. Her face was branded with his love.
Her cheeks were aglow, chafed from his beard. Her lips were
bruised bright pink from hours of kissing and the look in her
eyes reflected a whole afternoon of the finest love he'd ever
made. "You should hide all the guns and sharp objects," he
whispered against her mouth.

"You worry too much," she said. "I'm an adult."

"When am I going to see you again?" he asked her.

"Soon."

"I just want to keep you flat on your back for a month."

She laughed at him. "Luke, don't ever let anyone tell you
you're not romantic." She gave him a peck on the lips and got
out of the truck to go inside.

No one seemed to be around, which suited her. She really

didn't feel like walking into dinner in progress with Vanni, Paul and Uncle Walt. In fact, there was no activity in the kitchen and she wondered if everyone had gone to Jack's. She went to her room, pulled off her jacket and boots and flopped on the bed. She stared at the ceiling dreamily. After about ten minutes, she heard a door open down the hall. Vanessa, looking sleepy, peeked into Shelby's room. "I thought I heard someone come home."

"I didn't think anyone was here," Shelby said.

"Oh," Vanni said through a yawn. "Matt's having an extra-long nap and I kind of shared it with him." She rubbed her eyes, then looked at Shelby. "Oooohh," she said. "It happened."

"And happened and happened and happened," Shelby said and laughed as she kicked her legs on the bed.

Vanni came into the room and sat on the side of her bed. "Welcome aboard," she said with a soft smile. "How do you feel?"

"Like I've had sex all afternoon with a brand-spanking-new vagina. I might have to take a long soak in the tub."

"Was it okay?"

"Indescribable. Like I've never really been alive before today. Vanni, he was so good to me…"

"You aren't falling in love with him, are you?" Vanni asked. "Because I get a sense about Luke, that he might go a little hard on the heart."

"Yeah, he gave me that talk. He doesn't like to commit or get tied down." She laughed again. "The least of my worries," she said.

"Oh, baby, see—I was afraid of that. I don't know if you're up to that."

"You wanted me to be a virgin forever? If he makes me cry, I'll get over it, but I have to tell you, he doesn't treat me like a man who's going to break my heart. Besides, if he does, haven't you and I already been through way worse and recovered?" she asked.

"Yeah, we sure have," Vanni said. "He treated you right, I guess."

"Don't tell anyone and ruin his reputation, but he's the sweetest man I've ever known. He's afraid Uncle Walt is going to shoot him."

"Daddy sure worries the boys." Vanni laughed, remembering when Paul was afraid of the same thing.

"Where is everyone?" Shelby asked.

"Paul's not home from work yet and I don't know where Daddy is. I'm thinking of starting dinner. Have any ideas?"

"Yeah," she said, sitting up. "I'm going to soak in the tub for an hour, and then I'm going back."

"So soon?"

"I can't help it. I just have to. You and Paul are great company, but I want to be next to that man." She grinned. "You think Uncle Walt will have a fit?"

"Don't worry, he may not even be home himself," she said, shaking her head. "He's pretty savvy about this kind of thing. He didn't say too much when Paul was sneaking down the hall into my room. You slip out if you want to. I'll handle the home team."

"Thank you, Vanni," she said.

She had to go back. Not for more sex; she couldn't take any more. She wanted to know how he'd receive her. Would she be welcome? Was he done with her now, at least for today? She had many curiosities about his world—he warned her not to count on him, then treated her like a queen. He hadn't promised to love her, but he said such tender, lovely things to her—that she was beautiful, that he'd never had a sweeter experience, that he didn't want her to leave. Could he say those things and not care?

After a long soak, she went to the kitchen where Vanni was at the stove and Matt was in his high chair. Paul sat at the kitchen table with the newspaper spread in front of him. He was still in his dusty work clothes; she'd been tying up the bathroom. He looked up at her and his smile of greeting changed slowly into a look of surprised recognition, his mouth open slightly. She must be beaming.

She poked through the wine rack and pulled out a bottle. "Think Uncle Walt can part with this?" she asked Vanni.

"Sure. Take it."

"Don't wait up," she said.

"Shelby," Paul said. He stood up from the table and went to her, draping an arm around her shoulders. "You know if you need anything, anything at all, you can call me." He dropped a kiss on her brow.

"Wow. There aren't many secrets around here."

"No one said anything," Paul said. "No one had to."

"Did anyone warn Vanni when you were sneaking into her bed at night?" she asked softly. "Paul, he's wonderful, but I'm not naive. I understand what kind of man he is." She shrugged. "Right now, he's what I want. And he's very good to me."

"He'd better be. You can tell him, if he isn't, he'll answer to me."

"I don't think I'm going to have to tell him that." She rose on her toes and kissed his cheek. "Now let me be. I have a man in my life. At last." Maybe not for long, she reminded herself. But at the moment—a good man.

Okay, the joke's on me, Luke thought.

Shelby had left his bed and he'd taken her home at about four o'clock and he had hated it. He was not nearly ready to let her go. Far from cured of her, he wanted her more than ever. And not just her body, all of her—her sweet laugh, her soft mane of hair, her gentle and secure way of dealing with him and everything else in her life. He had warned himself not to get involved with someone so innocent and it had turned out *he* was the innocent—not prepared to feel such a rush of emotion. Every time he remembered her voice whispering, "Show me, Luke. I want to learn what makes you feel good," it sent a ripple of desire shooting through him that almost overpowered him, leaving him weak in the knees.

He hadn't gone to Jack's for his beer tonight. He didn't feel like being around anyone, unless it was Shelby. Right now when he thought of her, his eyes steamed with lust. He felt electric shocks soar through his whole body. He couldn't be in the same room with her and keep his hands to himself. So he'd stayed home to feel those things in private, undistracted.

He went to Art's cabin and helped him fix some chicken and dumplings with vegetables out of a can. They talked for a while about what they'd do around the cabins in the morning, then Luke went back to the house. He made himself a sandwich, drank a beer, took a shower, content to be alone. His mind was whirring with the memory of holding her, touching her silky skin, feeling her warm, fragrant breath against his chest. He could still smell her, taste her, even after the beer.

He had never felt like this before in his life. Never.

Wearing just a pair of jeans, no shoes or shirt, he sat on the sofa in his small living room in front of the fire, feet up on the ottoman, holding a beer by the neck of the bottle, thinking of nothing but her awesome body, her luscious lips, and all too often, the way he felt inside her. Had he warned her to be careful of him, that he was a heartbreaker? Jesus, he was an idiot was what he was. Thinking there would never be a woman he'd want to hang on to. Thinking he'd take his taste and move on.

He heard an engine and headlights bounced through the front window. He stood up, holding his breath. For a moment he was sure Walt had come for him; come to work him over for touching Shelby. He heard a soft knock at the door. When he opened it, she stood there, a backpack slung over one shoulder and that alluring smile on her lips. He felt his chest expand in ways he didn't recognize and knew that his eyes had grown molten and dark.

"You're here," she said.

He opened his arms and she stepped into his embrace. "Where did you think I'd be?"

"I don't know." She looked up at him. "Out for the evening? Prowling?"

"Baby, you worked all the prowl out of me this afternoon." He pushed the door closed without letting go of her.

"I probably shouldn't have come back."

"Why not?"

"Well, I might've had a little too much of a good thing. I'm spotting and I'm sore," she said.

He ran a hand across her cheek, lifted her chin and placed a soft kiss on her lips. "I'll just hold you. We wouldn't want to do any damage. I'm sorry if I made you sore."

"It wasn't so much you as the newness, Luke. You were careful. But I just wanted to feel your arms around me some more." She laughed and buried her face in his chest. "I wanted to smell your chest."

A deep sigh escaped him and he tightened his arms. He was just beginning to admit it to himself—he was in love with her. Totally gone. "Where does your family think you are?"

"With you. For the night, if you want me to stay."

He held her away from him and frowned. "You told them?"

"Is that all right?"

"I don't care who knows—but what about you?"

"I didn't have to tell anyone," she said. "Paul and Vanni took one look at me and told me to be careful. They all think I'm so fragile and you're a rogue. I'm not." She smiled. "And you're not."

He pulled the backpack off her shoulder and put it on the breakfast bar. "I was hard on you earlier, Shelby. Trying to push you away, trying to scare you. I'm sorry."

She shook her head. "Luke, I had made up my mind. Couldn't you tell?"

It was just beginning to dawn on him. "When did you decide?" he asked her.

"Not right away. I had to get to know you a little. And—" she laughed "—there was that tool belt."

"You had a job for me to do, didn't you, Shelby?"

"I did." She smiled. "It had to be someone irresistible and experienced."

"Sometimes I don't think. I can be insensitive. Careless with feelings," he said. "Weren't you afraid I might hurt you?"

"Not for one second," she said, shaking her head. "I brought a bottle of wine…"

"I'll open it for you, pour you a glass and finish my beer." He took her jacket, hung it on the back of a chair and started to unbutton her shirt. "Let's get into bed."

"I'm not kidding," she said. "I may have overdone it. See, I shouldn't have come…"

"I just want to feel you against me. I just want to touch you a little. I'm not going to do anything that will make you sore. I want to get you better." He kissed that delicious mouth. "You might need a few days, but I don't want to be away from you."

"But won't that just make it too tempting? Naked in the bed?"

"Nah. You're important to me. I'm going to take good care of you." He opened her shirt and lowered his lips to her breast.

"God," she said in a breath. "It might be too tempting for me."

He lifted his head and smiled into her eyes. "Don't worry, honey. I know how to take care of that." He turned her toward the bedroom. "I'll bring you a glass of wine."

Luke was locked in an incredible dream, with ecstasy overpowering him. His entire body was quivering wildly, madly, as the woman in his dream worked on him. He was close, ready to let himself go in a climax so huge it would rock the bed. The sound of his own groan woke him and he realized it was not a dream. He looked down at that honey-colored head of hair and gasped. "Shelby!" He reached down, grabbed her shoulders and pulled her up toward him. "Shelby, come here." He pulled her face up to his. "Honey, what are you doing?"

"Did I hurt you?"

"*Hurt* me? Sweet Jesus!"

"I've never done that before, so I wasn't sure…"

"Why are you doing it now?"

"Well, I've never slept with a man before and you were keeping me awake, poking me in the back." She smiled at him. "You don't hesitate to take care of me…"

"Shelby, do you realize what almost happened?"

She smoothed her hands over his chest and gave his lips a little tug with hers. "I'm inexperienced, Luke, not ignorant."

He caught her to him, holding her close. "Aw, baby."

"Was I awful? Maybe you should tell me what to do."

"Awful?" He laughed. "I almost lost it in my sleep!"

"That means it was okay?"

"You don't have to do that. This is all so new for you…"

She smiled at him. "Turns out it feels almost as good to please you as it does to be pleased by you." She gave him a little kiss. "Relax." And she slid down his body. Her lips brushed against his belly and he shuddered involuntarily. His head dropped back and he groaned. In one day, his life had changed too much to comprehend. No way he could deserve this woman and her unselfish passions. In no time his world exploded and he saw stars. Then he felt tears in his eyes and knew it wasn't from the orgasm.

She slid up and lay atop his body. She pecked at his lips. "I think you liked that."

"God," he said, unable to catch his breath. "I'm dead, that's what. And against all odds, I was sent to heaven."

"That good, huh?"

"Not just that. Everything. I've never had a day like this in my life."

"I thought you had lots of days like this," she said.

"Never. Baby, never. I'm afraid I'm going to wake up." He brought her mouth onto his and kissed her deeply, holding her tightly against him. He hadn't expected the most mind-blowing sex of his life and the sweetest woman on earth dishing it out.

"And I think now I might be able to get a little sleep," she said with a soft laugh. Then, with her lips against his ear she whispered, "Luke, thank you. You've made it all so wonderful, so good. Hold me," she said. "Let me fall asleep against you, in your arms."

He held her there, like that, stretched over his body, her head resting against his shoulder. She might weigh a hundred and ten pounds to his one-eighty, and she fit against his chest perfectly. He ran his hand down her back and over her soft bottom, stroking her, listening as her breathing evened out, as she sighed in her sleep.

This is the best thing that's ever happened to me, he thought. *I hope I don't screw it up.*

12

Walt went to the stable in the early morning and found Shelby there, mucking out a stall. He jumped in surprise when he saw her. "Morning," she said brightly.

"When did you get here?" he asked her.

"Not that long ago. Maybe a half hour. It was such a beautiful morning, I decided to come right down here, see what I could get done. Then I'll shower off the stable and have some breakfast."

He stepped toward her, frowning. "Shelby, you weren't home last night."

"You mean this morning, don't you? Because you weren't home last night, either."

"Shelby—"

"I was with Luke. But just in case you wondered or were worried, I told Vanni where I was going."

"All night?" he asked.

"All night," she said firmly, giving her chin a lift. He was quiet for a long time, looking at her from under those fierce, hooded brows. Finally she leaned on her shovel and met his eyes fearlessly, stare for stare. "You have something you want to say to me?" she asked.

"Let's go for a short ride...talk about some things..."

"I'm going to pass on the ride, Uncle Walt. I have some things I'd like to do this morning. But we can take a few minutes for you to get this off your chest."

"I don't know where to start." His expression softened. "Shelby, honey—"

"Walt," she said, purposely omitting the Uncle. "Let me help you, because we're going to get this over with quickly. I like him. He's very nice to me. I haven't been impetuous—I gave Luke a lot of thought. There's no question in my mind—he's a good man. I know he comes off looking like a reckless tough guy, just like a lot of the men in this town at first glance, but he's not that way with me. He's very thoughtful and considerate. He's real worried about you, however."

"I don't dislike the man. It's just that I don't know him real well. And I know a lot about men like Luke, I've commanded hundreds of them."

"You mean men like *you* and Luke—soldiers. Men who fight battles, go to war, get a little roughed up, seem to manage on very little conscience..." He hung his head briefly. "You can thank Vanni for already having this conversation with me—about soldiers, how they're trained, how they live, that edgy, son-of-a-bitch personality they learn in the army. You have a little of that in you, too, don't you, Uncle Walt? Covering up your softer feelings? Being hard and resilient and not letting yourself feel guilty about the damage you have to inflict? I suppose it goes with the territory." She stepped closer to him. "I spent a lot of years around you when I was growing up. I saw young G.I.s shake in their boots when you walked past them, but you always treated Aunt Peg and Vanni like precious jewels. And just like you, Luke has a sweet side."

"I promised your mother I'd look out for you, watch over you…"

"And so you are," she said. "I'm sure you'd be more comfortable with me right now if I'd stayed home and waited for some nice young man from church to come by the house and ask your permission to take me out for a buggy ride—but it's not going to be like that, thank God. I was attracted to Luke Riordan almost right away. The attraction is mutual. I'm having a romance, Uncle Walt. At *last*, I'm having a romance. I'm way overdue—and you're not going to make me feel guilty or make him nervous. I appreciate your concern, but it's up to *me*."

Whew, Walt thought, resisting the urge to take a step backward. "If I'm concerned, it's only because… Aw, honey—I just want you to be happy… I don't want you to be hurt. You might be getting in over your head…."

She took another step toward him, looking up at him. There was absolute conviction in her eyes. "You thought I'd save myself for marriage?" she asked, lifting one eyebrow.

"I'm a lot of things, but I don't think anyone could accuse me of being foolish or old-fashioned." She just tilted her head, questioning him. "Or impractical," he added grudgingly.

She laughed at him, though softly. "I'm not so sure Luke's going to hurt me," she said. "Regardless, there isn't much anyone can do about that. I don't know if you can understand this, but I'm glad that I can finally take my romantic lumps just like all the other girls have." She looked up at him earnestly. "Why does everyone think I'm such a wuss? You think the last five years have been easy? You think it doesn't take a brave girl to spend the night with a man when my overprotective uncle might be at home, pacing, loading his shotgun? Believe me, even if Luke Riordan breaks my heart, it's going to be a lot easier in the end than some of the stuff I've been through the last few years. This is a new adventure for me—and you're not going to bully me out of it. Man, if anyone's earned the right, it's me!"

"And all your plans?" he asked. "Travel? School? A new life?"

"I think it's ridiculous to even ask," she said. "Women don't have to choose between a relationship and education, Uncle Walt. I don't have to give up anything."

Walt reached out a hand and lifted her thick braid off her shoulder, caressing it between his thumb and forefinger. "I'm not here to bully you, and I don't think you're a wuss. In fact, I think you're pretty tough stuff. I guess I need to assure myself you're wise to this. Sometimes these adventures can scar the heart."

"I'm not afraid of that," she said, shaking her head. "I wouldn't be the first. Vanni said her heart was broken a hundred times."

"Her mother handled most of that," Walt said with a shrug. "You're stuck with me."

"You're not a bad guy to be stuck with."

"Just be careful." He reached out and touched her cheek softly. "I keep forgetting how strong willed you are. Luke Riordan might be sorry he got himself into this…this…"

"Romance," she finally supplied. "Really, I can't believe you're having such a hard time with this. I'm seeing someone, Walt, just like you are. It's not as if he's married or a priest or anything." She lifted one eyebrow at him. "Everyone in this family has someone, even eighteen-year-old Tom. You'd better get used to the idea I'm no different than anyone else."

"You're a little different," he said with a smile. "Better, probably."

"Phooey. I just want to be *normal*. Are you going to behave yourself?"

"What are you getting at?"

She crossed her arms over her chest. "You know *exactly* what I'm talking about."

"I just want to be sure you're all right," he said. "You're a grown woman. If you've made up your mind, I'll just hope all this works out for the best." He leaned down and kissed her forehead. "Are you going to be home tonight?" he asked.

"I sincerely hope not," she said. "I'll let you know."

Luke was up on the ladder, scraping old chipped paint off the eaves of number three when the general's Tahoe pulled up to his house. He had been expecting this, but he wasn't sure how it would happen, or when. Luke climbed slowly down the ladder. He tucked in his shirt and mopped his face with a rag.

"Luke," the general said. He did not extend his usual hand.

"Sir."

"My niece hasn't been home until morning the last few days."

"You aren't armed, are you, sir?"

"I knew where she was, of course. She was considerate enough to tell the family so we wouldn't worry. But I thought you and I should have a little talk."

"Go ahead, sir," Luke said. He hoped it didn't show that his stomach was twisting. Not because he was afraid of the general—he knew Walt wouldn't really shoot him—but because he was afraid of the general somehow convincing Shelby she was making a big mistake. He'd barely gotten into this with her; he was a long way from being ready to give her up.

Walt's cheeks darkened with a ruddy stain as he said, "She's been with you every night and she hasn't been riding. I don't know what to think—that she's not sitting a horse."

Luke looked down and found his own cheeks warming. "Sir, I can honestly say, I haven't ever been this uncomfortable in my life..."

"She says her back's bothering her..."

"Then maybe her back's bothering her..."

"I want something understood. Shelby might seem shy and sometimes not real sure of herself, but she's very stubborn. She does as she pleases. She always has. She might go at it quietly, but once she's decided, that's it. I tried like hell to talk her out of putting her life on hold to care for her mother. Midge could have gone into a nursing home, at least at the end. But I didn't make any headway because Shelby's mind was made up." He took a breath and shook his head. "I wasn't sure getting involved with you was the best idea, even though I don't dislike you."

"I didn't want her involved with me either, sir. But as you say, she's stubborn."

"Well, that gets us straight to the point—I can't accuse you of coercing my niece or taking advantage of her. I was more than a little aware that she had you in her crosshairs, and I could see she was hell-bent."

"Seems you're right, sir."

"It appears the die is cast. She's made herself clear—she plans to spend a good deal of time under your roof. When she's here, Riordan, you'd better be a gentleman."

"Absolutely, General."

"I'd be curious to know what kind of plans you have where my niece is concerned," Walt said.

"Due respect, sir, it would be wrong for me to discuss any plans with you before talking to Shelby. And at the risk of being indelicate, Shelby and I have barely—"

"That'll do," he said, holding up a hand. "I know how that sentence was going to end. Leave it at that."

Luke took a breath. "What I meant to say is—we're just getting to know each other." Luke stepped forward. "Sir, I've probably been around more than a father or uncle would prefer, but I'd like you to know that Shelby is treated with absolute respect when she's with me. I consider it my responsibility to see she's protected, that she's safe with me. I treat her with great care."

"You damn sure better. I love that girl. She's very special."

"Yes, sir. Very special."

"I'm not an idiot about relationships, son. I have two kids who have been through a few—my daughter has already buried a husband at her young age…"

That grave, Luke thought. He would have to remember to ask Shelby about it. Luke had assumed Paul was Vanessa's first husband.

"I understand things don't always go smoothly," Walt was saying. "Sometimes these things don't work out, I'm not naive about that. This thing with you and my niece, it'll either be a lasting thing or not—that's yet to be seen. But if you do anything terrible to her…" He sucked in his breath. "You know what I'm talking about?"

Luke frowned. "I'm not sure I do…"

"You abuse her, hit her, cheat on her and give her something, treat her with cruelty, or—"

"For God's sake!" Luke said, cutting him off and stiffening indignantly. "What the hell are you *talking* about? What kind of man do you think I am?"

Walt shrugged and said, "Well, I don't have any reason to suspect you of foul behavior, yet, but after all, I've seen a lot. I've had a lot of different kind of men in my command. I thought we should understand each other."

"We understand each other! I wouldn't do things like that to any woman! Jesus!"

"Good, then. Because I'd have to kill you."

"I'd have to *let* you!" Luke said passionately. He took a breath. "Due respect, I've known a real horseshit general or two. Sir."

"I felt the need to clear the air on a couple of issues."

"Consider it cleared!" He rubbed a hand along the back of his neck.

"Well, I didn't come here to try to talk you out of seeing my niece. Given the situation with her mother passing not too long ago, I feel a little more protective than Shelby is comfortable with. I didn't think it would hurt for you to know—I have limits."

"So do I," Luke said calmly but vehemently.

"Then I guess we're clear." He turned as though he would go.

Luke watched his departing back and in a split second thought about how he'd feel if he had to turn Shelby over to some guy.

"Sir," Luke called. When the general turned back, Luke said, "Now that we've faced off on this and both hold Shelby's well-being as the most important thing, I'd like you to know some things. Shelby could do a lot better than me, we both know that. I didn't mislead her, I avoided her and discouraged her. I've been completely honest with her; I'm not a good catch and I'm not looking for a permanent relationship. I'm sure Shelby had no trouble believing that. But it's not my intention to treat her badly. Jesus, she'll get the best I have. If it's any comfort, my mother would *kill* me if I ever abused a woman. If she failed to kill me, my brothers would do the job."

"Good," Walt said, a smile tugging at his mouth. "I can appreciate a close family."

"I might be a scoundrel, but I'm a fairly civilized scoundrel." Luke stuck out his hand. "I wish we could be friends. For Shelby, at least."

Walt hesitated, but he took Luke's hand. "Behave decently," Walt said.

"Yes, sir," Luke said. "You, too."

After putting in a long day of work on the cabins, Luke went to his house as the sun was lowering in the sky. He laid a fresh fire in the hearth and took a shower. Just as he was getting out, he heard his front door open. Wrapping a towel around his waist, he left the bathroom in time to see Shelby coming in with a brown sack. "Wow," she said, looking at him. "How's that for timing?"

"Whatcha got there?" he asked, hands on his hips.

"When I left the clinic, I stopped by the bar and got us some dinner so we could stay in tonight. I'm tired. I brought some pie so Art can have dessert with us if he wants to."

"He'll want to. Art has never turned down a slice of pie."

She looked down his body and laughed. "Luke," she said, shaking her head. "I don't even have my jacket off and you're popping out of your towel."

"Well then, take your jacket off," he said. "Will dinner keep for a little while?"

She put the sack on the table, shrugged out of her jacket and walked into his arms. "I put in a long day and the clinic was busy—I've been around babies and sick people. Can you give me some time to freshen up?"

He gently touched her lips with his. "Sure. Help yourself."

"I won't be too long," she said, slipping past him and into the bedroom to take off her boots and clothes.

Luke went into the kitchen and peered into the sack of take-out dinner. He pulled out the pie and put it in the fridge, then sniffed the remaining contents. It smelled delicious, but Preacher never put together a mediocre meal. He got down a couple of plates, pulled some flatware out of the drawer and opened two beers. Then he heard water running in the tub and headed toward the bathroom. He caught the scent of something feminine. Shelby had brought a couple of her things with her a few nights before—shampoo and lotion and such. He told her to leave it—something he'd never invited a woman to do before. Things like that always made him claustrophobic, but this time it made him feel extremely good, as though he wouldn't have to release her too soon. As if holding her shampoo and lotion hostage meant she would stay with him for a while.

He entered the bathroom just in time to see her lowering herself into the tub. Her long hair was pinned up on her head and there were bubbles. It was in his mind to pass her a beer and sit on the closed toilet lid to talk with her while she was in the bath, but then another thought was inspired. Luke had never in his life even contemplated a bubble bath. He put the beer on the sink, dropped his towel and got in.

"You're going to make a flood!" she said with a laugh.

"This tub isn't quite big enough," he complained, sitting to face her, the faucet jabbing him in the back. He pushed his long legs past her hips, lifted her legs to drape them over his thighs and pulled her toward him, into his arms.

"You're acting crazy," she said, laughing.

"I'm impatient," he said, his lips on her neck. "I can hardly get through the day, waiting for you."

"I'm not quite freshened up yet," she said.

"I'll help with that," he said, picking up the soap. He ran the soap smoothly over her shoulders, down her back, over her breasts, under her arms, bringing low, delighted hums from her when he lathered her up. Then he took the face cloth and gently rinsed her. "I want to tell you something."

"Another one of those talks? More conditions?"

"No. I visited a clinic in Eureka. Right after our first night together. I had a screening for STDs. To be sure, though I was already pretty sure. I wanted you to know that despite my shady past, I'm okay. You're not in any danger that I'll pass anything to you."

"Aw," she said, pulling him closer, chest to chest. "That was thoughtful."

"No one's ever been inside you before me," he said. "I want to keep you completely safe."

"I appreciate that."

"I got the results just in time. I don't have a condom in this tub," he said. "But there's that other matter..."

"I'm on the pill. I took care of that."

"You didn't tell me," he said.

"Sorry. I didn't think about your concerns—I was handling mine."

"Good news to me," he said. Then, after leaning in for a deep kiss, he said, "I meant to tell you another thing—your uncle visited me."

"He did? He shouldn't have done that. What did he say?"

"That he knew where you've been every night. And that he didn't much like the fact that you weren't able to ride."

"Oh God," she moaned.

"It was by far one of the worst moments of my life."

"I'm sorry, Luke. I'll talk to him—"

"No, don't. We worked it out."

"How?"

"Well," he said, pulling her close him and gently rocking her against him. "I refused to explain, he threatened me with dire consequences if I abused you or treated you cruelly, I tried to reassure him that I can be civilized if I concentrate, and in the end, we actually shook hands."

"God," she said. "Luke, Uncle Walt and I already had our standoff about this. He told me to be careful of you and I told him he wasn't going to bully me out of whatever relationship I chose. He promised to behave himself."

"You stood up to him?" Luke asked, smiling. "You defended me?"

"Does that surprise you? That I can stand up for myself? Really, does everyone think I'm a spineless little twit?"

"Nah, you're just too sweet. And Walt wanted to be sure you're safe with me."

"Did you tell him the truth? That I'm not? That you're dangerous and wicked and a real shark with women?" she asked playfully, tugging at his lower lip with her teeth.

"No one has to know, do they?" he asked her. "That I was the first one to—"

She leaned back, looking at him. "Why? Do you want it to be a secret?"

"I'd like it if that belonged to us. You and me. Private. Personal. It's so damn special." He grinned. "I've never had an experience like this in my life," he said. "And I've had a ton of experience."

"And I've never had any," she said.

"But I've never been with anyone like you," he told her. "You're amazing. You drive me crazy. You've got me playing house, for Christ's sake. I don't do things like this."

"See? I tried to warn you. Maybe I should have given *you* the talk."

"Yeah, I never saw that coming," he said. "Your uncle also wanted to know what plans I had with you. I told him that was for me to talk with you about."

"Luke, you shouldn't lie…"

"I didn't. Right now I plan to make love to you till you beg me to stop."

"Aw. Well, that's today. You'll probably be tired of me in two weeks. Remember, you don't stay involved for long."

He ran a hand down her chest, over a breast, down to place a palm over her soft mound. "How are you down here?"

"Fine. Good."

"Not sore? We getting you healed up?"

"You've been very considerate. I didn't know I could function on so little sleep, but I happen to like it." She laughed. "More than I thought I would. I never thought I'd be back every day. I guess I'm being a real pig about it."

"Go ahead. Be a pig about it. I can take it." He rubbed her gently. "You're opening up. Blossoming."

"Mmm."

He lifted her and brought her neatly onto his lap, slipping inside without difficulty. "God," he whispered. "Sweet heaven." Then with his mouth drawing on her nipple, his finger massaging her and his hips gently pumping, he loved her deeply and smoothly. She held his head against her breast and rocked with him, making all the wonderful little noises he'd grown to love. In a few short and breathless minutes, she had risen to that pinnacle of pleasure that caused her insides to tighten and pulse. She pulled his head harder against her and he pushed more deeply inside, letting himself go in a blast of heat that blinded him for a moment. He clung to her, panting. Recovering. Wanting the moment never to end.

And then he heard her giggle. "Someone's going to have to wipe up the floor…"

"Hmm."

"Luke Riordan, you're in a bubble bath."

"Yeah," he said, breathless.

"What would people think? Big, tough, womanizing Black Hawk pilot, in a bubble bath."

"You better not tell or you'll be punished," he said, still catching his breath.

She giggled again. "That might be interesting. I never know what you'll come up with next."

Late in the night, long after dinner and some time in front of the fire, Luke was lying in bed, his head propped on a hand, staring down at the sleeping form of Shelby. She was curled on her side, her beautiful, smooth back and perfect bottom against him, and he could see her profile. She slept like a baby, content, peaceful and drunk on sex.

He had known from the moment he saw her that she was dangerous, but he'd had no idea how lethal. She had pulled feelings to the surface that he thought he'd been in control of and now it was here—he felt it all and he was completely lost. Terrified. He adored her. He couldn't stand the thought of this ending.

He had felt something almost this deep and powerful once before, when he was much younger. He had been twenty-four when he found the beautiful, raven-haired Felicia. In her arms, in her body, he had come to life. He'd never fallen so hard before, and certainly not since. He had been surprised by the passion and commitment he felt, but he let it sweep him away. He loved her hard for a year, and then he had to leave on a mission. He went to Somalia. When the conflict was at its worst, it was her face in his mind that helped him get through, gave him purpose, something strong and powerful to fight for. He had pledged his life to her; he was going to love her till the day he died.

When he got home he found out it had all been a lie; she had never been his. She'd been unfaithful since before he left;

she cut him loose the first day he was back. It had been an ugly, bitter parting that left everyone scarred—mostly him.

To say his heart was ripped apart didn't touch it. For a couple of years at least the pain was so bad he thought it might kill him. When the pain stopped, he was empty inside. He made a firm resolution: that would never happen to him again. His involvement with women was purely recreational from that point on. He wasn't about to be vulnerable to a woman, open himself to that kind of pain.

Yet beside him, all gentle and sweet, was an incredible woman. He wanted to pull her into his arms, tell her how much he loved her, how far he'd go to make her happy, beg her to either change her plans or include him.

But he wouldn't. It was too risky. Another deal like the last one would kill him. He wouldn't give his heart.

The problem was, without meaning to, without wanting to, he had.

Walt Booth had watched the evolution of Muriel's renovation for almost six months; he'd helped with some of it, but she was extremely protective of her work and wanted to be able to take credit for doing it herself. As he witnessed, he learned a few things. One—gutting and remodeling, upgrading, modernizing, might be expensive, but it was easy. And such houses, like his, were a dime a dozen. All you needed was money and a builder. What Muriel was doing—restoring it to its former pristine beauty—was an art. Well—it was largely restored. She had new appliances and wasn't about to be sitting on spindly settees or sleeping on a hundred-year-old mattress. She couldn't wait to get her flat-screen TV, stereo and DVD equipment, all of which would be kept in antique wardrobes.

It was mid-November when she called him and said, "What are you doing?"

"I'm babysitting while Vanni runs into town. She'll be back soon. Why?"

"I want you to come over," Muriel said. "As soon as you can."

She never had to ask him twice. When he pulled up, she was all bundled up and standing on the porch of the big house, waiting. Her hands were plunged into her pockets, she was stamping her booted feet and her breath was swirling in steam around her.

He got out of the Tahoe. "What's the matter?" he asked, walking toward her.

Her face lit up in that brilliant smile of hers. "Matter? God, nothing! Walt—it's done. *Done.*"

Muriel had the upstairs finished to her satisfaction at least a couple of months ago, but she'd never moved out of the refurbished bunkhouse; she hadn't wanted to move that furniture out and live in a mostly empty house when she was perfectly comfortable where she was. She just kept working away.

"Are you ready?"

"Ready," he said.

She swung open the front door and he was standing right in a living room—no fancy foyers in old farmhouses. The dark wood floor gleamed; the baseboards and crown molding were the same dark, varnished color. She'd needed his help to lift the heavy sections of crown molding, but she'd fit it herself, using her very own circular saw. The walls, textured by her own hand, were painted green. The banister had been stained and varnished to match the walnut trim and molding, and the wall of the open staircase was a dark beige, the ceilings a lighter beige. Straight ahead, the same color scheme as the living room, the dining room was framed by a walnut arch.

She must have recently installed the sheer, lacy curtains that were pulled back from the windows. The hearth was framed in the original, thick dark wood mantel.

The kitchen was bright yellow, some of it papered in a design of old-fashioned yellow roses. The cupboards and counters were the originals, sanded and stained, but she'd pulled the cupboard doors apart and installed dark glass panels to replace the old, buckling wood. The sink and appliances were new white, but she kept the sink pump handle right where it was. She'd even sanded and stained the windowsills and frames. And the light fixtures that hung over the kitchen, dining room and breakfast nook were rewired antiques. There was a door to a pantry and a door to the cellar.

"You are amazing," he said.

The upstairs was equally impressive—the shining hallway floors, three bedrooms all painted different colors, a bath much too small and compact for a movie star down the hall from the largest bedroom. No master baths or walk-in closets here. But every detail of the original house was polished, varnished, painted, papered. It was beautiful. It looked like a museum piece.

"This will be my room, at the top of the stairs," she said. "I bought a bunch of quilts, but I bought them from a real quilter, so I'm only cheating a little bit. And throw pillows in petit point—actual antiques. I've been collecting them for years. I have a new floral-print duvet and matching sheets— I bought ten extra top sheets. Instead of wallpaper in here, I'm gluing sheets to a couple of walls. And I have old pictures of my parents and grandparents and great-grandparents to hang on the staircase wall. We have some Native Americans way back in the family tree and, remarkably, have some pictures of them. I also have a couple of old country watercolors I picked up years ago and took special care to preserve for this moment."

He shook his head and chuckled. "This is not how a woman nominated for Oscars is supposed to want to live."

"Phooey. There's a lot more to me than Oscars. Though I have to admit, it really pisses me off that I never got one." She smiled up at him and put her arms around his waist. "I've had some special pieces of furniture in storage. The movers are coming tomorrow. Will you stay with me when the bed's made up?"

"I will gladly stay with you in your flowery bedroom. And if I ever get rid of my houseful of offspring, you will stay with me in my bold and manly master bedroom with convenient master bath and big doorless shower."

"I will." She grinned.

"Muriel, this house… It's beyond my wildest expectations. You're gifted. Your talent is unsurpassed. I just can't express how impressed I am. And proud. I'm just so proud of you."

"Thank you. I'm proud of me, too. We should have a drink and cigar."

"I'd never have thought to bring cigars," he said.

"Not to worry. I bought us a bottle of Pinch and box of cigars. I'll leave all the lights on in the house. We'll sit on the bunkhouse porch, freeze to death, have a scotch and a Cuban and stare at the house. Is that brownish-lavender porch the best?"

"Cubans? You have Cubans?"

"I do. You don't think Mike V. will arrest me, do you?"

"If he finds out, it'll be tough to keep the local marines off your porch."

She chuckled. "I want to have a housewarming after the furniture is in and pictures hung. Do you think anyone would come?"

He frowned. "You're Muriel St. Claire. I think the whole town will come."

"Really?" she asked, surprised. "That would be so wonderful." Then her brow wrinkled as she thought it over. "What will I do for food?"

Luke and Shelby fell into the nice little pattern of new lovers, with Shelby sleeping over almost every night. Then she would start her day real early, going first to Walt's stable to help with the horses, maybe have a ride and breakfast with him, shower and grab a change of clothes. Next she'd go to town where her main industry was keeping Mel's professional life manageable. She helped in the clinic, sorted and filed, watched the kids. Luke marveled at her energy, her industry.

Luke and Art worked together on the cabins every day and Luke took great pride in the fact that Art was quite functional. He wasn't a gourmet cook, but he could warm a nourishing dinner in the microwave a few nights a week, eating with Luke and Shelby the other nights. He showered and shaved daily, took good care of his teeth, laundered his clothes, fixed his bed every morning. Luke had stocked his cupboards with decent food and nontoxic cleaning supplies. Art had fruit to add to his breakfast and lunch. He kept his bathroom and little kitchen spotless with spray cleaner.

Art was absolutely competent to live on his own, as long as he had someone trustworthy nearby in case he needed advice or ran into a problem, or maybe to remind him of things like, "Time to wash the sheets and towels, Art." Luke told him that when the cabins were finished, Art could be the custodian. He'd make sure the trash was handled, that things were tidy, and they'd work together on upkeep, cleaning, yard maintenance, whatever needed fixing or painting.

"Do you miss your old friends at the group home?" Luke asked him.

He shrugged. "I miss Netta and Payne," he said. "I miss

my mom." Then he smiled. "But I like it here by the river. I like my own house where I don't have to sign up to use the washer."

"You're doing a great job for me, Art. Thank you."

"You're welcome, Luke," he said, beaming proudly.

At the end of her day, Shelby would either meet Luke at Jack's or pick up dinner and go straight to his house. They were together every day. They were outed. They were a couple and everyone in town knew it.

This was something Luke hadn't thought about, this couple status. But the price of holding her through the night was this public recognition. People were nice enough not to make too many invasive comments, though there were lots of jokes about the water in Virgin River. It seemed plenty of men had made their way to the little town looking for peace and quiet, maybe some hunting and fishing, and found themselves tethered to a woman. Luke was able to chuckle and ignore them because it gave him strange satisfaction to be connected to her in this way; he was oddly content to be able to put his arm around her in public, to not worry about being caught kissing on the porch. Shelby had him so loose and relaxed, he wasn't likely to complain.

When it was obvious to the whole town that Luke and Shelby were together, it was time to bring Art out of the closet, introduce him around, give him a chance to make friends, even if they were only casual friends. Art had been out at the cabins less than two months and of all the residents of Virgin River, only Shelby and Paul had seen him, knew about him. They'd been cooperative about staying quiet while Luke had been paying attention to newspapers, radio and TV to see if Art was being looked for. There didn't seem to be any missing persons bulletins.

Art already loved Shelby. If she had a short day at the clinic and the weather was nice, she would ride over to the cabins with Plenty in tow and put Art on the horse. He was like a one-hundred-and-ninety-pound ten-year-old and the guy's sheer thrill with it made Luke laugh until he had to turn away to not offend. Luke started to take Art to the bar once in a while to buy him a cold drink, maybe dinner with Shelby. It held positively no surprise that he was accepted very kindly.

It was seeing Art on that horse that prompted Luke to buy some fishing gear for the man, an inexpensive rod and reel he could keep in his cabin. He taught Art to drop a line first. Casting was more of a challenge, but Art loved learning new things. The river was close enough for Art to get in a little fishing when he wasn't working. He took to it right away. It made Luke happy to see the big guy wander down to the river on his own, independent and content.

There was a small town party out at Muriel St. Claire's house that Luke, Shelby and Art attended together. It was newly remodeled, or as the general insisted on pointing out, *restored*. Indeed, it looked like a brand-new hundred-year-old house. Even the pictures, which she insisted were of family members, were antique. The oldest were tintypes. Besides a modern sectional and chair, everything was vintage, even the huge, antique wardrobe that concealed her TV and stereo equipment.

Luke was astonished by the work she'd done, impressed, but some of the townfolk, especially the women, were looking for something a lot more Hollywood. Most of them already had all that old stuff—it had been passed down from generation to generation and they took it for granted. Of course, their old stuff hadn't been pampered and restored like Muriel's, but they were small-town folk and lusted after more modern furnishings. What they wanted to know was, had she dated Clint Eastwood or Jack Nicholson? When she replied she hardly knew them, though she'd been in films with them, they seemed disappointed in her. For a movie star, she wasn't all that provocative.

At least a hundred people wandered through her open house and she beamed every time surprise was expressed that she would prefer this old farmhouse to a big marble palace in Hollywood.

Life was exactly as he liked it. Being a man, he wasted no time thinking deeply about it; feelings weren't exactly something men spent a lot of time pondering. All he wanted was for nothing to change.

To that end, he called his mother and explained that he wouldn't be able to come to Phoenix for Thanksgiving. It turned out it would only be Sean this year anyway; Colin was in Iraq, Paddy out to sea and Aiden was pulling call at the hospital over Thanksgiving to get Christmas off. His mother was disappointed; she hadn't seen him since August. So he told her about Art. Of course, Maureen Riordan told Luke to bring Art with him. "I don't think I can do that, Mother," Luke said. "He's on the run from a group home because someone abused him. I'm pretty sure I'm not breaking the law by giving him shelter, but I don't think it would be a good idea to take him out of state. At least not until I've had a chance to get his situation sorted out a little, which is going to take some investigating and probably legal help. It's just one Thanksgiving. I'll probably see you at Christmas. Be a big girl. Don't nag."

"I don't nag," she said.

"Oh, you nag." He laughed. "There's no mercy in it."

"I don't want you to be alone on Thanksgiving," she said.

"I'll be fine, Mother. Don't worry."

But Luke wasn't going to be alone. He was going to the general's house, and he was bringing Art. The invitation had come through Shelby and he recognized right away that it was mandatory. He'd rather not get any more enmeshed with the family, but it was impossible to avoid. When it came to living in a place like Virgin River, you were enmeshed the day you hit town. It was all right—a holiday dinner wasn't too much to ask. Art was welcome and Luke happened to like the general and the Haggertys. He couldn't deny that if Shelby had been his young cousin or niece, he might feel just as protective as they did, yet they'd managed to act as though they respected her choice and treated him fine.

Just as he was coming to accept it all, Luke's well-organized life was derailed by a phone call from his brother Sean.

"So, you put in a no-show for the turkey," Sean said. "What's up with that? You're stateside, you're not that far away...."

"I have things to do here, Sean," he said. "And I explained to Mother—I can't leave Art and I can't take him on a trip."

"So I heard. And that's your only reason?"

"What else?"

"Oh, I don't know," he said, as if he did know what else. "Well then, you'll be real happy to hear this—I'm bringing Mother to Virgin River for Thanksgiving."

Luke was dead silent for a moment. "What!" Luke nearly shouted into the phone. "Why the hell would you do that?"

"Because you won't come to Phoenix. And she'd like to see this property you're working on. And the helper. And the *girl*."

"You aren't doing this to me," Luke said in a threatening tone. "Tell me you aren't doing this to me!"

"Yeah, since you can't make it to Mom's, we're coming to you. I thought that would make you *sooo* happy," he added with a chuckle in his voice.

"Oh God," he said. "I don't have room for you. There's not a hotel in town."

"You lying sack of shit. You have room. You have two extra

bedrooms and six cabins you've been working on for three months. But if it turns out you're telling the truth, there's a motel in Fortuna that has some room. As long as Mom has the good bed in the house, clean sheets and no rats, everything will be fine."

"Good. You come," Luke said. "And then I'm going to kill you."

"What's the matter? You don't want Mom to meet the girl? The helper?"

"I'm going to tear your limbs off before you die!"

But Sean laughed. "Mom and I will be there Tuesday afternoon. Buy a big turkey, huh?"

Luke was paralyzed for a moment. Silent and brooding.

He had lived a pretty wild life, excepting that couple of years with Felicia, when he'd been temporarily domesticated. He'd flown helicopters in combat and played it loose with the ladies, taking whatever was consensually offered. His bachelorhood was on the adventurous side. His brothers were exactly like him; maybe like their father before them, who hadn't married until the age of thirty-two. Not exactly ancient, but for the generation before theirs, a little mature to begin a family of five sons. They were frisky Irish males. They all had taken on a lot: dared much, had no regrets, moved fast.

But one thing none of them had *ever* done was have a woman who was not a wife in bed with them under the same roof with their *mother*.

"I'm thirty-eight years old and I've been to war four times," he said to himself, pacing in his small living room, rubbing a hand across the back of his neck. "This is my house and she is a guest. She can disapprove all she wants, work her rosary until she has blisters on her hands, but this is not up to her."

Okay, then she'll tell everything, was his next thought. Every little thing about me from the time I was five, every young lady she'd had high hopes for, every indiscretion, my night in jail, my very naked fling with the high-school vice-principal's daughter.... Everything from speeding tickets to romances. Because that's the way the typical dysfunctional Irish family worked—they bartered in secrets. He could either behave the way his mother expected, which she considered proper and gentlemanly and he considered tight-assed and useless, or he could throw caution to the wind, do things his way, and explain all his mother's stories to Shelby later. Including the story about Felicia.

It really didn't make sense for Luke to expect his mother to be a prude. She was obviously much too with it for that. She was a beautiful, statuesque sixty-one-year-old woman who'd been widowed at fifty-three when Luke was only thirty, and remained single and devoted to her military sons. She still had her hair dyed the flaming red of her youth. With some ambivalence, he sometimes wished his mother would find a romantic interest that would take her mind off her boys and their personal lives.

Maureen Riordan was smart, energetic and funny. She was fearless; despite her commitment to her Catholic faith, she had some rebellious ideas. After five sons in ten years, the priest had told her to keep the faith and reject birth control, and she had told him to do something to himself that was never again repeated. But there hadn't been a sixth child. Getting down to it, she didn't have that many flaws—just this rigid set of principles she could be coerced into being quiet about if her demands were met. And there was her relentless dissatisfaction with her sons' inability to marry successfully and bring her grandchildren. That was getting real old.

The boys ranked thusly: Luke, Colin, Aiden, Sean, Patrick. Ages thirty-eight to thirty, down the line. All bachelors. Maureen might be getting a little bewildered and desperate.

As it stood, they had a firm family law that had evolved through bitter fights—no one told embarrassing or family secrets to newcomers without paying, and paying dearly. Frankly, Luke thought the story about his mother standing up to the priest about birth control was hilarious—but *she* didn't find it funny. And a trade was a trade. He could keep her quiet by respecting her principles and not telling stories on her. He could keep his mother's mouth shut by not sleeping with Shelby while she was in town. For *five* nights.

He was going to have to kill Sean.

"Shelby?" Luke began while she relaxed in his arms in the aftermath of yet another amazing sexual experience. "There's a complication with Thanksgiving."

"Hmm?" she asked sleepily.

He took a breath. "My brother Sean is coming. And bringing my mother."

She lifted her head. "Wonderful," she said, smiling, lying back down.

"It's not wonderful," he said miserably.

She laughed. "What's the matter, Luke? That's not bad news. I'd be so happy to meet your mother."

"Yeah, but... See, she's a little on the rigid side..."

Shelby laughed again. "Okay. Like Uncle Walt doesn't get a little stiff? We'll just set two more places. It could be fun. Stiff Uncle Walt and rigid... What's your mom's name?"

"It's Maureen, but we're not going to do that. We're not getting them all together, like one big happy family. You know how I feel about stuff like that. I don't like setting up those kind of expectations.... This isn't... This can't be..."

She laughed some more. "Will you please stop being so paranoid? It's not an engagement party, it's *Thanksgiving*. We bring together people who are important to us. You're also bringing Art—and he certainly doesn't complicate the whole family thing. My God, Luke. Lighten up."

"It screws up my head, thinking about getting our families together. Maybe you've accepted me the way I am, but I'm not convinced your uncle has. And I *know* my mother hasn't."

"But that's not an issue. That would be their problem. We've been over this— I know you pretty well, despite your efforts to be my greatest mystery."

"You do, huh? Still, this whole family thing… It's not what I had in mind."

"I know," she said. "What you had in mind was picking up a girl from out of town, having her in your bed at night and far away the rest of the time, with no connection to your day-to-day life. Unfortunately, we're from the same town right now. And we have all the same friends."

How did she know that? he wondered. He had never explained what he'd originally hoped this would be.

"But if you'll just relax, everything will be fine," she said. "We're all good friends and neighbors. Let me ask you—would your mother mind coming to our house as opposed to having a nice private turkey with you, your brother and Art?"

He was quiet a moment and then said, in a pout, "No. She'd love it."

She giggled. "Oh, I see. You're afraid she's going to like me…."

"Shelby, stop it. You know what my problem is with this."

"Well, I guess your problem is with your mother, because I certainly haven't given you any trouble. You and I—we knew what we were getting ourselves into. I have plans, you have plans, this is temporary. Isn't that what you said? Temporary. So. It's just a couple of families getting together for Thanksgiving." She grinned at him. "I like Sean. He's cute."

"I think he's an ugly, stupid asshole."

Shelby laughed at him. "There is going to be one inconvenience," she said.

"Yeah? What's that?"

"I'm not going to be able to spend the night with you while your mother's here."

He propped up on an elbow and looked at her. "You're not?"

She shrugged. "I'm sorry. It's a little old-fashioned, but that's a bit too much for me. She's your mother. I can't stay here any more than I can bring you to my house while my Uncle Walt is down the hall. I hope you understand."

"But Shelby, they *know* we're...what we are."

"Not quite the same thing," she said. "I'm not doing it under the same roof with them. Maybe if we actually lived together, as in set up housekeeping, changed addresses, etcetera. But no—we're a dating couple having sex. I'm not doing that with your mother in the same house."

"If you can't..."

"Sorry. I can't. Out of respect. That's just it. I won't."

"She's staying five nights," he said, running a hand along the hair that fell over her shoulder. "Five."

"Well, I guess you'll be some kind of maniac by the time she leaves. Maybe I can get Mel to prescribe something so you don't go out of your mind."

"That's what you want?" he asked. "For us to be apart for five nights?"

"No, that's how it's going to be, Luke. We all have our ground rules. Now I want you to relax. It's just dinner. It'll be fun."

"Sure," he said.

There were two reasons he hadn't been able to think of a way to explain why he couldn't cross that line with his mother, either. He was stunned that Shelby hadn't used the opportunity to pull him into a more serious relationship. And, he didn't want to sound like a wussy mama's boy.

But, he thought, it's not supposed to be like this. This isn't the way women acted. She was too cool. It was almost as though she wasn't madly in love with him. She was deliberately passing up an opportunity to trap him.

Muriel and Walt spent a whole day driving through the mountains, looking for garage sales and antique shops. He'd never in his life done anything like this. Nor had he ever cooked for a woman or helped her restore a house.

She was folding and refolding a Garberville newspaper in her hands. "Okay, there's a barn sale up the next road about a half mile...."

"What can you possibly need from a barn sale?"

"As I've explained fifty times, you just never know. I once bought an incredible hundred-and-fifty-year-old pine dry sink from a barn sale."

"Your house doesn't seem to need more furnishings."

"But this is what I do! Like some women drink martinis, I shop for antiques and collectibles."

"You also drink martinis."

She grinned at him. "I pride myself in being well rounded."

He pulled off to the side of the road. He turned and looked at her, resting the wrist of his left arm on the steering wheel. "Muriel, have you had invitations for Thanksgiving?"

"A few," she said.

"Are you going south for the holiday?"

"I haven't decided," she said. "A few friends were very thoughtful to think of me."

"Mind if I ask? What friends?"

"No one you know, Walt."

"Just the same..."

She took a breath. "Susan Sarandon extended an invitation to join her family. Lovely family. Love those kids. My friend George has reservations at a nice restaurant for a few friends—"

"George?"

"Not a boyfriend. Clooney, George Clooney. Very nice man. Very attached at the moment and a tad young for me. He's dating a woman in her thirties, I could be her mother. I actually met George many years ago through his aunt Rosemary. And there was a call from an old, old friend—Ed Asner. He has a small family gathering at his house. And of course Mason would like me to join him and his fourth wife and her grown children and grandchildren." She chuckled. "We're so modern, aren't we? The ex-wife is invited to dinner all the time. Of course, twenty percent of me is very appealing to her, I'm sure." When Walt looked perplexed, she laughed. "His commission, Walt. That's what he gets when I work."

"Hmm. So, where are you going?" he asked.

"I'm not sure. Why?"

He was a bit uncomfortable. He looked away briefly. "We're hosting Luke Riordan and his family. If you'd like to join us, that would be wonderful."

"Walt?"

He turned back toward her, meeting her eyes, her smile. "What?"

"Are you hoping I'll decline?"

"Why would you say that?"

"You wouldn't even look me in the eye when you asked me."

"Oh," he said. "Sorry. It's just that, I know you want to keep us...casual."

"When did I say that?" she asked with a laugh.

"When you said you'd been married five times and were done with that shit. I believe that's a direct quote."

That amused her. She reached over and put a hand on his thigh. "Walt, it would take a lot to get me to ever consider marriage again. I've been through the wringer on marriages. I say 'I do' and there's a cosmic explosion turning fabulous, sexy men into incorrigible animals or complete idiots. I'm cursed—I wouldn't do that to anyone. But I'm not avoiding a good relationship. And this seems as though it's shaping up to be a very good relationship. I'd love to join you for Thanksgiving dinner. But since we both know my limitations, I'll be in charge of cleanup."

His black brows lifted and he smiled. "Really?"

"Why not?"

"I'm not Susan Sarandon or George Clooney for one thing."

"Or Ed Asner, who is *very* special to me. But you are Walt Booth, and you rank right up there. But be careful, Walt. People will think we're serious."

He grinned at her. "At the risk of scaring you to death, I'm very serious about you, Muriel. And a good relationship is exactly what I'm in the market for. That, and a decent dishwasher."

13

When Sean and Maureen arrived late Tuesday afternoon, Luke was ready for them. The house was cleaned from top to bottom and, though there was still a lot of renovation to complete, the walls were textured and painted, the floors sanded, stained and varnished and the kitchen rebuilt. His furniture was good stuff—it made the place look better. He would put his mother in his room and his brother upstairs. Since there was no furniture in the second upstairs bedroom, he'd take the couch. He had logs in the fireplace, wine chilling in the refrigerator, steaks to put on the small grill he'd purchased…and he'd told Shelby she would meet Maureen Wednesday night because he'd want a little time to visit with his mother first. That wasn't the reason, of course. He could have asked Shelby to come over right after she finished in town on Tuesday, but that might look eager, and Maureen didn't need any encouragement.

Much as he resented the intrusion, he was actually thrilled to see his mom. He figured in about two days he'd be less thrilled, but when she stepped out of Sean's SUV, he beamed. Damn, she sure didn't look sixty-one and on both blood pressure and cholesterol medication. And you'd never take her for a woman who'd been a stay-at-home mom raising five very high-maintenance sons. She looked sophisticated even though she wore jeans, boots and a leather jacket. The thing that really melted him was his mother's smile, her eyes. Her smile was so stunning and bright; she had large, strong, white teeth. And Luke couldn't remember a time her green eyes hadn't sparkled; now they crinkled just a little bit in the corners when she grinned.

"Luke! Honey!" she called, running up onto the porch and embracing him.

He held her in his arms for a long minute. "How you doing, Mom?"

"I couldn't get here fast enough, that's how." She held him away from her. "You look okay. I was afraid you'd be thin and pale."

"Now, why would I be thin and pale?" he asked. He glanced over her shoulder to see Sean struggling with multiple suitcases from the back of the SUV. "Jesus, how long are you staying?"

"Just until Sunday—but it was hard to know what to bring for a place like this."

"So you just brought everything?"

"Funny," she said. "So where is Art? And Shelby?"

"Shelby?" he asked.

"I heard all about her from Sean. Pretty little thing, the only niece of a general, young, great on a horse, crazy about you, etcetera…"

"Mom, she's not here. She's at home. I asked her to come over tomorrow night to meet you and we've been invited to her uncle's house for Thanksgiving."

"Oh," she said, sounding disappointed. "I was looking forward to cooking for you."

"We can do that," he said hopefully. "I'm sure they'd understand—we don't see each other that often."

"Don't be ridiculous. I have plenty of time to cook and leave you leftovers. And what are we to bring to Shelby's family for the meal?"

He frowned. It might not take two days for that excitement to wear off, after all. "Wine. I bought it."

"We'll have to take something else," she said. "Pies, beans, bread, something."

"Let me get the luggage, Mom."

"Fine. And then show me this wonderful place."

Luke went down the steps while his mother went directly into the house to look around. There's one thing about having five boys with a strict father—Maureen was not to insult them by lifting a finger while they were around, except in domestic ways. They wouldn't let her haul groceries or luggage while any of them were present. So Luke went to the back of the SUV where Sean was unloading way too many suitcases for five nights. "You'd think she was taking a fricking cruise."

"Your death is going to be slow and painful."

"Aw, come on! What's up your butt now? You had plenty of time to get used to the idea. And she's thrilled to be here, you can see that."

"You told her all about Shelby? I didn't even tell *you* what was going on with Shelby! Can't you ever keep your mouth shut about anything?"

"I beg your pardon—I fly a spy plane. I have a very large security clearance. I told her about Shelby to piss you off."

He grinned. "Did I hear right? We're going to the general's for dinner?"

"Listen to me carefully, because if you screw this up I really will kill you. She's young and inexperienced, not my type, I'm too old for her and it's not serious. Her uncle is trained in hand-to-hand combat and he doesn't like that she likes me. It's not the usual thing, so just keep your big mouth shut. You hear me?"

"Whew, this is making you testy," Sean said with a smirk. "That means it's heating up. Where's Art?"

"In his cabin. I'll go get him as soon as we get these bags in the house." Luke hefted two. "Jesus, where did she think she was going?"

"She plans to be at her best for your new friends. You know, you could have avoided all this by just going to Phoenix for two days."

"I've been trying to avoid you for years, but you just won't go away," Luke grumbled. "This was your idea and you know it. Don't screw with me."

Sean stiffened. "In three seconds we'll be back twenty years, rolling in the dirt. Let's not do this to her, huh? She really gives a shit what's happening with you. I don't, but she does."

"Ach," Luke said, hefting a couple more bags. He took them up on the porch and said, "Put her stuff in my room. You're upstairs. I'm going for Art." He went down the steps to the cabin next door.

Luke gave two taps and opened the door. Art was sitting on the edge of his bed, made up tidily every morning, just waiting. He was all cleaned up, his sparse hair slicked back and wearing the new pants that Luke had purchased for him. His hands were clasped in front of him and he seemed to be terrified. "Art?" Luke asked.

"Are they here now?"

"They're here. You ready to come say hello?"

He stood up nervously and rubbed his palms down his trousers. He nodded too vigorously.

"What's the matter? It's just Sean and my mother. You know Sean. You got along fine. You worried about something?"

He shook his head forcefully. Luke stepped toward him. "Look, you're shook up about something. What's got you so upset?"

"Nothing. I had a shower. I didn't eat sandwiches, like you said."

Luke smiled. Art loved his bologna sandwiches. "You look great. I just wanted you to be hungry for dinner and you wouldn't be if you filled up on sandwiches. You'll have some steak with us."

"Steak is hard. I had it. I don't work the knife that good because I didn't use it that much, and steak gets too big for my mouth. My head's big but my mouth is small, that's what Stan said."

"You worried about that?" Luke asked, smiling. "I'll help with that. You'll work the knife fine—you do everything else with tools just fine. We'll get the steak small enough for your mouth. By the way, I don't buy that, that your mouth is small. I listen to you all day long, and I wouldn't call it a small mouth. Come on, you're the first person my mother asked about."

"My mother's gone now," he said.

"I know, Art. You'll like my mother. She'll like you."

"I'm not like everyone else."

"I told her you had Down syndrome, Art. She knows all about that. We had a good friend with Down's growing up—you're not going to disappoint anyone. You're perfect. She'll like you very much."

"You think?" he asked.

"Is that what you're worried about? Aw, it's going to be

fine—my mother is a very nice person. To people other than her sons, anyway. Come on, let's get on with this so you can settle down. I don't think I've ever seen you nervous. You act like you're scared."

"I had a shower," he said. "And didn't eat the sandwiches. One, I had one."

"It's okay." Luke laughed. "Were you hungry? Because around here you eat when you're hungry. You don't get in trouble for that."

"I know," he said. "I know." And he twisted his hands.

"Jesus, we better get this over with," Luke said. "She's not the queen of England. Calm down."

Art moved slowly. As Luke walked to his house, he had to pause and wait for Art several times and it was not far. By the time he opened the door to his house, his mother and Sean were working their way into the wine.

"Well, hello," Maureen said brightly. "You must be Art."

Art stood just inside the door, looked down at the floor and nodded.

"Then come in. I'm so happy to finally meet you. I hope you're hungry—I think we're going to a place called Jack's."

Luke shot a glance at Sean and scowled. This could really screw up his plan to have his relationship with Shelby appear casual. Sean shrugged and glanced away.

"I like Jack," Art said tremulously.

"I have steaks," Luke said. "I thought we'd stay in."

Maureen came out of the kitchen and went to Art. "Steaks will keep—we want to do the town. Are you a little shy, Art?" she asked him softly.

He nodded, but not quite so ferociously.

"Well, you don't have to be shy with me, because I've been looking forward to meeting you. And I hear you've been a big help to Luke."

Art lifted his eyes and said, "You're not the queen of England."

Maureen gave Luke a withering stare from narrowed eyes, something she had perfected by the time he was seven. It was that warning glance. The boys called it the "don't fuck with me" look, but Maureen had never in her life uttered that word.

"But I almost am, Art, so I trust you to be very sweet and nice."

He nodded.

"Of course you will," she said. "Now, do you have a hand-shake or hug for Luke's mother?"

He just stood there, uncertain. Maureen wrapped her arms around him, pulled him close and rocked him. "Ah, yes. So wonderful of you to help Luke. So wonderful to meet you."

When she released him, he said, "My mother's gone now."

"Is she dead, Art?" Maureen asked gently. And he nodded. "Then I'm so sorry. And you must need a mother's hug even more." She grinned. "Let's have another." And he freed up his arms to hug her back.

Luke found himself smiling in spite of the fact that he was trying to remain insulted by the whole invasion.

The one thing that would make any man—at least a normal man—happy, was tougher than a two-dollar steak for Luke to swallow. Maureen won them over. Not just Shelby, not just Shelby's family, the entire town. To be fair, Maureen hadn't met every resident of Virgin River, but she'd met the crowd Luke considered to be his new friends. And she not only im-pressed them, she made Luke look good.

They started out with dinner at Jack's the first night she was in town and of course Shelby was there when they came in, so the introductions began early. Of course, why wouldn't Shelby be there? She had nothing better to do; she hadn't been invited to Luke's. Her face lit up in a way that made Luke feel guilty; Sean grabbed her and hugged her like they were old friends, then made the introductions himself because he was like that—out in front, the gregarious one. The general wandered in with the famous Muriel and they all stayed for the usual gang dinner with Mel and Jack, Brie and Mike. Maureen couldn't be kept out of the kitchen, asking Preacher and Paige a lot of questions about the operation of the bar and while doing so, holding their new baby. Luke peeked into the kitchen to see what she was up to and got the hell out of there before she started harping on the fact that she had five healthy, handsome, successful sons and no grandchildren.

Maureen had a gift for getting to know people, for putting them at ease and showing her finest qualities. For example, she kept Art near her and was often seen holding his hand, something that showed her kindness, her tenderness. She made the general laugh, endeared herself to Mel and Brie, nurtured and courted Shelby, and she was best friends with Muriel in minutes. A covert glance at the general told Luke he was close to thrilled with Luke's gene pool.

Dinner the next night was an intimate family meal with Art and Shelby included—the steaks that had been kept waiting. It was then that Luke learned more about Shelby's life than he had made time to ask. Shelby's cousin Vanni's first husband, Matt, was a fighting marine who lost his life in Baghdad; Paul was his best friend and the best man at their wedding. After Matt was gone, it was Paul who was with her for the birth of their child and, after a lot of stumbling, finally confessed to Vanni that he'd loved her since the first moment he'd laid eyes on her—but Matt had gotten to her first. No self-respecting man invades his buddy's territory. And now they were together, Paul parenting his best friend's son. The romance of the story made Maureen sigh and fan at tears that gathered in her eyes.

Shelby shared other stories of the town—how Mel came to Virgin River after the violent death of her first husband, the saga of Brie and Mike, how Preacher found Paige and built a life and family he never expected to have. Maureen was enchanted by the history of Luke's friends, history Luke hadn't even known. Luke knew few of the details about the people who'd become his friends. Men don't share stories in the same way women do.

Thanksgiving Day was a stellar success at the general's house. Maureen met the rest of the family, there was a lot of laughter and the family stories that were shared were the safe kind, unlikely to ruffle any feathers. He was proud of his mother. She was a force of life, with her strong good looks, humor, compassion, energy. And there was not so much as a glimpse of her rigid side. It was obvious after getting to know her even a little bit that she was on the proper, straitlaced side, but she only judged her sons, no one else.

With a jolt, he realized—she gave him credibility. He'd been accepted well enough, but he remained a mystery to the Booth household, to the town. Known as a career soldier, single but interested in women, solitary, he presented himself as the kind of guy it wasn't easy to get close to. Enter Maureen, and he becomes a beloved son, the kind of generous man who would take on Art, a safe man for Shelby, a normal guy from whom good things should be expected. The way he was regarded by the general and Paul took a slow but noticeable turn; they treated him like one of the family, like someone they could trust rather than someone to be suspicious of.

Any normal guy would be grateful. Relieved. But for Luke it presented complications. It was bad enough worrying about Shelby's expectations, but he could keep that under control. He didn't know what the hell he'd do with the expectations of her family, of an entire town who'd recently begun to see him as a trustworthy man with honorable intentions.

It left him quiet. Morose. And at the same time, very ready for Maureen and Sean to go, give him back his private life with Shelby, who he was aching to hold, to make love to.

And finally Sunday morning came. The bags were packed, Art had breakfast with them before heading down to the river to fish, and Sean was ready to take his mother to the airport. He'd drive her to Sacramento and put her on a plane to Phoenix, then he would make the trip back north to Beale AFB where he was stationed.

Luke took a mug of coffee out onto his porch. The sun was shining, but it had gotten cold. He had a morning fire blazing in the hearth. It wasn't long before Maureen came outside, wearing her jacket, holding her own cup of coffee.

"All set?" Luke asked.

"Ready. Sean's using your shower. He should be done in ten, fifteen minutes. I thought maybe you and I could have that time. We haven't really talked."

"We've been together for five days," he said with a shrug. "Almost a record." But he knew that wasn't what she meant.

"It's been a long time since Felicia, Luke," she said gently. And she lifted her cup to her lips.

"Long time," he agreed. "I'm over that."

"She was the exception, not the rule," Maureen said. "You shouldn't assume relationships can't work just because you were treated badly by one woman."

Luke said nothing, but what he wanted to scream was *Badly? Badly? I thought she was having my baby and I came back from a war to find out it wasn't mine!*

"Shelby is a wonderful young woman. You're good together."

"Mother…"

"It isn't just her. Oh, it's obvious she loves you. But it's also you. The second she's near you, all those tense lines in your face relax and you soften up. That grumpy, self-protective shield drops and you're warm and affectionate. She's good for you, she brings out your best, makes you fun. You have something special with her."

"She's twenty-five."

Maureen shook her head. "I don't think that's relevant. It doesn't seem to have anything to do with how you two communicate…"

"There are things you don't understand about Shelby," he said. "She's not just young, she hasn't had many relationships. She's been taking care of her mother and hasn't really looked at the world. In a lot of ways, she's a child."

"I know all about her mother, but she's no child," Maureen said. "It takes maturity and courage to do what she did. So she didn't have a lot of relationships with young men, it doesn't mean she lacks worldly experience. And your age doesn't matter to her."

"It will. I'm too old. I'm not going to stand still while she gets older. She'll be thirty-five and I'll be almost fifty. She'd find herself with an old man."

"At fifty?" She laughed. "I liked fifty," she said with a dismissive shrug. "Fifty was good. I was only twenty-three when I married your father and I never thought of him as too old for me. To the contrary, it made me feel better in so many ways, to be with a mature man, a man of experience who didn't have doubts anymore. He was stable and solid. It brought me comfort. And he was awful good to me."

Luke straightened his shoulders. "I'm not getting married. Shelby will move on, Mom. She wants a career. A young husband. She wants a family."

"You know this?" Maureen asked.

"Of course I know that," he said. "You think we haven't

talked? I didn't lead her on. And she didn't lead me on. She knows I don't want a wife, don't want children..."

Maureen was quiet for a long moment. Finally she said, "You did once."

Luke let go a short laugh that was tinged with his inner rage. "I'm cured of that."

"You have to think about this. The way you've managed your life since Felicia hasn't exactly brought you peace. I suppose it's normal when a man gets hurt to avoid anything risky for a while, but not for thirteen years, Luke. If the right person comes along, don't assume it can't work just because it didn't work once, a long, long time ago. I know this young woman as well as I ever knew Felicia. Luke, Shelby is nothing like her. Nothing."

Luke pursed his lips, looked away for a second and then took a slow sip of coffee. "Thank you, Mom. I'll remember that."

She stepped toward him. "It's going to hurt just as much to let her go as it hurt you to be tossed away by Felicia. Remember *that*."

"You know, I don't think I'm the one guilty of assumptions here," he said impatiently. "What makes you think all people want a tidy little marriage and children? Huh? I've been damn happy the past dozen years. I've been challenged and successful in my own way, I've had a good time, good friends, a few relationships..."

"You've been treading water," she said. "You're marking the years, not living them. There's more to life, Luke. I hope you let yourself see—you're in such a good place right now—you can have it all. You put in your army years and it left you with a pension while you're still young. You're healthy, smart, accomplished, and you have a good woman. She's devoted to you. There's no reason you have to be alone for the rest of your life. It's not too late."

He'd met her soft gaze while she talked but now he turned away from her instead of arguing. He didn't see it that way; he thought it *was* too late. What he saw was a beautiful young woman agreeing to life with him, having a child or two, then waking up one morning to realize she hadn't really lived yet. She'd have gone from her mother's sickbed to Luke. She would still be young, beautiful, vibrant and sorry she hadn't looked a little further, for someone with more to offer her. Maureen was wrong. If that happened, if Shelby gave him a few years and then came to her senses and walked away, it was going to hurt a lot more. A *lot* more.

She spoke quietly to his back. "Listen, I have no idea what possessed Felicia to do the things she did. She could have had everything with you—finding a man who knows what he wants and cherishes it every day, that's not easy. But she was so foolish and shortsighted. On a stupid whim she gave it up. Maybe she thought she had logical reasons. She had a chance to have it all. But she walked away from a good man, a good life, a hopeful future."

Luke turned around and there was anger in his eyes. "Stop it," he said. "You don't have to draw me any more pictures. I *know* Shelby is nothing like Felicia."

"I wasn't talking about Shelby," Maureen said. "I was talking about *you*. In this case you'd be the one in love who, on a stupid, illogical whim, throws it away. Think, Luke. Don't throw away the best chance at happiness you might ever get."

"Stop it," he said softly, in a desperate plea.

Maureen wasn't easily intimidated. "You've held on to this anger way too long. It's time to let yourself have the life you really want."

They locked eyes for long seconds. Then Sean bounced out of the house, all smiles. "Well, we ready to head out? Mom? Luke?"

It took a second for them to recover themselves. "Sure am,"

Maureen said, handing off her coffee cup to Sean. "Just let me go down to the river and say goodbye to Art."

"Yeah, I should do that, too," Sean said, handing Luke the cup. "Then let's make tracks, huh?"

Luke waited by Sean's car until they came back. His mother was smiling that enormous smile of hers, green eyes twinkling. "Luke, honey, it was wonderful. I love your house and cabins, your town, your new friends. I think if you decided to stay right here, you might like it." She went to him and gave him a kiss on the cheek. "Thank you so much for everything. I'll talk to you soon."

"Real soon," Luke said. "Sean, drive carefully. Get her there in one piece."

Luke was brooding long after his mother and brother left. He knew what point she was trying to make. He could even give her credit for making some sense, but what she didn't understand was that even if he could work up the courage to take that kind of risk, it was impossible for him to put Shelby through a challenge like that. She was young and fresh. He was not. He was seasoned, bruised and holding back how he felt was by now a habit.

He could've worked on one of the cabins, but he didn't. He puttered. There weren't even breakfast dishes to clean up—his mother had done that. He laundered the sheets and towels. He wandered from the house to the porch and back again. At one point he saw Art come back from the river. He waved at Luke and went into his cabin for a while, then back to the river. Lunch break? Luke thought about getting him a little more gear just to ring his chimes—maybe a canvas vest, a creel, a fancy fisherman's hat.

Luke loved his mother so much. He held her in such high esteem, and he hated that he'd disappointed her. It wasn't a question of what he wanted, it was a matter of survival—didn't she get that?

She really annoyed him with her theories. He had to remind himself where she was coming from. She wasn't like women of his generation. She'd been considering the convent, although he'd seen pictures of her and she was a beautiful young woman; boys and men must have been after her all the time. But, being the prude she was, she hadn't slipped an inch. Although she wouldn't speak of indelicate things, Luke's father had said their mother was pure as the driven snow. Luke took that to mean a twenty-three-year-old virgin, a rarity in these days. Luke didn't run into women like that.

Until lately.

But that was a whole different thing—Shelby. She wasn't necessarily a virgin because she had been saving herself, but because she'd had no opportunities. That was what Shelby needed now—opportunities. Education, career, experience and, yes, a few more men so she could learn for herself what worked best for her. It wasn't a good idea for a young woman of Shelby's intelligence, curiosity and gratitude for the good things in life to get herself stuck. Just because Luke was the first didn't make him the best. God, he was hardly the best....

Still, there was a part of him that wished his mother's fantasy could be real—that you accidentally find this person, this one ideal person, and you dive in, not wasting a minute, and make her yours. And then everything for the next thirty or forty or fifty years is just one big lovefest. Unfortunately, it wasn't just his bad experience he drew from. He'd been around a lot of men the last twenty years and too few of them had relationships that held strong; too many had been fucked over by a woman. Being a big tough guy, he didn't get into emotional conversations with men by habit, but as a matter of fact he'd held a few young, sobbing soldiers as they grieved lost love.

The same men who could go into a bloody battle fearlessly could be brought to their knees by a woman who couldn't keep her promises.

His mother didn't know what she was talking about. His mother didn't understand him, he groused. She meant well, wanted the best for him, but she was pie-in-the-sky delusional.

And then Shelby drove up to his house. It was early afternoon and Shelby had known his mother and brother were scheduled to leave in the morning. She came. He stood from his chair on the porch and watched her get out of her Jeep, her hair full and free as he liked it. She wore tight jeans and boots, a down vest over her turtleneck sweater, and she stood there beside her car, smiling at him. She could have waited for him to show up at Jack's, or to call her and tell her the coast was clear. But she didn't wait, she came.

"Where's Art?" she asked.

"Fishing."

"Good," she said, grinning.

He forgot everything he'd been dwelling on. He smiled at her and never even felt all the tension drain from his face, his neck and shoulders. He laughed and hooked his thumbs in the pockets of his jeans. She slammed her car door and ran up the porch steps; she lunged at him, her arms around his neck, her legs around his waist, her lips on his lips. She laughed against his open mouth, but only for a moment.

He devoured that sweet mouth, holding her up. He couldn't move from his spot on the porch. All that was important to him at the moment was having her in his arms, tasting her, smelling her, feeling his mouth on her mouth. "I'll slow down," he promised against her lips. "I'll take some time."

"It's okay," she said in her own breathless whisper. "You don't have to slow down for me, because I'm in a big hurry."

"Oh God," he whispered, weak. "Are you sure?"

"Sure I'm dying for you, Luke."

"God," he said again. And he found his way into the house. He carried her like that straight to the bedroom and fell with her onto the bed.

"I couldn't get away any sooner," she said while pulling at his clothes. He began to peel away her clothes at the same time. The vest and sweater went first; his shirt was flung from the bed to the floor. "And I wasn't exactly sure when—"

He stilled her with his mouth on hers, hungry and aching.

She wrestled free of his lips and said, "Boots, Luke. We have to get rid of the boots."

He laughed a loud, lusty laugh. "Be interesting, doing it in only boots. Let's take off the jeans and put the boots back on..."

"Someone could get hurt," she said. "Hurry up."

He thought he'd die, having her like this, rushing him, needing him. "This an emergency, honey?" he asked her.

"Oh, man," she said, tugging at his lips. "Boots. Take care of the boots!"

He got an evil, amused glint in his eyes. He pulled off his boots, then hers, very slowly. It was fun, Shelby in a wild state. Holding her pleading eyes in his hot gaze, he grabbed her wrists, held them over her head and gently kissed her body, on top of her bra, on her belly, on her chin, on her neck. She laughed at him. "Will you *please!*"

"Need something?" he asked teasingly.

"I've been turned on all day, just waiting for you to be alone again."

He leisurely unsnapped her jeans and slipped his hand down over her flat belly.

"Luke!" she scolded. "We can play later!"

It made him laugh. He released her arms, pulled off the bra, pulled down the jeans and got rid of his own. Against her lips he said, "I'm going to last two minutes."

"I think I have one minute in me," she answered.

He lifted her legs for her, teased her a little bit, and then he went in for the kill. But Shelby was way ahead of him, hungrier than he was, which seemed impossible to him. Her legs came around his waist and within seconds she was astounding him with a shattering climax, sending him reeling into another world. He groaned low in his throat while he held on, letting her ride it out. And when she was on the way down from the experience, he let go. A week of tension, worry, doubt and paranoia pulsed out of him. He was in the only place he wanted to be.

Then there was the part he'd come to love as much—holding her while she returned to the world, conscious of their surroundings, relieved and appeased, flushed, happy. She laughed softly. "That was embarrassing," she said. "What have you done to me?"

"Nothing you didn't do right back to me," he said. He gave her a kiss. "I missed you."

"Yeah, but it was a good week," she said. "Whew. We're too new to have separations like that, I think."

"I hated my mother every night," he said as he slipped out of her.

"Aw. She's great. You're lucky, you have a wonderful mother."

He settled onto his side and pulled her close. Funny, the thing that came to his mind first was that he had learned more about Shelby's life by listening to her talk to his mother than he had from their time together, which had been intense and intimate. Something about that made him feel bad.

"Tell me about your mother," he said, hugging her.

"She was fantastic. If my mother had lived, our mothers would have liked each other. Before she got sick, she was such a bundle of energy. She was beautiful—I'll show you pictures sometime. She always worked. She had to, of course—my dad left us before I was even born. My Uncle Walt was a huge help, but still... Even though she worked full-time, she still made it to every concert or game or school thing I had going on. Not only did she make time for me to have girlfriends over, we were like chums. Everyone else hated their mothers, they were fighting all the time, but I was shopping and going to movies with mine." She got a little sniffly and said, "I'm so damn grateful we had that when I was a teenager. It's not the usual way, you know."

"I know," he said, brushing her hair away from her face.

"You do? Were you fighting with your parents?"

"I have four brothers. Everyone was fighting. We still fight."

"Aw, how can you say that, now? Sean is so sweet...."

"Stop saying nice things about him," Luke said. "He's a troublemaker. So tell me some more."

"You sure? It's boring."

"Not to me," he said.

"Well, after she slowed down and needed me, we couldn't get out much together anymore, but that didn't keep us from having fun. We both loved to read—I read to her till late in the night. I read all of *Gone with the Wind* and *Anna Karenina*, even though we'd both read them before. We loved those old, rich, deep, complicated romances. And we used to watch chick flicks—and cry. Then we'd talk about them—about what the girls did that was stupid, what the guys did that was inadequate, and of course what they did totally right. We'd develop our 'perfect man' fantasies around those characters. We were kind of alike, you know. She hadn't had a perfect man, either. We'd talk about the best things a man could say to just bring you to your knees. Like the Jerry Maguire line—you know?"

"Who's Jerry Maguire?" he asked, running his hand over her bare shoulder.

"Tom Cruise," she said.

"He's short."

Shelby grinned at him. "So am I."

"Stop," he said, laughing. "What did he say? What was the line? I'm always looking for a good line."

"You *complete* me."

Luke's eyebrows rose. "Really? What does that mean?"

"You make me *whole*..." He frowned at her. "I'm not a whole person without you. You know."

"Oh," he said. "I don't think I could pull that one off."

She laughed. "We used to make up our own best lines. And talk about what the perfect man would be like."

"What was your perfect man like?" he asked.

"Nothing like you," she said. "But then everything changed and it became you...."

"What was your perfect line?" he asked.

"It's just silly...."

"No, tell me. I want to know."

"It's just a line. A fantasy line. You can't steal it—it wouldn't be the same if I fed it to you. And if you use it on some other woman, I'm going to tell my Uncle Walt you did something *horrible* to me so he kills you."

"Shelby, we're naked and just had unbelievable sex—death threats right now are rude. Mind your manners. Tell me the perfect line."

She was quiet for a minute. She chewed on her bottom lip a little, thinking it over. Then in a very soft voice she said, "You're all I need. To be happy." Then she lifted her eyelids and connected with his eyes. She smiled shyly. "Just a line. Writing screenplays or romantic novels was once on my to-do dream list."

He ran his hand over her honey hair. He kissed her temple. "Shelby," he said softly, "I think you're all I need to be happy."

She looked at him for a long time. She smiled into his eyes.

"In my fantasy, he doesn't say 'I think.'" Then she laughed and said, "So—did your mother convince you to go to Phoenix for Christmas? She said she was going to try."

"I might go—but for two days. I'm not doing this five-day thing again. I can't take it when we're back together. You almost killed me." He grinned. "Do you realize you went from self-conscious little virgin to aggressor? Shelby, you've come out of your shell. Way out."

"Maybe you brought me out, ever think of that?"

"You must've been ready."

"Oh, I was ready," she said. She put a hand against his cheek. "For you."

It was the Saturday following Thanksgiving and Walt wasn't sure he could remember ever lying in bed with a naked woman in the middle of the afternoon. When he was a young man, not only was the army working him to death, the first baby came along soon after he and Peg married and from that point on their lives were entwined with family and the demands of a military officer's life. When he became a general, he also had an aide and some household staff. It wasn't that they were inhibited, neither of them were, but the second they tried something as daring as showering together, one of their teenagers would come home unexpectedly and bang on their door, yelling, "What are you *doing* in there?"

There was definitely something to be said for being consenting adults of a certain age. He chuckled to himself.

"Something's funny?" Muriel asked, nuzzling closer.

"Yeah. You and me. Stealing sex in the afternoon with a couple of lazy dogs sleeping at the foot of the bed. This is good, Muriel. Good. And I'm glad there are no ceiling mirrors."

She laughed at him. "Me, too. Let's not think about what we must look like."

"Maybe not what we used to look like, but you still have the body of a girl. You do."

"Know what I like best about you?" she asked. "Your intelligence. Even though you're a liar, you know exactly what to say."

"Well, this might be the wrong thing to say, but I'm going to say it anyway. I haven't had sex since Peg died. Until you."

She tilted her chin up, looking at him. "Walt, I haven't had sex since *before* Peg died."

"Really?" he asked, surprised. "That's amazing. You're made for sex."

She frowned. "There was probably a compliment in there somewhere."

"I'm serious. You're a wonderful lover. Partner. That's not too encroaching, is it? Partner?"

"It doesn't cross the line, but it rushes right up to it."

"You don't want to think of us as casual...."

"I don't," she said. "Casual is coffee or drinks. Intimate is—"

The phone rang in her bedroom. She rolled away to pick it up and Walt grabbed her arm, pulling her back. "Intimate is what?"

She smiled at him. "Very, very nice. May I answer the phone now?"

"Any of your close friends or family members dying?" he wanted to know.

"Not to my knowledge."

"Then how about we don't—"

"Walt, I'm answering my phone," she said, rolling away from him. "Hello?" she said into the phone. "Hi, Jack, what's up? Oh really? Is his name Mason? Yes, you can give him directions, he's my agent. And Jack—thanks for asking first. That was thoughtful of you. He could be anyone, you know." When she rolled back to Walt, she just sighed. "A man in a funny hat driving a Bentley just showed up at Jack's asking if he knew where I lived. Mason."

"What's he doing here?"

"Hell if I know. But I suspect he's got some big idea or script or something and thought if he pressured me in person, it would make a difference. It won't."

"Why'd you tell Jack to give him directions?"

"All right, now listen. Mason can annoy me with his focus on my career even after I'm trying to get away from movies, but he's been a good and loyal friend for over thirty-five years and—"

"And an ex-husband," Walt pointed out.

"We hardly notice that," she said. "Seriously, I owe Mason. He's gotten me out of some tight spots. My business can get real complicated. And he might get a little zooped up over projects that aren't all they appear to be, but if he ever sees that something isn't going as it should for my career, he steps in like a lion and gets it handled. So let's get dressed and be cordial. Hmm?"

"Tell you what," Walt said. "Let's meet him in our birthday suits so he knows how it is with us. How about that?"

"That's just plain cruel. You're the only one I plan to subject to that sight. Now, be civil to Mason. He'll go away much sooner if you just play nice and let me handle him."

"I'm going to slip into the shower," Walt said.

"Oh, come on. You're being a little obvious, don't you think?" she asked, drawing up her jeans.

"When he asks who's in the shower, you'll say, Walt—my beyond-casual and not-legally-partnered boyfriend who isn't going away without a fight anytime soon."

"Fine." She laughed. "Be sure you're dressed when you come downstairs."

Muriel let Mason in the front door ten minutes later. She

hugged him; he fussed over her beauty, though she wore no makeup and hadn't had a manicure or pedicure in months. He was shorter than her, wore a cashmere sports coat, Gucci shoes and a burgundy beret on his balding head. He had a salt-and-pepper beard and crystal blue eyes that were looking a little too alive. He either had a special script or was on crack.

By the time she was serving him a cup of tea in her brand-new kitchen, Walt appeared. Dressed.

"Mason, I'd like you to meet Walt Booth, my—"

"Significant other," he said, putting out his hand. He glanced askance at Muriel with a lifted brow, challenging her. She just shook her head and chuckled.

"Walt is my neighbor and very good friend. Very. Good."

Walt helped himself to a beer from her refrigerator, demonstrating that he was not a guest.

"Now, Mason," Muriel said. "Let's skip the suspense. What brings you all the way to Virgin River."

"Okay, here it is. I hoped you'd come to the house for Thanksgiving so we could talk about it, but since you didn't... I have an Oscar script, written for you. It's a romantic comedy, but it's got some serious teeth. Jack Nicholson wants you to costar. Only you. He's prepared to go to contract if you'll take the part. This is your shot, Muriel. This is it. I know I've thrown you a lot of crap that you turned down, probably wisely, but you have to look at this one. The producers are loaded and are courting three of the best Oscar-winning directors in the business."

Dead silence and absence of movement reigned. Muriel knew the fact that she said nothing caused Walt to stiffen nervously. He was no doubt accustomed to her saying no immediately.

"You brought the script?"

"Yes. Read it. At least talk to them. No matter how you

feel about working, if I let you turn this down without thinking it through, I should be jailed as a fraud."

She stood. "Well, then. Let's get you comfortable in the
guesthouse. Walt, stay put. I'll be right back. This way,
Mason," she said, exiting the kitchen and leading him through
the front door.

She took Mason and a couple of suitcases to her old abode
and came back ten minutes later with a script. Walt was seated
at the table, waiting.

Without preamble, she said, "Here's how this kind of thing
usually goes. I could love everything about this project and
after I make a commitment, Nicholson and the directors all
disappear and we have to make do with whoever will step up
to the plate. When I was actively working, I could afford to
take chances like that—we'd always salvage a decent film in
the end. But without even looking at this," she said, holding
up the script, "I'm damn sure not leaving my horses or my
new house or *you* for something that isn't carved in stone. Do
you understand, Walt?"

"He's staying?" was all Walt said in reply.

Mason Fielding only stayed overnight and at midmorn-
ing the next day was on his way back to L.A. Early in the afternoon, Walt rode Liberty up to Muriel's house and waited
while she saddled her Palomino mare, Sweety. Buff had to
stay behind, but Luce was out in front, blazing their trail along
the river until Muriel cut loose that piercing whistle of hers,
bringing the Lab back to heel.

The air was cold; the steam rose from the horses' nostrils.
There was no snow yet, but if the clouds rolled in, the air was
cold enough to support a nice white cover.

"Did you look at that script?" Walt asked her.

"Uh-huh. Read it twice."

"Twice?" he asked, astonished.

"It's not a shooting script. It's just a hundred and thirty-five pages of dialogue. I read down the middle."

"Any good?"

"Very good. It could use a tweak or two, but it's inspired. The writer's been coming along. This is pretty much what everyone's been waiting for from her."

"Her?"

"A woman, yes. This would be only her second feature film and her first was highly acclaimed. She was a very young playwright when she began her career. Now she's about my age."

"Hmm," he said, knowing so little about this business. "Good enough to consider?"

"Good enough to talk about considering it. I haven't said anything to Mason yet. I'm still in the pondering stage."

"When you say talk about considering it, what does that involve?"

"Getting all the principals together in meetings, ironing out details, determining stars and supporting cast, directors, etcetera."

"Does that mean going back to L.A.?" he asked.

"Maybe not. Actors and directors are often on location when deals are being set up. Conference calls work just fine. This is the kind of script that, done well, could be everything. But if a couple of things slip through the cracks or the right cast can't come together for the production, could be just another mildly entertaining film."

"Aren't a lot of scripts like that?"

"Not really, no. You know what most of them are going to turn out to be from the get-go. This one really does have great potential. But I think the thing that appeals to me the most—I could play myself."

"As in—yourself?" he asked.

"An unfancy woman who lives in the country and isn't crazy about a lot of Hollywood flash. I think the script flirts with being autobiographical. It's about a writer who hates Hollywood and lives on a nonworking farm with animals who are pets—dogs, horses, goats. Because she's gifted, an actor comes to her asking her to write a script that will make his career before it's too late—he's no longer young. They have nothing and everything in common and the relationship is complex while they hammer out a script together—sometimes hilarious, sometimes very sentimental and touching. Passionate in places. Lots of emotion. And no backless gowns or jewelry."

"You're thinking about it," he said.

"I can't help myself. I've always seen myself in roles like this, with the right people involved, but they rarely presented themselves. It's a life-transition film, like *On Golden Pond* with slightly younger lead actors."

"Making a comeback?" he asked. "A starlet returning to the big screen?"

She shot him a look of horror. She reined in her horse. "All right, let's get something straight. I'm not an aging starlet and I wouldn't consider it a comeback. I'm an actor and to me this is serious work. A challenge I'm up to. In my business the opportunities that are truly good are rare. But I'm no aging starlet, Walt. I work for a living. And the job isn't easy. But the rewards, if you do the job well, can be good. Not the least of which is pride."

"You'll have to cut me some slack," he said. "I don't know much about your business. I didn't say you were an aging starlet."

"You thought it," she said.

"You can't prove that."

She let out her breath. Slowly, as if deciding on something. She eased up on the reins.

"Hmm. Sounds like you'd like to do it," he ventured.

She was quiet for a moment. Then she said, "Like the main character, I wouldn't like being away from here." She looked at him. "I wouldn't like being away from you, either, and don't let that go to your head."

That brought a small smile to his lips. And then he laughed. "Well, I'll be."

"Inflated your ego, did I?"

"Not that," he said. "I had a moment of déjà vu. I don't know how much you know about the military, Muriel, but each special training program or promotion or new assignment incurs another commitment. To go from captain to major gives the army four more years of you. Go to flight school, sign up for four more years."

"I see. Your déjà vu?"

"The first twenty years were a no-brainer. I already had eight and owed four more when I met Peg. When I hit my twenty and could retire on a colonel's pension, Vanni was eleven and Tom wasn't even a twinkle in my eye. I had the potential to go further and, like your script, it could all fall apart at any moment if the right players weren't on board. Or I could go all the way. Not only that, my assignments were getting more complicated—the Pentagon, war zones, attaché to diplomatic service abroad. Every time I reached one of those forks, I'd sit down with Peg. I'd tell her what was involved, tried to be frank about the sacrifices that not only I but the whole family would have to make, and I'd always wrap it up by saying, 'I can stop right now and be happy. If you ask me to say no, I will.'"

Muriel was gloomily quiet. She wasn't giving him that kind of choice. Even though she liked her life right now, she'd decide for herself.

"Now, Peg, she was a very independent woman, but in

some ways she was dependent on me. Naturally. As a partner, a father to her children, a provider—she needed me. And
I needed her. In the end she would always say—you have to
fulfill every ambition you have, go where you can do the most
good, and we'll stand behind you while you do. And she never
once made me regret it. Sometimes it was damn hard on her."

Muriel chewed on that for a moment. "She must have been
a remarkable woman."

"She was," Walt said easily. He reached over to her and
grabbed her hand. "So are you, Muriel. A remarkable woman.
It's my turn to say it. You have to fulfill every ambition. I
wouldn't like being away from you, either. But I'll be right
here, rooting for you every step of the way. Proudly."

She looked at him with absolute love, though neither of
them had uttered such a binding word. Her eyes glistened and
she had to purse her lips to keep them from trembling. Men
had said wonderful things to her over the years, lavish compli-
ments about her beauty and wit, but never anything like this.
She blinked. She took a deep breath. Then she said, "Stop it.
I don't cry. Not unless the director says, 'Cry.'"

Walt laughed at her and leaned over, sidling up against
her and, with an arm around her shoulders, pulled her near.
"Would you have to be naked in this one?"

"Briefly. Would that bother you?"

He grinned devilishly. "Not in the way you think."

14

For the couple of weeks following Thanksgiving, things around Virgin River were far more hectic than usual and every hand was needed. It started with the erection of a huge Christmas tree between the bar and the boarded-up church. As Luke understood it, this was only the second year the town had put up such a tree, and it was a major project. Every available man was needed to chop it, haul it into town, stand it up and, with the use of a rented cherry picker, string the lights and decorate the highest parts. It was trimmed in red, white and blue and hung with gold stars and military-unit patches. It was meant to be a tribute to the men and women who stood the watch, and when Luke saw what they were doing, it made him feel, without a doubt, he'd chosen the right town. It was the first time he'd felt truly at home in years.

Right after the tree lighting, there were three new residences finished and three families to relocate before Christmas. Luke was more than willing to help.

Preacher and Paige had to be moved back into their new enlarged quarters behind the bar. Then Paul transferred his small family along with furniture into his house on the other side of the general's stable. And finally, the Valenzuelas were moved into their new home next door to the Sheridans. Throughout this process, Brie was much in evidence, staying busy while she got ready for two major events—moving into her own new house and giving birth. A number of people watched over Brie protectively, making sure she wasn't taking on too much. Mike Valenzuela was always within earshot of his wife and Jack kept a close eye on his little sister.

Brie had put the last piece of folded clothing in the last drawer when her first labor pain hit—two weeks before Christmas. Jack, almost as excited as if it was his own child coming into the world, told everyone who came in the bar that Brie had been in labor most of the day. Mike called him with updates. Whoever heard of a bartender reporting on centimeters and time between contractions? But Jack did.

That's when things took a crazy spin that Luke allowed himself to be swept up in. Shelby was looking after Mel's little ones so she could attend Brie in childbirth, so Luke happened to be at the bar when the call came that Brie was in the last stages of labor. The place came alive. "Mel says she's getting close," Jack reported. "Let's go!"

Luke had no idea what was happening. He meant to quietly slip away so these people could live their lives, when Preacher called him to the kitchen and started snapping orders. "Luke, help me pack this stuff up. You can take the food so I can help Paige load up the kids. Jack will get some good liquor and cigars. Paige—call Paul and Vanni and tell them it's happening. They'll make sure the general gets the word." Luke had no choice but to do as he was told; he boxed up what Preacher pulled out of the freezer, refrigerator and pantry—barbecue, buns, chips, pickles, creamy coleslaw, pie. He added salmon fillets, seasoned and ready to broil and a big container of rice and peas. A bag of premade salad and a big cheesecake. He saw Jack hurry past him with a box of liquor and cigars. It took only a few minutes before Preacher said, "See you out there."

"Where?" Luke asked dumbly.

"Brie and Mike's. We're having a party."

"A what?"

Preacher drew a patient breath. "Brie's having the baby. We all go when there's a baby, if it's not the middle of the night. But they've barely moved in—I don't know what they have for food and drink. I think there's a little more than usual here. We can leave some behind."

"Wait a minute," Luke said. "Isn't she in the hospital?"

"No," Preacher answered, as if confused by the question. "She's going to have the baby with Mel and Dr. Stone at home. Enough talking."

So he went, and all the way there he was thinking, *I hope they don't make me get too close to this thing.* He decided straight off, he wasn't sticking around. This whole baby business wasn't his cup of tea.

He found the house filled with people—Vanni and Paige were in the great room with small children—one in a swing, two in playpens, young Christopher on the couch watching an animated movie. Jack held David balanced on his hip in a kitchen full of men. Preacher was setting up pans on the stove, the general was mixing drinks and Paul was putting out small plates, napkins and utensils. Luke put down the large box of food and said he'd just get going.

"Oh, hell no, you're not going anywhere," Jack said. "My sister's having a baby, her first, and this is the cheering section."

"Wait a minute here," he said. "I'm not real big on babies. We've been over this—I have no idea what to do with them."

"Well, for God's sake, we're not going to make you do anything." Jack laughed. "You know how to eat, raise a glass, smoke a cigar? The delivery team is taking care of the messy stuff."

"Shouldn't it be real quiet around here? Fewer people?"

"We'll be quiet, we'll stay out of the way." Preacher handed Jack a bottle for David. "This guy's going to break in the new crib. Say good-night, David." The boy had the bottle in his mouth that fast, leaned his head against Jack's shoulder sleepily and opened and closed the fingers of one pudgy little hand, holding his bottle with the other.

"What if she…" Luke couldn't go on.

"What if she what?"

"Screams or something," he said squeamishly.

Jack put his free arm around Luke's shoulders. "See, you need to be here, buddy. It's time you learn about the cycle of life. You never know, this could happen to you someday."

"This is not happening to me someday. I'm way past all this."

A few male heads came up. There was some subdued laughter. "Is that so?" Jack said. "Cry me a river, pal, I was over forty when Mel tripped me up. We're all about the same age around here, except Preacher. He's still a pup, even though he looks older than the rest of us."

Walt handed Luke a drink. "I was forty-four when Tom was born. I think I'm holding up all right, to tell the truth."

"You're going to have to come up with a better excuse," Jack said. "Besides, I've been wanting to ask you something."

"Yeah? What?"

"Well, I have a situation. We usually go to Sacramento for Christmas, but with no doctor in town and Brie just delivering, my family is coming here. There's a ton of them. I have the guesthouse for my dad, a couple of rooms if we double up the kids, and the cabin is free again. And this is a new Valenzuela baby coming—wanna bet we'll be seeing a ton of Mexicans around here? Mike's family is bigger than mine. Buddy—we are out of space. What's the status of those cabins? Got any ready to rent?"

Luke lifted his eyebrows. This was unexpected. "Tell you what I've got," he said. "They're habitable and the new appliances have been delivered but not installed, they need inside paint, and furniture has been ordered, not delivered. Thanks to Paul, all new roofs, windows and doors. The countertops and cupboards are installed, but I'm still working on baseboards. I put in new hot-water heaters."

"If you had a hand with the paint and appliances, think you could free up a couple by Christmas?" Jack asked.

"I don't see why not," Luke said. "If furniture can be delivered quickly. But, Jack, even with your help, that would be a push."

Paul moved closer. "Where's your furniture coming from? Maybe we can pick it up with one of the company trucks."

"Eureka. Beds, sleeper sofas, small tables and chairs, etcetera. It was the next thing after paint and appliances."

"Then we'll get it done," Jack said. "That would be perfect. Otherwise, we're going to have to hang all these people from the trees. Be right back," he said, taking David off to bed.

Then suddenly Shelby appeared in the kitchen. She was smiling a sweet, secret smile, a very special light in her eyes. "I didn't think you'd be here," she said.

"Neither did I."

To the men in the kitchen she said, "Mel said to tell you it won't be much longer. And she said you are *not* to get drunk."

"We don't get drunk at birthing parties," Preacher said indignantly. Then he looked over his shoulder and said, "Except Paul. He got toasted after Matt was born, but that was a whole different thing."

Luke was focused on Shelby's smiling face. "What are you doing?" he asked.

"I was helping with Mel's kids so she could be with Brie, but now that Vanni and Paige are here, I can observe," she said. "Brie said it would be all right. I've never seen a birth."

"You're up to that?" he wanted to know.

"Of course," she said. She gave him a kiss on the cheek. "I'll see you later."

Luke made fast work of his first drink and was nursing his second, through many jokes and soft, respectful laughter, when Mike came into the great room holding a very small bundle wrapped in a pink receiving blanket. Mike went to the women first—Paige and Vanni. While they were murmuring, smiling, beaming, the men moved in a crowd out of the kitchen to have a look at what Mike had for himself. The look on Mike's face was a combination of exhaustion and exhilaration—just what would happen to a guy who'd just helped and worried his way through labor with his wife while she produced this, his first child. His smile was huge; his eyes were bright inside and weary on the outside.

And that's when Luke started to remember. So long ago. So deep and buried. He migrated to Mike and the baby, smiling sentimentally, gently tugging back the pink wrap to get a better look at her. He even heard himself say, "Good for you, man."

When Felicia first told him there was going to be a baby, she'd been real upset. It was unplanned, she wasn't ready. But he had felt something inside him grow proudly. She told him to keep it to himself, she didn't want everyone to know before she even got used to the idea. But back then he'd been so bonded with his men, his boys, he wasn't into secret-keeping, especially about things like this. He told them all; they toasted him, got him a little drunk and drove him home.

Against her wishes, he'd called his mom and dad, his brothers. He had been all puffed up on testosterone pride, life had taken on new meaning for him. He never even tried to understand her cranky behavior—he was a young buck with a baby coming and she was pregnant—what was to understand? He put up with her pissy mood; he tried to be patient. He watched her begin to grow.

She told him it was a boy and it seemed like seconds after he learned the news, he got the call. Somalia. But it wasn't supposed to be long—it was a peacekeeping mission. They'd make a presence there with the Marine Corps and he'd be back quickly. He felt he could do anything because waiting for him were his woman, his son. That euphoria stayed with him for so long, he assumed that was the way all men felt when they struck oil.

But it was ugly in Somalia; lives were lost in Mogadishu and it was in many ways a miracle there hadn't been more casualties. When he got home the first thing he could fill his eyes with was his wife—she was huge. He should've looked at her eyes first, but he couldn't help himself.

"It's not yours," she said. He wasn't sure, but he thought she said that before she even said hello. "I didn't want to tell you while you were on a mission, but you're back safe now. We're over. I'm leaving. I'm going with the father. I'm sorry it happened this way. You shouldn't have been bragging about it. I told you not to."

In a flash he wondered how that came to be his fault—being proud? At first he thought she was joking, some really sick joke. Then he thought there was a mistake; when had she had time for another man? He'd been making love to her con-

stantly. Next he thought she couldn't have done that to him—
not while he poured every cell of his body into adoring her.

He wanted to kill someone. Her, maybe. Or the father, who
turned out to be an officer in his command, a man whose orders he was obligated to follow. A man who'd been with them
in Somalia, knowing every day that he had a baby coming
with another man's wife.

The months that followed blurred as he drank too much,
avoided people, got in random fights, buried himself in a
dark, black loneliness and wished he was dead. Before he got
to remembering the scandal, the shame of having been made
to look like a complete fool, the sympathy and pity, he felt a
hand on his shoulder. "How about that, huh?" Jack said to
him, bringing him back. "When have you seen anything as
sweet as that?"

Luke pushed it all back down again. Thirteen years had
made him very adept at that—shoving it underwater where
it should all just drown. He smiled. "Lotta black hair on that
little head," he said.

He briefly remembered how the happiest day of his life had
been when his transfer orders finally came and he could get
away from Felicia and her new partner. By that time he was
lucky he had a career left in the army. He'd been completely
out of control there for a while and had been disciplined more
than once. Given that he'd performed heroically in Somalia
and came home to a wife, nine months pregnant and leaving
him, his commanders cut him a little slack. Moving gave him
a second chance, helped him pull it together.

He wanted to leave the Valenzuela house; he was exhausted.
But there was that bold press of men, converging on him,
catching him up in their celebration. While he'd been drown-
ing in the past, Muriel St. Claire had arrived and was now
gathered with the men. There was food to eat, gossip to pass

around. He was eventually pushed out on the porch where cigars were clipped and lit. Rather than going with the women, Muriel stayed with the men, accepting her cigar and drink, making them chuckle. If they were a batch of women, the childbirth stories would start, but there were only a few such comments; Jack had delivered his own children, Preacher had almost fainted when Paige gave birth. Dr. John Stone joined them for a cigar, and talk went back to all the work left to be done to get Luke's cabins ready for the Sheridan and Valenzuela clans to hit town for the holidays.

Luke had no idea if he'd been unusually quiet. He glanced at his watch and was stunned to see it was almost midnight—that was a little scary. Hours had passed and he'd been in the past, not real conscious of what had been going on around him. Then Shelby was beside him, looking up at him. "She's beautiful, isn't she?"

He put an arm around her shoulders and laughed. "Shelby, babies are like puppies, there's no such thing as an ugly one." He put his cigar in the ash can. "I'm going to head home."

"I'm not needed here anymore. Want some company?" she asked him.

He gave her shoulders a squeeze. That was exactly what he needed—someone soft, warm and safe. This young woman had an uncanny ability to make everything in his life feel right. Good. "You bet I do," he said.

15

Jack Sheridan must have been more serious about needing room for his family than Luke realized. The day after Brie's childbirth, he showed up in the morning with Paul and six men in three pickups. It was the sound of the trucks arriving that brought Luke out of cabin two. As the men clambered out, he grinned. "Looks like a barn raising."

"Might as well get it done. Show us what and where," Jack said.

First Luke showed them Art's cabin, which was finished. Luke was no decorator, but it had all new furnishings, appliances and fresh paint. Art had a new queen-size bed, a table with four chairs and a large chair with ottoman and reading lamp. There was a new stove and microwave, a small refrigerator that slipped under the kitchen counter. It boasted wooden blinds on the windows and a patterned area rug. Art was all stocked with dishes, glasses, sheets and towels; in the large bathroom were a small washer, dryer and closets. All the men walked through, poking around, nodding.

"Luke, this came out real nice," Jack said. "You did a fine job here."

"I'm no professional, but they've come a long way since we bought 'em."

He showed them a partially finished cabin—new baseboards, paint and appliances, but that was as far as he'd gotten. Then he showed them an unfinished cabin. The appliances sat in the middle of the room, uninstalled. Blinds that he ordered were still in long boxes, ready to be hung after painting, area rugs were rolled against the wall and cans of paint were stacked next to a couple of folded tarps.

"Looks simple enough," Paul remarked. "Two days. Maybe four, if we need extra supplies."

"Four days?" Luke repeated, stunned.

"It's all moving and cosmetic. We're kind of fast." He grinned. "We do this a lot more than you do."

"Since there have only been one or two painters here, there are only the two tarps," Luke pointed out.

"Not a problem, we came prepared, even brought some baseboards in case you didn't have enough. Now, if you're not worried we'll screw it up, this might be a good day for you to go over to Eureka and set up a pickup for that furniture and get anything else you might need for these cabins."

"Leave you working?" he asked. "I couldn't do that to you."

"Wait till you see my family. And the Valenzuelas," Jack said. "Go. Buy sheets and towels."

Luke thought about this for a very short time—he had other important errands in Eureka. It was high time he plunged into an investigation of Art's job and group home there. He had to know the man's past in order to help with his future. Buying sheets, pillows, towels and dishes wouldn't take any time at all. "You sure? Can you keep an eye on Art in case he gets a little excited with all the people? Sometimes he's too much help, you know."

"Sure, he'll be fine. Where is the good man?"

"If he's not here, he's at the river." Luke grinned. "I'm not getting so much help since I bought him that rod and reel, but the freezer's full of fish. I have a feeling some of it's going to be coming your way at the bar."

"We never turn down handouts," Jack said, hefting a ladder out of the truck.

As Luke stood and watched, they all started hauling tarps, ladders, toolboxes, brushes and rollers out of the truck beds. He wandered down to the river and found Art.

"Hey, Art," he said. "How are they biting today?"

"Okay," he said, throwing out a line and slowly reeling it in.

"Jack and Paul and some men have come to work on the cabins." He laughed at the way Art's head jerked toward him and his eyes lit up. "I'm sure they'd want you to help out if you feel like it."

"Do they want me to?" he asked, pulling in his line.

"Sure, but you'll have to let them tell you what they need the most help with. Huh?"

"Okay," he said, grinning happily.

"I'm going to run over to Eureka to get some supplies. Need anything?"

He shook his head. "Maybe I'll get a lot done with Jack and Paul," he said.

"I bet you will. Come on, I'll walk back with you."

Art really enjoyed being around people, especially people who treated him with respect, and whenever there were men at work, he eagerly, though shyly, loved to pitch in. It sometimes made him a little clumsy.

Luke only needed an hour or two in some big box stores to load up a couple of carts with things for the cabins. What he really wanted to do was visit a certain little grocery store. He had tried not to dwell on what Art had gone through, but he had managed to have a couple of conversations with him that gave him enough information to figure out where it was. Griffin's Grocery on Simmons Street.

It wasn't a bad grocery store, if a little on the worn side. He glanced around and then grabbed a cart. It took him twenty seconds to pick out a bagger who had Down's and in the produce section there was a woman he asked a few questions and by her slow and difficult answers, grappling for the right word, he suspected some kind of disability. Then he noticed her name tag—Netta. This was someone from the group home Art had said he missed. So Luke asked, "Who's your manager here?"

"Uh-huh, uh-huh, Stan. That's Stan."

"And where would I find Stan?" Luke asked.

She shrugged and said, "Maybe in the back?"

Before Luke had a chance to search Stan out, there was a grocer beside him, asking, "Can I help you with something, sir?"

Luke smiled his most engaging smile. "I wanted to talk to the manager. This lady says that would be Stan."

This was a guy in his late thirties, sharp and clean, articulate, wearing a green apron. He returned the smile. "I'm the assistant manager. Anything I can do to help?"

"Not sure," he said with a shrug. "I just bought a small store in Clear River. Just a little neighborhood store, smaller than this. Thing is—I'm doing it on a shoestring. It's a real good gamble, there's no grocery in there right now," he said, though he had absolutely no idea if there was a grocery store in Clear River. "I'm going to hire a couple of full-time people and a few part-time people. I'm going to have to stay low budget for a while when it comes to payroll. I'm interested in this store's employees. They're nice, they look productive, they're challenged. I wondered how you go about finding employees like them."

The man kept an even expression. "You're right, you're looking for Stan. That's his project. His sister has some kind of home and he gives work to a lot of them. But you might want to think twice about that idea. If they get slow or confused, it can be frustrating. I work real well with them, but…" He shook his head almost sadly. "It bothers some people."

"My younger brother has Down's," Luke lied. "I'm up to speed on the problems."

"You have the patience for that, then?"

"Oh, yeah," he said with a laugh. "He's got a real good job now. Makes him so happy to be managing his own life. The guy has never missed work, does his chores around the house, always has money in the bank… He's a dream come true."

"The work has to be uncomplicated to start—like bagging. Opening boxes. Cleaning up. Even stocking shelves can get too complicated for some of them."

"Everyone has a different level of competence, but I understand what you're saying. So, where's Stan?"

"Follow me," he said. And Luke followed.

The surprises started immediately. First of all, Stan was a young guy, probably not thirty. He was slight—way smaller than Art—but scrappy-looking. He met Luke with a curl to his lip and furrowed black brows, suspicious at once. There weren't a lot of reasons for a man to be suspicious right off unless he was expecting trouble. His size only confused Luke for a second; Stan was the one in charge and knowing Art, he would never hit back, never strike. Art also wouldn't lie. He knew right away—Stan had punched Art.

Luke went through his spiel about the imaginary grocery store again, as convincingly as possible. He skipped the part about having a brother with Down's and concentrated on the hard work, minimum wage, reliable attendance, his need to stay low budget. Stan did a lot of head shaking and shrugging. "I can't help you, buddy," he said. "Eureka is a long way from Clear River and these kids don't drive."

They aren't kids. But Luke kept a smile on his face. He offered to buy Stan a beer to talk a little bit about the grocery business, since they weren't competitors. Stan warmed up at the suggestion of a beer and he agreed—it was time for a break. When they were leaving the grocery, Stan never told anyone where he was going and he glared at everyone. The employees here didn't seem happy, not even the good-natured assistant manager. To just peg Stan as an abusive jerk could be accurate, but it might be too simple. What Luke really wanted to know was what had happened to Art and why Stan hadn't reported him missing.

A glimmer of understanding came with a beer. "My sister has a group home for these retards. I help her out by giving her kids some work," he said. "Keeps 'em busy and out of the house."

"They ever give you trouble?" Luke asked.

"They bug the shit outta me. How many times you gotta show 'em something? Tell 'em? But you're right about one thing—they're cheap and they keep coming back. Maybe you could get someone in Clear River to start up a home. It's not like it's hard. Just has to be clean and pass inspection."

Luke had an instant image of someone completely unqualified to run such a home, doing it for the money, and it made him feel angry and ill. But he said, "That might be doable. I have an ex-wife whose always hurting for money...."

"There's an idea. Get the ex off your payroll."

"Maybe I could talk to your sister? Think she'd tell me how a person goes about that?"

"I'm sure she wouldn't mind. What else has she got to do while all her kids are at work, huh?" He gave an address and some directions, not far from the store. "Just tell her I sent you over, huh?"

"I appreciate it, man. You'll never know."

Luke dropped Stan at the store and immediately followed the directions he'd been given. When he knocked on the door another surprise almost blew him over. Shirl was even younger than Stan. She was maybe twenty-eight at a stretch, dressed in a tight, short skirt, V-neck sweater that showed off her boobs, ultra-black hair with a pink strip framing her face. This was not Mother Teresa. And, of course, she was chewing gum. He could barely get a glimpse, but behind her appeared to be a very small, tidy house with old, worn furniture. That was the first time he considered that the couple of challenged employees he'd seen in the grocery were wearing clean but well-worn clothes. Art had looked as if he'd been homeless forever, but he was merely dirty and his clothes had already been threadbare. Shirl didn't waste a lot of cash clothing them.

She opened the door cautiously. "Hi," he said, pulling out his wallet and flipping it open fast, shut again just as fast, officially. "I'm looking for Art."

"Art?" she asked, stepping back. "Who?"

"Art Cleary."

"Um… I think he's at work…"

"I've been there. He's not at work," Luke said.

She frowned. "Are you the guy with the new grocery store?" she asked in confusion. "My brother called me and said—"

"Well, that was kind of a story." He shrugged. "I'm with the agency. Looking for Art. Just a follow-up visit, that's all.

The paperwork on him shows it's been a while since he's had a visit."

"Okay, okay," she said tiredly, holding up her hands, caught. "What timing. He took off. Ah, it was just this morning. He said he was going to—he wanted to go see some really old aunt of his in Redding. I called there, no answer, and no answering machine—some of these people are real hicks. I was just about to call Social Services, but I'm sure he just hitched a ride to his aunt's and she'll make sure he gets back. I was giving him a chance to check in—I don't want him in trouble. What are you going to do, fine me?"

Okay, lie number one, Luke thought. Art had been with Luke a couple of months. "You know what?" Luke said. "You keep trying the aunt. The less said about this, the better for Art. The better for you, huh?" And he winked at her.

"Yeah." She smiled. "Really."

"Why don't you jot down that aunt's address and phone number for me? If I find him there, I can bring him back before there's any confusion about it."

"You don't have the address? She's next of kin."

"Save me some time, huh?" he said with a smile. "To tell the truth, I have a lot better things to do than track him down, but it's on my sheet." And Luke wondered how many challenged residents had run off or disappeared while Shirl and Stan pocketed the monthly stipend provided by social security or insurance or the state. What happened to their paychecks from the grocery store? Did Stan write them off and keep the money? "I'll work it out," Luke said. "There might be paperwork. Don't worry about it. You're a nice girl to take him in the first place. These folks get to be a handful," he added with a grin.

"Tell me about it," she said.

He didn't know about the others, but there was no sweeter

soul, nobody less trouble and more eager to please than Art. But he said, "I'll take care of this and get back to you. You don't have to say anything." He raised his eyebrows. "We don't want him in trouble."

"Right," she said. "Wanna come in? Have some coffee or…something?"

"Thanks, but I'm running behind. I'll come back though— how's that?"

Luke left Shirl and took a big truckload of supplies for the cabins back to Virgin River. He decided he wasn't going to take any chances—he'd get help from Mike and Brie. He'd wait till after Christmas, give the Valenzuelas some time with their new baby and all the visiting family, then pay a visit, explain in detail about the group home and job Art had come from and ask what he had to do to clear things up so Art could stay with him. And if it wasn't possible for Art to stay with Luke, his next residence would be safer—Luke would see to that. Between Mike and Brie, given their legal and law enforcement experience, they could at least help him figure out how he should proceed. And he'd like to get Stan and Shirl investigated—they were a couple of punk kids in charge of a lot of disabled adults. It smelled like they were working the system for profit.

Luke decided it would be necessary to go to Phoenix for a couple of days over Christmas. If he didn't, there was no telling how many Riordans might show up in Virgin River, and he didn't have the patience for that. Going to Phoenix would appease his mother and mollify his brothers.

With all that was going on over the holidays around his cabins, he needed to be sure everything was well organized, planned out. First of all, he had to be sure Jack and Mike Valenzuela could manage everything their families needed while Luke was away because Art certainly couldn't handle guests' needs.

As for Art—he'd be fine on his own for a couple of days, but Luke didn't feel right leaving him alone. Luke appealed to Shelby and the general. Art should have a holiday dinner, a few presents that Luke would provide before leaving town and some sense of family. He knew before even asking they'd be more than happy to welcome Art and see that he had a memorable Christmas.

And then there was Shelby. He racked his brain for a gift idea. He wanted her to know she was very important to him, but he was nervous about what to buy her. She was the kind of woman he felt like buying something flashy and sparkly for, but he just wasn't ready for something like that. Women saw things like jewelry as stepping stones to marriage, but things like sweaters sent the message you didn't care at all. So Luke went all out in the only way he knew how. It was more than he'd spent on a woman in over a dozen years, including his mother—he bought Shelby very special, six-hundred-dollar ostrich boots, handcrafted and stitched. He considered buying her a saddle, but the boots were more personal. They had their Christmas-gift exchange right before he left town, and when she opened her gift and saw the boots, she wept. No one had ever given her a gift like that in her life and he enjoyed success when she kissed all over him.

He took her into his arms, laughing sentimentally. "I've never seen you cry," he said, holding her close, rocking her back and forth gently.

"Oh, you'd have seen way too much of that a year ago...."

"But these are happy tears. That's different. That means I did good."

"You did very good," she said. "They're just amazing. Exactly what I would have had made for myself. Like my own skin. I could sleep in them."

"But someone could get hurt," he reminded her with a laugh.

She gave him a new leather jacket that was almost as expensive as the boots and just as personal. "It's okay if you don't wear it a lot. I know you love that flying jacket of yours and you're so sexy in it—but this is for when you're not on the bike. For those rare times you dress up a little bit."

He asked her about all those things she'd talked about doing before Doc had died and she'd become so busy helping Mel— the applications to college, for example. She told him she'd applied to several major California universities: Stanford, USC, UC Davis, San Francisco State. It was only Christmas—September was a long way off. "I also sent an application to Humboldt State University, right down the road, in case I decide to stay right where I am. They have a fabulous program for bachelor of science nursing."

That was his cue to say something about how much he'd like that, he'd like to keep her here forever. But something caught in his throat and he said, "Sounds like you've covered all the possibilities, honey."

It was only the three boys in Phoenix for the Christmas holidays, Luke's stay being the most brief. "With Art and cabins full of holiday visitors, I can't be gone long."

"And with Shelby there," his mother said while she blended egg nog.

But Luke said nothing. His mother and Sean brought up Shelby's name fairly often, but Luke wasn't participating.

Their traditions amounted to food and church and laughter. There was a call from Colin in the Gulf, another from Paddy aboard ship. Once those two calls had been handled, they were free to leave the apartment. On Christmas Eve, they refused to let Maureen cook, even if it was the one thing she most wanted to do. Instead, the boys took her to Ruth's Chris Steak House in Scottsdale where you could eat the filets with a spoon. Then back to her apartment complex where they played pool in the recreation room, all four of them.

Then there was midnight mass. This was where Maureen shined, presenting three of her five sons to her friends, to the priest, to the sisters she knew. "I'm going to hell," Luke muttered to Aiden. "I took Communion and I haven't been in a church since last time I visited Mom."

"Me, too," Aiden whispered.

"Me, three," Sean said.

And the three of them cracked up, laughing so hard they could barely stand, while Maureen glared at them.

The tradition in their family since they'd become adults was to open their presents after mass on Christmas Eve, but the presents were less important to the boys than the fact that now they could finally bring out the bottle and pour some healthy shots, since they were in for the night. They had purchased lavish gifts for their mother. Luke had gotten her a gift certificate to the Chanel counter at Dillard's. Aiden had bought an expensive Lladró sculpture for her collection. Sean gave her a new iPhone.

The brothers gave each other modest gifts. Luke got a subscription to a motorcycle magazine and a sweater that was as ugly as a ball of string. Sean gave Aiden a subscription to *Penthouse* magazine.

"What the hell," Aiden said, looking at the gift card. Aiden was thirty-four, an OB-GYN in the navy, a doctor responsible for active-duty military women and a lot of the wives of marines and sailors, although he himself was alone.

"I thought you might like to know what women can look like when they don't have their feet in the stirrups."

"Thoughtful," Aiden said. "How can I ever thank you?"

Luke simply gave his brothers shirts, but Maureen's gift to her three sons stole the show. "It's for the Camelback Spa," she said proudly, passing them their individual envelopes. "They're open from eleven to three on Christmas Day and I made you appointments. I had to do it months ago. While I'm making the turkey and trimmings, you can go have massages or facials, manicures."

They looked at each other with wide eyes. And each one said, "Thank you, Mom, that's wonderful," "That should be cool, Mom, thanks," "How original, Mom—thanks a million."

"Now, I know you think you're too manly for facials, but try it. You'll love it!"

And on Christmas Day, while Maureen was making the turkey, Aiden, Luke and Sean found a bar that was open and drowned their guilt that they were not in a spa having facials and manicures. When they got back to Maureen's apartment, she fussed over how relaxed they all looked.

The Christmas dinner was, as usual, fabulous. Maureen loved nothing so much as fussing over her family and they all ate too much, which pleased her. Luke would be the first to leave, the next morning. Home to Virgin River. As his last day with his mother and brothers wore on, he grew more and more pensive, thinking about how Shelby had said after the first of the year, she'd be moving on. When everyone finally went to bed, he fixed himself a drink and sat up in the dimly lit living room of his mother's apartment.

Aiden found him there, sitting in the semidark, nursing a whiskey. Aiden fixed himself a matching drink and went into the living room, sitting down across from him. He was one of the brothers who'd tried marriage. It had been brief, during his residency, but in his case the breakup was his idea and he couldn't get out of his mess fast enough. He didn't suffer anything afterward but relief.

"So," Aiden said. "We could talk about it."

"Talk about what?"

"Why you look like someone shot your dog. Shelby, I assume."

"Nah," Luke said, taking a drink. "That's not serious."

"I guess that has nothing to do with your sleeplessness or your mood then. Trouble with the cabins? The town? Your tenant/helper?"

"Aiden, there's nothing bothering me, except maybe that I've been working my ass off for three months getting a house and six cabins rebuilt and furnished."

Aiden took a sip of his drink. "Twenty-five, so Sean and Mom say. And gorgeous."

"Sean's an idiot who can't mind his own business. She's just a girl."

"She's just a girl who has you looking a little uptight."

"Thanks," he said, standing. "You don't look that great yourself—I'm going to bed." He threw back the rest of his drink.

"Nah, don't," Aiden said. "Fix another one. Give me ten minutes, huh? I can just ask a couple of questions, right? I'm not like Sean, I'm not going to get up your ass about this. But you haven't talked about it much and I'm a little curious."

Luke thought about that for a second and against his better judgment, he went into the kitchen and poured himself a short shot. He went back and sat down, leaning his elbows on his knees. "What?" he asked abruptly.

Aiden chuckled. "Okay. Relax. Just a girl? Not serious?"

"That's right. A town girl, sort of. She's visiting her family and she'll be leaving pretty soon."

"Ah—I didn't know that. I guess I thought she lived there."

"Long visit," Luke said. "Her mother died last spring. She's spending a few months with her uncle until she gets on with things—like where she wants to live. College and travel and stuff. This is temporary, that's all."

"But—if you felt serious, there isn't any reason you wouldn't let it...you know...evolve...?"

"I don't feel serious," he said, his mouth in a firm line.

"Okay, I get that. Does she? Feel serious?"

"She has plans. I didn't trap her, Aiden. I made sure she knew—I'm not interested in being a family man. I told her she could do better, I'm just not built that way. But when I'm with a woman, I know how to treat her right. If she needed something permanent, she was in the wrong place. That's how it is."

"Never?"

"What do you mean, never? No one in this family is interested in that."

"Bullshit. I am. Sean says he's having too much fun, but the truth is he has the attention span of a cabbage. But me? I'd like a wife, a family."

"Didn't you already try that once?" Luke asked, sitting back in his chair, relaxing a little bit since the attention had shifted to Aiden's life.

"Oh, yeah—I tried hard. Next time I try, I'm going to see if I can find a woman who's not certifiable and off her meds." He grinned. "Really, that's what happens when you ignore all the symptoms because she's such a friggin' miracle in bed, it causes brain damage." He shrugged. "I'm on the lookout for that."

Luke grinned. "She was hot."

"Oh, yeah."

"She was worse than nuts."

"Nightmare nuts," Aiden agreed. "But this gorgeous twenty-five-year-old—she's real sweet, I hear."

"Fucking Sean…" Luke said, shaking his head.

"Not Sean. Mom."

"Almost as bad," Luke said. "You know Mom—she's been on this marriage-and-grandchildren campaign for a long time."

"So, she's not sweet?" Aiden asked.

"Sweeter than honey," he admitted. "But there are other things about her—complications. Her mother had ALS and Shelby was her nurse for years till she died—the girl's had no life. She dropped out of school and hardly left the house. Her idea of a big night was reading to her mother or watching a DVD with her. She's had her freedom for about six months and it was a hard freedom—that's why she's with her uncle, recovering. Making a transition. To hear her tell it, it's not easy to go from being needed twenty-four hours a day to having no one to take care of but yourself. She's a young twenty-five, as in, not a lot of life experience. She's a little bit like a prisoner on parole."

Aiden's mouth was open slightly. "Jesus." He took a breath. "Mom knows this?"

"Sure she does. They talked a lot, which wasn't a great idea. Mom loves her. She'd like nothing better than to reel her in." He shook his head. "Bad idea."

"Whoa, sounds like she had a rough time. How's she doing? With the transition?"

He shrugged. "Good, I think. You'd never know it—that she's been through all that."

"What was the problem? Not enough money to put the mother in long-term care?"

Luke was shaking his head. "Plenty of money—her uncle wanted to put the mother in a nursing home. But Shelby wouldn't have it. She was committed. She says her mother was her best friend."

Aiden was quiet for a long moment. Finally he said, "This sounds like an incredible young woman."

"She is that. Very mild mannered—hard to guess she could have that kind of conviction. Stubbornness."

"Strength," Aiden added. "Commitment."

"Well, you'd have to be strong to do that, right? Yeah, she's very strong, but she seems fragile." Then he grinned. "Unless you see her on a horse. She's a hundred and ten pounds, and on a horse, she's Annie Oakley."

Again Aiden was quiet for a moment, sipping. "What are you going to do?" he asked quietly.

"Do?" Luke repeated. "Nothing."

"Nothing?"

"She needs to get on with her life. She's behind. You can relate—I can relate. Remember being set free from medical school after years of no life? What did you do?"

"Married a nut job," he said, smiling blandly.

"Shelby put in her time, did the right thing, took good care of her mom, and now it's her turn. She's going to go back to school. She says she's going to be a nurse, but you watch—she'll end up a doctor or something. She's quiet, but scary smart. She has money from selling a paid-off house—so she can travel all over the world, pay for a dozen years of college. You know how important that is, we've been all over the world and it's worth seeing."

Aiden laughed. "I hope she sees better parts than we did. You saw a bunch of deserts, I went to sea, medical officer on a ship..."

"But it all counts. Life experience—it's worth it. She's

young—she has time to look around. I'll tell you what—that girl's going to have men hunting her down, she's that good-looking. She never had that before. In high school she was shy, had a couple of short-term boyfriends, but she lost a lot of shyness, got tougher and more aggressive while she was taking care of her mom and had to go up against doctors and therapists and hospitals and insurance companies." His eyes glistened proudly. "Believe me, she's ready now. It's her time."

He's letting her go, Aiden thought. *For her, though it's going to kill him.* Aiden leaned back in his chair and sipped his drink. "What if she just decides to stay? At her uncle's place? Forever?"

Luke laughed. "She's not going to, that would be a waste."

"If she did?"

"Look, I admit it—I got a little comfortable. The whole chase is a little boring and it wasn't exactly a punishment to have a sweet, pretty girl right there, handy. But that's just convenience, I'm winding down a little. There's this nice little bar in Virgin River—bunch of townpeople go there at the end of the day—real good people. They have the best food on the planet and the jukebox hasn't been turned on once since I hit town. A couple of marines run the place, so we connected. It spoiled me for entertainment, I lost interest in noisy, smoky bars with slutty girls looking for a pickup. I've been thinking... If I can rent out those cabins...work and live there, grab a beer at Jack's, hunt and fish... I'm telling you—it's almost a perfect life. You'll have to come up sometime."

Aiden let him think about that for a minute. Then he said, "How old do you have to be to appreciate that as a perfect life?"

Luke laughed. "About thirty-eight, twenty years of army, four wars. But now I'm thinking about staying in one place a while. I might look around for some flying in the area, something like medical-airlift transport or something."

"Could someone like me get into that? Small town like that?"

"They have a midwife and everyone loves her." Luke laughed. "You'd have some stiff competition."

"What I mean is, could someone younger than thirty-eight want that life? Or do you have to be this crusty, beat-up old grunt?"

Luke got the point and his lips went back into that firm, nonnegotiable line.

"Do you suppose young women ever choose that life over Ph.D.s or world travel? Think that's ever happened?"

"I think young women like Shelby might think they want that life and two years later realize they threw away their *real* life and they're stuck, and everything would go to hell at that point."

"But that's a guess," Aiden said. "And this is a remarkable, committed, stubborn, aggressive woman who's been up against a lot and knows what she wants."

"You tricked me," Luke said. "You said you were going to be a little curious but now you're up my ass."

"What are the odds you're ever going to run into someone like her again, once she leaves Virgin River? If you let her get away?"

Luke stood up. He put his drink, what was left of it, on a coaster. "But that's not the point," he said. "I'm going to bed."

Late on Christmas Day, Shelby leaned on the corral fence and watched as her cousin Tom kept an eye on Art astride Chico. Ever since first seeing Chico, Art had wanted to ride him, but Chico was a lot of horse for Art. Tom, however, was more than happy to spot that. And when they were done,

Shelby would take Art back to his cabin and Tom would go into town and find his girl.

She jumped when she felt a hand on her shoulder. With the noise of churning hooves in the corral, she hadn't heard Vanni's approach. Shelby turned toward Vanni and then turned back, giving her cheeks a quick wipe.

"Come on," Vanni said. "You can't pretend. Something happened between you and Luke."

"Nothing. Really, nothing."

Vanni turned her around. "Something," she insisted. "Did you have a fight?"

"No, nothing like that. It's just that…" Her voice trailed away.

"What, honey? What happened?"

Shelby's eyes welled anew and she shrugged. "Oh, well. I miss him."

"It's a couple of days, honey. That's all…"

"I know." She sniffed. "It would have meant the world to me if he'd called to wish me a merry Christmas. But I haven't heard a word out of him. He loves me like I mean everything to him, but he never says the words. I don't know why. Why, Vanni?"

Vanni ran a gentle finger along her cheek, wiping off a tear. "Baby, I don't know Luke like you do."

"It's almost as though he tries to keep this distance between us…"

"You said you wouldn't cry."

"No, I didn't. I said if he made me cry, I'd get over it. I still don't have any regrets."

"It hurts, huh?"

She took a deep breath. "I guess I'm as naive as everyone thought. I fell in love with him. I didn't mean to."

"Aw, baby," Vanni said, pulling her into her arms.

Shelby put her head on Vanni's shoulder. "It's going to be real hard to give him up." Then she let out a little huff of rueful laughter. "It's going to be real hard if he lets me go. But... I'll get over it. What are my choices? I couldn't have done anything differently."

The day after Christmas, while Walt was babysitting so Vanni could spend some time working on the wallpaper at her new house, Shelby drove over to the new neighbor's place. She banged on Muriel's front door and heard the sound of welcoming dogs inside. Muriel beamed when she pulled the door open.

"Any chance you have a cup of coffee?" Shelby asked.

"Sure. Come in. Everything all right?"

"Well, not exactly. Thing is, I need to talk to someone who's not a member of my family. About Luke."

"Gosh," Muriel said. "I'm honored. I would've expected you to go to Mel. The two of you are awful close."

"True. But she's got a lot of family in town right now," Shelby said. "And I just thought, maybe... I don't know, Muriel. Maybe you can tell me something I don't already know. About...you know...men."

"You do realize I've been married five times and never could make it work," Muriel said on her way to the kitchen. "It wasn't my fault, I swear it, but still..."

"I think maybe I've been a fool," Shelby said.

"Oh, now, *that* I've been a hundred times. I am an expert." Muriel laughed, pouring Shelby a cup of coffee. "Just tell me what's going on. I won't breathe a word to anyone. Especially Walt."

Shelby ran it down quickly. She met him, fell for him, bought into that whole never-settling-down program because she had big plans of her own and she didn't regret it. Now she wanted more, but he was still in that same place, while she was suffering. "When he said he'd never put down roots and didn't want that whole marriage-and-family deal, I really thought that meshed pretty well with what I was looking for. At the time, anyway. He never once lied to me, Muriel. He didn't lead me on and he's always treated me like pure gold. Maybe I was the one who lied to him—I thought that worked for me. But things changed. I still want to travel, go to school, but I also want the whole deal—a partner, a family, the security of a relationship I can trust. I don't want to be with a man who's just going to dump me right about the time I think I can't live without him."

"Oh, little darling," Muriel said. "I wanted all those things, too."

"You did?"

"I did. It didn't work out for me. I hope it works out for you."

"But you've had such an amazing career!"

"I was real lucky that way," she said. She reached across her kitchen table and grabbed both Shelby's hands. "I have some bad news, my sweet girl. One—you can't change people. If he doesn't change himself, you're flat out of luck. And two—you want what you want. Need what you need."

"I keep looking for a compromise..."

"Shelby, there are many compromises in relationships. You learn to live with men's underwear on the floor just shy of the hamper, toothpaste spit on the mirror, and you learn to keep your mouth shut while he drives around in circles for hours because he won't ask for directions. But the things you feel in the marrow of your bones, the deep and meaningful desires that will make your life complete—there's no compromise in it."

"No?"

Muriel shook her head. "You can force yourself to go along.

You might even find a way to force him to go along. But there's bitterness in it. It's not worth it."

"I guess you didn't go along," she said. "Do you have any regrets? About being alone?"

"I'm not alone, Shelby," she said patiently. "I'm on my own—there's a difference. And I have the most wonderful family of friends. It is so much better than having a man I'm not compatible with, even if I thought I adored him. Believe me."

"Of course," Shelby said. "I so love the way you see things...."

Muriel laughed. "I've had so much practice at *seeing* things. Far more than I'm happy about."

They talked through a whole pot of coffee, about Shelby's life, about Muriel's. It surprised Shelby to have anything at all in common with this Hollywood icon. After a couple of hours, Shelby asked, "What am I to do?"

"Oh, you'll know what to do. Don't be hasty, sweetheart. But don't wait too long. There will be a moment of clarity, my little darling, and it will come to you that it's time to take care of yourself. You don't have to give up your dreams, Shelby. Never take scraps. Never."

16

Right after Cameron Michaels had a nice holiday in Portland with his parents, brother and sister and their families, he drove to Virgin River, towing a U-Haul with his books, computer, bedroom furniture, clothes, TV and stereo equipment. He'd traded his Porsche in for a Suburban with all-wheel drive for getting around the mountains, valleys and foothills. When he pulled up in front of Doc's house, Mel came out onto the porch immediately, all smiles. "Welcome, Doctor," she said.

Shelby stepped out of the clinic right behind her. "Hey, Cameron," she said. "How was the drive?"

"Not bad," he said. "At least the sun's out here. It's wet and ugly in Portland."

"Leave the trailer and everything," Mel said. "I'm going to grab the baby and walk over to Jack's. Then the guys will help you unload. You're going to stay with us at the house tonight, until we can get your bedroom set up."

Shelby turned and went back into the clinic.

"I don't want to impose," he said.

Mel laughed. "Let me get this right. You're coming to work in my town for a pittance and you don't want to impose? You'll stay with us at least tonight, longer if necessary."

Shelby was back with little Emma cuddled against her, Mel's coat draped over her arm and the clinic keys in her hand, which she used to lock the door.

Mel put on the coat and took the baby from Shelby.

"Where's the little guy?" Cameron asked.

"With his dad, serving. He's in the backpack. So—you settled up all your affairs without difficulty?" Mel asked.

"Slick as grease. Had an offer on the house in three days, sold most of the furniture and put some favorite things in storage up there, traded in the sports car for an all-wheel-drive vehicle and had Christmas with my family."

They began walking across the street to the bar. "What did they think of this idea?" Shelby asked him.

He chuckled. "They think I've completely lost my mind. And maybe I have. But what the hell, huh?"

"I really can't figure out why you did this," Mel said.

"Same reason you did, Mel," he said.

"Nah, couldn't be. My heart was in pieces. I had to go someplace simple and quiet to get a handle on my life. To heal. To be alone and not so obviously alone."

"Same reason as you, Mel," he repeated.

She stopped walking. "Ho boy," she said. "There's more to this story."

"Yeah, we'll get sloppy some night and compare our broken hearts. How's that?"

She tugged at his sleeve. "This doesn't have anything to do with any of our, ah, mutual friends, does it?"

"No, Mel. This has nothing to do with Vanessa." Shelby's eyes grew very round and Cameron looked at her. "Before Paul got smart and told Vanni how much he loved her, I had a couple of dates with her. That's all—a couple of dates. She disappointed me when she picked the other guy—but she didn't break my heart. No worries."

"Shew," Mel said. "Had me worried there for a second. I mean, the gossip in this town is good, but it shouldn't be *that* good!"

Cameron laughed. "This is going to be great. I'm going to learn to fly-fish on my days off."

"You'll have plenty of those," she said, stepping up on the bar's porch.

Cameron apparently didn't think there was anything odd about the number of cars and trucks at the bar and on the street, but then he wasn't up on the seasonal activities. From January to June things were usually pretty wet and quiet around Virgin River, hunting done and the fishing pretty much closed. But when he walked into the bar, a bar stuffed with people, a cheer and greeting erupted. He stood just inside the door, stunned, while the din slowly subsided. Jack came around the bar, little David squirming around in the backpack. "Come on in, Doc. Welcome."

Next came Paul, his hand outstretched, then Vanni with a hug and kiss on the cheek, and Walt, pulling him into a hearty embrace. Preacher just about broke his ribs with his hug, then there was Paige, Mike and Brie with a brand-new baby. Next came introductions to friends and neighbors from all over town and the outlying ranches. A cold draft was pressed into his hand, there was a hearty and delicious buffet set out and lots of handshakes, grateful pats on the back. Among the crowd were doctors June Hudson and John Stone and their families, offering services and assistance at the call. June's dad, Doc Hudson, offered to come out to Virgin River for a while and visit with him on the subject of country doctoring and maybe a trip out to the river. "We can get your angling up to speed before the real fishing starts," he offered.

Cameron ate, drank, got to know the people from town and felt, for the first time in a very long time, a part of something personal and important. Something both hearty and delicate. There were very few single people among this happy throng, but it didn't affect him in the way being out with his married partners had depressed him, made him feel like he didn't belong anywhere. Here, he felt like one of them, though he was absent a partner with whom to share it all.

At some point in the early evening, Mel told him Jack would bring him home and she'd see him later. Jack helped settle his family in the Hummer so Mel could take the babies home to bed. Little by little people bid good-night and wandered off and then at nine o'clock the bar seemed to empty of patrons, bidding him good-night and expressing, again, their grateful thanks and earnest welcome. And then it was down to Jack, Preacher and Cam.

Jack got down a couple of glasses. "We usually pour a shot at the end of the day, after the bar clears out. I'll drive you out to the house if you're up to one more."

"You bet," Cameron said. "Jack, this was great, what you did."

Jack tipped a bottle of good, aged Glenlivet over three glasses. "I didn't do it, Doc. These things happen when word gets out. It's a real spontaneous place."

"God, they're wonderful," Cam said.

"They don't have much money, they're not real sophisticated, they haven't read the classics—most of them haven't, anyway—but this place has heart. It's a simple thing, really. They can't feed your pocketbook too much, but they know the value of friendship and gratitude. You'll never get hungry or lonely. That's what the town gets by on. You'll like that."

"I've never felt unappreciated in my work, but this is something new." He lifted a glass toward Preacher and Jack. "To new beginnings," he said.

"To satisfaction," Jack added.

Cameron drank to it. "I'm really glad I did this."

"Had to be a big risk, Doc," Preacher observed.

"Was it for you?" Cameron asked him.

"Naw," Preacher said. "Once I got up here and saw what Jack had set up, it was a no-brainer."

"I can see that," Cameron said. "Thank you for giving me the chance," he added.

Luke had drawn Shelby away from the party welcoming Cameron Michaels just after the crowd had begun to disperse. Luke took Art in his car and Shelby followed him out to the house and cabins in her Jeep. Once there, she went first to Art's cabin to make sure he was all settled.

"Doing okay, Art?"

"I'm doing very good," he said, grinning.

"I thought I'd check on you before turning in for the night. Sleep tight, okay?"

"Don't let the bedbugs bite," he said, echoing something she often said to him.

She laughed. "I won't. Don't forget your prayers."

"I don't ever," he promised.

"And don't forget to brush and floss."

"I don't ever," he said.

Then she went up on Luke's front porch, where he was

waiting for her, grinning. "I thought I saved his ass, but it's you he worships."

"I don't think it's quite as serious as that," she said, letting him enfold her in his embrace. "Eventually you should talk to someone about him. Let his people know where he is, maybe have him evaluated. I'm sure they won't have any problem with him being here, as long as he's safe and healthy."

"Yeah, I got a start on that. I found out where he's from—not a good place. I'll talk to Mike and Brie about how to get him out of there," he said, kissing her.

She pulled away. "And keep him?"

Luke shrugged. "It's not like I'm going to adopt him. I'll give him a place to stay and he'll do chores. But he shouldn't have to do chores for someone who hits him." He kissed her again and then he pulled her into the cabin.

"But you'll be responsible for him?"

"Shelby, it's not exactly a strain on me. He doesn't need much watching, just a safe place."

"And when you sell the cabins and leave here?"

He shrugged. "If that happens, it shouldn't be any trouble to find him a good place. One I'm sure isn't some Social Services scam."

"But aren't you worried that will hurt him? Confuse him?"

"I know how sensitive he is—I'll treat that carefully. But I think maybe I'll put off worry until it's necessary."

Shelby had known him a few months, a couple of months she'd known him intimately, and for her it had been thrilling. The way they came together was so amazing to her; just thinking about him filled her with shivering anticipation. She had no regrets about waiting so long to find out what this was about because she was certain it could never have been like this with any other man.

To her it was a miracle. Fate, putting her with the one man

perfect for her. When he touched her, she believed he felt the same way. But he gave no other sign.

After the lovemaking, he held her close to him. He could never stop kissing her, touching her, stroking her. It mystified her that he could be like this—so tender, so involved in her, so loving—and yet not in love at all. She wondered how he did that. She thought if she understood it, maybe she could walk away without being torn to pieces over him.

She rolled over and wriggled on top of him, lying prone, lifted up, braced on his chest, looking into his eyes. "There's a new doctor in town and Mel won't need me so much anymore. I've been here since August. There's less and less on my schedule every day."

He ran a big hand down her spine, over her smooth bottom. He gave her a lusty squeeze. "I'll keep you busy some of that time," he said with a laugh.

She gazed down into his eyes, so filled up with love for him. How could he not know? She wouldn't tell him she loved him first. She couldn't ask him; her pride wouldn't allow it. But she wasn't too proud to give him a chance. "All my applications to nursing programs have been sent out—now I'm just waiting to hear. And remember, I even shot one in to Humboldt State U, in case you come to your senses and decide you can't live without me. They have an excellent program."

He pushed her hair back over her shoulder. "I bet there are lots of excellent programs out there, aren't there?"

She nodded and tried to send him a mental message. *Say* it, she thought. Tell me you love me; tell me you wish I could stay right here. With you. "And the one right here is as good as any of them."

Instead of talking, he tightened his arms around her and rolled with her until she was beneath him. Then he covered her mouth in a deep, hot kiss. And his hands began to move in long, slow, thrilling caresses, his fingers gently probing her again.

With a sigh of disappointment, she yielded to him, filling up on sensation, knowing in her heart this might be all she ever had of him.

Abby had called Vanessa from her parents' house in Seattle on New Year's Day. "What are the chances you're up for a little visit?" she asked.

"Perfect," Vanessa said. "Your timing is great! We just moved into our new house before Christmas and there's still lots of stuff to do around here. Between trips to the coast to shop and putting things right around here, you can help me."

"I'd love to help," Abby said. "How soon can I come?"

"As soon as you like," Vanni said.

"Then get the sheets on the guest bed, I'll be on my way in a few days."

On her travel day, Abby kissed her parents goodbye in the driveway at dawn and headed south. The second she got into the car, her tummy muscles relaxed and she felt herself expand into the pants with the elastic waistband. She had a cooler packed with food and drinks and only stopped for gas and more potty breaks than seemed fair. By early evening, she was driving past the general's house, around the curve past the stable and down the road to a brand-new house. She gave her horn a toot and got out of the car. Vanessa came out to greet her, her smile bright and happy. As Abby walked toward Vanni, the latter stopped suddenly, eyes wide. Abby hadn't put her coat on and stood before her friend, running a smooth hand over a very slightly rounded belly.

Vanni recovered herself and wrapped Abby in her embrace. "You didn't say you were bringing company," she said with a soft smile.

"Vanni, I'm in a terrible mess," Abby said.

"You'd better come in, honey. I get the sense you want to talk about some things."

Vanni had something that smelled delicious in the oven, Matt was crawling around the living-room floor and pulling himself up on the furniture, and Paul, Abby learned, was not yet home, very likely having stopped off at the bar in town for a beer with his friends.

"Why didn't you tell me?" Vanni asked.

"I'm pretty embarrassed for one thing," she said. "I'm in some trouble, for another. The only people who know about the pregnancy are my parents and my doctor. And now you."

"You know I'd do anything to help you, but not talking about it isn't going to work much longer."

Abby shook her head. "At Nikki and Joe's wedding, you all knew divorce was in the wind. I couldn't stand to talk about it—but the marriage to Ross was *long* over by that time. If you keep up with any tabloid news, you know he had been living with another woman for more than six months by the time our divorce was final."

"Sorry, honey—I just don't see any tabloids."

"Well, I should have dispensed with that divorce immediately. The day he asked me, I should have signed the papers." She laughed suddenly. "Did I say he asked me? His lawyer asked me. A threatening and hostile man, he called weekly. I let the machine pick it up. I haven't heard from Ross in forever. More than a year by now. Don't ask me why I waited— I didn't want him back in my life. I think I was just stunned senseless and couldn't move. Plus, I felt like such a fool for marrying him in the first place, thinking I knew him when clearly I didn't. It just ripped me up. As soon as I got back to Los Angeles after the wedding, I signed. A little over a month later, I was a free woman."

"I think you're better off," Vanni said.

"Oh, I'm sure of it. Did you know that I met him while he was in recovery from drug addiction? For a little while, he was wonderful. Sweet and charming and going to meetings every day. By the time we'd been married six weeks, he was back on tour, using again. But I screwed up, Vanni. I signed a prenuptial agreement. A very simple and uncomplicated one—if I remained faithful during our marriage, in the event of divorce I could collect alimony. There was no reason for a promise like that to make me nervous.

"But—his lawyer presented me with bills. Credit cards— credit cards that I didn't even have! I immediately owed thousands of dollars, tens of thousands. I needed that alimony. To pay my share of *his* bills."

"Oh God, the turd! Of course you did," Vanni said. "You shouldn't feel guilty about that."

"I don't," she said. She smoothed her hands over her belly. "This happened right before I signed the papers, before the divorce was final. It's irrelevant that he was already living with another woman."

"Who's the father?" Vanni asked as delicately as she could.

"I'm not able to talk about that, Vanni. I'm sorry. It was, in fact, a one-night stand with a complete stranger. A completely lovely, tender stranger. If I wasn't pregnant, I'd get in touch with him, get to know him better. I could take my time figuring out if he's really a lovely man—months and months longer than I gave Ross. But now it's too big a risk," she said. "He would know he's the father. And what if he's not as wonderful as he seemed? Vanni, I don't really know anything about him except that he was nice to me for one night. Jeez, Ross was nice to me for longer than that and look at what he turned out to be. I just can't take the chance. I can't subject the babies to that."

"Babies?" Vanni asked.

Abby looked down. "I just found out. Twins," she said.

"Holy cow."

"I know. That's why I'm so big already."

"So—what's your plan?" Vanni asked.

"I have to hide out somewhere until the babies are at least a few months old. I figure after they're here, no one on Ross's legal team can prove I defied the prenup and ask me for the alimony back—but if anyone representing him discovers I'm pregnant, they might be able to subpoena tests to determine when I conceived. It was a little more than a month before the divorce was final—I'm scared to death that can be proven. Vanni, I can't pay those bills I'm stuck with."

"Have you asked anyone? Like your OB?"

She nodded. "It's possible to determine the date of conception from prenatal records. I need to disppear until those bills are paid and I stop accepting the alimony, until the babies are older and Ross's lawyers lose interest...

"So," she went on, "I took a year's unpaid leave from the airline and I'll look around here for something to rent. My change of address is to my mom's in Seattle and she'll collect my mail and send it to me. I put my mom on my account in Seattle, and to keep the trail cold, she'll wire me cash for my living expenses. Just six more months. Or so." She got tears in her eyes. "Vanni, I don't want his money. But I don't have any other way to pay those bills, to live."

Vanni reached out and put her hand over Abby's. "Don't you dare feel guilty about that! Good God, Abby—he cheated on you, lied to you, used drugs..."

"Yes, but I got pregnant." She shook her head. "Except for that money I need to cover his bills, I'm going to find a way to give it back to him. Eventually. I don't want his money. It's like it's stained. I just have to get beyond this. Then..."

"And you're not renting something! You're going to stay right here with us!"

"Oh, I can't do that—"

"You're not staying alone, pregnant with twins! I won't allow it! Paul won't allow it! We're going to get you through this, help you regroup. We have a wonderful nurse midwife—Mel. You met her at Nikki and Joe's wedding. But there's also a fantastic OB right down the road in Grace Valley. And recently, a new pediatrician in town. An old friend, actually. So you see, everything is going to work out."

Abby's face melted into tears and she leaned into her hands, sobbing. Vanni immediately enfolded her in loving arms. "It's okay," she whispered. "No crying! We're having babies! Wonderful little babies." Matt crawled over to Abby, pulled himself up on her knees and began to pat her thigh, babbling. "That's right—we never cry about babies."

"Oh God, Vanni. I didn't know what I was going to do. I not only shouldn't be having one—there's no way I should be having two! And God help me, I want them! I want them so much!"

Abby settled in with Vanni and Paul and got comfortable, feeling safe for the first time in weeks. She wasn't quite ready to be introduced to the town. When they made their occasional trip into Virgin River to have dinner at Jack's, she declined. She was still feeling embarrassed and shy about presenting herself as a single mother even though in this day and age it was hardly a rarity.

Later in January she was due a prenatal exam and made an appointment with Mel Sheridan. It was time to consider her delivery options and resume her prenatal care, which she would pay for in cash.

When she had her appointment with Mel, she was as captivated as Vanni promised her she would be. And the professional way in which Mel handled her was refreshing. "Single mom, huh? That's got it's challenges, but you're a lucky woman. Twins, good friends, perfect health, I can't think what else you need."

"I'm pretty nervous about the birth. I want them to be full-term, healthy, and then…"

"Have any idea how you'll take care of them and work?"

"As soon as they're big enough, I'm going home to my folks. My mom will help. She's very excited."

"That's a good plan. With a supportive family, you should be able to work things out. There are options for you—you can have John Stone in Grace Valley deliver you at Valley Hospital or I can attend you in birth with John's assistance. I don't administer anesthesia, but honey, these are twins—they're going to be smaller than the average birth. Probably quicker and earlier. We'll keep up with ultrasounds to make sure they're in the right position. And we have John Stone, in case we need anything special, like a cesarean. He's wonderful. As luck would have it, we have a fabulous pediatrician. Did you know that Paul assisted in Vanni's delivery of Mattie?"

"I heard something about that," she said.

"It was a wonderful birth. We had a birthing party. Everyone was there, at the general's house, waiting. Paul thought he couldn't handle it, yet he was perfect."

"This might be my only childbirth experience…."

"Oh, don't try to plan ahead like that," Mel advised. "You're young. Fertile. You have a few years to change your mind."

"This took me by surprise," she admitted.

Mel laughed. "Yeah?" she said. "Both of mine took me by surprise, and I'm the expert. Get dressed and I'll see you out front."

Abby was feeling real good about her appointment as she

dressed. She even felt better about coming out to the town. This was going to be okay, she decided. People were nice, accepting. Mel was everything a woman could want in a midwife—warm, humorous, delightful.

When she walked out front, Mel was waiting at the reception counter with Abby's chart. "Everything looks great, Abby. Do you have enough vitamins or can I hook you up with a refill?"

"I'm good," Abby said. "I brought a big supply from my last OB."

"Good, then."

At the exact moment Abby's eyes grew round and startled, so did Cameron's. They locked eyes. Cameron was sitting behind the reception counter at the desk, looking at the computer. He'd been with a patient in an exam room when she came in and hadn't seen her.

Mel noticed they were looking at each other and said, "Abby, meet Dr. Michaels. Cameron, Abby MacCall."

He stood. "Hello," he said.

"Nice to meet you," she said.

He came around the desk and put out his hand, which she took after some hesitation. "Abby... MacCall, was it?"

"Yes. Hi."

"You're staying here in Virgin River?" he asked.

"I'm visiting friends," she said.

"I'm new here myself," he said. "You're going to like it."

"Hmm. Well, I'm not staying long. I'd better get going."

"See you around," he said.

"Sure." And she nearly ran out the door.

Cameron's eyes were locked on her departure. When the door had been closed a few seconds, he pulled his eyes back to Mel's.

"I thought she was here for the duration. Something weird just happened there."

"Yeah," he said. "How far along is Abby?"

"Four months. Why?"

He dropped his gaze, looking briefly at his feet. Then he lifted his eyes to Mel's. "I know her. I know her pretty well, but I haven't seen her in about...four months."

"I'm a little confused."

"Four months," he repeated.

"You'd better clarify yourself."

Cameron had had an indoctrination with Mel, training in this clinic so to speak, and knowing that she kept everything about patients strictly confidential, he said, "I think I might be the father."

Mel's eyes grew round and her mouth hung open. It took her a moment to recover.

"Where's she staying?" Cameron asked.

"Vanni and Paul's."

"Oh fuck," he said. "That baby's mine," he said, shaking his head.

"Babies," she corrected. "It's twins."

He straightened abruptly, shocked. "Double fuck." He took his coat off the rack inside the front door, picked up his medical bag, which would be like an extension of his arm from now on, and said, "I have to step out for a while. I don't know how long I'll be. I'm not expecting patients."

"Um, wait," Mel said. "Just one second." She dashed behind the desk and got into the supply cupboard. She pulled out a couple of large plastic bottles of prenatal vitamins. "Here," she said, tossing them to him one at a time. "If you find yourself in a delicate spot, you can always pretend you're delivering these."

"Thanks, Mel. Hey, I'm sorry..."

She smiled. "Can I assume you two don't have a...relationship?"

He returned the smile, but his was hurt. Melancholic. "Don't assume anything right now. Except—we've got a...situation." And then he was gone.

The knock on the Haggertys' front door came not ten minutes after Abby returned from her visit with the midwife. She ignored it and kept folding her things to put into a suitcase. She had come home to find the house deserted. The doorbell rang, then there was more knocking, but Abby didn't respond.

Rather than being worried about another confrontation with Cameron, the thing that occupied her most was what excuse she'd give Vanni for leaving so abruptly. She wasn't prepared to say, "The man who knocked me up lives here!" Next, she worried—where would she go now? Nikki and Joe in Grants Pass was out of the question—too close to the scene of the crime. Cameron knew Nikki was Abby's friend. Maybe some anonymous little town down the coast where she didn't know anyone.

The knocking had stopped. Seconds later she heard, "You don't have to run."

She jumped in surprise and whirled around, her face ashen. "How did you get in?"

"The key under the flowerpot," he said. "Same place I always kept mine. Pretty unimaginative. And pretty rare, this door locking in Virgin River. Abby, it's too late for you to run."

She lifted her chin, but her eyes were moist. She put a protective hand over her tummy.

He stepped into the bedroom doorway. "What are you so afraid of, Abby? You think I'd do something to hurt you? You know better than that. If I meant to hurt you, I had a perfect opportunity in Oregon."

"Cameron, look, this is real complicated, and I can't let it get more complicated. Please."

He shrugged and put his hands in his pockets. He leaned against the door frame. "Catch me up a little—tell me why you'd be so damn afraid of me making your life more compli-cated. And stop packing, for God's sake. I'm not the enemy."

She crumbled to the bed and, putting her face in her hands, began to weep. Cautiously, not making any fast moves, Cam-eron sat next to her and put an arm around her shoulders. "I'm not going to say or do anything to make you nervous or afraid," he murmured. "If you don't want anyone to know about us, about that night, I'll never breathe a word," he said softly.

"I never meant that night to happen," she said, lifting her head to turn teary eyes to him. "I wasn't waiting for you in front of the elevators. I was going to my room. I wasn't about to spend the night with a stranger."

"How did that night happen? How does a good friend of Vanessa's end up in my town?"

"We were all there—it was our best friend Nikki's wed-ding. Joe is Paul's best friend. Even Jack and Mel were at the wedding."

"Are you kidding me? And I didn't see a single familiar face."

"I wish you had," she sniffed. "It would have saved us both a world of trouble."

"I didn't force you. It wasn't a bad night for you. Not bad at all. And you already know—for me, it was wonderful."

"It was a huge misunderstanding," she said. "I've just been through a horrific divorce, complete with tabloid pictures."

"I know. I read all about it. I was looking for you. I wanted another chance with you," he said.

She turned toward him, desperately grabbed the front of his jacket in both hands and said, "If you know who I am, where I am and that I'm pregnant, and if you tell anyone those details, it could be very, very bad for me. You have no idea how bad."

Cameron wanted to know everything, but there was no mistaking panic. If he backed her into a corner, even slightly, she could get away from him again. "I think you're okay here, Abby. I don't think anyone in Virgin River will make the connection."

"But you did," she said, letting go of his jacket.

"Yeah. But I was looking for you. And not for a bad reason."

"I don't even know you!"

"Well, that's arguable. But we'll go with your perception for now—you don't know me well enough to give you peace of mind, but I'm pretty easy to check out. Probably lots easier than you were. So—you're hiding? From him or from me?"

"I didn't even think I had to hide from you. I had no idea you were here. Really, this can't get out. Please don't ask me why."

"A sticky prenup, I gather..."

"Oh God! Who told you about that?"

"I read it in *People* magazine."

"Oh my God! How many people do you think *know* about that?"

"I don't know, but no one here will realize you're that woman. I recognized your face on the cover and read the story because I was hungry for details. Not that I got any—just the bare facts, which struck me as disgraceful. He left you after a few weeks, moved in with another woman and filed for divorce. There was mention that a prenuptial agreement might be a reason the divorce was delayed, but I have no idea how that plays into your drama. All I know is that the shit bag married you and left you. And I consider him scum of the earth for doing that. Not to mention a fool."

"And I'll be in a huge mess if you share that with anyone."

"Okay," he said, nodding. "I'll be sure and not write home about you."

"Funny," she said. "This is serious."

"All right, we'll get serious. You're not my patient, but anything that happens in that clinic is confidential. Mel and I have access to all the records and they're protected by privacy. Even if I wanted to gossip about you, I can't. But there's no rule against talking to you—and I have a personal stake in this. I have a feeling this has everything to do with me."

"They're not yours."

He smiled patiently. "Yeah, they are, but don't panic. Right now making sure you're all right is the only thing that concerns me. I'm not going to get pushy—I understand how you must feel about it being just one night, unplanned, accidental. Abby—I'm sorry. This is my fault. I talked you into it, I had the condom accident…"

"I had the pill accident," she relented. "I was taking antibiotics."

"Well, that explains it. You didn't know about the contraindication?"

She shook her head and sniffed. He produced a handkerchief and she wiped at her eyes and nose. "I'm not even sure they told me at the clinic. If they did, maybe I wasn't paying attention—I was getting ready to go to that wedding and my own marriage was over. It was a stressful time and I had an ear infection. Really, I was half-deaf."

"So why are you here?"

She shrugged. "I have to go real low profile right now. Oh

hell, you're going to find out anyway. I hope you turn out to be someone I can trust because—"

"Didn't I show you that?" he asked as gently as he could. "I tried to."

"Yeah, well, Ross showed me that, too. For at least a couple of months he was the sweetest man I'd ever known. A couple of months later he was back with the band, using drugs, his life a train wreck."

"Okay, point taken. But I don't think I have much in common with him. I don't have a long history of infidelity and drug use, for one thing...."

"But see, I don't really know that."

"Like I said, I'm real easy to check out. You could start with Vanni."

"Vanni?" she asked, surprised.

"Yup. Her first husband's mother tried to fix us up and we dated a little, before Paul. I had a practice in Grants Pass for several years—ask the doctors there. Check with Mel—she hired me. I'm here for a year."

"What *are* you doing here?" she asked.

"Their doctor, a man I knew briefly, died a few months ago. They needed help and I happen to love this place. You'll see— it's kind of special. Now, tell me about this problem you have. Not the pregnancy, that's not a problem. What has you hiding out in Virgin River, afraid someone will recognize you?"

She sighed deeply and let it out. Her choices were few at this point. At least if he knew why she was so afraid he might keep his big mouth shut.

"And that's what has you so wound up? Abby, that's only money."

"*Only* money? It's a ton of money! I didn't stick him with any debt, but I feel lucky it was only a fortune in credit-card bills! I suppose a rock star can run up a big tab."

"Abby," he said calmly. "It's legal details. It can be handled. We just have to figure out the best approach and—"

"Stop! This is *my* problem! I need time to breathe!"

Cameron wasn't too worried about things like prenups and credit-card debt. It wasn't that he thought he could buy their way out of this mess; he didn't have a ton of money. But he was sure there was a compromise in there somewhere. His biggest concern was getting the mother of his twins to trust him a little. He put a large hand over her slightly rounded middle. "Have you been seeing a doctor since the beginning?" Again she nodded, but this time she lifted her eyes. "And everything is going fine? You're feeling all right?"

"Fine," she said. "If I didn't miscarry from being a nervous wreck, I guess I must be in good shape."

He smiled. "You should have called me. I could have helped."

"I was afraid to get involved with someone I didn't know. I already screwed up on that once. You could be a lunatic for all I know."

"I could be, but I'm not."

"I can't be sure of anything. Anyone. You have to understand that. Don't take it personally—there are very good reasons for me to be cautious."

"I smoked a little pot in college," he said with a smile. "Otherwise, I'm relatively safe."

"Relatively?"

"Yeah. I've been known to do insane things like chuck a thriving practice to come to a town of six hundred for practically no money because it's quiet, clean and the people make you feel useful. My family thinks I've lost my mind," he added, laughing. "Other than that, I haven't had a severe personality shift since puberty."

"When I saw you at the clinic, it scared me to death," she said.

"That's the first thing we have to work on," he said. "There is absolutely no reason to ever be afraid of me. I would never hurt you. Why would I? What would that get me? I'd like a chance to get to know you a little bit. I told you that back in Oregon, that I'd like to know more about you. I'm not going to screw up that chance by being cruel. Forceful." He grinned. "You have that list. Forceful isn't on it."

"And you have very good manners," she added softly. And for the first time that day, she really looked at him. He looked different from that night. He was dressed in jeans, a denim shirt, laced boots.

"You have to promise you're not going to run away," he said. "We'll act like we just met, you don't even have to tell Vanni you knew me before. You're not my patient, it's not a problem for me to want to get to know you. I'll see you around. You'll show up at Jack's sometimes, and I get dinner there. And if I see you there sometimes, maybe we'll be friends. That's why I was trying to get in touch with you. Just to see you again. Give it a chance." He smiled at her. "Come on. You like me. You know you do."

"How are you going to explain some interest in a single, pregnant woman?" she asked him.

He laughed. "Abby. Look in the mirror."

"I should get out of here before there's trouble...."

"No, you can't go," he said calmly, firmly. He really didn't want to play hardball with her, but he shouldn't have to tell her what she would be able to put together after she thought about it a while—he'd turn the earth upside down to find her if she was carrying his children. Cam had the DNA to prove he was the father. "You have to give this a little time. I have a vested interest here."

"That's exactly why I didn't call you. It scares me. What if

I get to know you and decide you're just not the kind of man I want involved with my children?"

He smiled and lifted one eyebrow. "Really? And what if I get to know you and decide you're not the kind of woman I want raising mine?" The surprise was evident in her eyes, as was a little fear. "Just because I'm not carrying them and birthing them doesn't mean they're any less mine."

"Oh God," she moaned.

He stood up, grabbed her hand and pulled her to her feet. He slipped an arm around her waist and pulled her carefully against him, holding her sweetly, tenderly, lightly caressing her back until she seemed to calm and lean against him. He pulled back and looked down into her frightened eyes. "I just want you to remember one thing," he said softly. Then he lowered his lips to hers in a gentle kiss. Then he pulled back, smiling into her eyes. He kissed her again, again gently. And then he came down on her lips in a more serious kiss, moving over her mouth carefully, sensually, until her arms slowly and reluctantly encircled him, her eyelids dropping closed. He stayed on her lips until she kissed back, letting him open her lips. He tilted his head for a better angle, enjoying her response. Not knowing when he'd get a chance like this again, he stayed with that kiss for a long time, tasting her mouth, being tasted by her. When he released her mouth, he smiled. "Ah," he whispered. "You do remember." And he kissed her again.

He released her grudgingly. "That's a good place to start. Nothing to fear, everything to gain. Now, I'm going to get out of your hair so you can unpack."

17

The Valenzuela baby, Ness, was almost six weeks old when Luke called and asked if he might stop by with Art. Art was very excited; he got himself all cleaned up, put on freshly laundered clothes, his new heavy jacket and wiggled in the truck all the way there. "Settle down a little," Luke said with a laugh. "You know Mike and Brie. It's just a baby."

"I won't touch it," he said by way of a promise.

"If you want to touch the baby, you have to ask politely. And if the answer is no, it's no."

"Okay," he said.

"And we should be kind of quiet around the baby," he said. And Art nodded.

Luke invited Art to carry the brightly wrapped gift, all pink bows and gewgaws with a pair of crochet booties tied into the bow. When Mike opened the door, Art pushed it at him proudly. "Thanks," Mike said with a laugh. "Would you like to come in?"

"Okay," Art said. "I'll be quiet. Can I touch it? The baby?"

Mike held the door open. "My wife handles all special requests. But she's very generous. Let me get her."

Mike dropped the gift on the coffee table and disappeared into the house. A few seconds later he was following Brie into the living room. She held the wrapped baby against her shoulder. She grinned at Art and said, "It's so nice to see you, Art. How've you been?"

"I've been very good."

Brie lowered the baby. "Well, Art, meet Ness. And Ness, this is Art."

"Oh," he said a little breathlessly. "Oh."

"She's sleeping. When she's awake she has a very big cry."

"Very big," Mike affirmed. "When she's fifteen, she's going to kill me with it. It's already one of those girl-screams. Terrifying."

"Art, if you'd like, you can hold her."

Art got a stricken look on his face for a second. Then he wiped his hands on his trousers and put them out, palms up.

"No." Brie laughed. "Not like that. Come over to the rocker, take your jacket off and sit down. Get comfortable. I want you to hold her like this," she said, demonstrating cradling the baby in her arms. Art very quickly positioned himself in the rocker and got his arms ready. Brie placed the baby in his arms and said, "Now, don't squeeze her—she's very fragile. And hold her just like this."

He stared down at the baby for a second in awe, in wonder, and then he lifted his eyes to Brie's and broke into a huge smile. "She doesn't feel like anything!" he said softly.

"I know. It takes some getting used to." She sat down right beside Art, just in case he needed her.

"Can I get you something to drink, Luke?" Mike asked. "And Art, when you're done holding the baby?"

"I'll hold the baby," Art said. And then very quietly he said to her, "Shh. Don't let the bedbugs bite."

That dug into Luke. It left him speechless for a moment, seeing Art so tender and sweet with the baby, echoing Shelby's words. Then he recovered himself and said, "Ah, no thanks, Mike. But we did have another reason for coming to visit. Me and Art, we might need a little advice."

"Sure," Mike said, sitting down. "What can we do?"

Luke sat forward a little in his chair. "I haven't explained the details about how Art and I were introduced," he began. To curious townsfolk, he had said that Art "turned up" and could use some work. So he told the real story, from finding him sleeping in one of the cabins, a black eye, on the run, to how he gave him shelter for chores. Then he ran down his visit to Eureka, to the grocery store and the group home. "Art's mother's gone now and he doesn't want to go back to that group home, doesn't want to work for Stan at the grocery store, and I'd like him to stay where he is. He's a good friend and a big help. But we don't want to break any rules or laws. I need to know who to talk to, how to proceed, so we do it right."

Mike said, "Whew. Complicated."

"If he has to go back to a group home, it can't be that one. And if there has to be a next one, I'll visit him every day to be sure it's all right, if I have to. I'd really like to make arrangements for him to stay in Virgin River where he's pretty happy. But we have to do it right."

Brie gave her attention to Art and very gently asked, "Art, how old are you now?"

"Thirty years old. November seventeen. We had a cake, me and Luke and Shewby."

"Did you earn money at the grocery store?"

He nodded.

"And did you sign your paychecks so they could be cashed?" Again he nodded. "Did you sign any other checks?" He nodded again. "And who did you give the checks to?" Brie asked him.

"Shirwey or Stan," he said.

"And did they give you money?"

He smiled and nodded. "Fifteen dollars every week."

"Okay, Art—do you happen to know—are you a ward of the state? A ward of the court?"

He furrowed his brow.

Brie, a former Sacramento prosecutor and currently a consultant to the Humboldt County D.A.'s office, looked at her watch and then turned her attention to Luke. "I can run this by the district attorney, but here's my guess—Art is a thirty-year-old man. An adult. He might be collecting social security benefits because his parents are deceased and he's disabled. He could be in a group home that's subsidized by the state through social services, but if he's not a ward of the state, he's not obligated to stay there. If he leaves, the subsidy ends and he gives a change of address for his benefit checks. The D.A. can find out his status.

"That other matter," she went on, "should probably be turned over for investigation. I can still get the D.A. on the phone. Do you have some names for me?"

Luke pulled a piece of paper out of his jacket pocket—names, addresses and phone numbers for Shirley and Stan—and handed it to Brie.

"Mike?" she asked, standing. "You're in charge."

"Sure," Mike said, but he waited until Brie left the room before he very casually and unobtrusively moved himself to the chair near Art, just in case there was a reason to be close, though Art was doing great with the baby. He balanced his elbows on his knees, clasped his hands together and leaned toward Art. "So, Art. That your first baby?"

Art grinned. "Uh-huh. Is it your first baby?"

"It is my very first. We did very good for our first, wouldn't you say?"

"Very good," he agreed. "I like how her hair stands straight up like that." Then he focused his eyes on Mike's. "I can stay with Luke now?"

"Everything's going to work out fine," Mike said. "You asked the right person. Brie knows everything about everything."

Twenty minutes passed and Art didn't tire of holding the sleeping baby at all. Then Brie came back into the room. "Well, it's all good. Art can live wherever he wants to. You'll have to go to Social Services and collect copies of some of his vital papers—birth certificate, social security benefit change, new picture ID in case he ever wants to travel via airlines, a whole bunch of stuff. He should start receiving his benefit checks a few weeks after you complete that. If you want a subsidy for giving him housing..."

"I don't need that," Luke said immediately.

"Rethink that—health care is part of the subsidy and that's important. Unless he becomes your dependent and you can put him on your military health care. In any case, you'll have to apply to either one. A little paperwork will tidy things up." Then she grinned. "Okay, a lot of tiresome paperwork."

Luke stood. "Stan and Shirl?"

"It's being looked into. From the reaction of the D.A., I'd say their party's just about over."

"Jeez," Luke said, running a hand over the short-cropped hair on his head. "I had no idea it was all going to be so simple!"

"Yeah, well, I know the right people here now," Brie said. She leaned down and ran a hand over her daughter's head. Then she leaned down and gave that little head a kiss. When she straightened, Art bent his big head and gave the baby a small kiss. "Welcome to Virgin River, Art," Brie said with a smile.

That night Luke couldn't wait to tell Shelby how smoothly things appeared to be working out for Art, thanks to Brie.

"So he can stay with you forever?" she asked.

"Forever's a long time, but he can stay here while he wants to," Luke said.

"But what about when you sell the cabins?" she asked.

"Well, they're not for sale yet," he said with a shrug. "If I do sell them, I can find a place for Art that's safe and secure."

"If," she said, her heart racing suddenly.

"I think I've gotten kind of comfortable here." He laughed softly. "Surprises the hell out of me. I thought I'd be stir-crazy by now."

"You were talking about a flying job. Have you applied anywhere?"

"I've talked to a couple of outfits that have openings—a news chopper in Dallas. A rescue outfit in Georgia. Nothing has my name stamped on it yet. I've only been out of the army six months. There's plenty of time. Right now the important thing is that Art feels okay."

Shelby didn't say anything right away. She waited for him to say something about them—their future. About it being important that she felt okay. About having plans that included them both. But nothing came. Because nothing had changed.

"While I'm here," Luke said, "I should be able to keep an eye on Art, it's not like he's high maintenance."

"Well," Shelby said. "That's great news. I'm sure you'll be very happy together."

Loving Luke was like a drug for Shelby. She wasn't sure exactly how long to stay in this relationship or how to let it go, but one thing she did know for sure, he wasn't offering her anything more than what they had together, and what they had wasn't binding in any way. It was more than just sex, but intimacy with him held her captive. There was also affection.

In terms of companionship, friendship, she felt secure; it was clear he cared about her. The problem was that without words of love, without commitment, the day could come without warning that he would say, "I don't feel enough to keep this going any longer." And that day would kill her.

It was that moment Muriel had warned her about. The moment of clarity that signaled it was time to think about moving on.

The weather had been fairly mild until late January and then a blast from the north covered the mountains and brought in February with rain, snow, sleet and ice. The days were short and, given the overcast, dark. The snow didn't stick for long but the ice was unpredictable and treacherous. The California Department of Forestry was clearing the mountain roads of debris and spreading sand along the steep and curving roads. There were more than the usual number of one-car accidents caused by poor visibility or slippery roads. Everyone in Virgin River was bundled up.

Shelby headed for town one afternoon to spend some time talking with Mel; Mel was always compassionate but straight to the point with her advice. Uncle Walt warned Shelby to watch those patches of black ice. All the way into town, she was rehearsing what she would say, how she would explain that nothing had gone wrong with Luke, but it also hadn't gone quite right. That Luke was ready to take care of Art and make sure he had all he needed, but hadn't even said he would miss Shelby—that said it all. She needed to be told she was loved. She didn't think that was greedy.

She slowed as she saw something up ahead that looked like a pile of trash by the side of the road. Also, some dirt on the shoulder was visible through the snow. Then from that pile at the edge of the road, there was movement. As she drew near, a child stood up while another person remained down. She hit the brakes and skidded, so she eased up through a possible spin until she stopped safely.

She jumped out of the Jeep and what she saw stunned and confused her. A little girl, maybe six years old, stood beside a teenage boy who sat on the ground, gripping his shoulder with one hand and grimacing in pain. He had a gash on his head and his arm hung at an unnatural angle. The little girl was sobbing, tears running down her cheeks. Her eyes were wide and frightened.

Shelby knelt beside them. She ran her hands over the little girl's head, shoulders and arms. "What happened here?" she asked them.

"The bus," the boy said, turning his head to point down the hill. Halfway down, a hundred feet at least, that big yellow bus was balanced very tentatively, the back end up against a huge tree, the front end pointing downward. If one thing shifted, that bus could head down the hill like a torpedo, hitting every tree and bump in its path before crashing at the bottom, a long way down.

"Holy God," Shelby muttered. She bent to the boy, who grimaced in pain again. "Are there kids on the bus?" she asked.

"It's full o' kids," he groaned. "When it slid off the road, we started to get out the back emergency door." Tears ran down his cheeks from the pain. "I only got Mindy out before the thing shifted and slid farther." He groaned. "I took a dive."

"And crawled up the hill?" she asked.

He nodded. "If they try to get out, it could go. My arm. It's outta the socket. You gotta pull it hard. Get it back in."

"Hang on, buddy," she said. "Just hang on." She walked over to the edge of the hill, framed her mouth with her hands and yelled as loud as she could. "Don't move! I'm getting help!" She helped the boy to his feet, then took the little girl's hand. She opened the back door of the Jeep for them.

He struggled to get in. "Can't you do this arm?" he asked. "All you have to do is—"

"We're only a couple of minutes from town, just hang on and let a doctor do it. You can make it. Work with me here," she said. Through some slipping and sliding, she got them into the Jeep. She punched the odometer to zero to record the exact distance to the scene. As she headed the rest of the way to town, she asked a couple of questions. "You have any idea how many kids are on the bus?"

"I don't know exactly. Some didn't go today because of weather," he said. "About twenty. Mostly the little ones."

"Do you know how it happened?"

"Ice," he said simply. "We fishtailed. I thought she had it, but then the back end of the bus slid down the hill. Lucky we weren't crushed, me and Mindy. We were coming out the back."

"Do you know if anyone else is hurt in the bus?"

"I didn't see anything after it started down the hill."

"Mindy? You okay, honey? Anything hurt?"

"My knees," she cried. "I want my mommy!" Tears ran down her chafed cheeks.

"How long ago?" Shelby asked the boy.

"Not too long. You came along right away."

"Sheer luck," she said. "I'm so glad I did." As she neared town, there was sand sprinkled on the road. But what she saw panicked her—parents waiting inside their cars for the bus to bring their children. At least they were inside the cars and might assume the bus was running late because of weather. She hoped they'd take no notice of her hauling kids into the clinic at the other end of the block. She pulled up in front. "Stay right here while I get the doctor. You have to give me sixty seconds. Can you do that?"

"Yeah," the boy said. "Hurry."

Shelby ran into the clinic. As she entered, Cameron came

out of the office and Mel came from the kitchen. Shelby tried to keep her voice calm. "I've got two kids in my Jeep. A little girl about six, scratched up, a boy about sixteen, gash on his head and dislocated shoulder. The school bus went off the road. Four point six miles west of town. Twenty kids are trapped in a bus that's balanced against a tree and could slip down the mountain any second."

"Jesus," Mel said. "Let's get the kids in here," she said, heading for the door.

Shelby grabbed the sleeve of her sweater. "Listen, there are parents waiting at the bus stop. If they figure out there's an accident, they're going to rush out there, maybe attempt a rescue, maybe cause that bus to dislodge and crash down the hill."

Mel looked at Shelby calmly. "Call 911. Then call Jack and tell him about the accident and where to go—tell him about the parents. He'll know what to do. Then call Connie at the corner store and tell her we have an emergency. Ask her to walk down here, calmly, as if nothing's wrong. We'll take care of the kids in your Jeep and the minute they're stable, we'll have Connie stay here and head out to the scene. Got that?"

"Got it," Shelby said, heading for the phone.

She was already on the phone to Jack when Mel and Cameron were bringing the kids into the clinic. She watched Cam take the boy into the treatment room as Mel took the little girl into the exam room. Shelby was on the phone to Connie when she heard a loud cry from the treatment room—Cameron had likely yanked that shoulder to pop it back into the joint.

Shelby paced for a couple of seconds, waiting. Then she picked up the phone and called Walt, sending him out to help. Then thinking that if anyone had heavy equipment that could be useful, it would be Paul; she asked her uncle to find him in case he could help. And then, thankfully, Connie came in the door. Right at that moment, Mel came out of the exam room and faced her.

"We have a school-bus accident," she said, reaching for her coat. "First aid will probably be necessary. Maybe triage. We have to go out there right away. There's a small child in the exam room—her name is Mindy. She appears to be all right, just some scrapes, but you have to get her help to contact her mother. Cam's treating an older boy. Someone has to stay here in the clinic, Connie. My kids are sleeping in the kitchen, due to wake up. Call for help if you need to, but I need to have Shelby with me. Can you manage this?"

"Sure," she said, shrugging. "I'll give Joy a call right away. She'll come."

Cameron came out of the treatment room. "Connie, sixteen-year-old boy in the treatment room. He has shoulder pain from a dislocation, repaired, and bandage on his head. I gave him pain medication and told him to stay right where he is, resting. You can call his parents, but I don't want him to leave until someone can look at him a little later. Tell him to be patient—it'll either be one of us or paramedics." He reached for his coat and medical bag. "Let's go."

Jack was the first to arrive at the scene of the accident, Preacher not far behind him. He got ropes and pulleys out of his truck bed, rapidly secured it to a tree and rappelled down the hill to the stranded bus. The hillside was slick with ice and snow and he slid around, landing on his knees more than once. He was almost there when he glanced up and saw Preacher standing at the top of the hill, looking down at him.

The ignition on the bus was off. It just sat there, its back end up against a big tree trunk. There was no movement. He got as close to the driver's window as he could. "Molly?"

Slowly, cautiously, the window slid open. Molly looked out at him. She had a cut on her chin and a big, purple bruise on her forehead. "Jack," she said in a breath.

"Can you keep everyone in the bus still?" he asked. "We're waiting for rescue and paramedics."

"They'll be still. No one's moving. But we're pretty scared in here."

He heard some weak crying in the bus. "Yeah, I know. What have you got for injuries? Have any idea?"

"Past these first couple of rows, no idea, Jack. Everyone says something hurts, but they can hold still."

He glanced at the rear of the bus, hooked up against a big sequoia. It looked as if a little jostling could bust it loose and send it sailing down the hill. "Here's the thing, Molly—this bus isn't stable at all. It looks bad out here. We need rescue to brace the bus before taking people out. Understand?"

She pulled her head in and spoke to the kids, calmly and firmly. "We can't move a muscle," she told them all. "We have to be perfectly still until the bus is braced and can't slide. Rescue is coming. Then they'll get us out. Without moving a muscle, tell me you understand," she instructed.

Jack heard small, careful voices from inside. "How many, Molly?"

"Eighteen," she said.

"Okay, could be a while. Close the window. Don't let the heat out. I'll stay right here by your window until they get here. It's going to be okay."

She smiled weakly. "Okay," she said. And then the driver's window slowly closed.

The temptation to try to get as many kids out as possible was almost irresistible. And the thought that he could be holding himself here, hanging on to a rope, right next to the bus, and see it plummet down the hill and crash, was enough to make his insides grip and knot. The hardest thing about any kind of life-threatening situation was always the wait. Taking action, that wasn't as hard. Sometimes you just moved, not thinking, performing on instinct, getting it done. Doing nothing, waiting for help to arrive, it was just torture.

Jack moved to the right enough to brace himself against a tree trunk so he wouldn't have to hang on for the duration. He watched the bus, watched through the windows. It was cold as hell; he hoped they could do something before it became a toss-up as to what was worse, those kids plunging down the mountain or freezing to death in there.

It seemed a lifetime before he heard the sound of engines. "Preach—you have to keep everyone but emergency back! The kids in the bus are trying to hold still, and it's hard!"

"Yo!" he heard back from the top. "I've got help up here, Jack!"

Slowly the sky grew darker and it seemed an eternity before what sounded like heavy equipment started arriving— fire trucks, he assumed. Suddenly the dusk was lit by a blast of light coming from above; high-powered beams slanted down the hill, illuminating the bus.

It grew colder; the wind picked up. There was a sound from the top of the hill that sounded like a jackhammer. Finally two firefighters rappelled down the hill. One went to the driver's window while the other slid close to the side of the bus and used a flashlight to view the undercarriage.

A third man in heavy turnouts and boots came down the hill, being lowered by a thick cable. As Jack watched, the three of them went to work under the bus, attaching the cable to the axle with giant hooks. He couldn't resist checking his watch— they were at it for almost a half hour when two emerged from beneath the bus. The third said to Jack, "Can you get a child up that hill?"

"You bet," he said. "I can come back for more."

"We'll let you know," he said. Then he went to the rear of the bus and carefully pulled open the emergency door. The bus wobbled slightly, but held, secured by the cable.

The firefighter at the door shouted into the bus. "I need your attention, I need you to listen carefully and do just what I ask. The bus is still rocky, unstable. We're going to take you off now, one at a time. Slowly. And we have to take you from the front of the bus first, keeping the weight in the rear. You have to walk down the aisle one at a time, very slowly, very carefully. The next one doesn't start down the aisle till the one before is off the bus. Does everyone understand? If you don't understand, ask me now before we start." There was no response.

Jack shifted himself off the tree and held on to his ropes, moving sideways until he could get near where the firefighter was at the rear door.

"Okay, driver—how about you first," he yelled. "Show them how it's done."

"Driver last," she shouted back. "I don't leave my kids. Becky, you go. No one has to show you. When Becky's out, Anna goes. Easy does it. Almost over, kids."

As soon as the trembling little girl cleared the door, the firefighter grabbed her, passed her to Jack. "Hold on around my neck, angel," he whispered. "Almost home." And as he slowly pulled himself up the hill, the rescue team was moving down past him, rappelling gear and harnesses in place.

The sight at the top of the hill almost threw him into a state of shock. The lights that flooded the area were Paul's construction beams; the cable that held the bus was attached to a brace that came off a forklift that had been bolted right into the asphalt, also Paul's. In addition to rescue equipment, there were vehicles everywhere. A paramedic rig and fire truck sat right at the top of the hill. Next to it on one side the Grace Valley ambulance with Docs Stone and Hudson at the ready; on the other side stood Mel, Cameron and Shelby beside the Hummer, the back hatch open. And there were so many people, it looked as though the entire town was present, all being kept behind a perimeter set up by sheriff's deputies.

As soon as he put the little girl on her feet, there was a huge cheer. Cameron rushed forward and scooped the girl up, taking her to the back of the Hummer to look her over.

Right behind Jack, another child was brought up the hill, and again the cheer. Slowly, one by one, eighteen kids ranging in age from six to sixteen, were delivered to the top of the hill. There was a possible broken collarbone, a few head lacerations, lots of bruises and scrapes, and one possibly serious head injury was rushed off to Valley Hospital by Dr. Stone in the ambulance.

Jack walked to the edge of the hill to watch the last passenger come up the hill, being aided by two firefighters. Molly. He reached out for her hand to pull her the rest of the way. Blood ran down her chin and had dripped onto her jacket. The second she reached the top, the town cheered.

She looked up at Jack with tears in her eyes. "Are they crazy?" she asked in a low voice. "I thought they'd tar and feather me!"

"For ice?" Jack asked.

"I swear to God, I was going slow, for the ice..."

"Molly, you kept your head. You kept eighteen kids still for two hours. You probably saved all their lives."

"Jack, I don't know that I was ever so scared."

He put a hand around the back of her neck and pulled her against his chest. "Yeah. Me, too." He took a breath. "Me, too."

Luke had gone to the bar, hoping to get dinner to take home for himself, Art and Shelby. Upon finding it closed, he heard about the accident and, like everyone else who heard, headed that way. There were so many people in the thick of a rescue that was well under way by the time he got there, he didn't get too close. He stayed back behind the perimeter tape, behind a crowd of parents and townsfolk, watching in fascination as a team that combined men from town—Paul and some of his crew, Preacher, the general, Mike V.—and the rescue team worked. They bolted down a brace, fastened a heavy cable from a huge spool and ran it down the hill.

While this was going on, he saw Shelby with Mel and Cameron, saw her rush forward to lead a child to the Humvee for medical evaluation and treatment. She was in the thick of it, helping to administer first aid, soothing crying children, calming disgruntled parents, snapping to attention with every request from either Mel, Cameron or even a paramedic. She looked as if she'd been doing it all her life.

Finally, after standing for well over an hour, his breath swirling around, he saw the firefighters bring up the bus driver, the very one who'd splattered him on his way into town. He'd been listening to the talk in the crowd of townspeople, that Jack had been down there, hanging on to a rope, keeping her calm while she had the bigger job of keeping all the children from wiggling around or trying to escape the bus.

He saw Jack give her a hug, then saw Shelby go to her, take her hand and lead her to the paramedic rig to have her bleeding chin looked at. Mel followed, watching them treat her injury.

People were beginning to leave, or follow their children to the hospital or take uninjured kids home. Road-construction barriers were set up around the brace that held the cable that held the bus; California Highway Patrol was directing traffic out of the area. And Luke walked toward Shelby as she was packing supplies back into the Humvee.

"Hey, there," he said. "What's new?"

She jumped in surprise. "Luke! How long have you been here?"

"Little over an hour," he said. "By the time I got here, the fire department, police and paramedics were all over the place and I had to stay behind the barrier with everyone else. I didn't want to distract you."

"Did you see that bus down there?"

"I didn't want to get too close. There was an awful lot going on."

"The floodlights are still on it. You should look. It'll scare you to death."

"So—what they're saying is, you found a couple of hurt kids who got out before it slid down the hill and went for help."

Before she could answer, Mel was beside them. "Correct," she answered for Shelby. "You would have been impressed, Luke. She never flinched. She knew all the right things to do and remained perfectly calm. Efficient, skilled, confident." Mel smiled. "She's going to be an incredible nurse. You should be so proud of her."

"I am," Luke replied. "And not at all surprised." He draped an arm around her shoulders.

And Shelby thought, *Oh God. I have to get this over with.* She didn't need advice from Mel or anyone else. She'd given him every chance, but he never said a word about how he felt about her, not a syllable about wanting a life with her. She had to make herself move on before she couldn't. Tears gathered in her eyes. "Let me finish up here, Luke. I'm going to follow Mel and Cameron back to the clinic, help clean up the Humvee, restock it. I'll catch up with you later."

"Are you crying?" he asked softly.

"I might be overwhelmed."

He frowned slightly at the glistening in her eyes. "Sure," he said. He kissed her forehead. "Take your time."

18

A few days later found Shelby in the stable in the early morning. No one in the Booth family was riding; just walking from the house to the stable to tend the horses was torture. Walt had put a coffeepot in the tack room because he couldn't keep a cup hot when carrying it from the house. Even though the stable was heated, Shelby wore heavy gloves, a scarf around her neck, her suede jacket…and her ostrich boots. She wore them all the time.

Walt came into the stable while she was feeding the horses. "Hey, I'm way ahead of you," she said.

"You usually are. Damn cold out there."

"It's not the tropics in here. Let's get a cup of coffee while these horses feed. I have something great to tell you."

He lifted an eyebrow and threw an arm wide for her to precede him into the tack room. She poured a couple of mugs and dressed one with powdered cream and sweetener for her uncle. "I talked to one of the administrators at San Francisco State. It's not official, but it looks like they're going to let me in. And if they do, she said I can enroll for summer classes if I feel like it. And as soon as I get down there, she'll write me a pass to audit. It wouldn't hurt to sit in on a few classes. That might give me an edge." She grinned largely. "I won't be too far away, Uncle Walt. I should see you, Vanni and Paul pretty often."

"And what about Humboldt State?" he asked. "You mentioned..."

"I think San Francisco might suit me better," she said. "More potential social life, for one thing."

"It's just that Humboldt is right here," he said. "Close to the people you love."

"I know. And I've been so happy here with you, Uncle Walt, but I'm ready to spread my wings."

He thought about that for a moment, then said, "That's good news, Shelby," he said, toasting her with his coffee cup. "To you."

"Thanks. Thing is, I'm going to want to go early to find a place off campus. There's housing—mostly dorm housing—not available to me until next fall when I'm a full-time student. But I've been thinking about it and I don't think I'm up to that lifestyle, seven years older than the average freshman. This is good, that I'm kind of forced to find my own place. I can always change my mind later, move onto campus, but I bet I stay in my own place. Maybe I'll have roommates at some point, if I find students I have something in common with, starting with age and maybe life experience." She smiled. "To all of you I'm so young, to them, I'll seem old."

"I can understand that."

She looked down into her cup, then up. "I'm going to want

to go real soon, Uncle Walt. Get settled in. Meet people. You know."

"What's real soon?" he asked suspiciously.

"Real soon," she repeated. "But first, I'm taking that vacation I promised myself. I'm going to spend two full weeks on the beach in Maui." She laughed. "If I wasn't tempted to do that before, this weather for the last couple of weeks sure sealed the deal. I have to see the sun again!"

"You deserve it. When do you suppose you'll do that?"

She gazed up at him with clear eyes. "Right away. A couple of days…" He was speechless; his mouth might've dropped open slightly. "I made all my arrangements. Did you know you can do all of that on the computer?" She laughed again. "Everything from plane tickets to hotels and car rentals."

He frowned. "Yes, I knew that."

"Well, I've never gone anywhere. Not since I went to spend summers and holidays with you as a kid and you always sent the tickets. Really, it's so slick. Punch in a few dates and times, give 'em a credit card and—"

"Shelby," he interrupted, "what's this about?"

She fixed her lips into a tight line, sighed, then said, "It doesn't seem like it, but I've been here six months. It's time for me to get on with things."

"I realize that, but this is abrupt."

"I apologize, it must seem so—but I've actually been working on the details and didn't want to say anything until I had an agenda. I hope that doesn't upset you, Uncle Walt, because I'll be back to visit. No reason I can't. Not now."

"Your mood's been a little different lately…."

"I've been thinking so hard about this," she said with a shrug.

"You don't have to tell me, but does Luke have anything to do with this?"

"No. No, of course not."

"You sure about that?"

She turned away from her uncle. "I've been thinking about things and…" She turned back. "Listen, it's tempting to just stay here, like this, forever. I could travel from here, go to school from here… There's no future in it, that's all. I'm thinking like a boxer—I want to go out a winner."

"Has he hurt you, Shelby?"

She shook her head. "Just the opposite. Things are nice enough that if I stay in this pattern for six more months, I might stay for six more years. But, Uncle Walt, it's never going to become all I'd like it to be. It won't change. My clothes will hang in your closet and I'll spend most of my nights at his house. In the long term, I'm looking for something more than that.…"

Walt pursed his lips and shook his head. Under his breath he muttered, "That sorry son of a bitch…"

"Now stop," she said firmly. "You're surprised by this? Be fair—I had a big crush on Luke. He was always wonderful to me and it would probably be just fine with him if I didn't move on. But it's going nowhere. In the end, I'd be selling out. That's not what I intend to do."

He looked at the floor and shook his head. Then he took a slow sip of his coffee.

"Remember that song, Uncle Walt?" she asked him. "'Me and Mrs. Jones, we got a thing going on…?' Me and Mr. Riordan, we have a thing going on…and the next man in my life is going to be more than a thing. I want the whole deal. And Luke said from the start, if I was looking for something like that, I wouldn't find it with him. Really, if I'm honest with myself, I never doubted that."

"This is your decision, then?" he asked.

"Oh, absolutely. I haven't even mentioned this to Luke yet. And you're under strict orders—you are *not* to treat him like he's done something wrong. Do you hear me? Because if you do, you're going to be in big trouble with me. Are we clear?"

"If that's what you want."

"It's what I want." Then she laughed. "Give him a year, he'll be so damn sorry he let me go."

"You think so, huh?"

"Oh, you bet. He'll manage to find women—he's good-looking and can be real charming. But he won't find one like me. And once I make a clean break and get myself in a new life, he's gonna be shit outta luck."

Walt chuckled. "You're a lot tougher than you look."

"Yeah, I know. You shouldn't underestimate me so much. It's your biggest mistake. And it'll be Luke's, too."

"Honey, all I want is that you be happy. If these plans make you happy, then I'm on board. Just as long as he hasn't hurt you."

"He hasn't. He's been great to me. But I want more than he has to give. I want it all, Uncle Walt."

"Then you go get it. And let me know what I can do to help."

"Sure," she said. She glanced around. "I can finish with these horses in five minutes. Go read your paper."

"You sure? I could help you—"

"Nah, I'm almost done. Go," she said with a laugh, taking the coffee cup out of his hand. "I got it."

He kissed her brow. "You're incredible, Shelby. I'm proud of you."

"Thanks, Uncle Walt," she said. "That means a lot."

He left the stable. She watched out the door as he trudged up the hill. When he was far enough away, when she was sure he wasn't coming back, tears welled in her eyes and rolled down her cheeks. Then she went to Chico, clung to his neck and sobbed against his cheek.

★ ★ ★

Luke was just pulling a shepherd's pie Preacher had made out of the oven when he saw the glow of headlights flash by the window. He took a bottle of merlot he thought Shelby would like from the rack and got the corkscrew out of the drawer, but the front door didn't open. He stared at it expectantly and when she didn't come in, he went to the door and opened it, stepping outside.

Her Jeep sat right in front of the porch, but she didn't seem to be there. He was just thinking she must have gone to invite Art to dinner when he caught sight of her sitting in one of the chairs on the porch. She was bundled up in her suede jacket, a thick scarf around her neck and her hands tucked in her pockets. "What are you doing out here?" he asked, confused. "You must be half-frozen."

"I was going to knock in a second," she said.

"Knock?" He laughed. "Since when do you knock?"

"Luke, I'm not coming inside tonight."

"What?" He stepped toward her. "Shelby, what's going on? I have a fire—"

"Really, I knew this was coming, but when the bus went down the hill, full of kids, it was a defining moment for me. I'm going to do that—help to save lives. Oh, I hope I don't see any more buses go down a mountainside, but if they do, they'll need someone like me to help, and that's what I want to do. Luke, I…" She took a breath. "I know you care about me a lot. Hard as you try to hide it, I know you do."

"'Course I do," he said, taking a step toward her.

She stood from the chair. "Remember when I said that I wanted to fall in love someday? But that I didn't expect it from you? When I said it, it was true. But then I fell in love with you. I didn't do it on purpose, but I did. And you didn't love me back."

"Shelby, I loved you every night, sometimes more than once a night."

She laughed at him, but there was definitely no humor in it. "Yeah, I know. You sure stepped up that way. Thing is, I need to hear that you love me, that you want a life with me. I need more than sex every night. I'll be honest with you, it's hard to give that up, though."

"Then don't," he said, reaching for her.

"I want to hear that you're in love with me, too. I want a true partner and family, Luke. A child, at least one child."

"Shelby, honey, you have plans! School, travel, a career as a saver of lives—"

"That's exactly right, and you know what? We girls don't have to choose between education, careers and family anymore. It's a brave new world, Luke. I can travel, get an education, train for an exciting career and have a solid relationship, too. Just like the boys do. Look at Mel. Look at Brie."

He hung his head, looking down.

"You don't have to say it. You were clear from the beginning—that just isn't going to happen with you. So I'm taking off. I came to say goodbye. I'm leaving in two days for Maui. That vacation I've been kicking around. I'm packing up the car, driving to San Francisco and picking up a flight from there. Then I'll go back to San Francisco and look around for an apartment. Maybe get a part-time job and audit some classes while I wait. San Francisco State is going to take me."

"Shelby," he said, stepping toward her. He reached for her hand and when she didn't meet him halfway, he pulled her hand out of her pocket and drew her toward him. "I'm freezing. Come inside. Tell me about your plans."

"I want this to be quick. I want you to remember me strong, sure of myself. You're probably better at saying goodbye than I am. I don't want to get all worked up."

"I never say goodbye," he said. He pulled her into the house and kicked the door closed behind her. He faced her and held both her upper arms in his hands. "Isn't this kind of sudden?"

"Oh—I've known for a while this was coming. This was the best I could do. But I wanted to tell you a couple of things. It just matters to me that you know…. I don't have any regrets," she said. "I know I didn't give you much of a choice—I was so determined that you were going to be the one, my first man, my first love. And I was mostly right—you made everything perfect. I don't think I'll live a day without remembering, without feeling your arms, your lips… Thank you, Luke. For treating me like you loved me. Every time you touched me, I believed you loved me."

"What are you saying? That you're not coming back? Ever?"

"I'm sure I'll be back to visit the family, but not until I think I can do that without getting in your space. I mean, when I move on, you move on. I understand that. There will be another girl's shampoo in your shower before I—"

"I don't let just anyone keep shampoo in my shower," he said. He pulled her close, put his arms around her. "Shelby, take off your coat. Stay with me a while."

"Nah, I'm afraid if I stay even five minutes longer than I have to, I'll never have the courage to go." She pulled back and looked up at him. "I knew you were completely honest with me, Luke. I understood—you just like things free and easy, you don't want all the complications that go with taking on a commitment to a woman. You don't want a family. I guess not everyone does. I knew it, but inside there was a tiny little voice that kept saying, but he loves me enough for that to change. I thought maybe you could be that guy—the guy who'd say the perfect thing and keep me forever…."

He ran a hand through her hair. "Shelby, honey, I told you

I was a bad choice if you were looking for those things. I'd make the promises if I could keep them."

"Oh, you make them and keep them. You do it all the time. You promised me you'd never let yourself be tied down to a woman, and you meant it. I thought the right woman might change that, but… I realized I was kidding myself when you told me what you'd done for Art. You not only took him on and cared for him, but made a commitment to him, to be sure he was taken care of forever. That's when I knew for sure—it wasn't really commitment that has you running scared. It's making a life with *me,* that's what you can't do. Something must be missing. I'm just not enough for you to take that kind of risk."

"Nothing was missing," he said. "Nothing. But I'm not a good bet and you have things to do. I saw you out there at the accident—you were born to help people. You have to go after that life, and you should see more of the world than you have. Shelby, the possibilities for you…"

"If that's what it was, we'd talk about how to make all that happen. Together. There are a million ways to work this out, you and me. Except…there really isn't a you and me. Not like I hoped there could be."

"You think you're ready for something like that, but you're not. You were just born, baby. You have to get out of the nest now. Fly."

"Oh, Luke, I'm not a newborn. I've been places that I pray, by the grace of God, you never go…. When I thought about it—you've made many commitments, not the least of which was the army. Brothers, business partners, friends. But Art was the one that made me really sit up and take notice."

"Art's different, Shelby. He has nowhere else to go. And if I couldn't take care of him, I could find him a safe place. It's not the same, you have to know that. And the army? Aw, hell, Shelby—they had me, I didn't have them. It's service or AWOL."

"Bull. Everyone gets a discharge date, unless they re-up. You were committed. And I'm proud of you for that, I'm proud of you for everything, especially for Art. If I don't go soon, I'm afraid I'll stay here forever without ever hearing you say the things I need to hear. And that, more than anything, will break my heart."

He shook his head, his eyes pained, but he didn't let go of her. "I knew in the end I'd hurt you, and I never wanted to hurt you. Shelby, I want everything for you."

"I believe you. I absolutely do. You couldn't have loved me the way you did if you didn't care, if you weren't sincere. If I'm hurt, it's just because you're so damn hard to give up. And I'm so damn in love with you." A tear ran down her cheek. She pulled away from him. "Be safe, Luke. I know I'll think about you all the time."

"What about Art? Aren't you going to tell Art where you're going? What you're going to do?"

She shook her head. "God, I can't," she said softly. "I'll fall apart. Luke, please, tell him for me. Tell him it was sudden and I'll write to him. Please?" She was edging away from him and he abruptly pulled her back. He held her tight and covered her mouth in a searing and desperate kiss. In spite of herself, she returned the embrace and opened her lips to him, but a whimper escaped her. While he kissed her, Luke could taste her tears. When he released her lips, she dropped her head against his chest and for just a moment, she cried. It was very brief; her struggle was courageous. She pulled away from him and in a whisper said, "Goodbye, Luke. You were everything. You were all I needed. I'm sorry I wasn't enough for you. Maybe someday you'll meet someone who is."

When she went out the door, he stood there for a long time.

He heard her Jeep start, saw the headlights strafe the windows as she backed away, listened while the engine noise grew more faint and finally disappeared. And still he stood there. Then he hung his head.

Despite the wicked chill in the air, a few people from Virgin River braved the cold to gather together for dinner at Jack's. Vanessa and Paul took Abby with them and while they were there, Mel and Cameron came over from the clinic. Mike V. stopped by for a beer before heading home where, he said, their baby daughter would no doubt be screaming like a banshee. Walt passed through only long enough to pick up some takeout for an evening with Muriel. Vanessa was pleased to notice that Cameron took a chair beside Abby and was visiting with her. For a second there she had a hopeful thought—that maybe those two could—

But then she noticed something in the way he seemed to gaze into her eyes and she seemed to lower her lids almost shyly. Abby was not shy. Sure, she was vulnerable right now and probably not in the best shape to receive the attentions of a single man, but... Cameron leaned toward her to say something quietly and Abby smiled and nodded. And then he touched her thigh under the table, giving her a soft and reassuring pat that turned into a brief caress. And Vanessa had to concentrate not to stare.

No one stayed late, the weather was just too frigid. No one seemed to notice that Vanni was unusually quite. Once they were home, Vanni settled the baby for the night and Paul fell asleep, sitting up in bed with a book in his lap. She crept out of her room. Abby was still in the living room, curled up on the couch in front of the fire with a throw around her shoulders.

Vanni went to the couch and lifted a corner of the throw, snuggling close.

"What's the matter?" Abby asked. "Couldn't sleep?"

"No. I've been thinking…"

"What's got you thinking?"

"Math."

Abby laughed. "Well, I can't help you there. I was never good at math."

"You left Nikki and Joe's wedding reception. We knew you were depressed, we all knew you and Ross were on the skids even though you wouldn't talk about it. We thought you went to your room to suffer in silence and even talked about trying to draw you out, but in the end decided sometimes a girl wants to be alone, to lick her wounds, think, maybe even cry."

"Well…"

"And now I'm thinking, what are the chances you met someone that night, in Grants Pass? Someone so nice, so sweet. So sexy and handsome that you were tempted to actually pass some time with him. Someone I know."

"Vanni…"

"He's a good man, Abby. A very good man. He's come to help our town. He courted me a little and when he realized I was in love with Paul, not only did he back away like a gentleman, he helped us—more than once."

"Vanni, I don't really know him."

"Then I suggest you get to know him. Real soon. I could tell by the way you two looked at each other—there's something happening there. You have his babies inside you, don't you?" Abby looked down. "Well, if, worst-case scenario, you can't fall in love with him, at least you can let him be a father to his children. He's not a slimeball like Ross—he's decent. And I happen to know—it would mean a lot to him."

There was a long period of silence. "Do you think everyone knows?"

Vanni was shaking her head. "No one knows you like I do.

And remember, I know him, too. Lucky guess. Plus, I was in Grants Pass. Abby, you're going to have to deal with this. Does he know?"

"It didn't take him long to guess," Abby said. "Just exactly what I was hoping to avoid."

"Well, kiddo, that ship has sailed. How in the world did this happen?"

Abby shrugged. "He was alone in the bar. So was I. We spent a couple of hours, just the two of us, talking. Laughing. And my head was so screwed up, I let myself be coerced upstairs to his room. I never meant that to happen. It was a mistake."

"I don't know about that. Sounds like it could have been fate. So, what's the plan?"

"He doesn't think it will raise many eyebrows if we become friends, get to know each other a little bit. But, Vanni, you have to understand something— I'm not diving headlong into another relationship with someone I don't know very well. It's going to take time and it may not end up being the fairy tale you'd like it to be. We were two disappointed, needy people that night. That's all. In a practical relationship, I'm not sure we have that much in common."

"Hmm, I can think of a couple of things."

When Walt got to Muriel's house, the dogs rushed to him, but Muriel didn't. He found her sitting at her kitchen table with a notepad and glass of wine. He hefted his sack. "I brought you meat loaf and garlic mashed from Jack's."

She looked at him across the cheerful kitchen and said, "I'm doing it, Walt. I'm going back to L.A. to work."

When he thought about it, he'd expected this. She was enchanted with the script from the moment she read it. And he knew she wouldn't sell out, so it must have come together in a way she thought was worth her time and effort. He put the sack on the counter and went to the cupboard and got down a glass and that special bottle of Pinch she reserved for special occasions, pouring himself a drink. Then he sat at the table across from her. "Tell me about it."

"I probably should have talked to you about it sooner, when it started to look like it was going to work to my advantage. But I try not to get stupidly optimistic about possible deals. For just about the first time, it turned out I was the last hold-out. The actress waiting in the wings for the part was Diane Keaton. It's a good part, Walt. A good opportunity."

"Why don't you seem happy?"

She shrugged. "It wasn't how I thought I'd spend the next six months. It's going to be a lot of hard work. And later, when the film is out, there will be promotion—that's also a lot of hard work. And none of it can be done here. I'll be in L.A. for some of it and on location in Montana in spring and early summer."

He took a bolstering drink and then reached for her hand. "We've been over this, Muriel. If you feel strongly about doing the film, I'm behind you. If you have worries, I don't want one of them to be me."

She smiled a small smile. "I have to leave tomorrow to begin rehearsing."

"Tomorrow?" he asked, shocked. "My God! Should you be packing?"

She shook her head. "No need. I just have to get together my cosmetics. I can take the dogs with me—I had them put it in my contract that I'll have help with pet care. They'll send someone to stay in the guesthouse and take care of the horses. And—"

"Why don't you need clothes?" he asked.

"I have a place in Los Angeles. A small but very nice condo. I left behind a full closet—those clothes wouldn't work for me here and the clothes I wear around here won't work for me there. I figured in a year or so I'd empty the place out and either rent or sell it, but now it'll come in handy. I've let a couple of friends use the place for visiting relatives, so it hasn't gone to waste."

"You never even mentioned it," he said, and for a moment he was grateful for that. If he'd thought all along that she still had another home, he might not have been so optimistic about their chances.

"Really, I didn't think I'd ever use it unless I was in L.A. visiting or something…"

"Muriel, are the dogs going to be a problem while you're making this movie?"

"No," she said, shaking her head. "I'll have some long hours, but the studio will make sure there's someone assigned to walking them, feeding them, all that. I just won't get to run Luce or train Buff like I'd planned to."

"Let me keep them for you. Let me take care of the horses."

"Walt, I can't ask you to—"

"You didn't ask, Muriel. Really, it's selfish. I don't want to think of someone else living in that bunkhouse or the dogs pooping on concrete somewhere when I can run them along the river. Besides a little babysitting, what do I have to do? Shelby's gone, Vanni and Paul have their own place, I take care of horses every day anyway…"

"It's a lot of bother, Walt."

"I offered. No strings," he added. "I didn't offer so that you'd feel obligated to me in any way. I mean, who knows? Jack Whatshisname might turn out to be just what you've always dreamt of."

"You jealous of him already?" she asked.

"You're goddamn right," he said, leaning back in his chair,

drawing those fierce eyebrows together. "He's going to spend the next six months with you and I'm not."

"Well, he doesn't stand a chance," she said softly.

He thought, this must be how Peg felt when he was leaving for a long remote tour, as though there was a chance he wouldn't come back to her. "I've been down this road," he told Muriel. "Separations for work. It's not easy, but it's highly survivable. Do you need a ride to the airport?"

"That would be nice. It's just to Garberville."

"Picking up a charter?" he asked.

She shook her head. "They're sending a jet."

His eyebrows shot up. "I haven't been down that road," he said, shaking his head. "You want meat loaf? Or do you want to go upstairs, let me peel your clothes off and tell you goodbye properly?"

She grinned at him. "Let's think about meat loaf for breakfast."

"Good idea," he said, standing. He reached for her hand. "Come on, honey. This is my last chance to pamper you before your Oscar. What time does your flight leave?"

"When I get there."

The next morning, Walt drove her to the Garberville airport where there was a Lear waiting. The pilot and cabin steward, nicely uniformed, were waiting at the bottom of the airstairs and they fussed over her very impressively. She had only one small bag and traveled in her jeans and boots, leather jacket and cowboy hat. She kept them waiting while she gave Walt a long, deep kiss goodbye. "If there's a break in the filming, I'll be up for a visit. And I'll call you when I get there."

"Muriel, stop being reluctant and sad. You want this and I want it for you. You're good, that's why you're getting this chance. Knock 'em dead. And if Jack Whatshisname makes a play for you, tell him to fuck off. You have a boyfriend already."

She laughed. "I'll be sure to tell him."

"And I'm a good shot."

"Yeah," she said. "Thanks for taking on the animals. They mean a lot to me."

"Me, too," he said.

He stood there in the blistering cold until her private jet took her away. He watched it until it was out of sight. All he could think was, what if she doesn't come back? What if she really does get that Oscar and is lured into one more and one more and one more? A private jet came for her and she didn't even have to pack. And having her own jet didn't make her the least intimidated or uncomfortable. This was Muriel's real life.

What the hell was I thinking I could mean to her?

What if she's all done being mine?

Mel heard a truck pull up in front of the clinic and thought it must be Bruce bringing mail and asking after specimens to be delivered to Valley Hospital. She walked out onto the porch, but didn't recognize the truck. She frowned as a woman got out of the passenger side. This was an attractive woman in her early thirties—trim, brown hair, pink cheeks. She looked up at Mel and smiled somewhat shyly. "Hi," she said.

Mel frowned, then returned the smile. "Hi. How can I help you?"

"Oh, you already have." She took two steps up onto the porch. She wore light makeup, slim jeans, a long-sleeved turtleneck shirt and down vest.

And then it dawned on her. Cheryl Chreighton! Her transformation was nothing short of astonishing. In just a few months' time her complexion had pinked up, her eyes were clear, she'd dropped about twenty-five pounds—probably most of it the edema that she carried from drinking—and she was not just clean, but actually groomed and styled. Someone had cut her hair and showed her how to fix it. She wore women's clothes and a very happy smile. "Oh, dear God."

"Absolutely," Cheryl said. "Dear God and you."

"Look at you," Mel said in a breath.

"Thank you," Cheryl said solemnly. "This is because of you."

"No, it's *you*," Mel stressed. "All I did was make a few phone calls. You did the work. Have you come home?"

"No," Cheryl said with a laugh, shaking her head. "This isn't a good place for me. I have a job and a place with some roommates. Not exactly a group home, but close—we're in recovery. Not much of a job, but I don't need much of one right now." Cheryl swallowed and looked down. "I doubt I'll ever come back here," she said. "There aren't any meetings here or anything." She looked up bravely and gave a shrug. "I don't think I'd be happy in a place where I used to be the town drunk. Not just an average town drunk, a below-average town drunk."

"That wouldn't matter, you know that. But the meetings—you need the meetings. Recovery without aftercare is like major surgery without stitches."

Cheryl chuckled. "Yeah, you got that right."

"How long has it been?" Mel asked.

"A hundred and twenty-seven days. I don't think we can count the day you took me. I was blitzed. I don't see a time I'll be skipping those meetings, even though I really don't want a drink today…. Mrs. Sheridan, what I have right now, I don't want to give it up. I'm at meetings all the time, sometimes twice a day. If it's forever, that's okay."

Mel almost said, "Call me Mel," but caught herself. This was Cheryl's show; she could do anything she wanted. "Good for you," she said, smiling. "Wonderful."

"I have to see my parents. I haven't seen them since I left here that day with you."

"I'm sure they'll be so happy to see you...."

Cheryl laughed. "Oh, I don't know. My mother thought the whole rehab thing was crazy and my dad thought we were doing pretty good the way he doled out the booze on his terms so he thought he had it under control. That might explain a few things. And they're not well, either of them. I need to see them, but I can't stay here. I wouldn't come alone, though. My sponsor is with me."

Mel leaned down a bit to peer into the truck. A silver-haired woman sat behind the wheel and gave Mel a brief wave and she thought, ah good. A mature woman, hopefully with years of sobriety under her belt. That would give Cheryl a good shot at success.

"And there are amends," Cheryl said. "I'm not sure I can cover the whole town, but I wanted to catch you and Doc, maybe Jack..."

Mel was temporarily shocked and for the first time realized she'd come onto the porch without a coat. She shivered. Tears gathered. "Cheryl, my God, I'm so sorry. Someone should've gotten word to you. I'm surprised your parents didn't— Doc passed away suddenly last October. We don't know why. His heart maybe. Or a fatal stroke. There was no autopsy...."

"Doc? Gone?" Cheryl asked.

"I'm sorry," Mel said. Mel blinked and a tear escaped. "He was so happy you decided on treatment. He'd be so proud of you."

"God," she said. "Isn't it amazing how fast things can just shift? He was always kind to me...." Cheryl shook herself. "Well. I can't remember if I ever did anything terrible to you that I should make amends for, but—"

"You didn't," Mel said quickly, shaking her head. "In fact, you were nice to me. You offered to help me with babysitting a long time ago. You cleaned out that horrible cabin Hope McCrea gave me as my free housing."

"I don't remember about babysitting," Cheryl said.

"Trust me. You were nice to me."

"Thanks for that," Cheryl said. "But Jack—I know I was a thorn in his butt. I wonder if I should go see him, tell him I'm sorry about that."

"You should definitely see him, though I already know he's not holding any grudge. But it would make Jack so happy to see you sober and well. It would be a good thing."

"Are you sure?"

"I'm sure, Cheryl."

"That's amends to you, too—I made a pass at Jack. I mean, I want to tell him it was just booze. I'm not really insane." Then she smiled. "Well, no more than the average drunk."

Mel let go a small laugh. "That must have happened way before I found him—you have no amends to make to me. And I'll bet Jack understands. Still, you can't imagine how happy it would make him to know you're in recovery. Cheryl—I never told him I took you to a treatment facility."

"You didn't?" she asked, shocked. "I thought the whole town knew!"

"Not from me or… Doc. We don't talk about clinic business."

"Wow. I didn't expect that."

"Well, now that you know, you can expect it. In fact, I never heard any talk around town. After all, it wasn't the first time you slipped away for a while." She grinned.

There was a quiet moment between them as they just looked into each other's eyes. Then Cheryl said, "Thank you, Mrs. Sheridan. It was a real good thing you did for me."

Mel felt her gut clench and tears threaten to flow. Those had been Doc's exact words! How he would have enjoyed seeing her like this, so different, so attractive and talking so smart. Mel liked to think maybe Doc did see. "I'm so glad it worked out, I'm proud of you. Go. See Jack and your folks. Have a nice visit. Will you stop by sometimes? When you visit your parents? Tell us how you are?"

Cheryl nodded. "Sure. If you want."

"I want," Mel said. "That would be nice."

When Mel went back inside the clinic, she went to Doc's old office, which she now shared with Cam. There were no patients, the kids were napping, Cam was off on errands. She was alone—free and clear. She put her head down on her arms and cried. Cried happy tears for Cheryl and special tears for missing Doc, knowing what it would mean to him to see one of his own coming out of such a dark time. God, to look at the woman was inspiring! To listen to her speak, so astounding! She was a whole new person. And she was young yet; she had a chance for a full and productive life.

Mel was consumed for at least a half hour. Then she heard the sound of a vehicle and thinking, again, it might be Bruce with mail, she wiped her eyes and walked out on the porch. This time it was Bruce. He handed her a packet of mail. "Any specimens?" he asked.

"Not today," she said.

"Good. I get off early."

As he jumped back in his truck, she looked at the front porch of Jack's bar. He walked outside with an arm draped over Cheryl's shoulders. They stopped, hugged, and Cheryl bounced down the steps to the waiting truck. The truck backed away.

Jack stood on his porch, looking at his wife. Even from across the street she could see the tenderness in his smile, the pride and gratitude. Cheryl had told him everything. He lifted his hand to Mel. And she lifted hers.

19

Aiden Riordan pulled up to Luke's cabin and blew the horn before getting out of his car. Luke came out with a perplexed look on his haggard face.

"What the hell are you doing here?"

"You haven't answered the phone in ten days!" he said angrily. "You know, answering machines work just fine out here!"

"Phone's out," Luke said, turning to go back inside.

Aiden rolled his eyes, shook his head and followed. He walked into the house behind Luke and pulled off his leather gloves as he looked around. Luke sat on the sectional, staring at him from beneath angry, hooded brows. "Nice," Aiden said. Then he walked over to the kitchen phone, looked at it and plugged it in.

"You're going to be real sorry you did that," Luke said.

"What's the matter? Getting a lot of calls?"

"I would call them attempts at calls. I don't want to talk. That includes you, by the way."

"Yeah, well, you're stuck with me," Aiden said. He went to the refrigerator and grabbed a bottled beer, popped the cap and went to the living room. He sat and without even bothering to take his jacket off, he said, "So. She left you."

"What are you talking about?"

"I'm talking about the perfect nymphet, Shelby. She left you and you're going down the shitter." He took a drink of his beer.

Luke silently and meanly glared at his brother.

"She left you, you're miserable and completely fucked up. I had to come all the way up here to make sure your ten-day-old dead body wasn't in this house and you're not being at all cooperative or hospitable."

"No one asked you."

"Well, Jesus, I *know* that! God forbid the firstborn ever show weakness or ask for anything. You're the steel man, right? Give me a break, Luke. Look at you. You augered in. Crashed."

"I've been working," he said.

"Bullshit. The work's done. Tell me what happened."

"Nothing happened," Luke said. "It's been kind of quiet around here. I didn't feel like talking to anyone. That's all."

Aiden looked down and shook his head with silent laughter. "Brother, you give me no credit. You think I took emergency leave to come up here and save your life without knowing anything? I called that bar—that sweet little bar you like so much? Where they haven't seen you in a long time? I talked to Jack a while, got Walt Booth's number and talked to him, too. Here's what happened—Shelby went to Maui for a warm, sunny vacation before heading to San Francisco to get an apartment for school that's not starting for *months*. She got out of town. Since we had this talk once already, I can guess why. You pushed her away. You wouldn't tell her how you feel because you think it's a mistake for *her*. And you're still scared every woman you meet is going to do you dirty. You're still making decisions for other people without getting their opinion. Now she thinks you don't care about her and so she took you up on the challenge and she left. Got as far away as she could. And now you're in the shitter!"

Luke glared at Aiden for a moment before he said, "I'm going to fucking kill you."

Aiden sat back in the chair and grinned. He took a slug of his beer. "Oh yeah? And why is that?"

"You called the *general*? About *me*?"

"Yup. And the bartender. But I got the call from Sean who got the call from Mom and you should just be glad Paddy and Colin aren't stateside or they'd be in it. Now, why don't you just answer the fucking phone and tell people you're busy and can't talk? What the hell are you doing?"

"Save my *life*?" Luke asked. "Emergency leave? Save my *life*? What the hell are you talking about?"

Aiden sat forward and grew serious. "Look, we've been here before. We were all young, true, and the circumstances were entirely different, but try to imagine what it's like to see your big brother—the guy you most admire in the world—hit the skids and just about sink out of sight. Scared the shit out of everyone. That's not going to happen again. No one is going to let it happen again."

Luke took a breath. "Look, it's not a big deal. Shelby was just following through with her plans. She wants to travel, go to school. I'm adjusting. Gimme a week. It'll be fine."

Aiden stared at him for a second. "Aw, bullshit," he said.

Before Luke could respond, the phone rang.

"See? God*damnit!* Why'd you plug that thing in?" Luke roared.

Aiden went to the phone. He said hello. "Yes, Mom, I'm

here—he's fine. Yes, fine. I took his pulse, he's alive, he'll be fine. Yes, Mom. Yes, Mom. *Mom!* I just got here! Would you let me— Yes, Mom. Goodbye. I love you, too." Before he could get back to his chair, it rang again and Luke groaned very loudly. Aiden picked it up and said hello. "Jesus, I just got here! Will you give me ten minutes to find out what the hell's going on? Yeah, he's fine! I'll call you back. Now leave us alone!"

Aiden went back to his chair, his beer.

"See?" Luke said.

"Yeah, but you obviously unplugged the phone after all the calls started. You never bothered to tell anyone you were fine. What if Shelby called to say she'd thought it over and decided to sit it out here until her classes started? What's the deal?"

"She wasn't going to call."

"What if she did?"

"That wouldn't be good for her."

Aiden was stunned silent for a minute. His mind was whirring. Then he was slowly overcome by a sly grin. "Oh man," he said. "You wouldn't be able to keep yourself from answering the phone if it rang, hoping it could be her, so you unplugged it."

"You're out of your mind..."

"You'd rather have her think you weren't here. That a day or a week after she left you, you got it together and you were out looking for girls. Jesus, Luke." He laughed. "What if she wanted some more time with you? Huh? What if she wanted to give you some more time with her to work out your issues?"

Luke shook his head helplessly. He got up from the sectional and went to the kitchen to get a beer. He went back to the living room. "That would be a bad decision."

"Okay, now we're on the same page. You're looking out for her. You going to come clean with me, or do we have to have six more beers to get there? Because I don't drink a lot anymore. On call all the time, you know…"

"I thought I explained this," Luke said, sounding annoyed. "She's a beautiful young girl. She might be a chronological twenty-five, but subtract a few years of her being tied to an invalid. She would be carded in most bars. I was almost her first flirt! She should do things! Experience things! She's been patient and dedicated a long time—she has to get out there and…"

"And not take a chance on you and then realize in a couple years that she was hasty," Aiden supplied.

"Aw, what the hell," Luke said, standing up and running a hand across the back of his neck. "She's not ready to make that kind of choice. She might think she is, but she's not!"

"Because you weren't?"

"She's too young!"

"Because you were?"

Luke didn't respond. He turned his back on his brother.

Aiden stood up and approached Luke's back. He put a hand on his shoulder and squeezed. "You weren't too young when you married Felicia. You weren't too naive or inexperienced when you were twenty-five. You had it all—you were sharp and loyal and you knew how you felt. You had enough passion and commitment to never change your mind. You got screwed up by someone who wasn't your match. I'm sorry, buddy, but it wasn't your fault. Jesus, will you ever let yourself off the hook for that? You didn't cheat on her! She went out on you!"

"She wasn't enough," he said. Then he laughed ruefully and shook his head. "That's what she said to me…."

"Felicia?"

Luke turned around. "Shelby. She said she knew she wasn't enough…."

"Oh, Christ," Aiden said in a breath. He thought for a

second and said, "Okay, look, let's not just get tanked and whimper. Let's go out, get a decent meal, maybe have a conversation that doesn't include yelling, and when I'm satisfied you're all right and won't unplug your phone anymore, I'll get out of your hair."

Luke answered with a weak nod.

"Want to go to that bar you like so much?" Aiden asked.

"No," he said immediately. "I need a little more time on that. Let's go over to Fortuna. There's a fish place..."

Aiden drove Luke to the next big town over and they ate at a nice little restaurant near a wide river. They ordered the same thing, which happened a lot in their family. There were things Aiden wanted to understand, but knowing Luke it wouldn't work to just come out and ask him. So Aiden got him talking about the town, the people, the cabins and what he thought he'd end up doing with the property.

The mission when he bought the house and cabins was to turn them for a profit as soon as it was reasonable to do so. Now Luke was thinking about taking a year to see what booking them as vacation rentals looked like. There wasn't a motel or bed-and-breakfast in Virgin River and it could be a highly profitable venture and not too much to manage. If it worked itself into a decent income, he might try to buy out Sean and run it as the sole owner. It would be the most settled Luke had been in more than twenty years.

Luke was ready to put down roots. He was just scared to death to ask anyone like Shelby to take that on. Because she might change her mind. And that would kill him.

So then Aiden got a little brazen and said, "There must have been something about this Shelby that really tripped you up. It's not like you to get mixed up with some local girl, especially one with a general for an uncle."

Luke chuckled. "Her looks. The first day I passed through

town, I ran into her twice. I thought she was about eighteen and, brother, I knew better."

"She was the only pretty girl in three counties?" Aiden asked.

"I couldn't tell you," Luke said. "I think I hit my head or something. I had a bad case of tunnel vision. I tried like hell to talk myself out of it, but it wasn't long before all I could do was finish what I'd started. You've been there."

"Been there," Aiden agreed. After all, he'd *married* a woman because of tunnel vision. "And that's when you started to lose interest?"

He was quiet for a second. "You don't lose interest in someone like Shelby. No matter how hard you try."

Aiden took a chance. "Been a while since you felt something like that, I guess."

Luke leveled his gaze across the table at Aiden. "I know what you're doing. I don't want to spend a lot of time talking about this. I don't need the aggravation. What I need is time."

"You fell hard," Aiden said.

"It happens. Now, that's enough."

"I just want to be sure you're going to be able to move on without…" His voice trailed off.

"Without going completely crazy? Listen, I think I learned a few things, Aiden. This is as bad as it's going to get. Until it gets better. Leave it alone."

"Damn shame you couldn't just go with it, Luke. There's at least a fifty-percent chance you're all wrong about her, about yourself, about the way the whole thing could turn out. You might've been happy every day of your stupid life, and now you're just working on getting over her."

"There's the thing, Aiden. Fifty-percent chance one of us is right. We just don't know which one."

After breakfast the next morning, Aiden threw his duffel in

his car, shook his brother's hand and said, "Go after her, Luke. Tell her the truth, that it scares you to death but you want her."

Luke just smiled. "Thanks for coming, Aiden. I know you only want to help. Drive carefully."

It was almost time for Shelby to leave Maui, but she wasn't sure if she was ready and was considering another week before embarking on San Francisco. She didn't know if the rest and sunshine was helping or if it would be better to take on a new challenge.

She'd packed everything at her uncle's, loaded the Jeep and drove to San Francisco to fly to Hawaii so she wouldn't have go back to Virgin River to pick up her car, her things. Her Jeep was in the long-term lot at the airport, waiting for her next step toward that new life, the one that didn't interest her at all. The tall trees and mountains called her and the noisy din of the city didn't sound appealing. Nothing could be as good as the quiet, the clear sky, the natural beauty that had surrounded her. She missed the horses. She missed so much...

She had chosen her vacation accommodations carefully—a hotel on the beach with a decent restaurant. She thought she'd do a little sightseeing around the island, but hadn't. Reading a lot was part of her plan, but for the first time in her memory, her mind wandered too much to escape into good fiction. Even when her mother had been at her worst, she had been able to read; it had brought her great comfort to fall into a good story. The hotel restaurant was exceptional, but she still yearned for some of Preacher's food and a blazing hearth, the laughter of friends, the touch of a lover's hand under the table. Except for breakfast, most of her meals were delivered to her by room service. She was very alone, hidden behind her dark glasses, which was the way she wanted it.

Every day she walked along the beach as far as she could go, sometimes for a couple of hours. She'd lounge on a chaise on the beach and soak up the sun, sometimes relax under a cabana, her eyes closed so she looked as if she was napping. Resting. But she was bleeding inside. If anyone looked closely, they'd catch the occasional tear rolling into the hair at her temples. The crying—it was so much more than she'd imagined it could be. She was so busy holding it together while she was around her uncle and cousin, she'd had no idea how much emotion she'd been struggling with. The crying started as soon as the plane's landing gear came up and in spite of her best efforts, she sobbed half the way to Hawaii. Luck was on her side and she was seated next to a kindhearted older woman who put an arm around her and said, "Oh, darling, there's no mistaking a broken heart."

The best fiction in the history of the world had not adequately conveyed just how much a broken heart could hurt or how much crying was involved. It was a kind of death made worse by the fact that there hadn't been a death at all, unless you accounted for the demise of perfect happiness.

"Beautiful day," a man's voice said.

She turned her head to see him sitting on the chaise right beside her. There were dozens of available chairs on the beach and around the pool and yet he had to choose this one. "Beautiful," she said quietly, turning her head back, trying to ignore him.

"I hear it rains here all the time. Have you seen much rain?"

"Please," she said. "I was napping."

"Think you'll be done napping by dinnertime? I'd love to take you to dinner."

She turned her head, lifted her glasses and said, "No, thank you." Again she turned away.

"Then maybe I could buy you a drink? A mai tai or Bloody Mary?"

Without looking at him she said, "Do I have to move? Or will you?"

He chuckled. "Nothing shy about that, Shelby."

She jumped in surprise, sitting up a little. "Did someone tell you my *name?*" she said, stricken. The last thing she needed right now was to feel at some kind of risk. She was alone here, depending on the hotel staff to be sure she'd be completely safe.

"No," he said. "I already knew your name. I asked where I could find you. They're very protective here, but when I described you, the towel kid knew where you might be."

She sat up, her mouth open.

He put out a hand. "Aiden Riordan," he said. "How are you?"

Stunned speechless, she slowly put out her hand. He was a nice-looking man, but didn't resemble either Sean or Luke. He was dark-haired with heavy black brows, green eyes like his mother's and a very pleasant smile. "The doctor?"

"OB-GYN, in fact. Nice to meet you."

"What…? What in the world are you doing here?"

He gave a slight shrug. "I thought someone ought to explain Luke, if that's possible."

Still in something of a state of shock, she sat sideways on the chaise, facing him, her feet in the sand. "Did he send you?"

"Oh, no." Aiden laughed. "In fact, when he finds out, it's gonna be ugly. And maybe this was just a waste of my time, but I have a feeling there are some important things you don't know about him. On the other hand, I'll bet you know things about him I don't even want to hear."

"Oh, this is…this is *crazy!*"

"Tell me about it. We have some loudmouths in the family, but it's kind of unusual for the boys to get into each other's business to this degree. Luke's kind of a special case, though."

"Why is that?"

"Well, did he ever happen to mention he was married when he was much younger?" Aiden asked.

It took her a moment to absorb that. "Well, that would explain a few things," she finally said.

"The explanation gets more complicated. You've probably heard a hundred nasty divorce tales, but this one combined a lot of events that worked out badly for Luke, and I think it's safe to say he's got some residual effect from it."

She looked down. "I guess he didn't trust me that much," she said. "Or he might've told me."

"It has nothing to do with trust, Shelby. He was trying damn hard to keep from getting too close to you. It didn't quite work for him—you should see him. He looks like a dead man, he's so miserable."

She scooted forward. "When did you see him?"

"A couple of days ago. And no, I didn't tell him I was going to try to find you. He wouldn't have endorsed this idea."

"Is he okay?" she asked, concerned.

"Nope. He's a mess. I guess he could recover," Aiden said. "But we have to talk, you and me, and then what will be, will be.

"Luke got married when he was about twenty-four. He was a brand-new Black Hawk pilot and he married a girl he met in Alabama—a real pretty Southern belle who turned his world upside down. Prettiest girl in the South, maybe. They dated, started making plans right away, had a wedding a few months later and he was the happiest man alive. Since he was the oldest, the rest of us were watching every move he made. We all wanted to be like Luke—he was so sure of himself, so well equipped. All the boys wanted to go into the military, excel, get a million ribbons and promotions, marry the prettiest, sexiest girl on the map, grab on to that perfect life filled with challenge, adventure and passion."

"Something went wrong, I gather," she said.

"Oh, boy. Let's see, Colin was in the army, stationed on the other side of the country, I was in my last year of undergrad at the time, Sean was only nineteen and at the air force academy. Patrick was in high school. And Luke had a baby coming. First baby in the family, a son. First marriage for anyone. Luke was on top of the world, so happy, so in love, so excited about the baby, and then he was sent to Somalia, to Mogadishu. You ever see that movie *Black Hawk Down?*"

"I did," she said. "I don't think I want to see it again...."

"Luke got shot down over there, had some injuries, but he's the bravest man I've ever known. That was a horrible experience for the army—everything bad that could happen, happened. But he somehow got through it, performing heroically. He saved lives and was decorated for bravery. He got home as fast as he could because his son was about to be born. He was undoubtedly still battle scarred when he faced another battle. He wasn't home five minutes when his wife told him the baby—which was conceived months before he left for Somalia—wasn't his. She was doing some captain. One of Luke's superior officers, in fact. A man Luke went into war with, took orders from on occasion. And she was leaving Luke to go with the baby's father."

"God" was all she could say.

"It humiliated him, this tough young soldier. He was your age at the time, Shelby—twenty-five. There was a stir on the army post—an officer messing with one of his men's wives. It wasn't only a divorce, it was just about front-page news, there were rumblings about pressing charges against the captain and Luke looked like a fool. He wasn't close to being done dealing with war. He had some issues from that at the same time. Broken heart, scandal, humiliation, disappointment, PTSD from battle, grief from watching comrades die." Aiden took a breath. "He was suicidal."

"Luke?" she asked. "That's so difficult to imagine. Anger, I can see that. But—"

"It didn't present itself in a typical way. He went down like a torpedo—drank too much and drove, almost flew drunk, but someone pulled him off the flight line. He got in fights—he seemed to go places where he could count on getting the hell beat out of him by at least several men. He picked the fights. He landed in the hospital a couple of times, injuries from fights, from a one-car accident. He probably wouldn't tell you this, but he told me. He just wanted to die."

She took a moment to absorb that, then said, "No wonder he won't have a close relationship..."

"There are a lot of things that can screw a guy up, but Luke had a full menu. It wasn't just a bad marriage, Shelby, but everything, with a no-good cheating wife in the middle of it. It took a couple of years for him to get straightened out. He changed everything—he stopped being calculating and just took too many chances, and he moved real fast. It turned out he couldn't give up women, but he seemed to give up attachments."

She tilted her head. "That explains so much," she said. "He told me he didn't fall in love, went through women like a shark goes through scuba divers...."

Aiden smiled. "That sounds like Luke."

"I absolutely believed him," she said. "I thought I could handle that. And then I stupidly thought something was different for him with me. That's where I screwed up." She took a breath. "I must have blown his mind with that talk about children...."

"What talk was that?" he asked.

"I told him that I wanted a committed partner, at least one child. He said it was never going to happen with him, but I thought..." She shrugged.

"He's been saying that for quite a while. Maybe he believes it by now, but when he thought he had a child coming, I never saw a happier man. I'm sorry he lost that."

"He made the excuse he was too old. I guess if he trusted

me, he could have told me about his marriage, his reasons, given us a chance to work through it…"

"Yeah, well, he has a lot of denial about that. And, by the things he said, it sounded like he started out protecting himself, but later in your relationship, he was protecting you."

"Me?"

"He told me about your mother, about how dedicated you were for a few years, that you didn't have any real freedom… My condolences, by the way."

"Thanks. Maybe you'll understand this, since you're a doctor—Luke sure doesn't get it. It wasn't a sacrifice. I wasn't held hostage. I was doing exactly what I wanted to do. I was very close to my mother. Helping someone close the door on this world and move on to the next—it's very special. Intimate. I wasn't giving anything up—I was getting something most people will never experience."

He smiled at her. "That's a pretty remarkable take on things."

"I'm not remarkable," she said with a self-effacing smile. "I was in a support group and learned an awful lot."

"You've had some tough blows in the last year," he said. "First, losing your mother. Then Luke."

Her eyes became moist, but she held steady. "I don't regret what I gave either one, Aiden. I wouldn't change any of it. I would never have left my mom in someone else's care. I couldn't help falling in love with Luke." She gave a tremulous smile. "I knew almost right away, he should be the one. My first love."

Aiden touched the hand that rested on her knee. "You never fell in love like that before, I guess."

"I never fell in love at all," she said. "It wasn't very long after high school that my life got pretty isolated, and I wasn't one of the girls who got around a lot in high school. Luke was right about one thing—I haven't lived much in those ways. I could've stumbled onto some insensitive jerk, but it was Luke. He was so good to me, so tender, so wonderful. I can't regret that," she said, shaking her head. "Much as it hurts now, I wouldn't take away one day with him. When he said he wanted to keep it just between us because it was so special, I guess I started to think his pattern of never getting involved could change…with me…."

"Just between you?" Aiden asked in spite of himself.

"That he was the first one. Ever." She dropped her gaze. "The way I feel, he's probably going to be the only one. Ever."

Aiden was silent, looking at her sweet face, stunned. After what Luke had been through with his wife, he stumbled onto someone pure? Untouched? Oh, man, no wonder he was so screwed up. He must have glimpsed a kind of impossible dream—a sweet and good woman who could be trusted, who would belong only to him. "Oh, Jesus," Aiden said, hanging his head. "No wonder this is so bad…."

"Huh?"

"Shelby, the girl he married—she was about the furthest thing from a virgin a guy can get. She was a sexy little flirt. She'd been around, and apparently never stopped getting around. You gotta imagine—Luke must have been thinking that if that one hurt, if something like that happened with you, it would kill him."

She shook her head. "I can't believe he ever thought I'd be like that…."

"I think it's time for us to have that Bloody Mary," Aiden said. "Take a walk on the beach. Then dinner."

When Aiden left in the morning to go to the airport, she hugged him goodbye like an old friend. They had talked the rest of the afternoon, through dinner, and then sat on the beach in the moonlight until very late. Most of that time was focused on Luke and her relationship with him, but also on the other brothers and Aiden's movement through medical

school and practice, aboard ship and at naval bases and Camp
Pendleton. And he learned about her childhood, her mother,
the rest of her family, her love for the mountains and rivers,
the horses, the quiet tranquility of Virgin River. They became good friends.

"I've had the strangest thought," she told Aiden as he stood
by his cab.

"What's that, sweetheart?"

"Luke's trying to rescue me by letting me go. He doesn't
want me to sacrifice anything, to give up anything, to settle.
But really, he's a mess. He's the one who needs to be rescued."

Aiden laughed. "Yeah, maybe. But since he'll never admit
it, it's probably impossible."

"Take care of him, Aiden," she said as he got in his cab at
the hotel.

"I'll do what I can," he said. "Will you go to San Francisco
now?"

"I might take another week. Really, there's no big hurry
for me to get there. I just felt like I had to be moving on, to
be doing something. It's strange how long it takes to forget."

"You don't forget, Shelby. You just adapt."

She laughed softly. "Thank you, Aiden. For coming all the
way here just to talk to me. You don't realize how much it
mattered, helped."

"I hope so, Shelby. Luke's right about one thing—you're
special. Best of luck."

"Same to you."

Luke was sitting in front of his fireplace, feet up, listening to
a CD while looking off at nothing in particular, when headlights dashed across his living-room window. It was wet out
there; he wasn't expecting anyone. He looked at his watch; it
was eight o'clock. If this was another brother or, worse, his
mother, he wasn't going to be able to control himself. He'd

been answering the phone, for God's sake. He hadn't been conversational, but he'd answered. It was still a little raw, this thing with Shelby, but he was making progress. He slept now at least....

He opened the door and saw the Jeep. She stood in front of it, leaning against the hood, arms crossed over her chest, getting wet in the freezing drizzle. His heart lurched. Almost three weeks since he'd seen her and his feelings hadn't given him a break. He still wanted her so bad it hurt.

"You never told me about Felicia," she yelled at him.

"That was a long time ago," he said loudly. "How do you know?"

"Never mind. Didn't you trust me enough to tell me?"

"It was years ago," he said. "It had nothing to do with anything." He took a step onto the porch. "I didn't hear anything about you coming back."

"No one knows I'm here," she said. "Do you think I'll be as bad as she was, is that it?"

"No. I know better than that. You think I'm the best you can do?"

She shrugged. Her hair was getting wet; her cheeks glistened. "What if you are? How did I screw up? I thought I showed you I knew exactly what I wanted. You think I'm fickle? That I'm too young and too stupid to know whether I really love someone?"

"You're not stupid— I never thought that. Young, maybe."

"Oh—you thought it was *puppy* love?"

"No, sir," he said. "Nothing puppy about it. Come out of the rain."

"No. Not until a couple of things are settled. If we can't come to terms, I'll go to the general's. But I'm not moving to San Francisco—I don't want to be there. I've never lived in a big city and I don't like them that much. What I like is *here*."

"Come up on the porch at least and we'll talk. Out of the wet and cold…"

"No," she said, holding her ground. "Maybe I expected too much too fast, but you expected too little. I don't want another man's hands on me. Ever. This is where the only hands I ever want are. Yours. Only yours."

He couldn't help but smile at her, standing so proudly, so stubbornly in the rain, arms crossed over her chest. "Then why did you go? I never minded putting my hands all over you."

"I needed a tan. And I thought you didn't love me. I want more than this—I want the whole deal. I want a child someday. It doesn't have to be soon—but I want a child, at least one, and it has to have a father, and that's a deal breaker."

He tipped back his head with a laugh. "Who do you think you are? Deal breaker?"

"I think I'm the only woman you've loved in forever. And you were going to pitch me out that fast, just because I make you nervous. I thought you didn't trust me, but now I think you don't trust yourself." She shook her head. "I don't want a man like that. I need a man with guts, who's sure of himself. Confident enough to stand by me. I need a man who's not afraid to take a risk or two for something important."

"I've taken a risk or two," he said. "And you don't scare me. Come up here on the porch."

"No. Not until you say that if we stay solid, there will be a real relationship and a family. I don't want any of this 'I don't get involved' shit. It's all crap, Luke. You can have some time to be sure, I'm patient. But I'm not giving you up."

He smiled at her. "I don't need time to be sure. I know how I feel."

"Still on that? Still that 'never gonna happen' bullshit?"

"Okay, I guess it could happen," he said. "If it did happen, it would happen with you. I just always thought you deserved more."

"More than everything I've ever wanted in the world? See what an idiot you turned out to be?"

He had to laugh. She was something, this woman. "Shelby, come here. I don't have to think about it—you're the most solid thing I've ever had in my life. Now come here."

"I thought I wasn't enough for you—but I was too much," she said. "And you don't get to decide what I deserve. What I deserve is a man who looks at me grow fat on his baby and feels pride. Love and pride."

"Okay then," he said. "I love you. Come here."

"Not good enough. You have to say something to convince me this is worth the gamble. I came a long way and I came alone. I was betting on you, on us. I love you and you love me and I'm sick of screwing around. Say the right thing for once. Say something *profound*."

He stared at her and his smile slowly faded. He put his hands on his hips. He took a deep breath and felt tears gather in his eyes. "You're all I need to be happy, Shelby," he said. "You're everything I need…"

He actually surprised her. Her arms dropped from over her chest and she gaped at him for a second.

"You're everything," he said. "It scares me to death, but I want it all with you. I want you for life. I want what you want, and I want it right now."

"Huh?"

"Everything, Shelby. I want you to be the lead in my shoes that keeps me on the ground. The mother of my children. My best friend, my wife, my mistress. It's a tall order." He took a breath. "If you won't quit, I won't."

"You're sure about that?" she asked him.

"Sure it scares the hell out me you'll change your mind? Or sure I want it all? Oh, yeah, honey. I'm sure."

"I won't change my mind," she said softly.

"I can't hear you!" he yelled. "I can't hear you because you won't come out of the frickin' rain!"

She ran up the porch steps and into his arms. He lifted her off the floor and went after her mouth hungrily. She cried against his lips. He had a tear or two he ignored, loving her tears of relief.

"Am I enough?" she asked.

"Way more, you always were," he said. "I want you so bad, I never wanted you to go. I don't know if this is fair to you—"

"Here's the deal—I decide what's fair to me, you decide what's fair to you. We stop deciding for each other. The idea is to work *together*. You're a little controlling...."

"I'm flawed in many ways."

"All I want is that you love me enough to make a life with me. It doesn't have to be tomorrow you make the promise, but you have to give us a chance..."

"It can be tomorrow. It can be tonight. Losing you almost killed me."

"Oh God," she whimpered. "Can you love me forever?"

"Probably longer. It's like I don't have a choice. Think you can handle that?"

She took a deep breath. "You just try me."

★ ★ ★ ★ ★